A Chasing After the Wind is Jim Carson's long-awaited novel and the first of his powerful trilogy.

No one should have to start life with a tragic loss, but Mack Shannon had no choice, it was as if he was born with a birthmark of a black cloud.

Sent by his Uncle Mickey to live at an all-boys Catholic orphanage, he meets his lifelong nemesis, Crazy Ray, a devious and unsavory character that causes him to be hunted and beaten for a crime he didn't commit. His uncle has had enough, and in the dark morning mist, after a second clash with the police, Mack is shipped off on a towboat downriver to Natchez, Mississippi to live with a spinster aunt on her 100,000-acre farm, Shamrock Plantation.

These misfortunes are like a disease with no cure, but Mack learns to use them as building blocks for the upcoming challenge of a once in a lifetime opportunity from his Aunt Irish.

Will Mack rise to the challenge of becoming greater than he ever imagined, or will he fall into the Memphis underworld of drug lords and hit men?

Praise for Jim Carson's
A CHASING AFTER THE WIND

What a rare treat Jim Carson is! Rarely do you find a new author with such a clean, crisp style—each phrase locking you into the moment with a sharp clarity. The pace in the beginning of the book has you breathing in gasps from the onset—high-intensity scenes empowered by remarkably descriptive prowess. The first quarter of the novel fairly races along before the author pulls back the throttle a little and begins to allow the reader into the depth of his characters. And the characters are skillfully brought to life—bright, dangerous, sexy, and manipulative. In *A Chasing After The Wind*, we watch a young, gritty Irishman rise from a "child of the street" to a man of power and wealth, but it's a tangled, vicious, sensual journey, with more twists and turns than a "Wild Mouse" roller coaster. Carson's style reminds me of a combination of Lee Child and Harold Robbins. His exacting knowledge of military tactics, aviation, boxing, skiing, automobiles, and weapons make the book "believable" on so many levels, and his sense of timing is impeccable. With the debut of this novel I'm left a little in awe. While I'm considered a "best-selling novelist" with ten books to my credit, I somehow feel, a year or two from now, I'll be saying with pride, "Yeah, I knew Jim Carson when he was just beginning..."

Michael Reisig, author of
The Road To Key West series

A Sense-Sational Novel. I read fiction with the expectation that the author will take me to a different place, not just tell me about a different place. If he doesn't, I don't bother to read anything else that he writes. In "A Chasing After the Wind," Jim Carson meets my expectation. I could feel the heat against my face in the burning house. I could smell the fear and the burnt gunpowder with my face in the grass at the park. I could feel the cobblestones bump under my tires at the

Memphis riverfront and smell the Mississippi River. His protagonist, Mack, and I drank a cold Guinness at the local pub. We told lies and laughed. I look forward to all the other places Jim will take me and to meeting many more interesting characters. This is an author I will come back to as often as he writes because he meets my expectation.

—Robert, MD, December 16, 2014

Jim Carson has done some real fine work. A rare flare for descriptive expression and an astute observation of humanity, bold, colorful, primitive, yet far from naive. Jim's a seasoned, saging son of the South.

—Pejuta, January 14, 2015

From the very beginning, the book grabs the reader's attention and continues to hold it throughout each chapter! It is a feel good book, in that the character progresses from an uneducated boy to a worldly man, with all that it entails. Great read!!!

—Ruth K. Dec. 2014

The real deal. As a frequent action reader of many great authors to include the late Tom Clancy, I found "A Chasing After the Wind" to be fresh and exciting. As an active duty Solider, my deployments are frequent with multiple long plane rides, this book is entertaining and will be added to a must re-read on my next trip. I believe the passion and knowledge throughout the book made it come alive. I would highly recommend this to my community of peers and look forward to the next book by Jim Carson.

—Captain D. Parnell, January 8, 2015

An awesome read! Looking forward to many more novels by Jim!

—Sara Morris, November 2014

A CHASING AFTER THE WIND

A NOVEL BY
JIM CARSON

A CHASING AFTER THE WIND
Copyright © 2014 by Jim Carson

ISBN (hardback): 978-0692315514
ISBN: (paperback): 979-8-89965-053-6
First Edition, 2014. All rights reserved.

BABY DRAGON PRESS, Inc.
3984 Tutwiler Ave.
Memphis, TN 38122
www.jamesacarson.com

Edited by Jonathan W. Thurston
Cover design by the Damonza.com team

Printed in the United States of America
10 9 8 7 6 5 4 3 2 1

For my mother
Lorraine (Bell) Carson
"She watched over her brood like a fierce mother hen."

King Solomon

"I wanted to see what was worthwhile for men to do under heaven during the days of their lives. I had seven hundred wives, three hundred concubines, and a harem...the delights of the hearts of man. I denied myself nothing my eyes desired; I refused my heart no pleasure. Yet when I surveyed all that my hands had done and what I had toiled to achieve, everything was meaningless, a chasing after the wind."

Contents

PROLOGUE

"OHH NO," ROSE said, lifting the heavy covers. "Who wet the bed this time?" She crawled out from under the quilts and stood on the cold linoleum floor, as she searched for the wet spot on her flannel nightgown. The only light was a dim orange glow coming from the old fireplace of the shotgun house.

She stepped over two sleeping toddlers, wrapped in blankets on a pallet of cardboard. While searching under the bed for her pink rabbit slippers, she felt something cold and wet and jerked her hand back. On her knees, she peered under the edge of the bed and saw the black hair of her little brother. He was curled up in a tight knot, squeezing her fuzzy rabbit slippers, his large green eyes dilated in the dark.

Rose sat on the floor, shivering as the freezing air oozed up through the cracks in the linoleum. "Come on little Mack," she patted the floor, "it's okay. We'll get you some dry underwear." She took his hand as he scooted from under the bed and crawled into her lap.

"Rosy's toes are freezing. Can I have Fuzzy Rabbits?"

Sitting between her legs, he gave her one slipper at a time. Once they were on her feet, she wiggled her toes, making the rabbits' ears move.

She picked up her smiling brother and flinched from his wet bottom. He wrapped both arms around her neck and held tight to her long braided ponytail. She carried him to the bathroom, wiping his nose with the dry part of his nightshirt.

"What happened?" Kathleen asked, as she stood in the doorway of the bathroom, rubbing her eyes. Rose's mother held a patch quilt over her shoulders.

"Mack couldn't get the covers off quick enough to make it to the potty." Mack stood on the toilet seat naked while Rose washed him down with a warm washrag. His long tee shirt and soggy briefs lay on the floor at the base of the toilet.

"I'll get him some dry underwear," Kathleen said.

Rose wrapped Mack in a towel and carried him back to the bedroom while Kathleen gave a spoon of cough syrup to one of the neighbor's boys she was nursing back from the whooping cough. Looking over her shoulder, Kathleen said, "Rose, take those towels and cover the wet spot on the bed. It's too late to change the bedding; you can do that in the morning."

"Mama, it's so cold in here," Rose said.

"They're supposed to turn the heat back on tomorrow; I paid the bill today. Now, hurry up and get under the covers. It's going to be a hard freeze tonight. Did you leave the faucets dripping in the bathroom?"

"Yes ma'am. Mama?"

"What, honey?"

"Are you going to work late tomorrow?" Rose asked.

"No, only the seven-to-three shift." She bent over and kissed Rose and Mack, tucking in the covers. "I'll put some more wood in the fireplace before I go back to bed."

She felt the head of one of the children on the floor to see if he had any fever, and then tucked the blankets tight around the other two sleeping in the rollaway bed. There was no money for doctors, so Kathleen, a pediatric nurse, was "Doctor Kate" to all the sick children in the neighborhood. "Mama?"

"Yes, Rose?"

"I left my rabbit slippers on."

"That's okay. You'll need something on your feet tonight."

"Can we put the Christmas tree up tomorrow, when you come home?"

"Yes, we can. Now go to sleep."

"I love you, Mama."

Kathleen, half asleep and exhausted from working a double-shift at the hospital, shuffled into the other room, stoked the smoldering embers at the bottom of the grate, and broke up some kindling to fuel the fire. She glanced at the six-foot Christmas tree standing in the corner and noticed that some of the sprigs were already turning brown. She wished she had put the tree in a bucket of water to keep it from drying out, but like most things it could wait till tomorrow. Kathleen struggled with a heavy log, dropping one end on the burning kindling and lifting the other end; she tilted it to the back of the grate.

That should keep us all warm till morning.

Rose, wrapped in quilts, watched her mother kneel at the foldout couch to say her prayers. Kathleen's head nodded a few times before her overworked body gave way, and, with prayers forgotten, she crawled onto the fold-out mattress and was dead asleep...her rosary falling to the floor.

Rose turned and whispered to Mack as he played with her long, braided hair, "You want to climb over to this side so we can snuggle?"

Mack crawled over Rose, burrowed himself into her opened arms, and whispered, "Sing me a song."

"What's the magic word?"

"Pleeease."

"Okay. But then you have to go to sleep, promise?"

"Promise," Mack said.

"You are my sunshine...my only sunshine...you make me happy...when skies are gray..." Rose kissed Mack on the head and continued singing.

Mack whispered the last fading verse along with Rose, *"Please don't take...my sunshine...away."*

Lying huddled on their sides, they watched the red-hot glow of the fireplace, their eyes heavy, surrendering to a deep, warm sleep.

No one saw the burned kindling under the log crumble and fall through the grate causing the log to fall forward rolling out on to the floor, where it lay smoldering...underneath the Christmas tree.

It was as quiet as a graveyard except for the deep snoring of Private Tony D'Agostino. He was stretched out with his short legs crossed and his feet propped up on a scarred desk. His wide bottom hung over the chair as he leaned back on the two rear legs. An opened Sears Christmas catalog rested on his stomach.

Tony jerked upright, almost tipping over backwards, when he heard the swinging doors open behind him. He watched Captain Jack Kelly shuffle across the floor to the kitchen, kneading his stomach with the knuckles of his right hand. His ulcer must be acting up; he often said it felt like a rat trying to eat a hole out of his gut.

Tony looked up at the clock; it was 2:35 a.m. "What's the matter, Cap...can't sleep?"

There was no answer. Tony heard the familiar sound of running water, the stirring of baking soda in a glass, and within a short time, a loud burp. Tony waited, knowing there was more to come. He suppressed a laugh as a thunderous fart boomed off the walls of the small kitchen.

"How about some fresh coffee, Cap? It won't take but a minute."

Captain Jack stood over the stove emptying the thick dregs of coffee into his mug. His baggy long johns were so twisted that the rear hatch rode the middle of his right thigh. He bent over and fished around the top of his sock until he found the pack of Camel cigarettes. He shook one out of the pack, stuck it in his mouth, and lit it from one of the stove's burners. Setting the empty coffee pot down in the sink, he took a long drag, and started coughing. He coughed up a glob of dark phlegm and deposited it expertly into a metal trashcan. Straightening up, he took a deep breath, then added three tablespoons of sugar to his black coffee and shuffled over to the kitchen table.

"Yeah, go ahead, make a pot. I'm not going back to bed, it's too quiet." He looked up for the first time from under wild-growing eyebrows, smoke blowing out of both nostrils. His thinning red hair was mashed flat in the back and sticking up in the front.

Tony filled the coffee pot with water and almost missed setting it back on the burner when one long ring of the fire phone blasted the silence, signaling a fire. He raced to the desk, jerked up the phone and shouted, "Six's?" With a pencil in hand, he flipped all the lights on in the bed hall upstairs and wrote on a scratch pad. He hung up the phone and hit the turnout bell, opened the overhead door, and yelled over the PA system, "House on fire at 939 North 7th Street...Six's and Four's Pumper, Truck 2, Salvage 1, and Battalion Chief responding."

Captain Jack was like the old-time fire horses that turned into thoroughbreds when they heard a turnout bell. He stood erect, eyes focused and alert. He took a long drink of his coffee, dropped his cigarette in the cup, and walked over to the stove and turned the burner off. Tony's hand was trembling when he handed him the address of the house.

"Relax, Tony, we didn't set the fire; we're going to put it out."

Tony ran out the double doors and climbed onto the rear of the pumper as groggy men dropped out of a hole in the ceiling, sliding down the fire pole one after the other.

Captain Jack climbed inside the cabin of the Peter-Pirsch pumper as the long nose of the Waukesha engine leaped out the overhead door.

The record-breaking freezing temperature slapped Tony in the face with the shock of an ice-packed snowball. He struggled to hide his head under the canvas that covered more than a thousand feet of sardine-packed hose. Over the roar of the engine and the siren, only God could hear Tony's words, as he made the sign of the cross.

"Hail Mary, full of grace. The Lord is with thee." As the pumper swung north out of the fire house, a rookie firefighter, Joey Davies, fought to hang onto the hand-rail, banging into Tony, "Man, I almost didn't make it back there. I thought they waited till you signaled with the rear horn back here?"

"Not Captain Jack. He walks; you run. He don't wait on nobody; in the shower or sitting on the shitter...seconds to the Captain mean life or death," Tony shouted in the rookie's ear.

The driver downshifted to slow the heavy pumper as it swung west on Guthrie, a short alley over to Seventh Street, and saw the bright pink glow of the sky at the end of the street. He shot a quick look over at the Captain and saw him buckling the flap around the collar of his turnout coat.

"You know where the plug is, right?" The Captain shouted over the noise of the radio and the growling engine.

"Yes, Sir, corner of Henry." Standing on the brakes, the driver wheeled the huge machine to a stop in the middle of the intersection with the rear end of the pumper facing the burning shotgun-houses, three of them bunched together.

Captain Jack picked up the radio microphone and in a clear, calm voice reported, "Six's on the scene. Three, one-story frames on fire, one fully involved, laying an inch-and-a-half." Hearing another siren close by, Jack added, "Four's pumper, lay two lines into Six's at Henry and come on to the fire. I may need your booster...I don't see anyone outside." He tossed the mike on the seat and was out the door before the pumper stopped.

"I knew it was too damn quiet," Jack mumbled as he pulled on his gloves. The smell of burning pine and tar permeated the air, and the sound of the burning houses howled through the quiet neighborhood.

Captain Jack waited while Tony loaded the hose on the shoulder of the rookie standing on the ground at the back of the pumper. He then shouted to the driver, "Move out!" The pumper jumped forward and raced down the street, spitting hose out the back end, headed for the fire hydrant.

Captain Jack turned to the rookie, Davies, "Okay, Sonny, let's earn our paycheck."

A wall of deadly heat from the burning house stopped the rookie in the front yard, and he dropped the bundle of hose and pulled his collar up and his helmet down to keep his face from being scorched. Orange flames leaped out exploding windows, and heavy black smoke surged out the eaves and curled up over the roof, engulfing the moaning house as melted asphalt shingles dripped off the roof's edge, like black raindrops.

"Spread out the hose. I want one nozzle in the front door and the other in the back. I'm going to check the rear of the house." Captain

Jack raced down the side of the house, turning his shoulder and helmet away from the heat. At the back door, black smoke gushed from underneath the door and around the frame. Sitting on the top step, he took a couple of deep breaths then pulled off one of his gloves and cautiously touched the brass doorknob; it was blistering hot. He ran his hand lightly over the wooden door and could feel it pulsating, ready to ignite. He inched himself up with his back to the doorframe; shutting his eyes to the heavy smoke. "Fire! Fire!" He shouted, banging on the side of the house, "House on fire! Get out, get out!" The scorching heat burned his lungs as he shouted, and then with his ear pressed against the door, he listened for any sounds of life. He scooted down the steps and ran back to the front yard, taking note of the fire and smoke now lashing out every window on this side of the house, threatening the house next door.

Tony hung onto the back of the pumper, dodging the unfolding hose snaking its way down the street as the brass couplings from each section banged on the pavement. When the pumper stopped in front of the fire hydrant, Tony grabbed a plug wrench, and slapped it over the top of the hydrant, and turned the operating nut. After a few turns, he knew they were in serious trouble.

"Where's the *water?*" The driver shouted.

"The plug's *frozen.* Bring me that Molotov."

The driver jerked a rear compartment door open, yanked out a burlap sack, and raced around the front of the pumper to the fire hydrant.

"Is it full?" Tony asked, grabbing the string and pulling the slipknot while untying the sack. The driver lifted a fruit jar with kindling taped around the outside and full of gasoline. He slid the jar back in and Tony tied the neck of the sack. Taking his Zippo lighter from his pocket, Tony lit the top of the sack and threw it, smashing it against the back of the fire hydrant. The exploding flames engulfed the hydrant and immediately Tony heard the water rushing up from underground with ninety pounds of pressure.

"Water coming," Tony said, as he stepped over to the fireplug and kicked the burning kindling and glass to the side. He took off running down the middle of the street, racing the water to the fire as it filled each section of hose.

Captain Jack ran back to the front where he had left the rookie and found him with Bobby Yarbrough, the Captain of number Four's pumper. "Where's the water?" he shouted, his frozen breath fanning both of them.

The rookie was bewildered. He stood shivering, holding the nozzle and looking down at the limp, dry hose.

"Jack, your boys were hooking up to the plug when we dropped our lines." Yarbrough said.

"Give me your booster; I can't wait any longer," Jack shouted.

Each pumper carried a 100-gallon tank of water. "That's not enough water, Jack. You could burn up in there. Hold on a minute, water's coming."

"We don't have a minute. There's people in there."

All Tony heard over the noise was Captain Jack shouting, *"Booster,"* and he came running with number six's booster hose and a fire ax and stopped between the two captains.

Jack turned to Yarbrough, "Bobby, this boy's a rookie," nodding toward Davies, "put someone with him, and when you get water, keep that booster tank full."

Jack grabbed the nozzle of the booster from Tony and ran for the front door with Tony dragging the hose behind him.

"Cap, the plug was frozen, but we got water coming now." Tony was breathing hard.

The heat stopped Jack ten feet from the front door. He squatted down under the heat and smoke and opened the nozzle. Turning the setting to a fog, he duck walked behind a shield of fine spray, and shut the nozzle off at the porch. He couldn't see Tony but felt him holding on to his coattail.

"Keep low. We could get a backdraft here." Jack felt the screen door, shoved his hand through it, and grabbed the wooden frame, snatching it from its hinges. Reaching up through the smoke, he found the doorknob, but it was locked. He moved his hand higher on the door, felt a pane of glass, and shattered it with his helmet. Opening the nozzle he shoved it through the broken glass, whipped it around the ceiling and shut it off, conserving his 100 gallons of water.

"Hold this," he said, handing the nozzle to Tony. "Give me your ax." Jack took the blade of the ax and shoved it between the door and frame, popping the lock. He tried to push the door, but it only moved a few inches. Something was blocking it.

Both men crouched with their backs to the door and pushed it open wide enough for Jack to squeeze through on his belly, dragging the booster hose behind him. He could see the leaping flames in the far back room as the heat hit him in the face like a flame-thrower. He wrapped his upper arms around his face and pressed his nose to the floor as a large swoosh of fire and heat rushed over him, blowing the remaining glass out of the front door. Jack stuck the nozzle above his head, opened it on fog again and sprayed the ceiling from corner to corner before shutting it off. With the water vaporizing to steam, scalding pellets fell from the ceiling like granulated lava. Jack, with his nose still to the floor, sucked in the last bit of air remaining, but it was fouled air, that sweet, sickening smell that all firefighters dread. His stomach knotted up and he vomited all over the floor. Rolling over he touched the back of the door, and felt the small bundles stacked on top of each other. Choking through the smoke and vomit, he yelled for Tony, "Get in here."

Dragging them one at a time, he handed Tony each small body, burned flesh sticking to his gloves, and then carried the fifth one out on his back. Tony passed the bodies to a firefighter behind him and then helped pull Jack out onto the porch. Tony and another firefighter lifted the larger body from his back and carried it out into the front yard. Jack leaned back against the porch wall, taking a deep breath of fresh air. Through all the commotion he almost missed hearing the faint outcry, "Help! Oh God, please help me!"

Tony returned to the porch to find Captain Jack gone. "You let him go back in by himself?" he shouted at a firefighter standing on the porch.

Ducking under the bellowing smoke, Tony straddled the red booster hose and followed it back into the house. He kept his nose to the floor, sucking up the little air that was there while walking the hose hand-over-hand, feeling his way through the darkness; he hated this. He stopped, made the sign of the cross, and then his gloved hand fell on the ax he had left on top of the hose. Some of the floor had burned out in the front room, and the bottom of the fireplace had fallen half way between two floor joists, causing the brick chimney to tilt. He could hear Captain Jack shouting and searching, but he stayed with the hose, dragging the ax until he found him sitting on the floor, his back against the bedroom wall, coughing. Half of the bedroom ceiling had fallen in, and you could see a large hole burned through the roof and most of the smoke was pouring out through the hole, but the fresh oxygen was like throwing gasoline on the fire. The entire room was in flames.

Jack handed Tony the nozzle and started crawling across the room, sweeping his arms side to side until he found the bed. Roofing and burning rafters had fallen onto the bed, setting the bedding on fire. He squeezed under the first bed, stretching his arm out as far as it would reach, sweeping it from front to back, then moving over to the other bed.

"Time to go, Cap, I can't cut it anymore. We're going to burn up in this place."

Jack could taste the warm, watery substance running down his exposed face from the burst blisters. He reached quickly under the second bed, searching and his hand touched a soft bundle coiled in a knot. He yanked the metal bed away from the wall.

"Tony. Over here." Jack picked up the small limp body; her head drooped over his arm, her long braided hair hanging freely. He handed her to Tony.

"Get her outside quick."

"Cap, we got to go, *now*. The whole house is going to fall in on us."

"Go! I'm right behind you."

Tony headed for the front door, crawling with the young girl on his back.

Jack moved quickly through the black smoke, feeling his way back to the same bed, remembering—like a wild animal, they always hide in the darkest places when trapped. He ran his gloved hand down the wall to the baseboard and followed it to the corner, between the bed and the wall. His fingers clamped around a tiny foot sticking out from under a quilt. The foot jerked out of his grip and the quilted figure scurried back under the bed. Jack scrambled under the bed scooping the small bundle in his arm as the entire roof came crashing down.

"Cap? Cap? You all right?"

Jack wiggled out from under the bed, kicking a burning timber out of the way and dragging the bundle with him to the bedroom door. "I told you to get out of here."

Tony came crawling back to the bedroom door, coughing. "I'm not leaving without you. Come on, we don't have much time. The whole roof is gone in here, and the front one is about to go."

"Where's the girl?"

"I don't think she made it. I got her to the porch, and they took her. They've got water now." Water was pouring through the roof opening, burning them like steamed lobsters.

"I got to go, Cap." Tony was choking and vomiting.

Jack hovered on all fours over the quilt and followed Tony. He felt along the wall as he dragged the bundle, pushed it with his legs, and then the quilt was snatched from his hand. He looked down, not a foot from him, and stared into two defiant but glimmering eyes, buried in a soot-covered face.

"Where's Rosy?" The boy shouted.

Jack stopped and pulled the quilt over their heads, protecting them from the suffocating smoke and burning water. Lying face to face on the floor staring at each other, "What's your name, tough guy?"

"You fire man?"

"Yes, sir...firefighter, and I'm going to get us out of here, but you got to tell me your name."

"Mack," he said, coughing and slapping at the quilt to get it off his head.

"Hold tight there, Mack, we've got everyone out but you. Stay covered so you won't get burned, okay?"

Pushing Mack back under his chest, he crawled, hands and knees, when an explosion shook the house, lifting them both and slamming them against the wall. The ceiling joists and roof in the front room crashed down, then a loud crackling roar as the twenty-foot chimney exploded, shooting brick missiles.

Jack rolled over onto his back, half conscious. He fought to free himself from the quilt and felt for the small boy, finding him against the wall. He pulled his limp body over to him and pressed his ear against the boy's chest. His heart was beating strong and fast. He removed his glove and quickly searched the boy's head for blood or cuts and then his body for any broken bones. *He's okay, probably just a slight concussion; hell, my head's still ringing.*

He kept his nose close to the floor as his hand swept the area until he found his helmet, his throat and lungs scorched by the heat. He slipped his glove back on and rewrapped the boy in the quilt. One end of the ceiling was still attached to the top plate of the wall, creating a void and trapping them between the fallen ceiling and the interior wall. He started crawling to the end of the wall when hissing flames whirled around the corner, blocking his exit. He backtracked, the flames burning his face. He grabbed hold of the quilt and dragged it to the other end, but the fire was in full force now—blocking both ends of their escape. He moved back to the center of the wall, arched his back, and with both feet pushed as hard as he could on the leaning ceiling. It wouldn't budge. There wasn't much smoke now, but the heat was so extreme the wallpaper was igniting.

The booster? Falling on his stomach he squeezed under the collapsed ceiling. With his out-stretched arm, he searched along the edge, until his hand found the red hose. He yanked and pulled, feeding the hose through his hands, until he reached the nozzle. Leaning back against the wall with the hose between his legs he shouted, "Now baby, now..."

Jack jerked the nozzle open—no water. He slammed the handle shut with the heel of his hand and yanked it open again—no water! With raging fury, he banged it against the wall, opening and shutting it off again and again, but still no water. Burning embers, ricocheting off his helmet, caught the quilt on fire. He threw the nozzle down and pulled the blanket off the boy, snuffing out the fire. He unbuckled his coat and stuck the boy inside.

"Tony! Tooo'ny!" He shouted.

There was no answer.

Tony didn't make it: he was buried under a pile of chimney-bricks on the other side of the wall just a few steps away. Only his helmet, knocked to one side, lay uncovered.

The remaining roof collapsed, spreading fire everywhere, closing off their space to no more than the size of a closet. This is it, Jack thought, as he scooted backward away from the fire. Then his hand fell on the wooden handle of the fire ax—his fingers tightened around the handle in a death grip. Removing Mack from his coat, he dropped to his knees and chopped away at the floor. As chunks of wood flew, he thanked God for his hardnosed insistence that the men keep their axes sharp enough to shave with.

An opening between the floor joists appeared, and Jack tore off his coat and helmet and dropped through the hole in the floor pulling Mack, but his boot slipped on the mud and water under the house and he fell, banging his head and losing his grip on Mack. Struggling to raise up in the small space under the house, Jack felt a sharp blow to his chest and out of the smoke and debris he heard a voice demanding, "Where's Rosy?"

Mack had fallen through the hole and now sat up in the muddy water. As the two crawled through the mud, they emerged from under the house to face a curtain-wall of high-pressured water protecting the house next door. Two firefighters ran to help Jack as he carried Mack away from the burning house and guided them to the front yard, which was covered with fire equipment, ambulances, and people from the neighborhood.

Jack stood dazed, his blood-streaked eyes locked in a frigid stare, his wet hair frozen into red icicles. He had no eyebrows, his ears blistered and swollen twice their normal size, and patches of burst blisters hung from his face, leaving dark raw blotches.

"My God, man, what happened to you?" A doctor said running up to him.

Mack stood watching the burning houses looking for Tony, his wet long johns frozen on his body.

"Over here right away," the doctor called out. Two medics came running. "This man's in shock. Get him covered with some blankets."

"I'm all right. Take care of the boy here," he mumbled.

"Where is Rosy?" Mack was shouting while the doctor and medics rushed both of them into the waiting ambulance.

No one would realize until the fire was under control and extinguished, that a firefighter had lost his life. After twenty-four years of fighting fires, Private Tony D'Agostino's body lay alone, buried under a pile of chimney bricks and a collapsed roof.

Mack would not let go of Captain Jack's neck. They both sat in the front seat of the ambulance wrapped in blankets with the heater blowing on them. Mack was exhausted and rested his small head on Jack's shoulder, his face pressed against the window.

The driver backed over the fire hose and then pulled forward, crawling past the five bodies covered with blankets and lined up on the frozen ground. Mack lifted his head, checked each body, closing his eyes after each one, and in a low whisper begged mournfully,

"Please, please don't take my sunshine away."

The driver edged the ambulance over the curb and turned on his siren, drowning out Mack's scream as he looked back at the last body with one foot sticking out from under the blanket. It was covered with a pink rabbit slipper.

CHAPTER 1

BICKFORD PARK IN December looked like an unkempt graveyard. A thermometer, recessed in a rusted Coca-Cola sign and nailed to the door of the storage room, read 38 degrees. Multi-colored leaves blanketed the ground ankle deep. The net from the paddle tennis court, and the hockey sticks from the scarred hockey box were missing, stolen or locked in storage for the winter, and—most depressing of all—the drained wading pool lay empty, its blue paint curling up between the dead leaves.

The ten-acre park was vacant except for the five boys playing "overhead-tackle" football, a game where one boy, with his back to the others, throws the football over his head, and then everybody tackles the one who caught the ball. Isaac "Sonnyman" Brenner, a fat, dark, colored kid, wearing a new pair of high-top Converse tennis shoes, turned his back to the four other boys and threw the football high into the air over his head. Mack Shannon, a skinny Irish kid with a thick mop of black hair, gauged his leap as he snatched the football and landed on the run. He ran opposite from the designated goal line, a towering 200-year-old oak tree and a landmark for generations. He faked out the boys in pursuit, reversed his field, and headed for the big tree.

Ambling down the middle of the field with his eyes locked on Mack was Sonnyman. Anticipating Mack's fake, he grabbed him in a bear hug and drove him to the ground with the full weight of his body. All the other boys piled on, searching for the ball, like a rugby scrum. Mack let out a yell and coughed up the football as someone in the pile clamped down on his testicles. Another shout was heard as Mack bit down on an ear close to his mouth. The boys unfolded and Sweet Pea, an albino midget, squeezed from the bottom of the pile with one hand clutching the football and the other trying to staunch the trickle of blood from his ear. He chuckled as his child-like legs churned for the goal line.

Everyone turned when they heard the horn, four loud musical notes, like a calliope on one of the old paddlewheel boats downtown.

"Hey, Mack! Mack!" They heard someone shout.

Mack stood up, holding his testicles, while looking toward the darkening street.

"Isn't that Crazy Ray Flynn?" Sonnyman asked.

Mack watched as Crazy Ray got out of his car and stood on the running board waving for him. Mack showed no noticeable signs of fear, but like the bristling of the hackles on a dog's neck, the potential danger was widespread. Mack turned his back to the street. Feeling the cold, he tucked his sweatshirt into his jeans and walked over to the big tree; the other boys followed. Three-foot-tall Sweet Pea, with his white bushy hair like a boll of cotton, sat on his new football, leaning back against the tree.

"Too dark to play anymore, huh?" Sweet Pea said to no one in particular.

Mack picked up his Navy pea jacket and slipped it on, then pulled his watch cap out of his pocket and stretched it onto his head.

Standing beside Mack, Sonnyman said, "Trouble's coming, Sweet Pea, you'd better head on home."

Sweet Pea stood up. Without his glasses he had to walk closer and squint until he recognized the outline of the two figures heading toward him. He ran back to the tree, picked up his football, and ran into the wooded area of the park muttering, "Oooh shit, that's Crazy Ray and Dago."

Mack watched the two boys swaggering across the field.

Just like that old western I saw at the movies last week. Two gunslingers walking into town looking for the sheriff....The problem is...this is no movie, and they're calling my name, not the sheriff's. Fight or flight? It always comes down to that question.

Mack's answer was always the same: *never* run.

Dago wore sunglasses and walked two steps behind Crazy Ray, who was tall for his age and skinny, wearing an open, full-length black leather coat that dragged across the ground.

Mack had known Crazy Ray since the fourth grade at St. Jerome's Orphanage and School. He remembered a fire drill one day when all the kids marched out of the classrooms and gathered in the schoolyard. Crazy Ray crawled out onto the windowsill. Everyone in the schoolyard pointed up to where Crazy Ray was dangling his feet from the third floor window, smoking a cigarette. He had closed the window, and the sisters begged and prayed for him to come back in, but he threatened to jump if any of them opened the window. He finished his smoke, flipped the cigarette butt to all the kids watching below, and banged on the glass, commanding the waiting sisters to open the window. Father O'Brien paddled him so hard that Ray had to stand, using the same windowsill as a desk for two days.

Crazy Ray was a notorious bully, two years older than any other student, and he challenged Mack to a fight after school that same day, bragging to everyone how he was going to teach Mack a lesson. The whole school showed up—everyone that is, except Crazy Ray. Things were different now; Mack knew that Crazy Ray always carried a gun.

"Mack, why haven't you come by to see me, man? I left word at Mickey's and the boxing gym that I was looking for you, man."

Mack stood with both hands in his coat pockets, saying nothing, staring at Crazy Ray's dirty red hair that was tied in a ponytail. The heavy make-up he always wore failed to hide the deep acne scars covering his face.

Crazy Ray walked over to Mack, put his arm around his shoulder, and whimpered, "I needed you, Baby. I got a job just for you...it pays big bucks." Then without any warning, he exploded, flailing his arms and stomping his feet. "You're too good to talk to me?" The cigarette blasted from his mouth almost comically as he screamed,

"WHAT'S-THESE-NIGGERS-DOING-IN-OUR-PARK?"

Everyone stood rigid—waiting.

Crazy Ray, sticking his lips up to Mack's ear, "Why—are you—playing football—with these—*Jigaboos?*"

Sonnyman pressed his knees together to keep his legs from shaking. He could feel the hate in Dago's eyes burning through the sunglasses like a cutting torch. He lowered his eyes and, halfway down Dago's leg he saw the nose of a sawed-off, double-barreled shotgun sticking out of his right sleeve.

Sonnyman was afraid to breathe. Dago weighed over 250 pounds and was six feet tall. He was square—like a dump truck—and wore a large, loose-fitting mackinaw. His once dark crew cut was now bleached to a golden-yellow.

"Crazy Ray, I know you, you'd better leave them alone. I'm going to call the police," came a loud squeal from Sweet Pea, hiding in the woods.

Sonnyman saw the shotgun drop from the sleeve of Dago's coat and the red blast blow out the end of the barrel. He dove to the ground with the explosion still ringing in his ears.

"Come on out of there you little tree monkey. I see you!" Dago shouted, walking forward and firing the other barrel into the trees. The only two standing were Crazy Ray and Dago. Walking back, Dago opened the shotgun, and two empty shells flew out. He pulled two new shells from his pocket and shoved them into the barrels.

As the noise of the shotgun blast diminished, you could hear the little feet of Sweet Pea running over the dead leaves, heading out of the park.

"Everyone stay on the ground just like you are!" Crazy Ray shouted. He walked over to Sonnyman and savagely kicked him in his side. "Get your black ass over there with the other two niggers. We're going to teach you boys a lesson about playing in *our* park."

Mack started to get up, but Crazy Ray stomped him in the middle of his back, knocking the breath out of him. Then he felt the cold steel barrel of a pistol pressed into his neck. Crazy Ray knelt beside him and shouted, "*You*, don't want to be my friend anymore? *You*, don't want to help your old buddy? *You*, would rather play with the *nig'gers*?" Mack raged inside but said nothing.

Crazy Ray smiled as he pulled Mack up and jerked his cap off. He brushed the dirt from Mack's face and coat with the cap and said, "You know you're my main man, Baby. There's absolutely no one that can drive a car like you, and that's what I need. I swear, on the Sacred Heart, I won't touch one kinky hair on their burr heads if you drive for me, okay?" Mack didn't say no.

"*Alllll*-right then, it's a deal!" Crazy Ray started walking back to his car with his arm around Mack's shoulder and tried to kiss him, but Mack jerked away.

Dago, still guarding the boys with the shotgun, yelled, "Hey, Ray, what do you want me to do with these niggers?"

With his arm still around Mack's shoulder, Crazy Ray turned, pulling Mack with him and said, "Kill 'em."

Mack bolted from Crazy Ray's arm and raced toward Dago shouting, "Nooo." Dago sidestepped Mack's lunge and slammed him to the ground, pinning him there with his boot on Mack's neck.

Crazy Ray was bent over laughing so hard, he choked and fell to his knees coughing, then fell backward, still laughing. He spread his arms and legs like a snow angel and with an exaggerated Irish accent looked up to the sky. "Aye, me lads, as me mother would say, 'tis a heavenly night tonight." He laid spread eagle, listening to the soft sobbing of one of the boys, then got up and walked over to Mack.

"Mack, Baby, it's a joke. We're not going to kill anyone. You've been watching too many gangster movies. *We* are the good guys, man." Mack watched as Crazy Ray pulled the 38-caliber pistol from inside his coat pocket and tapped him on the shoulder as he talked. "But we got to teach these boys a lesson before we leave. Right, Dago?" Dago did not respond. "You niggers ever coming to this white man's park again?"

The two boys with Sonnyman answered without hesitation and in unison, "No sir, never."

"What about you, fat ass?" Dago shouted, tapping Sonnyman in the head with the barrel of the shotgun.

"Please. Please don't kill us."

"All three of you, take off your clothes," Crazy Ray said, waving his pistol. "*Now.* When I count to five, the first nigger that ain't completely naked, I'll shoot him." One of the boys was already down to his underwear before the count of three when Crazy Ray shouted, "*All* your clothes! Black-ass naked, all three of you and put them in a pile right here!" pointing with his pistol.

Mack cautiously stepped over to Crazy Ray, "Ray, please, I'm asking you..."

"*What?* What am I doing?" brushing Mack aside. "Dago, take their shoes and pull all the laces out. You three, get down," jabbing with his pistol toward the ground. Crazy Ray walked over to Dago, whispered something in his ear, then said out loud, "We'll wait for you in the car."

"Come on, Mack, like I promised, not a hair on their kinky heads." Crazy Ray pulled Mack by his coat sleeve as they walked to the car, telling him that Dago was just going to tie them up. He kept jumping around, punching Mack, shadow boxing and taunting him to teach him how to throw a left hook. "We got ring-side tickets to the Midsouth Championship—you going to beat that punk from Little Rock, right? I got money on you."

Mack paid little attention to Crazy Ray. He kept looking back, watching Dago tie up each boy with their shoelaces, face down, with their hands behind them.

A black cloud fell over the park as Dago, using the barrel of his shotgun, picked up some scattered clothing as if they were contaminated and placed them in the pile. Laying down his shotgun, he saw his two empty shell casings and picked them up and put them inside his shirt pocket. Standing over the pile of clothing, he unzipped the fly of his trousers and, with a smile on his face, urinated over the boys' clothing.

The four loud musical notes of the car horn broke the silence. Dago looked toward the street as he picked up his shotgun. Standing with his back to the boys, he breached the shotgun slowly and then closed it.

Sonnyman, face down in the leaves, heard the car horn and prayed that Dago would leave now. But tonight his prayers would not be heard as he felt the toe of Dago's boot close to his head. He looked up as he heard Dago open the shotgun, saw him push two shells from his shirt pocket into the barrels, and close it. Sonnyman felt the two cold steel barrels of the shotgun pressed against the back of his neck and waited. He heard the loud sound of the trigger pull. *Click*...his heart stopped beating.

"*Damn,*" Dago said, "a misfire. Well, that's why they have two barrels." He pulled the trigger on the other barrel. *Click.* "Well, I'll be damned, *two* misfires." Dago turned and walked toward the car, then stopped and breached the shotgun; two empty casings came flying out. "Luckiest nigger I ever saw," he laughed as he walked to the car.

Sonnyman did not breathe until he heard the car roar away with a parting blast of the musical horns. He rolled over on his side and coiled into the fetal position, shivering in the cold. He listened to the moans and painful sobs of the other boys. Tears streaked down his dirty face as his long, agonizing cry echoed through the trees and a warm flow of urine ran down the inside of his legs.

CHAPTER 2

MACK WAS HUNKERED down behind the wheel of Crazy Ray's 1934 Ford street rod 4-suicide door sedan with the motor idling. The car was dropped low to the ground, front and back, and powered by a 400 Chevy with 426 horsepower— a rocket on wheels. The only sound was from the three carburetors grumbling at having to sit and wait.

After letting Crazy Ray and Dago off on the street side of the American Snuff Company, Mack drove to the end of the building overlooking the river. He backed alongside a spur railroad track on the river bluff and parked at the corner of the building. From there he had a clear view of the back and the street side of the building. He didn't have a watch, but he knew it was after midnight and figured he had been there about ten minutes. It felt more like thirty. He didn't feel good about this, his stomach was in knots, but he was not going to back out. A much more powerful thought dominated his actions, creating an obsession...*revenge.* He needed revenge to cleanse himself. He would never again in his lifetime suffer the shame, the cowardly helplessness, he had gone through in the park; he would die first.

Mack felt wetness from sweat under both arms and checked the heater switch; it was off. He lowered the window to cool off, but the smell of the fine brown snuff blowing off the open windows, caked with dark brown powder, caused him to choke and cough.

On the weekends and sometimes after school, Mack worked at his Uncle Mickey's Pub a couple of blocks from here. The snuff workers, looking as if they had been dusted with dark brown flour, would line up three deep at the bar, downing one frothy pint after another of the dark Guinness. Mickey's Pub was an Irish neighborhood public house with ice-cold beer, Irish whisky, and lots of hot food served by hearty women. A clandestine back room served those with a betting nature.

Mack's left foot tapped the clutch pedal to the beat of the rumbling engine. He pushed in the clutch and pulled the floor shift down into first gear then moved it back to neutral. He noticed the sawed-off shotgun that Crazy Ray had taken from Dago sticking out from under the passenger's seat. He slid it under his seat and looked down the street; there was no one in sight. It was pitch black, with no streetlights and no lights on in the building. The only light Mack saw was a dim, hooded light above the side door.

The gunshot blast sounded like a cannon. Mack's heart rate doubled, and a chill covered his body; his sweat feeling like ice water. He bolted upright in his seat and stomped on the clutch and gas pedal at the same time, jerking the floor shift down into first gear. The Ford leaped forward. Mack speed-shifted into second gear and skidded around the corner. As the car hit hard pavement, he fought for control. His peripheral view caught two men as they burst out of the side door, struggling to carry what looked like bags of...*what?* Mack slid the car into the curb with a jolting halt, fifty feet from the door. He slung his left arm over the top of the seat and opened the back door and saw Dago, who was behind Crazy Ray, drop one of the bags. Still holding two of the bags under his arm, Dago kneeled down, trying to roll the dropped bag up his leg and under his other arm. The bag burst open, and a flow of shiny silver dollars poured out. Mack saw the night watchman stagger out the door with a gun in one hand and a bottle of whisky hanging at his side in the other. He wore a policeman's uniform with a large star-shaped badge pinned to his left coat pocket.

"Stop! Stop or I'll shoot your ass!" The watchman shouted.

Mack watched as he raised his gun and fired two shots into the air.

Dago lost it. Scared and enraged, he jumped to his feet screaming at the cop and dropped the other bags, which split open at the top, scattering coins at his feet. He reached into his coat pockets and jerked out two pistols, one in each hand, firing off alternating rounds while standing ankle deep in silver dollars. After emptying the pistols, he cried out like a wild man—falling to his knees, pointing the pistols to the sky, and continued to jerk each trigger over and over.

Mack choked down a scream when he saw the whisky bottle explode on the concrete walkway. He watched with his mouth open as the night watchman grabbed the left side of his chest and fell backward against the door, crumbling over.

Mack jumped when Crazy Ray dropped his two 50-pound bags of silver dollars on the back floor of the car.

"Go, man! Move it!" Ray shouted.

"What about Dago?" Mack watched Dago stuff his coat pockets with silver dollars.

Crazy Ray pounded Mack's head and shoulders shouting, "Go, you dumb ass. He's killed a cop. Get out of here, *now!*"

The car jumped forward, then stalled, the engine dead.

Crazy Ray went ballistic, hammering him with his fist and shouting to get the car started.

Mack couldn't think. He grabbed the shotgun and swung, catching Crazy Ray across his right ear, knocking him to the floorboard.

His first thought was that he had run out of gas. He checked the gas gauge, knowing he had filled it earlier. He knew then that it was flooded, the three carbs full of gas. He turned the key off and forced himself to wait a few seconds. What seemed to him a lifetime was less than a minute. He checked the rear view mirror and saw Crazy Ray sitting up holding his bloody ear. *Now,* he thought. Holding the gas pedal to the floor, he turned the key back on and the engine roared. He raced down the street, and without any warning, he slammed on the brakes. Crazy Ray shot forward almost over the front seat, and before he could protest, Mack shifted the car into reverse. Crazy Ray grabbed the back of the front seat and held on as the car backed down the street, weaving, with tires squealing and smoking. Lights from the little shotgun houses across the street came on as Mack backed over the curb and skidded to a stop next to Dago.

"Get him," Mack shouted. Dago was on his knees scooping up the silver dollars with both hands and putting them back in the bags.

Crazy Ray obeyed. Opening the back door, he reached out and grabbed Dago by his coat and dragged him onto the floor of the car. With Dago's legs still dangling from the running board, Mack stomped on the gas and whirled the steering wheel. The car jumped the curb, screeching down the street, fishtailing past people standing on their porches—a trail of silver dollars spilling from the open back door.

Mack was in a cold rage, no longer nervous, but mad and calculating. *Cop killers* dominated his thoughts.

Crazy Ray kicked Dago on the floorboard, shouting, "I told you— no guns!"

Dago, blocking the kicks with his arms, shouted back, "Oh yeah, and you said—no night watchman, right?"

Mack couldn't think, "Shut up back there, both of you." He slowed the car to the speed limit, then turned south on Second Street and stopped. He was in big trouble. His right foot twitched, tapping the brakes pedal. *What am I doing, sending a signal with my taillights?* He grabbed his leg and squeezed it until his foot stopped moving. He took a deep breath and exhaled.

Dago was on top of Crazy Ray now, holding him down shouting, "You never checked that place out, *did you?* You almost got us killed. Where was the payroll money?" He threw a hand full of silver dollars at Crazy Ray, "This...this pocket change." (Very few people outside of American Snuff Company's employers and employees were aware of their tradition of paying Christmas bonuses in silver dollars.)

Mack heard the sirens and saw the glow of red flashing lights one block over and shouted, "Shut up!" He spun around, the sawed-off shotgun shaking in his hand, "One more word from either of you, I'll shoot you both and dump you in the river. I swear to God."

Mack laid the shotgun across his lap, switched the headlights off, and turned west on Union Avenue. He coasted down to the foot of Union and crossed Riverside Drive down to the river. The car bumped over the sloped cobblestones as he focused on a plan, his eyes adjusting to the darkness as they passed the different boats docked along the waterfront. He spotted what he was looking for, pulled in, and stopped between two parked cars close to the river's edge.

He opened his door and pulled the shotgun out with him, holding it to his side. He stood holding the back door open and shouted for Dago to get out. Dago hesitated, glancing at the two pistols on the floorboard.

"Go ahead, pick them up. I dare you!" Mack raised the shotgun.

Dago grabbed the doorpost to pull himself up and out of the seat.

Mack stepped back and kicked the door as hard as he could on Dago's hand. He screamed, clutching his broken fingers as Mack pulled the door open and jerked him forward onto the cobblestones. Dago rolled to the rear of the car trying to get away, but Mack was on him instantly, stomping and kicking. Dago groaned, covered his head with his arms while Mack beat him with the shotgun.

In Mickey's Pub, Mack had heard many times the Irish saying: "Vengeance is a dish best served cold." *Well, not for me it isn't.*

Mack took a long step and kicked Dago in the middle of his back. He rolled over, hollering, and came up on all fours. Mack kicked him one last time as he scrambled down the cobblestones.

Crazy Ray had locked all the doors and was now in the front seat, searching for the keys. Mack dangled them in front of the window and tried to open the door, but Crazy Ray held the lock down. Mack slammed the barrel of the shotgun through the door window, shattering the glass as Crazy Ray scrambled to the opposite side of the car, but his long leather coat caught on the floor shift. Mack reached through the smashed window, opened the door, and stuck the shotgun in Crazy Ray's face.

"Get out!"

Crazy Ray scooted to the far corner of the passenger door and shook his head.

Mack stabbed the shotgun into Crazy Ray's forehead. He yelled, grabbing his head, trying to halt the blood spewing through his fingers like a burst water pipe. Mack walked around to the other side of the car, opened the door with the key, and grabbed Crazy Ray by his ponytail, pulling him out onto the cobblestones, kicking him over and over. Straddling him, he laid the end of the bloodied double-barreled shotgun on the bridge of his nose.

"How does it feel? Tell me, you piece of shit." Mack stood over him now, shouting, "Open your eyes!"

Crazy Ray felt the cold steel of the two barrels resting in his blood-filled eye sockets.

"If you so much as breathe a word to anyone about me being with you two tonight..." Mack lifted him by his leather coat and shoved him across the cobblestones. He stumbled and fell. "Now crawl down there with your buddy and there'll be two piles of shit." Mack watched as Crazy Ray hobbled down the bank, holding his bleeding forehead.

Mack was exhausted, his Irish temper spent, leaving him with a pounding headache. He brushed the shattered glass from the car seat, and drove along the riverbank searching. He stopped at the far end; *no cars or boats down at this end of the river.* He looked up toward Riverside Drive and saw what he was looking for—a level landing about halfway up the bank—a flat offloading area for bales of cotton when the river was up. He backed the car up onto the landing facing the river. Then he pushed the gearshift to neutral, removed his belt, and tied a knot around the handle of the sawed-off shotgun. With the car still running, he pushed the clutch in and shifted the car into second gear. Picking up the shotgun, he placed the barrels on top of the depressed clutch and then wedged the handle against the bottom of the front seat. He climbed out of the car, shut the door, and stood on the running board, listening to the rhythmic idling of the powerful engine he helped build from scratch. This wasn't going to be easy. He had keen memories of this car, but all those people across from the factory had seen it racing from the shooting. He reached through the broken window, careful of some jagged pieces of glass still stuck in the bottom guide, found the end of the belt and stepped back, jerking the shotgun free from the clutch. The car jumped forward and bounced down the riverbank until it splashed into the swift current of the Mississippi River. Mack stood on the riverbank, watching the top of the Ford sedan bob up and down, headed south. He added up his disastrous undertaking for the night: the hundred dollars he failed to collect for driving the car, a dead cop, the loss of the car with two pistols, one sawed off shotgun, his only belt, and a floorboard full of silver dollars.

CHAPTER 3

A WEEK HAD PASSED, and Mack had not seen or heard from Crazy Ray or Dago. He waited, alone, in a small room in the belly of the giant Ellis Auditorium. The Corinthian-designed auditorium, built in 1924, appeared to have surfaced from a Greek archeological dig. Perched on top of the river bluff overlooking the Mississippi River, the building covered one square city block. Tonight it would host the biggest fight of his life.

He sat on a metal chair, surrounded by lockers; a single light bulb hung from a black cord overhead. The walls, ceiling, and floor were all a dull gray concrete—not unlike a jail or a bomb shelter. He looked at his hands wrapped tight with white gauze between each finger and tape that crisscrossed up to his wrists.

What am I doing here? I should just get up and walk out. Yeah, sure...why not commit suicide while you're at it?

It was the night of the finals of the Mid-South Golden Gloves Championship. The main event of the evening was between Mack and twenty-three-year-old Rocco Montesi, known as "The Golden Boy"— a cocky ironworker from North Little Rock, Arkansas. They both weighed the same, 147 pounds, but Mack was four inches taller, at five-foot ten. The difference in the two was that Rocco looked like a grown man, with a developed body of defined muscles. Mack was a skinny kid, with very little muscle tone, but what got him this far was he hit as hard as a mule kicked.

Mack was nervous, not about fighting; he liked a good fight now and then, it tested your mettle. It was the prefight, the waiting, alone in this *dungeon;* too much time to think. And of course the embarrassment of not meeting everyone's expectations or doing something stupid, like getting knocked out in front of all your friends. His stomach was a cage of butterflies, multiplying so fast if he opened his mouth they would fly out. And if that wasn't enough pressure, a picture of the night watchman grabbing his chest and falling to the ground flashed before his eyes like a recurring news clip.

Twilly Kilkenny stuck his head inside the room and looked around before mimicking the ring announcer, "The *winner...*and new *Mid-South Welterweight Champion—Mack Shannon!*"

Twilly had a broad smile on his face with deep-set eyes that glowed with merriment. He waddled across the concrete floor carrying a brown shopping bag under one arm, his body shaking like a bowl of Jell-O with every step. His hands, fat and heavy, barely cleared the sleeves of his coat.

"Jeez! This place is like a crypt," Twilly shrieked with a high Gaelic accent.

Mack warmed with Twilly's presence, and the tension of waiting faded.

"Mackie, how you feeling me boy—a wee bit nervous? This is the worst part, the waiting. Here, turn around and let me massage those traps." Twilly set the shopping bag in the corner while Mack turned and rested his arms on the back of the chair. Twilly rubbed Mack's neck then moved down into the knotted rhomboids.

"Listen close, Mackie." Looking left and right, he whispered, as if someone might be listening. "We're going to make us some money tonight. I put a bet down of five big ones, and another big one if you knock him out. Plus, another hundred, with two-to-one odds, that you will knock him out in the first round. That's eight hundred, and you get eighty bucks in your pocket. And, as an added bonus—only if you knock him out in the first round—I have lined you up tonight with Miss Ruby. Heh, heh, heh, not bad, huh?"

Ruby was a twenty-six-year-old hooker, a regular at Mickey's Pub. Mack had fantasized about her for months, and Twilly had picked up on his erotic itch. Twilly had paid Mack some easy money in the past to run collections of bets when things were slow at the bar. But, truthfully, they were more like errands than collections. He gave terms to anyone who couldn't pay a bet; and if they still didn't pay, there was never any rough stuff. He had a simple philosophy: if you didn't pay, you didn't play—ever again. Mack often thought Twilly was a bookie, not so much for the money, but more for the contact and the favors he did for people, especially women.

"Get your Leprechaun ass out of here, Twilly," Sarge Smith said as he charged through the door and breezed by Twilly. "I told all you Irish mobsters to stay away from my fighters." Sarge removed the pair of twelve-ounce boxing gloves from around his neck and wiped the blood and sweat off with a towel. "You ready to kick some ass, Champ?"

Mack stood up and waited until Sarge opened one of the gloves and then shoved his hand deep inside and worked it around until it felt comfortable. He did the same with the other glove. They were still hot inside from the other fighter.

Sergeant Gene Smith was the boxing coach for the Front Street Gym where Mack trained. His thick neck sat on square shoulders, and a potbelly was starting to show. He yelled over his shoulder to the fighter who came in with him, "Make sure you have Doc look at that eye after you shower." Then he held up both hands in front of Mack with palms out. Mack threw a couple of punches, banging each opened hand. "That's it, make sure you follow that right with a left hook. And when you do, pop that left shoulder and hip into it. How the hands feel? You ready?"

Mack nodded and headed for the door, banging his gloves together. Sarge followed, spreading a dingy towel over Mack's shoulders, and stopped when he saw Twilly standing in the shadow of the overhead light.

"Listen, fat man, I thought I told you to get your ass out of here."

Unperturbed, Twilly sauntered past Sarge and stopped in between the two, turning his back to Sarge and handing Mack the brown shopping bag. "We'll celebrate at Mickey's after the fight." He turned, smiled at Sarge and ambled out the door whistling.

Mack handed Sarge the bag he held between his two boxing gloves and shrugged his shoulders.

"I wonder what the little toad has in here." Sarge opened the bag and pulled out a long, white satin boxing robe with green cuffs and held it up for Mack to read the name on the back. A pair of matching boxing shorts fell to the floor as Sarge held up the robe. On the back was the name, MACK SHANNON, with a shamrock between his first and last name.

"Well, I'll be damned," Sarge said, as he pulled the towel from Mack's shoulders and helped him remove his old workout shorts. He held the green boxing shorts while Mack slipped each foot through, working them up and over his leather protector. He opened the robe as Mack slid his gloves into the oversized sleeves of the most dazzling garment he had ever worn. Mack brushed his face against the shoulder of the satin robe, feeling the smoothness, while Sarge tied the belt in front, and then opened the door to the narrow corridor. Mack stopped in the doorway, turned his back to the cracked mirror on the wall, and smiled while looking at the large green letters on the back of his robe.

The north auditorium was full, and the crowd was wild and raunchy with everyone pushing and shoving when Mack came into view. This was the last fight on the card and what the crowd had been waiting for. Sarge walked behind Mack with both hands on his shoulders, guiding him through the mob and down the aisle. Mack walked with his head down, trying to stay focused, but the shouts broke his concentration.

"Kill the bum, Irish!"

"Great robe, Mack!"

"You the man, Shannon!" People reached over and punched him on the arms and others slapped him on his back.

Almost to ringside, Mack looked up and saw Ruby standing in the aisle; his potential prize for tonight blocked his way to the ring. She smiled at Mack, her legs parted, with both hands on her hips. Her weight shifted to one foot causing the silky red dress to pull up tight on one side. The hem of her dress sliced across the middle of one shapely thigh and coiled upward, around her small waist. Wearing red spiked heels, she stood the same height as Mack. Cheers and catcalls started when the crowd saw Ruby blocking Mack's path to the ring.

Mack stood smiling. *Man! What a body.* He held out his arms, gloves turned up, looking at the crowd as if asking, *What am I to do?* Someone in the crowd shouted, "Knock her out, Mack."

Ruby moved a few steps toward Mack, ducked under his arms like a boxer, bobbing and weaving, and pushed her body up through his arms until her lips reached his ear. Her hot breath whispered, "Knock the Wop out, Mack. You can knock *me* out later."

Mack stood rigid, feeling a red glow of embarrassment, thankful he was wearing the leather groin protector.

Sarge pushed Mack past Ruby, and the crowd hooted and hollered while Mack climbed up the wooden steps into the ring. The bell rang loudly until the crowd settled down and the lights in the auditorium dimmed to darkness, leaving only the large hooded light hanging above the center of the ring.

"Laaaadies and...gennnntlemen, this will be the last fight of the evening, of the Mid-South Finals..." the announcer began.

Mack paced from corner to corner on his side of the ring while looking out over the crowd. He stopped when he spotted Dago limping down the aisle with a cast on his right hand while balancing two hotdogs in his other hand. Mack watched as he moved across the second row from ringside and stopped next to Crazy Ray. They both stared up at him. Mack smiled when he saw the two red circles, scabbed over on Crazy Ray's forehead, from the shotgun. He was without a ponytail. His red hair was fluffed out and hanging down over his shoulders. With all the makeup he had on, he looked more like an ugly girl than a man.

"This fight is in the open division and is for the Welterweight Championship of the Mid-South," the announcer continued.

Mack shadowboxed his way back across the ring to his corner. Seated in the first row were Twilly, Ruby, Mickey's young blonde girlfriend, and Mickey himself. On the other side of Mickey, was Kevin O'Shea, the Commissioner of Fire and Police, the two of them with their heads together in conversation. The Commissioner, a large and influential politician, his bright bush of red hair a prominent trademark and noticed by the crowd as he nodded and waved, never slowed his talk with Mickey. Mack walked over and looked down at Twilly, and while holding the lapels of his boxing robe, he made a short bow, thanking him for the robe. Twilly pointed to Mickey, letting Mack know who was really responsible. Mack shrugged his shoulders and danced back to his corner after failing to get Mickey's attention.

"In the blue corner, weighing 147 pounds, wearing the green shorts with the white stripe, last year's City Novice Welterweight Champion and this year's City Open Division Champion with a total of 21 wins, 19 by knockouts, and no losses, the hard-hitting, Bluff City's own, Maaaack...Shaaaannon."

Mack raised his right glove in the air to the shouts of the crowd.

"In the red corner, also weighing 147 pounds, wearing the gold robe, the gold shorts and the gold shoes, three-time Lightweight Champion of Arkansas, two-time Mid-South Champion, fighting for the first time in the Welterweight Division, with 36 wins, nine by knockouts and three losses. Let's hear a warm welcome for our neighbor from across the river, North Little Rock's, Rooooocco 'Golden Boy' Moooonteeeesi."

Rocco danced around the ring to all four corners, throwing punches and raising his arms, his gold robe fanning the air as a large following from Arkansas chanted, "Golden Boy! Golden Boy!"

Mack had never been in front of such a rambunctious crowd. He realized now the embarrassment Twilly had saved him with only a bath towel for a boxing robe and an old pair of gym shorts. Mickey may have paid for the robe, but you can bet it was Twilly's idea. Sarge pulled the sleeves over the boxing gloves, and Mack disrobed.

"The referee for tonight's fight, and former three-time Open Golden Glove Champion, Chief Eddie Hamilton of the Memphis Fire Department."

The bell rang again, and the referee motioned the boys to the center of the ring. Mack noticed Rocky's broad shoulders, his powerful arms, and muscular chest with all the hair. He had never seen so much hair on a human body. The referee took the towel off Sarge's shoulder and wiped the excess Vaseline off Mack's eyebrows.

"I have already talked with you boys earlier," he said, looking at both boys with angry black eyes, "and you both know what not to do...no holding and hitting, no hitting below the belt line or when a man is down."

Rocco stared at Mack. It made Mack nervous, so he looked away and focused on Rocco's big nose and the outline of the dark shadow of his beard. Rocco looked up and said, "You mick bastard, I'm going to kick your ass all over this ring."

"Knock off that talk, Montesi, and listen up," the referee said. "If a man is knocked down, the other man goes to the farthest corner and stays there until I signal him back to fight."

Mack looked at all the hair on Rocco's chest, and stopped and stared at the faded red letters SWEET and SOUR tattooed above each nipple. *Damn, I bet that hurt.*

"No rabbit punches or hitting with the forearm or backhand. Is that understood? Now let's have a clean fight; touch gloves, go to your corners, and when the bell rings, come out fighting."

Sarge took a gob of Vaseline from the back of his hand and wiped it across Mack's eyebrows and over each cheekbone, making sure the referee wasn't watching. "Okay Mack, here's what I want you to do. When the bell rings, he will come right at you. Be looking for him to lead with a right; and when he does, I want you to drop back half a step and unleash your left hook, okay?" Sarge stuck Mack's mouthpiece in, and the bell rang for the first round.

Rocco looked like a wild bull coming out of the gate, charging right at Mack. True to Sarge's word, Rocco couldn't wait until they got to the center of the ring before he telegraphed his looping right hand. Mack, baiting him, leaned forward a little; then halfway through Rocco's swing he bounced the half step backwards. Rocco fell forward, missing with his overhead right as Mack's left hook exploded to the right side of Rocco's temple. The crowd went wild as Mack danced back to his corner while the "Golden Boy" lay face down on the canvas.

The referee stood over Rocco with one hand in the air, starting his countdown, raising a finger for each count, "One...two..."

Everyone in the auditorium was on their feet, screaming. Rocco rolled over on the canvas and rose up in a sitting position shaking his head.

"Four...five..." the referee continued to count, holding his fingers in front of Rocco's face. Rocco pushed himself up on one knee, grabbed the ring ropes and pulled himself upright on the count of seven. The referee wiped Rocco's gloves on his chest while staring into his eyes and asked if he was okay. He said nothing, wobbled, and nodded his head. The referee held up his hand as if the fight was over and led him to his corner, not letting him sit down. He signaled for the ringside doctor.

The crowd was quiet—waiting. "Doc" Malinsky, a balding, 60-year old general practitioner and ex-fighter, climbed the steps to the ring. He pulled a penlight from inside his coat pocket and examined each of Rocco's eyes. He took his hand and covered one of Rocco's eyes, then the other, and held up two fingers asking him how many fingers he saw. He asked him what his name was and the day, month, and the year. He then nodded to the referee that it was okay for the fight to continue. The crowd came to life with clapping, shouts, and whistles. The Doc, chewing on his unlit stub of a cigar, his expression never changing, maneuvered himself back down the three steps to his ringside seat.

Mack didn't wait. As soon as the referee shouted, "Fight," Mack was all over Rocco with lefts and rights to the head. Rocco crouched and went into a shell, his gloves covering his head and his elbows in tight to protect his body. Mack moved in close for an uppercut, and Rocco grabbed him, tying him up, leaning his weight all over him. Mack tried to pull loose, but Rocco was stronger and held on. The referee pulled them apart shouting, "Break." Mack stepped back, but Rocco leaped forward with an overhead right that tore open a two-inch gash in Mack's left eyebrow. He followed with a wild left hook that missed and then grabbed Mack to keep from falling. With his head buried in Mack's chest, he drove him into the corner of the ring and jerked his head up, butting him under the chin. Seeing the blood on Mack's face and on his chest, the referee leaped between the two and marched Rocco to the far corner of the ring, shaking a finger in his face, admonishing him.

Sarge was up the steps in a flash, hanging halfway in the ring and jumping up and down on the bottom rope, screaming to the referee's back that Rocco had headbutted Mack. Mickey and Ruby stood and shouted, "Foul! Foul!" at the judges. The crowd raged, throwing an empty whiskey bottle, a large paper cup filled with ice, and balled-up programs into the ring. The police moved down and surrounded the ring, displaying their nightsticks. A ringside official banged on the bell with his hammer as the lights came up, and the announcer climbed into the ring shouting for order.

The referee waved for Doc to meet him in the corner as he sat Mack on his stool. Sarge worked to stop the flow of blood pouring from the cut under Mack's chin. Twilly had moved amazingly fast for a fat man. He was up the steps, draped between the ropes with a glob of alum on the end of a cotton swab, and stuck it in the open cut in Mack's left eye. With a cotton pad pressed against the eyebrow, he slid the cotton swab out, holding the pressure on the bleeding cut.

Doc stopped at the foot of the steps and scanned the riotous crowd as a half-eaten hotdog fell short of the ring. His stoic nature calmed the crowd down as he grabbed the corner post, pulling himself up the steps.

"Let's see the eye," he said.

Twilly removed his compress and not a drop of blood was showing. Doc pulled a sterile pad from a box sitting next to the ring post and wiped the excess alum from the cut. "You think you got enough gook in this cut?" He pushed his bifocals up on his nose. "All right, now the chin?"

Sarge pulled the pad from the cut, and blood dripped onto Mack's chest.

"Mack, hold your head back where I can see under your chin." Doc took another pad and pressed hard against the cut, held it there for a moment, then wiped the pad away as he pressed his glasses up on the bridge of his nose, moving closer to the cut. He stood up and looked at Twilly and nodded toward Mack. "Do the same thing to his chin as you did to close that eye." He turned and said to the referee, "Eddie, the chin's okay, but if that eye opens up any wider, I want another look."

The referee walked to the far corner and took Rocco by the forearm and pulled him in front of each ringside judge. He motioned for them to deduct one point from their scorecards as a penalty for butting.

Twilly took charge, climbing into the ring, and switching places with Sarge. He was intent, pressing hard on the cut to stop the bleeding. Sarge held the jar of alum, sterile pads, and cotton swabs, assisting Twilly.

In a low, calming voice Twilly said, "Reeeelax, Macky, deep breaths, everything is going to be just dandy." Grabbing inside the front of the waist band of his boxing shorts and lifting him up, he said, "Lean back and stick your legs out, arms down...deep breaths now, in through your nose and out the mouth, sloooowly, attaboy." Twilly motioned to Sarge to take his place holding the compress under Mack's chin. He then took a wet towel from the ice bucket and spread it out over Mack's chest. With one end, he wiped the blood from his face and then his torso.

"This blood is nothing, a couple of small cuts, that's all. I've stopped the bleeding—nothing we can't patch up with a couple of butterflies, but forget all that. Listen to me, I want you to focus on one thing, you've got to finish this bum off now, this round. We've plenty of time, do *exactly* as I say."

Sarge leaned through the ropes listening to every word, while holding the pad under Mack's chin. Twilly directed Sarge to remove the pad. No bleeding; Twilly nodded.

Squatting down between Mack's legs, like a Sumo wrestler, Twilly took Mack's face in his hands, "Look at me! This Wop is a brawler, you understand, a street fighter. He wants to smash your face and rattle your brains any way he can. Do you want this fight?" He didn't wait for an answer. "We're going to kick his ass; payback, baby, for the cheap shot under your chin. The 'Golden Boy' will come at you the same way as before, his first punch a looping overhead right. I don't want you to move back this time, but forward. Just drop straight forward, slipping under his right and throw your right hand as hard as you can to his gut. When he folds—and he will fold—explode that left hook to his kidney immediately behind your right." Twilly almost fell backward, showing Mack how hard he wanted him to throw his punches.

"He will try to tie you up so move away quickly." Twenty years had gone by, but Twilly was back in the ring "fighting" again, with fiery animation. "When he unfolds, he will come at you swinging like a wild man, so do the same thing. Drop in forward, in close, and with your right, tear his ribcage loose this time. Then, immediately behind your right, like a slingshot, slam the left hook to the body again. Lift him out of his golden shoes, and move away quickly. No headshots until his hands come down. Then you know what to do, right?" Twilly threw four short combinations for illustration.

Sarge was having *déjà vu*. Twenty years ago in this same ring, he had experienced an unexpected and vicious body attack by a short, overweight kid, Twilly Kilkenny. He lost the Lightweight Championship, his very first loss, and so devastating to his ego it almost ended his boxing career.

The referee tapped Twilly on the shoulder. "Your boy ready?"

Mack stood, and Twilly took the mouthpiece from Sarge and stuck it in Mack's mouth. "Remember; body, body, body." Sarge removed the stool and held the ropes open for Twilly to climb out as the bell rang to continue the first round.

Mack waited. He stayed in his corner acting dazed, his hands down at his side.

Rocco moved quickly, sensing an easy kill to an injured prey, and swung his sledgehammer right for the fatal blow.

Mack couldn't believe the opening when he saw it. Rocco's midsection was like someone had painted a red bull's-eye on it that begged, *hit me here, baby.* Mack slipped under Rocco's wild punch and fired his right like a battering ram, his hip and shoulder the driving forces. When Mack's right fist smashed into Rocco's body, he felt the two lower ribs break as the glove tore through the mid-section. Rocco doubled and groaned dropping his gloves to protect his body. Mack stepped forward, shifted his weight to his left foot and drove the left hook up and behind Rocco's protecting elbow, deep into the kidney. Rocco winced with pain and tried to grab Mack as he danced out of reach. Both of Rocco's arms were down now as Mack stepped in with two stiff left jabs to the face, a right to the body and a jolting left hook that caught Rocco flush on the chin. His knees buckled, and he collapsed as if struck by a thunderbolt; both eyes rolled back in his head.

Mack's left eye was swollen shut. Blood and sweat spilled down over his heaving chest. He stared down at the motionless, "Golden Boy," then exploded with a vociferous roar, his head thrown back and both gloves high in the air.

CHAPTER 4

ICKEY'S PUB WAS packed after the championship fight. The crowd was celebratory, shouting words in Gaelic to Mack and Twilly. Demanding a toast, they forced pints of Guinness and shots of Bushmills in front of them. The ice packs had taken most of the swelling from Mack's eye, and, except for the two butterfly patches, he looked almost normal. His black hair was still a little wet from his shower, but his big smile mirrored his enjoyment of all the attention. Twilly pushed Mack through the crowd to the end of the bar where Sean, the bartender with a heavy black beard, smiled and pressed a button to unlock the door to the back rooms.

"Way to go, Mate," Sean said, patting him on the back.

Twilly and Mack hurried through the door of the smoke-filled room. A craps table in the center of the room was packed two rows deep, and a poker table was full with men standing and waiting for an empty seat. Wedged in the corner was a crescent-shaped blackjack table wrapped with four bar stools, all occupied. No one noticed Twilly stepping behind some heavy drapes and tapping on the hidden door. The doorman, an ex-boxer, smiled and feigned a punch at Mack as he followed Twilly down the hall to the rear of the converted house.

Mickey Montague was the brother of Mack's dead mother and more or less his godfather. His office was one large room with a thick carpet, a large desk, and leather chairs. Mickey sat behind his desk bent over a large plate of spaghetti and a full glass of Guinness. A spotless white linen napkin was stuffed into the collar of his silk shirt. The gold cuff links, the heavy gold watch, and the gold collar pin left little doubt that Mickey enjoyed being referred to as "dapper." Stacks of one, five, ten, and twenty-dollar bills, wrapped with rubber bands, covered a corner of his desk. Ruby, her arm draped around the back of the sofa, held a half-empty glass of red wine in one hand and a cigarette in the other. She smiled when she saw Mack, stubbed out her cigarette, and walked over and touched her wine glass to his beer glass, in a toast.

"Great fight, Champ."

"You can put that beer down right here, Kid," Mickey said, tapping the desktop with his fork.

"Let's all make a toast to the champ," Twilly said, holding his shot of whiskey in the air.

"Yeah, after he brings that beer over here."

Twilly emptied the shot glass in one gulp and banged it down on the desktop. "Back off, Mickey! Let the lad enjoy his one night of fame."

Mickey jumped up from the table shouting, "I told all of you I didn't want the boy drinking."

"Get off his back. A pint of Guinness is not going to kill him; you're just jealous."

"Who the hell is jealous?"

"You are, that's who."

So enthralled in their heated argument, neither Mickey nor Twilly noticed when Ruby grabbed her purse and jacket, took Mack's arm, and led him down the hall to the back door. "Come on," she whispered, "they'll argue for an hour before they realize we've gone." She opened the door and pushed Mack out into a four-car garage. "Open those doors, Champ, and let's go party."

Mack stood by the open doors buttoning his coat while watching Ruby back out the red Buick convertible. He closed the double doors and climbed in beside her as the top folded down and she eased the car down the alley.

"How you feel, Baby, your eye okay?"

"Has the swelling gone down?" Mack asked, feeling his eye.

"Looks good to me," she kissed two fingers and touched his eye with them as she turned south on Bellevue Street. "You want to hear a cool band, do a little dancing?"

"Sure."

"Look in my purse and pull out that brown envelope."

Mack opened her purse and found the envelope; it was stuffed with five-and ten-dollar bills.

"It's yours. Twilly told me to give it to you. He put an extra twenty in and said you deserved every penny." Ruby reached over and squeezed the inside of Mack's thigh, smiling. "That was some fight, Honey."

Her touch caused him to drop her purse, and he struggled to catch the contents.

"Hey, relax, the fight's over. Hand me that small change purse while you're in there, will you?"

Mack handed her the purse, and Ruby slowed the car while removing what looked like a hand-rolled cigarette, and lit it with the car lighter. She took a long drag, holding it in her lungs and exhaled.

"You ever get high?"

"No."

"You want a hit? This is some good pot."

"No thanks."

"You hungry?" she mumbled, taking another hit.

"A little."

"How about a couple of jumbo barbecues from Leonard's with onion rings? We still got time; they don't close till midnight. We can eat them on the way to the Cotton Club." Ruby took another long drag from the joint.

"Where's the Cotton Club?"

Ruby stopped the car in the middle of the street, started coughing, and couldn't stop. Smoke bellowed from her mouth and nose as she waved the joint in front of Mack for him to take. "Too much." She wheezed between coughs. "Damn, that's some potent stuff."

Mack held the burning joint and sniffed at the drifting smoke.

"Go ahead, take a toke; it won't kill you," Ruby giggled.

Mack hesitated and then handed the joint to Ruby, "No, thanks."

Ruby shifted the car into gear and turned down a side street, then into an alley and stopped. She switched off the lights, put it in park, but left the engine running. She slid over close to Mack and took the joint from him.

"I want to party hard tonight, so let's get high together. I'm going to take a small hit and put my lips against yours and slowly blow the smoke into your mouth. You exhale first and then inhale the smoke when I blow, okay—a little at a time."

Mack watched the end of the joint brighten as Ruby took a deep drag, held it, and moved her lips to his. She used her tongue to wedge an opening between his lips; and as his mouth relaxed, she let the smoke trickle into his. He felt her large breasts against his chest.

Mack closed his eyes, inhaled the sweet smell, and felt her soft lips and her tongue exploring his mouth. Then he started coughing. They were both coughing and laughing at the same time.

"You have to suck it in a little at a time. Now let's do it again. Don't forget to exhale before I kiss you." She took another long drag from the joint.

Mack didn't like the smoke, but her kiss so inflamed him that he didn't care. She poked him playfully as she held the smoke, motioning for him to exhale. "More," she mumbled, poking him faster.

When Mack had no more air and opened his mouth to inhale, she pushed him down in the seat and pressed her lips hard against his, blowing the smoke, and forcing it down deep into his lungs. Mack struggled, but Ruby held her mouth tight to his. He couldn't breathe; the full weight of her body held him down. He felt like he was drowning. He grabbed her by both arms and bucked her off, throwing her to the floorboard, then jumped out of the car and fell to his knees, coughing violently.

Ruby, her head halfway in the floorboard and her feet in the air, giggled, waving the joint, "You want another toke?" She laughed, pulled herself up, and stood on the front seat looking for Mack. "Ahoy there, mate!" She climbed over onto the back seat and saw him sitting on the ground. "Hey, you okay?" She sat on the fold of the convertible top.

"Don't *ever* do that again."

"Do what?"

"Hold me down like that."

"You didn't like it?"

He got up off the ground.

"You going to punch me out? I'd like that. Go ahead hit me. Hit me!"

"*Hit* you?"

"Yeah, it's okay if you want to."

"I'm not going to hit you," Mack swayed a little.

Ruby stood up in the back seat with her hands on her hips. "Okay then, how about that barbecue and a couple of Falstaffs? I'm bone dry. Come on, you drive."

Walking around to the driver's side, he let his hand drag over the hood, feeling the heat of the engine, and admiring the long lines in the design. He opened the door and pulled himself under the steering wheel, easily shifting into reverse. Ruby climbed over into the front seat, the whiteness of her thighs showing in the darkness as she slid down the back of the seat, her arm falling around Mack's shoulders.

"*Great* barbecue. This is the best I've ever had," Mack shouted into the swirling wind whipping through the convertible.

Ruby was laughing while feeding him. It was a turn-on for her, watching him high with the munchies—his serious mood turned playful, and the thought of seducing this young stallion, especially when high, was overpowering. The slaw oozed from her sandwich and she caught it, laughing, and licked it from her hand.

Mack saw a train up ahead as they were crossing the bridge over the Mississippi River into Arkansas. He threw his head back and howled like a train whistle, the cold air soothing on his bruised face. He blew the horn repeatedly as they pulled alongside the train. This was the old "Rocket" Streamliner, running on a wooden trestle across from them, a non-stop passenger train from Memphis to Little Rock. The engine was bullet-shaped and covered with polished aluminum, as were the passenger cars. The train engineer heard the horn and pulled three long blasts on the train's whistle. Ruby saw the engineer and waved; and when he waved back, she stood up and sat on the back of the seat smiling and waving with both hands. The engineer, seeing Ruby with her dress blowing up, blasted his whistle with five short blasts.

The train whistle drew the passenger's attention to look outside, and when they saw Ruby sitting on the back of the seat of the convertible they all waved from their windows. Ruby, loving the attention, stood up in the seat holding onto the windshield. Wobbling, she gathered up her dress above her hips and turned her back to the train and pulled down her panties, mooning them. Screaming with excitement, she hollered at Mack, "Go...Go...Go!"

Mack stomped on the gas pedal, she slid down the back of her seat, and they roared away from the train.

"Did you see the looks on their faces? Yaaaahoo!" Ruby shouted.

Mack stared like a wild bull seeing a red cape, as she pulled up her red panties covering the thick patch of hair bunched between her legs.

"Hey, watch the road." Ruby saw the speedometer was on ninety. She scooted over and wrapped her left arm around his shoulder and moved her right hand between his legs, squeezing, "Whoa, Big Boy, slow it down, we don't want to go to jail in Arkansas. Up here at the end of the bridge, on the right, turn there on the gravel road." Ruby sat back up, pulling her dress down.

Mack was so flustered he almost missed the turn, and jerked the wheel as he turned off the highway onto a dark gravel road that sloped down an embankment under the bridge. He stopped the car and let his eyes adjust to the darkness, scanning the beam of the headlights out over the treetops. Flashing the lights to high beam, he saw a white sign nailed to a large cypress tree with two black arrows pointing in opposite directions. One read, "DACUS FISHING CAMP," the other, "COTTON CLUB."

"What's that noise?" she asked.

"Sounds like the train." Before they could turn and look up, the train was over them. The noise was deafening. The ground shook and the wooden trestle swayed back and forth. "Must be doing a hundred," Mack shouted, the train gone before he finished.

"What did you say?"

"The Rocket, it must have been doing a hundred."

"Yeah...well let's do the same. I'm dying for a drink." She tossed the two empty bottles of Falstaff from the car.

"To the right?"

"Unless you want to go fishing."

There was a steep embankment on both sides of the narrow dirt road, and Mack could see only as far as the headlights reached. He drove about ten miles an hour, and as his eyes adjusted, he realized that he was driving on top of a levee.

He saw the blinking neon letters, COTTON CLUB, on the roof of a long wood-framed building with a gable at each end. Mack noticed that there were no windows on this side of the building and two doors, both in the front, almost side by side.

"Why the big letters?" he asked, thinking there was nothing out here but cotton fields as far as the eye could see.

"Beats me," she smiled, both high heels propped on the dashboard. "In case you get lost in the cotton fields, I guess."

Mack peeked at the exposed white thighs while she buckled the ankle straps. "Better keep your eyes on the road, or we'll end up down there picking cotton." Ruby laughed, not bothering to pull her dress down.

Mack coasted down the tractor road and off the levee onto a hardpacked strip at the end of the cotton field. The place was packed with cars and pick-up trucks. There were no parking spaces, so he parked at the end of two cotton rows. Ruby held onto Mack as she struggled in her high heels crossing the rows and maneuvering over the gravel parking lot in front of the club.

"And stay out!"

Mack jerked Ruby back when the door flew open and a fat man in bib overalls came tumbling out, landing in the gravel. "I warned you, Ol'man, 'bout feeling up those women—now you stay out of here till you sober up, you hear?" a huge black man barked, standing in the opened door, blocking out all the light.

"Who you calling, 'Old Man?' You couldn't throwed me out of here without hadn't you sneaked up and grabbed me from behind." The fat man made no effort to get up.

"Get your black ass 'way from here 'fore I call the sheriff." He sailed the man's hat out and slammed the door shut.

The hat landed at Mack's feet. He picked it up and reached over to help the man up. "Come on, Mister, give me your hand." Mack saw the shiny flash just in time to jump back as five inches of a straight razor swiped at his arm.

"Don't touch me, White Bread. Don't need your help."

Mack started to kick him, but Ruby grabbed him and pulled him away.

"Watch yourself here, Baby, this is not our turf." She slid her arm around his waist and pushed him through the front door into a small vestibule.

A heavyset black woman slid the glass window back, "One dollar cover charge each, or three dollar for the both of you." She stared at Mack with a serious look, demanding, "Ya'll together, ain't 'cha?" Then roared with laughter and smiled at Mack. "Give me two dollars, boy, and get your young ass inside." Ruby paid the lady and pushed Mack through the door when it swung open with a buzz. Mack heard the fat lady laughing, "White folk ain't got no sense of humor, *none*."

The place was dark. Mack didn't move. Ruby grabbed his hand and started walking toward the dance floor, a third the size of a football field. The place was swarming with people, and a cloud of cigarette smoke covered the ceiling throughout the room.

"I'm Bubba." Standing in front of Mack was the huge black man he had just seen throw the drunk out the door. "Any trouble, you come get me, you hear?" He grabbed Mack's hand, turned it over, stamped two large red C's, and did the same to Ruby.

"You want a pint or a fifth?" he asked, looking at Ruby.

"Fifth."

"What's your pleasure?"

"What you got?"

"You name it, I got it."

Ruby hesitated. Bubba jumped in. "I got ten-year Old Charter for twelve bucks."

Ruby nodded, handing him a ten and a five. "Keep the change for a table close to the band?"

"You the one, Baby Girl." Bubba turned to a waiter and gave him the order. "You follow me." He moved with familiar ease across the unlit dance floor, weaving in and out of the packed dancers. Ruby followed, pulling Mack behind her until he stopped and whispered to her, "Is this a colored club?"

"Yeah, and *we* be de colored..." Ruby laughed, pointing to her arm. Mack had a puzzled look on his face. She kissed him on the mouth, shaking her head and whispered, "*White*, we're the only color in here," pointing to her arm again and danced on through the crowd. They stopped at a table Bubba was towering over next to the dance floor. The waiter was right behind them balancing a bucket of ice, two glasses, two bottles of Coke, and a fifth of Old Charter. Dropping her purse on the table, she twirled and grabbed Mack before he could sit down and waltzed him to the middle of the floor as the singer moved into a new song. She pulled him in close and led him to the rhythm of the music, her body pressed hard against his, singing in his ear.

The stage was packed with musicians, and the music was soft and bluesy. "Oh Mack, I just love that song. Listen to the words…"

Mack held on to Ruby as she danced him all over the dance floor, turning and spinning with her head flung back. When they paused, her legs squeezed his leg, and she rocked back and forth, riding his leg to the music.

Mack looked around to see if anyone was watching. *The hell with it. He didn't know a soul in this place.*

Ruby put both arms around his neck and pulled him down close, breathing heavily and singing softly.

"Hold me closer, Mack."

He still had a buzz on as he moved with her, swaying to the rhythm of the music.

Ruby's head was on his shoulder. Her hot breath and wet lips moved over his neck. "I can feel every part of your body touching me. Can you feel mine?"

"Yes."

"Does it feel good?"

"Yes…"

"Tell me how it feels. I want to hear you tell me. Talk to me." He didn't know what to say.

"Relax, Baby, close your eyes, and listen to the music." She kissed his face and lips and ran both hands across the top of his shoulders and down the sides of his arms. She worked her hands inside his coat and around his waist, pulling his shirt out and, inch-by-inch, ran her fingers up his naked back.

Mack fought the wild thoughts running through his mind. Soon his body let go, he relaxed, and followed Ruby as she rocked him from side to side to the slow, melodious voice of the singer.

"Mack?"

"Huh."

"Have you ever been with a woman before? You can be honest with me…come on, tell me."

"Let's just dance, okay."

"Sure. It's okay. I'm glad. You're a gorgeous man." She hugged him, her lips touching his ear. She took his hand and moved it to her breast, "Squeeze it, Baby."

Mack was going crazy; he had never felt anything so soft, yet her nipple was as hard and erect as the thumb on his hand.

"Ohhh, Mack, harder. Squeeze harder," she whispered in his ear. "I'm going to teach you more than most men learn in a lifetime. Not because I was paid to, but because there is something about you that very few men will ever have." She leaned back, pulling his head down to her breast.

He couldn't help himself. He had dreamed of this many times—his lips on her nipples.

She danced away, swaying in and out of his arms, then pulled him close. "Tonight, when I saw you standing over that fighter, the blood and sweat running all over your body and your heart pounding...you were like a wild animal. I waited and when you stepped down from the ring and I threw my arms around you...your smell drove me crazy. Just standing next to you, the heat of your body started a fire so deep inside of me...no man has ever done that."

"I...ah."

"You have no idea what I'm talking about, do you? Believe me, women know—they go to bed at night fantasizing about a wild man like you."

The music moved to a fast song, and Ruby pulled him by the hand, dodging some gyrating dancers. "Come on, Wildman, let's get some fire water."

Leading Mack off the dance floor, she stopped short when she saw three black men at their table. Two were standing, and the third was reared back in one of the chairs drinking from their fifth of Old Charter. Ruby backed up.

"Uh oh, weee've got company. 'Little Mister Trouble' follows you everywhere, don't he? I'm going to find Bubba."

"What's the trouble here?" Bubba stepped forward from a dark shadow.

The one sitting at the table smiled, showing perfectly shaped white teeth, and continued to leer at Ruby as he sipped from the bottle of Old Charter. "There ain't no trouble, Mister, unless you start it." He was dark-skinned, with wide shoulders, and wore a black leather baseball cap cocked to one side on his shaved head. All three wore black t-shirts.

"Then what you doing at these folks' table, drinking their whiskey?" Bubba demanded, looking at Ruby's purse in the middle of the table. Mack saw two other bouncers move in behind the three men, and he tried to move in front of Ruby, but she pushed him back. Some dancers stopped and stood watching.

"It's called reparation, payback, *Nigger.* We taking what's owed us. What's your name?" the man sitting at the table demanded.

"I's the one ask the questions...who the hell do you think you are?" Bubba said.

One of the men standing said to Bubba, "Nigger, you better get on board. This here's Willie 'Nat' Turner."

"This club is for *our* people. Whitey got his own...they need to go, *now*," Nat said.

"Naw, that's not the way it works in *my* club. You're troublemakers; you the ones got to go, *now*."

"We ain't going nowhere," Nat said.

Bubba turned and saw one of his bouncers following an Arkansas State Trooper across the dance floor. Sergeant Billy Joe Wilson, dressed in the trooper uniform of dark brown pants, stuck inside tall boots, and a Sam Browne belt with a flap over the pistol holster. Bubba often thought their uniforms looked more like Nazi storm troopers.

Billy Joe stopped in front of the table, staring at the three men, and shot a look of scorn at Ruby and Mack. Mack turned his head away and withdrew a step. His first thought was, *are the cops looking for me?*

"We got a call there was a little trouble going on in here, Bubba?"

"You must have been hiding out in the parking lot when you got the call," Bubba taunted.

Billy Joe turned and looked up at Bubba. Standing only five feet, seven inches tall, Billy Joe's eyes burned with controlled anger. Bubba knew Billy Joe well and was aware of his zeal to practice his years of karate training on anyone who crossed him and tried to stay his distance.

"I asked Nat and his boys here to leave the club, and they say they ain't moving." Bubba shrugged his shoulders and headed back up to the front of the club waving his two bouncers to follow. Ruby snatched her purse from the table and pulled Mack with her as she followed Bubba.

"You boys causing trouble?" Billy Joe asked.

"Who you calling boy, Shorty?" Nat said.

"That's our whiskey he drinking," Ruby shouted back over her shoulder.

Most people who knew Billy Joe were aware of his Napoleon Complex, and Nat had just lit the fuse of a small package of high explosives. "Why don't you boys come on outside?"

"Like we told the big nigger there, we ain't going nowhere," Nat said.

Billy Joe stared at the three men. Slowly, a slight, undetectable grin pulled at the corner of his mouth and then disappeared. He tipped the brim of his trooper hat, turned and walked to the front of the club. Bubba was standing at the door with two of his bouncers. Ruby and Mack stood behind them.

"No one is to leave this building," Billy Joe ordered, as he marched out the front door.

Mack thought about the shooting at the snuff company—*I can't get arrested.* Almost in a panic, he grabbed Ruby's hand pulling her toward the door, "Come on, I got to get out of here."

"Naw, you ain't. Can't let you do that." Bubba moved in front of the exit door.

"You can't keep us here," Ruby said.

"You heard the man. He's out there in the parking lot, and he ain't leaving. Best you stay clear of him. He don't think too highly of white folks mixing."

"Is there a back door?" Mack asked.

"The only two doors in this place..." Bubba pointed to the entrance and exit doors, then leaned over and whispered to Ruby, "Things start getting rowdy round here, you take your friend there and head for the women's room, there's a window, you hear?"

Mack made a wild dash around Bubba for the exit door, and at the same time, two Arkansas State Troopers larger than Bubba charged through both doors, stopping just inside. Mack, slammed against the wall, stayed crouched, staring at the backs of the two cops, each cradling a Remington 12-gauge pump short-barreled shotgun. The lights in the club flickered on and off in rapid succession, and the band stopped playing when all the lights came up bright and glaring. The dance floor emptied, and the frantic crowd scattered like a kicked-over anthill. Marching through the door, four more State Troopers lined up across the front of the dance floor, each with a three-foot riot stick in his hand.

Ruby grabbed Mack and pulled him through the scattering crowd to the women's room, pushing and shoving to get through the door. Mack saw two women standing on the toilet inside the cubicle, pushing on a huge woman hanging halfway out the window. The woman was yelling, "I'm going to fall on my head." The two women kept pushing rolls of fat, a handful at a time, through the window. Mack braced himself against the cubicle door to keep from being crushed as a line of women pressed him forward. He heard clanking and metallic sounds hitting the concrete floor and looked down to see a small pistol, two knives, and a straight razor scattered on the floor.

Ruby turned to Mack and nodded toward the two women standing on the toilet as the fat woman hit the ground, swearing.

"They want you to go out first and catch them as they come out."

The two women stepped down and Mack stepped up on the toilet, noticing the bowl was stuffed with baggies of pot, a lot of loose pills, and what looked like a small bag of white power. He exited the window feet first and caught the two women as they came out head first, then caught Ruby.

"Let's go," Ruby said.

"What about the others?" Mack asked, looking back at a woman hanging halfway out the window, squealing.

Ruby shoved him forward, "Go! Let's get out of here."

Inside the club, Sgt. Billy Joe Wilson stood on the edge of the cleared dance floor, two steps in front of his four troopers. He surveyed the stampede, savoring every minute of his power to cause such disruption. Most of the dancers were lined against the walls, waiting to see what was happening. Billy Joe swaggered across the dance floor in measured steps with his troopers following.

The Memphis skyline reflected off the water of the Mississippi River as Ruby drove back on I-40, crossing the upper bridge, Hernando De Soto, into Memphis from Arkansas. The top and windows were up, somehow mirroring the sober mood of Ruby and Mack since exiting the Cotton Club. Ruby took the cigarette from her mouth and broke the silence.

"What time are you supposed to be back at the orphanage?"

"I can stay out till midnight. They're pretty relaxed, not enough help for all the kids they have. I'm on kind of a work release, sort of like out at the penal farm. Sometimes I stay overnight on the boat or with Mickey. I'm gone on the river a lot, especially in the summer and they trust me to sign in and out.

"It's after midnight now. Are they going to give you any trouble?" Ruby looked over at Mack scrunched down in the seat.

Mack didn't answer.

"I know you were expecting more tonight, but it's late, and I wanted our first night together to be something special, not rushed."

Ruby moved her hand from the steering wheel to Mack's leg. "I was hoping you would let me cook supper for you one night this week?"

Mack set up in his seat, hesitated, and then a smile broke out over his face. "Sure, what night?"

"How's Tuesday?"

"I'll be there. You have to tell me where."

"Can you come early?"

"I'm out of school at three."

"What time do you have to be back?"

"I can sign out for an overnight stay."

"Good. How about you come around six o'clock...that will give me time to clean up and start supper?"

"Sure."

"We'll have a good time. I haven't cooked for someone in a long time. How does steak, mashed potatoes with gravy, and English peas sound?"

Mack asked, "What's for dessert?" They both laughed.

CHAPTER 5

SAINT JEROME'S ORPHANAGE and School for Boys was on the corner of Poplar Avenue and McLean Boulevard in midtown Memphis. The perimeter of the twenty acres was marked by a high stone wall with the main gate on Poplar and a delivery gate on McLean. The top of the wall had a pointed ridge-cap of gray slate, matching the steep-pitched roofs of the four Gothic-style buildings inside the wall.

The Chapel was the smallest building and the most elaborately designed, with flying stone buttresses, vaulted cedar ceiling, and dark walnut floors. Tall stained-glass windows lined each side of the building, with the names of the donors at the bottom of each window in gold-leaf lettering. Tall oak trees hooded each side of the stone walkway leading to the Chapel.

The second building was a walled one-story convent that shielded the nuns and secured their privacy. The other two buildings were the school and the three-story dormitory that stood alone, sparse, without trees or any adornment in a dark corner of the property. Seventh through twelfth grade boys lived on the third floor. At the end of each hallway were exit doors leading to an outside fire escape. There were no doors on any of the interior rooms.

A black four-door sedan, with chrome spotlights mounted on each front roof post, turned into the driveway of St. Jerome off of McLean Boulevard. The driver turned off the headlights and coasted down the drive, stopping at the delivery gate in the rear of the orphanage. There were two men inside, both dressed in suits and ties as they sat in the dark car in silence. All that could be seen was the glow of the driver's cigarette.

The driver, Sergeant Patrick "Pat" O'Riley, of the Memphis Police Department, Homicide Squad, was a tall heavy-set man with drooped shoulders. He rolled down his window as he finished his cigarette and thumped it in the air, watching it as it hit the ground in a silent flash. Reaching under the seat, he pulled out a flashlight and checked the time; it was 1:20 a.m.

His partner, Butch Walker, reached over and covered the flashlight with his hand and gestured toward a car turning onto the drive. Halfway down the drive, the headlights went out as the car turned onto the grass and stopped with the front bumper almost touching the stone wall.

Pat reached over the back seat for his binoculars and quickly focused on a red Buick convertible.

"Good timing, it's our boy. Looks as if he's not only a fighter but a lover, too." He watched, with Butch stirring next to him, like a teenager. After a sufficient time of tormenting him, he handed the binoculars over. Butch snatched them from Pat's hand and, in a short time, he could hear Butch's heavy breathing as he watched their heads popping up and down in the car seat.

"Damn, Butch, how long has it been since you had any?"

Butch gave him the middle finger without taking his eyes away from the binoculars. "He's out of the car," Butch said.

Pat watched a dark figure climb from the bumper to the fender and over the seven-foot wall and out of sight. They watched as the Buick backed out onto the driveway and turn north onto McLean. Pat scooted down in his seat and tipped his hat over his eyes.

"Aren't we going after him?" Butch asked. "In about an hour."

"An hour?" After a moment Butch leaned back and tilted his hat forward, mimicking Pat, and soon was snoring.

An hour later, Pat opened his eyes and looked at his watch. *Right on time.* He grabbed his flashlight and the keys from the ignition, walked to the rear, and opened the trunk. He pulled on a pair of black gloves and removed a long crowbar, then slammed the trunk lid, causing

Butch to pop up in his seat. Rubbing his eyes, he watched Pat walk to the delivery gate and stick the crowbar into the padlock. With one quick jerk, the lock was on the ground, then he kicked the gates open.

Butch snatched open the glove box and found the flat leather slapjack and a roll of two-inch wide adhesive tape. He slipped the slapjack into his back pocket as he caught up with Pat, walking toward the rear of the dormitory building with the crowbar over his shoulder. The two walked up the drive as unconcerned as if it were the middle of the day, unaware that they were marching in step with one another.

They saw a small light at the corner of the building, looked in the window, and saw a nun bottle-feeding an infant while in a rocking chair. They moved to the fire escape, and Pat took the long crowbar, hooked the first rung of the ladder, and pulled it down.

Butch followed Pat up the fire escape to the third floor landing, where he turned to Butch and put his finger to his lips before opening the door. There were no lights except the red overhead exit signs at each end of the hallway. Pat waited and listened, his eyes scanning the layout, then nodded to Butch. They crept down the hallway, turning into the last room on the left. Pat stopped at the bottom bunk bed on the right, and Butch stood guard just inside the doorway. The bed was empty, but the covers had been thrown back. Pat bent over and shoved his hand down between the sheets; they were still warm. He dropped to his knees, searching under the beds but found no one. Butch pointed to the wall lockers as he slipped his slapjack from his back pocket but stopped when they heard the flushing of a toilet at the end of the hall.

Mack, half asleep, shuffled into the room. Butch grabbed Mack and clamped his hand over his mouth while Pat drove his fist deep into Mack's midsection. Butch, executing the final blow, came down hard on the back of his head with the slapjack...*Nobody gets away with shooting a cop; I don't care who you know.*

Mack's body went limp, slipping to the floor. Butch removed the tape from his coat pocket, tore off a strip, and stuck it over Mack's mouth. Rolling him over, he taped his ankles together and locked his wrists behind his back with the handcuffs Pat handed him. Butch lifted him effortlessly over his shoulder and headed for the fire escape. Pat looked around, and, finding the other boy in the room sleeping soundly, he moved down the hallway to the exit door. Standing under the red exit light, he checked the time, 2:33. *Thirteen minutes, not bad.* He opened the door and stepped out onto the fire escape.

With offices up and down the Mississippi River, from St. Paul, Minnesota, down to New Orleans, Li Fang managed Mickey's company, Malloy Marine Services. They serviced over two thousand miles of traffic on the Mississippi River, including delivery of fuel, food, water, medical supplies, mail, boat parts, towing, construction, and all emergencies, even taxi services. Each towboat captain called in his order a day or an hour in advance, and Li sent a boat out that ran alongside their boat until services were completed. He was proud that their food and services were equal to a four-star restaurant.

Li was a little man, with a round face and smooth skin, always pensive and hard to read; even up close you could not see his eyes, only two dark dots. He showed very little emotion, never running hot or cold. Every morning at daybreak, you could find him standing out on the end of one of the barges, a steaming mug of coffee in his hand. Territorial instinct rushed over him every time he saw a load of barges, sometimes five wide and as long as six football fields, laboring down the river like a floating island. The river was in his blood as it was in his father's blood and his grandfather's; both had been boat captains up and down the east coast of China.

The cold and throbbing pain brought Mack back to consciousness. He was curled up in a corner, his feet and hands still bound. He lay there on the floor, listening to a faint but familiar sound in the distance.

Some light came in under the door, and he saw that he was in a small room, maybe a closet. The room shook and rolled, and Mack heard the sound of water lapping the underside of the steel floor. He recognized the sound of twin diesels and the towboat as it pulled alongside and banged against the tires hanging from the barge. Mack pulled his feet up under him and tried to sit up, but fell back on his side. He could feel the pain and nausea building in his stomach, and looked to see if he had been stabbed; there was no blood on his white tee shirt or underwear. He forced himself to sit up and, leaning against some stacked boxes, he took a deep breath through his nose. His head pounded, a wave of sickness overtook him, and he vomited. With his mouth still taped, the vomit backed up and spewed from his nose. He fell forward on his knees and fought to inhale through the blocked passage...he was choking to death. He pushed himself up from the floor and leaped forward with all the force of his body and exploded through the door, falling into the middle of the room groaning and kicking, with vomit streaming from his nose.

"*What the*—is he having a fit?" Butch shouted.

Li Fang, reading a report as he walked into the room, stopped, removed his thick horn-rimmed glasses, and ran over and jerked the tape from Mack's mouth. A geyser of foul-smelling vomit spewed all over the room. Like a catfish thrown on the riverbank, Mack thrashed on the floor, gulping for air.

"Get those cuffs off him," Li ordered, as he unraveled the tape from Mack's feet. Butch, with a squeamish olfactory, threw the keys to Pat and rushed from the room with his hands over his mouth, gagging. Li took the keys from Pat and ordered him to the kitchen for some wet towels.

Standing at his office window, Li looked over the top of his glasses and watched the long black Cadillac bumping its way down the cobblestone riverbank. The car stopped at the foot of the gangplank to the barges. The rear door opened, and Mickey Montague stepped out. He turned and bent down as a beautiful young blonde, half his age, leaned out and kissed him. He returned her wave as the black sedan made its way back up the riverbank and pulled out onto Riverside Drive. He stepped over one of the mooring lines to the barges and, with a little swagger, made his way up the wide gangplank. Mickey was in great shape for a man his age and had a head full of white hair, an attractive contrast to his dark skin. He looked more Italian than Irish.

Walking up the gangplank, he looked up at the large block letters, double-faced, on top of the building spelling out the name "MALLOY MARINE SERVICES." This was for river traffic and for the downtown traffic along Front Street and Riverside Drive as well as for the windows of most buildings on the bluff. As he reached for the door, he stopped and whispered in Gaelic the script written above the door, *"Céad Míle Fáilte Romhat"* A Hundred Thousand Welcomes to You.

Mickey walked into his office, tossed his coat and hat in a chair, and sat behind his desk. Li poured the coffee while Mickey shuffled through the stack of papers that was next to a tray of ham and biscuits on his desk.

"You want to see Mack first or talk a little business?" Li said.

"How's he doing?"

"Okay...all things considered. He's a tough kid."

Mickey took a sip of the steaming coffee. "Any of this can't wait?" Mickey looked up from the stack of papers.

"Nothing I can't handle."

"Is Sergeant Pat still here?"

"In the kitchen." They both smiled. Mickey's policy was that all policemen and firemen had an open invitation to hot coffee, biscuits, donuts, whatever they wanted, 24 hours a day. Every Monday morning a dozen hot-out-of-the-oven buttermilk biscuits were delivered to the mayor's office and to the office of the commissioner of fire and police. As Mickey often said, it was "a small premium for such an important insurance policy."

Mickey looked at his watch. "He's not going to like this." He opened the bottom drawer of his desk, removed a bottle of Bushmills Irish whiskey, and poured a shot in his coffee. "Let me talk to him."

Mack walked in fresh from a shower, dressed in an open pea coat, sweatshirt, and blue jeans. His face was flushed from standing outside on the barge, and a narrow strip of tape was still over his eye, which was bloodshot and discolored.

"Sit down, Mack," Mickey said, nodding to one of the brown leather chairs in front of his desk. "How's that knot on your head? Stupid cops...they could have killed you. You want something to eat...coffee?"

"Those were *cops* who beat me up?"

"Sometimes they get carried away. I asked them to pick you up, not beat you up."

"Pick me up...for what?"

"For your protection."

"*Protection?*"

"Hold on now. Commissioner O'Shea and I...well, we both wanted to talk to you last night and tell you what a great fight you fought, but I turned around and you had run off with that...Ruby. You two got something going? Be careful; she's a wild woman. Anyway, I'm real proud of you. It showed a lot of guts hanging in there like you did after he butted you."

"What did you mean, *my* protection?"

"I'll get to that. First, let me say...well, being your godfather and all, I know I was supposed to be more of a father to you—look after you and all, but I never married or been around kids." Mickey opened the bottom drawer of his desk again and pulled out the bottle of Bushmills, took a healthy swig from the bottle, and poured another shot in his coffee. "I always tried to make sure you had everything you needed, you know, for school and such."

"What's this all about?" Mack stood up.

"*Sit* down and listen! See, see what I mean? I don't have much patience; this ain't easy."

Mack dropped back into his chair.

"I never told you this, but I was about your age when my sister sent for me to come to the States. She and her husband Joe paid my way over here and took me in. I was half-starved back then, sickly, weighed maybe 90 pounds. Ireland was having a bad time; there was no work, it was brutal cold and wet; no coal to heat with, very little to eat, and only rags for clothes. We had to steal cardboard to stick inside our worn-out shoes."

Mack shifted his weight from side to side in his chair, impatient, fidgety; he didn't need all this preaching.

"Yeah, I know, you don't want to hear about all that. Anyway, I was put to work the first day I was here as a kitchen helper on the old towboat, the *Irish Mist*. That's where Rosa Leigh got her name, Captain Irish, from that old 135-footer."

Mickey leaned back and put his feet up on the bottom drawer that he had pulled out.

"You remember your Aunt Irish, right? She took you to her plantation a couple times when you were younger?" Mack shrugged his shoulders.

"Anyway, I gained ten pounds the first week in that little galley— I never saw so much food. But then...Rosa Leigh's husband was killed while checking some barges that had broken loose and run aground. After that it was all downhill.

"The mortgage company called the note on their house, the utilities were disconnected, and the straw that broke the camel's back was that the bank came looking for the boat. Irish was devastated; there was no insurance, and she knew nothing about mortgages or running a business. But Joe had taught her how to pilot a towboat, and late one night, she woke me up with bags packed and a cop car waiting outside. This cop friend of hers took us to the *Irish Mist* and by daybreak we were halfway to Vicksburg. We lived on the boat, up and down the river, always moving and doing odd jobs: salvage work for insurance companies, towing other boats that broke down, any kind of emergency. We made twice the money we did pushing barges, but worked our asses off, 24/7. Of course, we were always dodging the repo-man until Li's father came along and loaned Rosa Leigh, 'Irish,' the money to pay the boat off. By that time, I knew every turn in the river, every bridge, and every sand bar. I had my Captain's license in less than two years; shortly after that we had two boats, then three, and we were passing each other on the river."

"Uncle Mickey, why am I here?"

"Okay...here's the deal." Mickey got up and walked around to the front of the desk. "I, ah...I know all about the shooting of the night watchman at the American Snuff Company."

Mack dropped his head and mumbled to himself. "*That's* what this is all about."

"Fortunately, the cop is not dead. He had a mild heart attack and was discharged from the hospital. When the police got on the scene, saw all the blood, and found his badge with a hole in it, they panicked. No one bothered to check and see that the blood was from his head hitting the sidewalk. He's a retired cop and, with all the confusion, word went out over the police radios that a cop had been killed in a robbery. It was all over the front page the next morning. The emergency room nurse found the bullet, a small caliber, stuck between his coat and shirt; he was lucky, or—I should say—you're lucky the bullet hit his badge and slowed it down."

"Honest to God, Uncle Mickey, I never got out of the car. I can't believe this! I just drove the car. I thought he was dead. I've been having these nightmares. How'd they know about me?"

"The police got a call from a bartender about a drunk that was buying everyone drinks with silver dollars. They picked your friend Dago up and, after two detectives roughed him up, he coughed up Crazy Ray's name and yours. Both of them confessed that you were the shooter who killed the night watchman."

Mack stared in disbelief with his mouth open but didn't say anything. Mickey continued talking, "Me and Father O'Brien were at Commissioner O'Shea's house all night calling in favors. When I couldn't find you, I sent Sgt. Pat over to the orphanage to bring you here until things settled down. Cops have a way of dealing their own swift justice sometimes, especially when one of their own has been shot."

"Mickey, I swear all I did was..."

"I know. The cops finally got the full story, and, as soon as they are released from City Hospital, there will be more charges filed against them. You should have known better than to run with such garbage."

"Is everything okay then?"

"Not quite." Mickey stood up with his hands in his pockets.

"You're going to have to leave Memphis."

"Leave? Where would I go? When?"

"You're leaving in a few minutes. Li is going to take you out in one of the delivery boats and put you on a towboat, the *Dan Quinn*, headed downriver to Vicksburg, then to Natchez."

"But why?"

"They still have a warrant for your arrest on armed robbery, assault with a deadly weapon, and some other charges. The best deal I could make was the Marine Corps or jail."

Mack jumped up from his chair. "The *Marine* Corps...I'm *not* going in the Marine Corps. All I did was drive a car."

Mickey held his temper. He sat on the corner of his desk and waited. "The big guy next to me at the fights, you've met him, Kevin O'Shea, the Commissioner of Fire and Police. He's a former Marine, and his son-in-law is a Marine recruiter down in Jackson; he'll take care of all the paperwork. The Commissioner, as a favor to me, got with the prosecutor's office and worked a deal to drop all charges and destroy any records involving you in this robbery if you leave town now and go into the Marines."

Mack sighed and shook his head.

"Your two buddies are headed for the Penal Farm. You can go with them, or you can leave on the *Dan Quinn*. It's up to you. That's the deal I agreed to."

"What about all my stuff, I don't have..."

"Listen to me, we don't have much time." Mickey said. "Sergeant Pat is in the kitchen. He has orders to see that you're on the *Dan Quinn* or take you to jail. I have talked with Father O'Brien and Sister Agnes George, and they will box up everything and send it to me. In a short time, you will be in basic training at Parris Island, South Carolina; you won't need money or clothes. You'll stay with my sister, your Aunt Irish, down in Natchez until the recruiter puts you on a bus for Parris Island.

"Your *sister?*"

"*Yeah,* my sister, *your* aunt. Don't be so damn negative. She's your mother's sister; that's all the family you've got."

"I don't remember her."

"Well, it's a good time to start. She knows you and has loved you from the day you were born, even wanted to adopt you, but I said no; she was sick at the time. She and Father O'Brien started that orphanage you live in, building one building at a time. She's been like your guardian angel, following your every move."

Mack's head throbbed. He rubbed his hand over the knot on his head where the cop had hit him.

"You okay? You want some more aspirin?"

"No. I want to know *why* I didn't have any say-so about all this? You, Father O'Brien, this guy, O'Shea, all of you get together and decide *my* future? *Order* me to go off and live with a strange woman and spend years in the Marines?"

"I left you alone a lot. We all did. I thought it would make you tough, independent, and it did. But you made a big mistake...almost deadly. You got in with the wrong crowd. I made the best deal I could make for you. But it's not too late. You *do* have a say in all this. In about five minutes, the *Dan Quinn* will be passing downriver, and you can be a part of her crew. Or I'm sure Sergeant Pat would enjoy beating on your ass some more while he takes you to the Penal Farm. It's your call. "

"I, ah...."

"Look, Mack, we all have your best interests at heart. Your Aunt Irish is expecting you, and she's extremely happy you're coming. You should get on your knees and thank her when you get there. She sacrificed a good part of her life for you. She lived on the river day and night, and she did the best she could. She and Father O'Brien worked it out—you were to live and go to school at St. Jerome—she would pay for everything: food, clothing, your books, whatever it took for your education. And there wasn't a lot of money back then. I was to work you on the river after school and during the summer, Li was to teach you the business end, and Father O'Brien was to see to your education.

"No one ever told *me* about this."

"What damn difference does it make—*it is what it is*—and you're being told now! You're going to live with your Aunt Irish until the Marines come after you." Mickey lowered his voice, "She's been a little sick again, but don't let that fool you. She's as tough as they come, shrewd, and looking forward to having you. Don't give her any trouble, you understand? Just because she's a woman doesn't mean you can't learn a thing or two. I've talked with her a couple of times this morning, and she will pick you up at the landing in Natchez day after tomorrow."

There was a knock at the door, and Li walked in carrying a small duffel bag. "The boat's ready," he said, looking at Mickey and then at Mack, both a little apprehensive. Li walked over, put his arm around Mack, and held up the duffel bag. "I packed you some underwear, socks, toothbrush, and things that I thought you might need—and a change of clothes." Li led Mack out of the office and in a low voice said, "Don't worry, I promise you I'll take care of everything; you'll be all right."

As they were walking single-file down the small hallway headed to the boat, they passed the kitchen. Mack saw the big cop, Pat, through the glass door. He left the kitchen, walked towards the exit door to the *Dan Quinn,* and stopped at the men's room.

Mack stopped and said, "I'll meet you at the boat. I need to take a leak."

Mack watched Li and Mickey continue down the hallway and waited till the door opened to the outside. Then he hurried down another hallway that wrapped around the kitchen but didn't see Sergeant Pat. He stopped outside the men's room, listening at the door. When he heard water running, he started searching the hallway. His eyes stopped on big red letters, "FOR FIRE ONLY," printed across the glass cabinet mounted on the wall. Mack turned the key in the lock and removed the pick-head fire ax. He stood with his back flat to the wall, next to the door of the men's room, holding the heavy ax at port arms, diagonally across his chest. The door opened, and Mack swung his hip and shoulder as hard as he could, like throwing a left hook. The flat part of the ax slammed into the face of Sergeant Pat, and he dropped like a dead man hit by a speeding truck. He didn't know what hit him. Mack stood over him, surveying the damages—a broken nose and a large gash over his eyebrow, spurting blood. He whispered to himself, *"Shhhhit! Did I hit him too hard?"* He dropped the ax, stepped over the cop sprawled halfway into the men's room, and ran down the hallway to the exit door. He took a couple of deep breaths, and stepped outside.

Mickey was waiting at the boat. Mack stuck his hand out, and Mickey took it and pulled him in close, his left arm around him.

For the first time, Mack didn't feel embarrassed about hugging a man.

"In a couple of years, which will fly by, you will see the wisdom in all this," Mickey said, released his hold, and walked back to the door.

Mickey heard the boat pull away as he stepped inside. When he turned the corner, he saw legs sticking out in the hallway. He rushed over, saw that it was Sergeant Pat, and noticed the ax on the floor beside him. The bleeding had stopped, but blood was all over his face, and a large blue knot was swelling rapidly over one eye. Mickey bent over and checked the pulse on his neck—it was strong, and his breathing was okay. He lifted Pat's legs and moved him inside the men's room. Pat moved, raising his hand as if to thwart additional blows, moaned something inaudible, and fell back to the floor. Mickey noticed a dark brown substance in Pat's hand and moved for a closer look. He smiled as a familiar smell satisfied his curiosity. Crushed between Pat's fingers was a chocolate-covered donut. Pulling a handful of paper towels from the shelf, Mickey stepped over Pat and out into the hallway, shutting the door behind him. He picked up the ax, wiped the blood off, put it back in the glass cabinet, locked it, and put the key in his pocket. Walking down the hall, he crumbled the paper towels into a ball and tossed an overhead hook shot at a 55-gallon drum parked in the corner. Looking back, he saw the paper ball bounce off the wall and fall into the drum. The old swagger was back in his step as he strolled down the hallway back to his office.

CHAPTER 6

"HEY! YOU MACK Shannon?"

"Yeah," Mack yelled. With daylight about 30 minutes away, and it raining so hard, Mack could only see the outline of a man on the barge. The tugboat rocked up and down and banged against the rubber tires on the side of the barge. The weather had turned rough during the night, and the blowing rain caused the river to crash high up on its banks. Mack rubbed his eyes from lack of sleep and waited; the next wave lifted the boat above the barge, and he jumped, grabbing the man's hand.

"Is that all the gear you got?" looking at Mack's duffel bag.

"That's it."

"Let's go."

Mack followed the man through the steady rain, watching him limp up the steps from the dock to the parking lot. He noticed the high heels and pointed toes of the man's boots as he climbed into an old Chevrolet pick-up, dragging his stiff leg behind him. He leaned across the seat and pushed the passenger door open.

"Hop in; that outside door handle is broken."

Mack threw his bag on the floorboard and climbed in.

"Name's Red...Red Bordeaux, like the wine," he said, sticking out his hand and smiling, showing his nicotine-stained teeth. "Careful when you slam that door. The window sometimes falls down inside, and it would be the devil getting it back up in this weather."

Mack shook the man's hand; it was calloused and his grip was vise-like.

"Damn, boy, someone beat the hell out of you or what?"

Both of Mack's eyes were bruised and discolored, with stitches over one eye and a Band-Aid under his chin. "It's nothing, just an accident."

Red took his cowboy hat, knocked the rain off against his knee, and slammed his door shut twice before it caught. Mack stared at Red, puzzled. Tight little curls, wiry and reddish-brown, covered his head; freckles sprinkled his sun-worn face. "You looking at my ear?"

"No," Mack shook his head.

"Well, it's okay; everybody stares at it." Mack stared at the ear—or half an ear; the top part of his right ear was missing.

"Ebony bit it off," Red said. "Clean and straight as if you drew a line and cut it with a pair of shears. I didn't even know it until he spit it out on the floor of his stall." Banging his hand on his left thigh, he said, "And one of his sons did this to my knee; slammed it into a corral post and crushed it like a pecan."

Red started the truck and, in low gear, pulled up the steep graveled riverbank onto a two-lane paved road. The rain came down in sheets. With the defiant noise of the truck's engine and the howling wind and rain, Red had to raise his voice with the speed of the truck.

"First time to Natchez?"

"Yeah."

"Do you ride?"

Mack looked confused, "Ride what?"

"Horses."

"No, I've never been on a horse."

"Really? Well today you'll get to see the most beautiful, graceful, and intelligent animal God ever made, the Tennessee Walker. I train 'em, buy and sell 'em, and breed 'em. We won the World Championship at The Celebration last year."

"Is that a rodeo?"

"Hell, no, boy, it's a horse show, just Tennessee Walkers. Ten days of partying and the best of the best Tennessee Walkers from all over the world."

"How far to where we're going?"

"To Shamrock...maybe an hour in this weather. You want a smoke?" Red pulled out a pouch of loose tobacco, and Mack shook his head. With his arm wrapped around the steering wheel, Red wiped the windshield with the cuff of his jean jacket and rolled a cigarette with his other hand. He stuck the cigarette in the corner of his mouth and lit it with a wooden match.

"A Tennessee Walker is a mixed-breed, like me. They are part Thoroughbred for their fire," showing Mack the burning match, "but mainly their heart." He stuck the tobacco pouch back in his left jean pocket and patted his heart. "Then there's the Morgan part in them; that's for size and strength, but mainly endurance, like this old Chevy here with 200,000 miles on her. Now, the Saddle Horse part is for the pleasure and easy riding, and the last is the Standard-Bred, for gaits, trotting, or pacing." Red continued to talk nonstop, driving slowly and never taking his eyes off the road.

Mack could hardly understand him. He spoke like a foreigner. "Are you from Ireland?"

"Ireland...why you say that? No, I'm from Lafayette...well, I'm really an ole Cajun, a Coonass, from Acadiana.

"When the Captain bought Ebony Fury, I was living at the Circle D over in Ponchatoula doing odd jobs. I lived in the barn, like one of the barn cat varmint killers. My first job was shoveling horseshit out of the stalls. Then I started feeding, washing, saddling, and whatever was needed. They had two tracks outside and one inside, and I would watch all the trainers, their different techniques, the good ones and the bad ones." The whole time Red was talking, he never took the cigarette from the corner of his mouth. Mack watched as the ashes crumbled down the front of his jacket.

"The Circle D was having a big auction in one of the outside arenas, and people from all over the world were there. I was in the barn brushing down Ebony Fury when Cap'n Irish walked over and asked me about Ebony. We talked for a long time. I told her he was not for sale, but the next thing I knew, me and Ebony were on our way to

Natchez. It was rumored that she paid over a hundred thousand for that horse, and that was the most..."

Mack faded. Turning his collar up, he scooted down in his seat. The warm air from the defroster weighed on his eyes, and the rhythmic beat of the only working windshield wiper hypnotized him into a deep sleep.

Mack sat upright and shaded his eyes from the bright sun; there had been no rain here. He watched Red open the double gates, and waved for him to drive the truck on through as he removed the mail from the mailbox. Mack slid across the seat and, without hesitation, put the truck in gear, drove across the steel cattle guard, and stopped on the gravel road. He noticed the printed signs, "PRIVATE PROPERTY—NO TRESPASSING," on each side of the gates, attached to the wood fencing. He smiled when he saw the green shamrock painted on the black mailbox. Red, with a handful of mail, closed the gate and climbed in on the passenger side.

"Welcome to Shamrock. You want to drive to the house?" Red said.

"Sure." Mack pushed in the clutch and eased into first gear.

"Straight ahead until you come to a fork in the road," Red mumbled, rolled his shoulder into the side of the door, and tilted his cowboy hat down over his eyes. Mack drove past cleared fields planted in cotton and watched the gravel road narrow into a red line on the horizon.

He had been driving for quite a while and wondered if he had missed a turn or something, but when he crossed a wooden bridge, Red pushed his hat up from his eyes. He fished in his jacket pocket for the butt of the cigarette he hadn't finished earlier and stuck it in his mouth.

"Are we still on the farm?" Mack asked, looking out each side of the truck.

Red nodded and pointed straight ahead with the flaming match he held for his cigarette.

Mack slowed the truck as he approached a wide fork in the road.

Red sat up, pointed to the road off to the left, and handed Mack his duffel bag.

"Just follow that road around the curve and through a patch of woods, and you'll see the house up on the hill." Pointing to the rear of the truck covered with canvas, he said, "I have to drop these supplies off at the barn and meet the vet about one of the horses. I'll come up and show you around the place after that."

Mack watched the dust roll from Red's truck as it bounced down the side road into the bright sun. He picked up his duffel bag, slung his pea coat over his shoulder, and started walking.

When he came to the sharp curve, the road narrowed into a tunnellike opening, leading into a thick patch of woods. He stopped when he realized everything had closed in around him. It was dark and damp, and the temperature had dropped about ten degrees. He stood looking up at the large virgin timbers that blotted out the sky with only a few thin rays of sun piercing the canopy. Spanish moss hung from the limbs of the live oaks that stretched out over the road. An eerie chill came over him as he shoved his arms into his coat and unconsciously quickened his pace. Large smooth stones covered with green moss and wet with moisture replaced the red gravel.

A distant rumbling stopped Mack in the middle of the road. He turned in all directions, listening, as a thunderous cadence grew louder. Surprised, he stumbled backward and fell as four horses roared from the darkness; hooves pounding, neighing, they zoomed by him like a passenger train and disappeared around the next curve. Mack lay there in a small swale on the side of the road, his arms covering his face. He sat up when he heard something in the undergrowth move close to his head. He swung his duffel bag at the movement, missing a large armadillo that hissed at him and turned away unaffected, continuing his foraging. Mack sat there in the ditch.

"Are you okay?"

Mack turned and looked up into a trickle of sun breaking through the treetops. A large white horse stood over him blocking the view of the rider.

"I'm Katherine Willingham...my friends call me Kate...and you must be Mack Shannon?" She laughed, seeing the confused look on his face.

Mack jumped to his feet and brushed himself off. Startled at Mack's sudden movement, the horse backed up, reared, snorted, and lowered his head, charging Mack. Kate jerked the reins back and held them as the steel bit cut hard on the stallion's mouth.

"Whoa, Roman. WHOA!" Kate shouted. The horse stopped. Loosening the reins and switching them to one hand, she leaned forward, hugging and patting his neck and whispering in his pointed ears, "Easy Roman, eeeazy." Her blond hair was tied back in a ponytail. "Sometimes I forget that Roman is a stallion. He's so sweet, and then he acts up like this to let me know he is still—*the man*."

Mack was speechless. His cockiness escaped him; both horse and rider were powerful images.

Kate laid the reins on Roman's neck and touched his side with the heel of her boot, turning him broadside to Mack.

"I'm sorry if my horses ran you off the road. They're on their way to the river to play. Every time they cross into this closed area—I call it the 'Enchanted Forest', they get spooked when they hit this old riverbed and run wild until they're through the other side."

Mack looked into the darkness of the woods. "I can understand that."

"I guess it can be a little spooky at times; obviously the horses think so. They smell the family of black bears that travel regularly across this creek bed. But I just love this place; it's a special section of Shamrock, a sanctuary for all of God's little critters."

"Yeah, talking about critters, I just saw the biggest rat crawling in the bushes there..." Mack held his hands apart about two feet.

"Really, are you sure it wasn't an armadillo? We have lots of those."

"I've never seen an armadillo; it had a long tail like a waterfront rat."

There was an awkward moment of silence; Mack struggled to think of what to say. "How did you know my name?"

"Mr. Bordeaux told me he had just let you off at the fork. Everyone has been waiting to meet you...and, ah, I wanted to, I mean, I thought I would be the first." Kate, hesitated, "I mean, maybe I could give you a ride to the house?" She pulled the tie from her ponytail.

"Sure," Mack said, searching how to get on the horse.

She slipped her boot out of the left stirrup.

"Do you ride?" Mack shook his head.

"If you give me your bag, then put your left foot in the stirrup here, I'll help you up." Kate reached down with her hand. "Grab the back of the saddle with your other hand and pull yourself up."

After a couple of tries, Mack was on the back of the stallion.

She handed Mack his bag. "Put your arms around my waist and hold on." She squeezed Roman with her knees and gave him a kissing sound, and he moved out in a smooth trot.

Mack, almost sliding off the back of the horse, grabbed Kate and held on as tightly as he could, his fingers brushing against the bottom part of her breast.

She took Mack's locked hands and moved them down a few inches. "You okay?"

"Yeah," he mumbled, trying to get balanced as he swung the bag over his back and wiggled closer to Kate. Her hair whirled across his face. He inhaled; her smell, her closeness, the rocking movement of the walking horse, fired his passion.

Kate could feel Mack's hot breath on the back of her neck. "Is my hair bothering you?"

Mack leaned closer, his lips next to her ear. "No."

Kate reached back and touched his leg, "If you squeeze tight right here, you can ride with your hands free."

Mack held tight as Roman broke out of the woods and turned up the hill toward the house.

When they reached the gate, Kate stopped the horse and looked over her shoulder.

"How old are you?"

"Ah, nineteen."

"You are not!"

"How do you know?"

"I know."

"Okay, I'm seventeen."

"Good, I am too. We are going to have a wonderful time while you are here; there's so much to show you. Let's walk the rest of the way to the house." Mack slid off the side of the horse, somewhat confused with this new intimacy.

Mack stood looking at a seemingly never-ending white brick fence on each side of a huge archway. Two rock columns supported the granite arch with the chiseled words EIRINN-GO-BRACH across the face.

Kate grabbed a small bouquet of roses stuck under the pommel of her saddle and jumped to the ground. "Here, I picked these for you to give to your Aunt Irish; she loves flowers. Do you know what those words say?" Kate asked, standing close beside Mack, looking up at the arch.

"I know that it's Irish. I think it means Ireland to the end, but I'm not sure."

"It means Ireland Forever," Kate said. "I just love it. *Forever...Ireland Forever.* Did you know that I am Irish?"

"Willingham is Irish?" Immediately he wanted to bite his tongue, realizing he may have hurt her feelings. He added, "Katherine sure sounds Irish."

"I'm so impressed; you remembered my name." Kate leaned over and kissed him on the cheek. Sticking her arm inside his, she started pulling him up the tree-lined drive, leading Roman by his reins. "Okay, how about half-Irish then." They both laughed. "I really do wish I was

Irish."

"Why?" He had never heard anyone say that.

"All of you are so proud of being Irish. Look at Aunt Irish. She's named after her own country."

"She's *your* aunt, too?"

"Not my real aunt, silly," she smiled and squeezed his arm. "Everyone calls her Aunt or Captain. She's famous you know...she's known from one end of the Mississippi River to the other. She's the first woman to ever own a fleet of boats and drive them herself."

"You mean pilot them."

"Whatever. Wait till you see the topiary." Kate skipped ahead.

"What's that?"

"You'll see." She stopped and waited on Mack. "Where is your mother, still in Ireland?"

"No. She died when I was young."

Kate reached out and wrapped her arm around Mack, "Oh, I am so sorry. I bet she was beautiful; you with all that black hair? What about your father...is he in Memphis?"

"I don't know. I've never seen my father. I think he lives in Ireland. They say he didn't like it here in the States."

"Oh, Mack! You poor dear." She put her arm around his waist, and they walked up the drive.

"Good morning!" Kate called out, waving at the two workmen standing on a wooden stepladder, trimming a tall shrub shaped like a giraffe. Others were raking leaves and cleaning flowerbeds.

"Good morning, Miss Kate. Good morning, Mr. Shannon."

"See, I told you everyone was expecting you. *Those* are topiaries," Kate said, stepping up her pace and pointing out each sculpture to Mack.

Mack stared up the long neck of the giraffe and, up on the hill, saw a large squatty bush in the shape of a giant turtle. There were other shapes throughout the yard.

"How do they do that?" Mack asked.

"I don't know. I've watched, and it takes a lot of patience. One missed cut, and a head or a hand is gone, and it takes years to grow back." Kate pulled Mack up the driveway, and he saw through the trees to the large white columns surrounding the two-story, antebellum plantation house with green shutters.

An old magnolia tree had grown into the side of the porch, and a low-hanging limb reached out into the yard, providing shade for a large table filled with food. A mosquito net hung from the limb protecting the table from birds and leaves. Two servants scurried back and forth from the kitchen, carrying a cornucopia of food from the house to the table.

Mack and Kate stood looking at all the food that had been placed on a triple-tiered lazy Susan. The smell of food weakened Mack and reminded him how long it had been since he had last eaten. Two wicker wing chairs stood across the table from each other.

"Can you believe all this food?" Kate asked, while tying off Roman to the porch railing.

A loud bark interrupted the two as they turned to see an enormous, black furry creature charging out of the woods toward them with lightning speed. Mack moved quickly in front of Kate and grabbed one of the wicker chairs to take the animal's charge.

"Bear!" A shout declaring authority called out. The animal froze, like a bird dog holding a covey of quail—no teeth were exposed, but his closeness was commanding. His small ears, clipped to a fine point, sat vigilant on his massive head. Spring-like hindquarters supported a chiseled body that was wrapped in a blanket of rough, thick, curly hair that failed to hide the powerful neck.

"It's okay. It's just Bear," Kate said, stepping out from behind Mack to hug the dog's imposing body.

Riding up behind the dog on a black horse was a broad-shouldered woman wearing an unbuttoned, leather vest over a cowboy shirt. She had strong legs that filled her khaki pants, the bottoms of which were stuffed into a pair of worn, green lizard cowboy boots. She dismounted the stallion with the grace of a professional horsewoman. A cigarette burned in the corner of her mouth.

"I'm Irish, your mother's sister; do we shake hands or hug?" She asked in a deep, Irish-accented voice, smiling and taking long strides toward Mack as she removed her cowboy hat.

Mack stood looking at the tall, muscular woman with very short, boyish-cut, gray hair. In the distance behind her, he noticed something move just inside the tree line. It was another horse with a rider dressed in camouflage. Mack focused on the outline and then the face; was it camouflage paint on his face or a black patch over his eye? Mack saw the horse move, and then they were gone, vanished into the woods.

Mack stuck out his hand.

Irish took Mack's hand with a strong grip, and pulled him to her, and wrapped him in a bear hug, "I've changed my mind. I want a hug. You're the spitting image of my Da, all that thick black hair and green eyes. Even with those cuts and bruises. Believe me, I've seen my Da with many a shiner." Stepping over to Kate, she said, "I see you met our neighbor, Miss Kate?" The dog walked a step in front of Irish. "You all sit down here before the biscuits get cold while I hustle up another chair I'm starving to death."

"No ma'am, don't you worry about me. I sure would love to eat, but I have to get my horses at the river and then back to school. I played hooky this morning, but I have a music class this afternoon that I can't miss. My piano recital is next week, and I hope you all can come?" Kate looked to see if Mack was listening.

"We'll see," Irish said.

Kate hugged Irish and then kissed Mack on the cheek and whispered, "See you soon, I hope." She untied Roman and walked off, leading him down the hill behind the house. Mack stood waving.

"Pretty little thing, isn't she? Sit down, Honey, let's talk and eat. Those flowers for me?"

Mack handed her the roses and sank down in the cushioned chair as he looked out at a distance, following the river as it snaked its way through high timbers and cleared fields. The dog insulated himself between the two chairs. "Is that the same river where her horses are?"

"Yep. You go ahead and help yourself. We're very informal around here." She waved her fork over the table and stabbed a biscuit. "The river down there is part of the Yazoo." She flipped her cigarette out toward the river. "You crossed it twice coming up here. It winds around Shamrock and separates us from the Willingham's property." Pointing with her thumb over her shoulder, "There's a trail at the back of the house that goes down to the bridge that crosses over to their place; she's headed back that way now. On this side of the river, there's a sandbar; the horses, kids, and even old Bear like to swim there." Irish snapped her fingers, and the huge dog bolted to her side and gulped a large biscuit she handed him.

Mack felt the dog watching his every move. He saw the fire in its deep-set eyes, shaded by the heavy furry-like eyebrows. Its presence was regal, audacious, willing to serve, but not subservient.

"This is my beloved Bear; he thinks he's human." As if understanding what Irish had just said, Bear shifted and plopped his huge head in her lap. She grabbed a handful of hair at the back of his neck and gave him a rough shake. "You give him a piece of that smoked ham, and you'll make yourself a quick friend. Don't drop it though, let him eat out of your hand."

Bear bolted when Mack held up the ham, and with his long, wolf like canine teeth, lifted the slice from Mack's hand, swallowed it in one bite, and sat on his hindquarters staring at Mack. "What kind of dog is he?" Mack asked,

"He's a Bouvier...from the Netherlands. He's trained in all three levels of tracking, obedience, and protection."

"He's the biggest dog I've ever seen. How much does he weigh?"

"Too much, I'm sure. Let me introduce you to Ebony before he gets too jealous." Irish whinnied like a horse, and the black stallion walked over to the table with his ears standing straight up, his nose flared and sniffing. Bear moved to Mack and plopped his heavy head in Mack's lap.

"Well, it doesn't take long, does it? Dogs, kids, and horses; they can size you up immediately." Irish lifted a wooden spoon full of ambrosia from a bowl on the table and poured it in her hand. "Here, sweet boy, we love you too." Ebony nibbled her hand clean.

"Is he the one that bit Red's ear off?"

"One and the same."

Early the next morning, Red, his wife Carmen, and their seven children stood lined up, watching Mack and Bear running down to them from the main house. Bear jumped and nipped at Mack's shirtsleeve. Mack stopped and looked at all the children while Bear continued his jumping and barking, wanting to play.

"Mack, this is my wife, Carmen, and my sons, Pedro, Pablo, Pepe, Antonio, my girls, Juana, Juanita, and the little one here is Rosa Leigh, after Cap'n Irish, but everyone calls her Stormy."

Mack shook Carmen's extended hand. She was a large woman, much taller than Red, with smooth brown skin and long black hair. She smiled every time Mack shook each child's hand as they were introduced. When it came to Stormy, Mack reached out to pat her on the head, and she shouted, "No!" Bear stopped his jumping.

"Sit!" Bear dropped his back legs, frozen like a concrete statue, and stared at Stormy.

"Come," Stormy ordered again, pointing to the ground beside her. Bear came to her and walked around her back and stopped at her left side, nudging her leg.

"Down," Stormy said. Bear plopped beside her with both paws out to the front, like the legs of a sphinx, his tongue hanging out.

"Come on, Mack, she's just showing off. Let me show you the barn and then where we live," Red said. "You kids get back to work."

"Is there a reason the last boy's name didn't start with a P?" Mack asked as they walked toward the barn.

"I don't know. Carmen named them. She's from down in Mexico, said they were family names, and if she was going to have them, she was going to name them; I don't know. It don't make sense to me. "

Walking through the open doors of the barn, Red started what appeared to be his standard tour speech. Mack followed with Stormy holding his hand and Bear trailing the three of them.

"The barn is 150 feet wide and 200 feet long; we can train the horses and never go outside. That's a great marketing tool when you're showing and selling champion-bred horses. On each side of the arena are twelve stalls, 14 x 14, with gates on the inside and doors to the outside arena. Most barns are all wood, but this one has all steel framing, with a brick exterior, on a concrete slab. Of course, we have a dirt floor in the arena and wood stalls, but it's basically fireproof. No fire department needed out here. Plus it's sprinkled, just in case. Most nights, there are over three million dollars' worth of insured horses in this barn."

Red stopped at the first stall. Soft music played throughout the barn as he named each horse's lineage, some going back over a hundred years. His children worked their chores, in and out of every stall, the boys cleaning and the girls feeding and watering. All of them, that is, except Stormy.

Red was sitting on the top rail of the arena wall, explaining the breeding process when a loud noise erupted, and the music stopped playing. Red immediately rolled off the wall into the arena and sprinted across to a center stall—Mack noticed the steel knee was of no hindrance to his speed in what appeared to be an emergency. Mack and Stormy jogged around the outer wall of the arena, following Bear to all the noise.

A 2 x 8 board was splintered and a jagged piece blocked the walkway between the stall and the arena wall. Inside the stall, crouched in the corner, was a broad-shouldered young man holding his ribcage, his eyes wildly searching for an escape route. His leather apron repelled the blood running down from the side of his face. Towering over him was Ebony's Storm, over a thousand pounds of muscle and black fury. His eyes bulged, nostrils flared, as he shook his mane from side to side and reared his body, pawing the air.

"Who's in there?" Red asked.

"The new farrier," someone answered out of the crowd that had gathered.

"I've told you all, over and over—*no one* is allowed in his stall without me being here. If that horse is injured, we'll all lose our jobs."

Mack remembered Stormy pulling her hand from his and only thought of her when he heard Red shouting.

"*Nooo*, Stormy!"

The little girl had opened the stall gate and stood very still inside the stall. Ebony's Storm rolled his eyes down and fixed them on her but continued to paw the ground with his lethal hoofs.

"Quiet! No one move or say a word!" Red ordered.

Stormy put her hand in the pocket of her jeans and removed some broken pieces of peppermint. The huge stallion stopped his pawing but continued swinging his head, back and forth, from the farrier to Stormy. The heavy breathing of the horse overpowered the quietness, except for the rhythm of a faint, singsong voice, "Ebbbbony. Peeeeppermint."

The huge nostrils of the animal twitched, and his lips rolled, uncovering his squared-off teeth. He backed into the opposite corner from the farrier and then moved forward to Stormy, shaking his head and showering her with sweat.

"Stop that!" Stormy said, spitting and shaking her curly black hair. "Ebony—I've got peppermint." She crept forward, holding out the candy with one hand and wrapped the other around the halter rope hanging from Ebony's Storm's neck.

Bear had bumped Mack's leg, but he paid little attention until Bear nipped him. Mack turned, and Bear ran to the exterior door, stopped, and looked back. Mack walked over, opened the door, and followed Bear to the outside arena. He found Bear squatted in front of a stall door with his large head resting between his front paws.

"What is it, Bear?" Mack asked and then realized he was at the outside door of the same stall as Ebony Storm. He cracked the door and saw Stormy holding Ebony's Storm by a rope and had the horse turned away from the farrier. Mack eased the door back and motioned for the farrier to come to him. The young man just stared at Mack, afraid to move.

Mack heard Stormy say, "I don't have any more—here, lick my hand." He watched while she walked him out of the stall.

Red had tried to intervene, but Stormy had barked at him, "I know what to do!" Acquiescing, he had moved everyone to the other side of the arena wall and opened the gate to the next stall.

Mack rushed in to help the farrier up, but Red stopped him. "If his ribs are broken we have to be careful he doesn't puncture his lungs. Let's check his head first, then his ribs. If he's okay, then we'll see if we can get him standing."

Stormy came running into the stall shouting, "Did you see me, Mack?"

"Yes I did. Weren't you scared?" Mack lifted her in his arms.

"Naw, we're buddies. He's named after me, and we have the same birthday."

"When is that?"

"I forgot. Come on I'll show you."

Mack started to put her down, but she shouted at him, "No, carry me!" and pointed to the stall door.

Outside of the stall door, she pointed to a brass plate with Ebony's Storm's name and date of birth.

"Is that when you were born?"

"No, silly..."

Red came out of the stall with the young farrier leaning on two other workers.

"Thanks," the young man grimaced, nodding at Mack and Stormy.

"Well, that ought to be enough excitement for this morning. Cap'n

Irish wanted you back up at the main house as soon as I could let you go. You'd better git," Red said, taking Stormy from his arms.

"I want to go with Mack," Stormy said.

"No, you have to stay here," Red said.

"No! No! No!" Stormy stomped her feet then ran to Mack, wrapping her arms and legs around his leg, looking up and pleading with tears in her eyes.

Red pulled her from Mack's leg and held her out, away from him, while she screamed and kicked the air. Red put her down but stood between her and Mack.

Mack stood speechless as Stormy threw herself to the ground, kicking and screaming and throwing dirt and sawdust in the air. He had never seen such a performance. *What a little firecracker.* Red had escaped to the top rail of the arena wall, like a thrown bull rider. They both watched while she covered her black curls in sawdust. Mack choked back a laugh before he backed away from the dust storm, realizing suddenly that both Ebony's Storm and Stormy were appropriately named. He turned and starting jogging back to the main house with Bear nipping at his heels.

CHAPTER 7

IRISH WAITED FOR Mack at the far end of the library, sitting in front of the fireplace. There was a knock at the door, and Carmen walked in with a tray and set it on the table next to Irish.

"Red called from the barn and said Mister Mack was on his way up to the house, and that there had been a little accident with the farrier, and...there was something else. Let's see, oh, he said Ebony's Storm was not hurt."

"That's good. Was the farrier hurt?"

"He didn't say. You want me to call down and find out?"

"No, Mack will know."

"Are you feeling better? Did you take your medicine?" Carmen pulled the shawl up and over Irish's shoulders.

"Yes, *Mommy*."

"Okay, okay, I just don't want you to catch a cold. Can I mix your drink for you?" Carmen looked at the exotic mixtures on the tray.

"No. I can manage, thank you. "

"Well, I'd better check the biscuits in the oven..."

"Tell Mack to come right on in when he gets here."

"Yes ma'am."

Irish had been planning for years, making notes from time to time, in preparation for this talk with Mack. She knew she would have to be diplomatic with her words and her tonal quality. In other words—curb her "Irish"—*don't raise your voice*. He would resent anything demanded of him, especially by a woman.

Mickey had done his part; he had *forced* Mack to be tough, independent, and street smart, and that worked for him; now it was Irish's turn. Mack was older now, and it would be harder. Any kind of force by her, he would reject, but she wanted him to be the best he could be. She wanted a Renaissance man, not some uneducated machismo. It would be a delicate endeavor—weaving Mack's strong manliness into a refined, worldly sage.

Irish picked up the bottle of absinthe from the tray Carmen brought in and filled the small bubble-shaped reservoir in the bottom of her glass. She put a cube of sugar on top of a slotted spoon and placed the spoon over the rim of the glass, then slowly poured ice water over the sugar cube. She leaned back in her chair and inhaled deeply the herbal aromas and flavors that blossomed from her *"La fée verte"* (the green fairy).

She lit a cigarette and sipped her drink.

There was a knock at the door, and Mack walked in with Bear charging past him.

"Good morning," Irish said, her voice deep and raspy. She flipped her cigarette into the fireplace and took a quick sip of her drink. "You two certainly hit it off. Shows he has good taste." Bear plopped at Irish's feet.

"Has Red got you on a horse yet?" She closed the old box her green lizard boots came in, set it on the floor, and patted the seat of the wingback chair opposite her.

"No, and I'm not sure I want to after seeing Storm go wild down at the barn."

"Is he okay?"

"Who, the horseshoe man?"

"No, Storm?"

"Not a scratch. He's double-tough, and so is that little girl, Stormy."

"Don't worry, you won't be riding one of the show horses, not at first. Is the farrier okay? That's what they call someone who shoes horses."

"Oh yeah, Red told me that, but I forgot. He was okay when I left. Storm kicked him a couple times, though."

"Horses are a lot like us. If a stranger walked into your house how would you react? But don't let that frighten you."

"I'm not *frightened*. I told him I'd ride tomorrow," Mack said, sitting down.

"Good, the sooner the better, everybody should know how to ride. And while I'm thinking of it, you need to start flying too. Go down to the airfield, just behind the barn. They're expecting you and will take you up. Those crop dusters are wild men, but they'll get you started."

"Really? Fly an airplane?"

"Sure, just don't kill yourself; those Ag planes are unforgiving. Have them start you out in our Cessna. Bear could fly one of those."

Pushing her glasses up on her head, she continued, "I hope you don't mind the fire. It's a little late in the season, but I need some warmth in these old bones. You've got a birthday coming up soon, right?"

"Yeah, next month."

"Have you thought about what you're going to do with your life? I mean, after the Marine Corps?"

"No."

"No idea of how you're going to make a living, support yourself?"

"Not really. Father O'Brien gave me this old book to read *Think and Grow Rich*."

"And did you read it?"

"Yeah, well, parts of it."

"And you want to be rich?"

"Yeah, doesn't everybody?"

"Yes *Ma'am!*" Irish corrected him. "*Mack!* Look-at-*me*. Look me in the eyes. Now, hold that look. No, don't look away, keep looking into my eyes and *listen*. Don't try to think of a response or a reaction, just relax, and listen to me, okay? Now say, 'Yes *ma'am*.'"

For the first time, Mack looked directly into her eyes. He felt a rage building up inside of him. *Who the hell does this woman think she is to tell me what to say? She wants a stare down; I'll give her a stare down.* He locked in on her large brown eyes.

"Mack, please don't challenge me. I'm not trying to intimidate you or change you. I want you to be all that you are now and more, *lots more.*"

Mack noticed the deep crow's feet at the corner of her eyes.

Irish leaned forward and spoke softly, "I want you to understand that when you say, 'Yes ma'am,' 'No ma'am,' 'Yes sir,' and 'No sir,' that these words are all signs of respect; just being polite, part of our proud Southern culture...not a sign of abdication or servility."

"Do I have to say this to everybody?"

"No, you don't *have* to say or do anything. Many people are satisfied with their current lifestyle and have no desire to put in the extra time and effort to compete with the best. I have plans for you to be much more than average. What I'm telling you are suggestions to save you some of life's hardships, so that you can grow, better yourself—socially and professionally—*and* without too many faux pas.

Mack frowned.

"Faux pas. In English it means a blunder, a slip of the tongue, an embarrassing mistake." She picked up a couple of 3" x 5" index cards and handed them to him. "A good habit is to write new words down or a saying or a reminder to study later. Faux pas is a tag sometimes, exposing your level of education. It could be table manners, poor grammar, or some breach of conduct." *Sweet Jesus, how many have I made?* "It will be like that in the Marine Corps, a standing order, that every first word out of your mouth will be 'Yes sir' or 'No sir.' Isn't it better to learn *now* than to have them beat on you every time you forget?"

Irish looked at the light bruising still under his eyes and the red cut line over his eyebrow. "Didn't you train and prepare for months before you fought that boy and won the boxing championship in Memphis? Wouldn't it be better to start now, preparing for that *rich* future? Things would be a lot easier for you." *Enough. I need to slow down with the teaching and preaching.*

There was a knock on the door, and Carmen came in with a tray of coffee and biscuits. Irish removed her drink from the tray and nodded that it was okay to remove the tray of water and the bottle of absinthe.

When Carmen closed the door, Irish leaned back in her chair smiling. "Help yourself," as she poured the coffee. "Okay, we've established that you want to be rich. How rich are we talking about, and are we talking about rich with money? Power? Knowledge?"

Mack tried to think of the right answer. "Money."

"How much money? A hundred thousand dollars, a half a million—how about one million dollars?"

"I'd take the million, sure."

"I like your style. What if you had to take a test first?"

"I'd probably fail."

"What if you had the answers?"

Mack waited...thinking, mindful of a trap. "Twilly always said, 'You get nothing for nothing.'"

"Twilly's a smart man—it would cost you."

"How much?"

"About ten years."

"Ten years!"

"You will be what, twenty-seven, twenty-eight?"

"I would have a million dollars?"

"A lot more than that, I hope. After Mickey, you're the only family I have."

"What do I have to do for ten years?"

"A lot. How about, whatever I say? Can you handle that, an old woman giving you orders? Better yet, can you *give* orders without looking back, without questioning yourself? Well, I'm getting ahead of myself; the Marine Corps will take care of a lot of that training.

"Let's see how you do with this hypothetical test question. Go back a couple of weeks ago. You're sitting behind the wheel of the car at the snuff company your two buddies are robbing...now don't get upset.

Hear me out. We're only imagining it happened this way. So, your two partners in crime are shot and killed. One throws a large bag of money in the back of the car as he falls to the street. The police catch you hours later after you've hidden the million dollars and offer you a deal if you tell them where the money is. Being seventeen and a first offender, your attorney tells you the most time you will serve would be ten years. Would you do the ten years or less and have a million dollars waiting for you when you get out?"

Mack didn't like the pressure he was feeling and didn't have the poker face to hide his emotions. Here he was trying to forget, and she's bringing it up again.

Irish felt the tension. "You don't need to answer now. Just think about it and compare it to my offer." She walked over to one of the bookcases, removed a large book, and laid it on the table. She dropped her glasses down over her nose and turned the pages to the first bookmark.

"Come over here, please; I want you to read something for me." Mack walked over and read as Irish pointed to each passage. "And God said, *Ask what I shall give thee.*"

"And here," Irish pointed.

"And Solomon said, *O Lord my God, thou hast made thy servant king. And I am but a little child: I know not how to go out or come in.*"

"And here," skipping certain areas.

"*Give therefore thy servant an understanding heart to judge thy people, that I may...*" Mack paused.

"Discern. It means, 'that I may know.'" Irish read, "*that I may discern good from bad.*"

Mack looked up, and Irish nodded for him to continue to read God's answer to Solomon. "And I have also given thee that which thou hast not asked, both riches, and honor: so that there shall not be any among the kings like unto thee all thy days."

"Do you understand what's happening here?" Irish asked.

"I'm not sure."

"Good, I'm glad you're honest." Irish walked to the fireplace and back to the table. "King David is dying and has just appointed his son, Solomon, King of Israel. He is twenty years old and his father has told him he is young, inexperienced and that his task is great.

"Now you're talking about pressure. Solomon was under the gun in front of all his people. Let's keep this in perspective. Here is a young man—not too many years older than you are now—that has been told he is King of a whole country, Commander in Chief, ruler of all his people."

Irish started getting into her story, gesturing and pacing, like a trial lawyer before a jury. "Solomon has to make life and death decisions for his people, hundreds of thousands of them. Questions and answers on what and when to plant and what to sell, trade, or keep at harvest time. Water was a big problem back then: irrigation, droughts, sickness, health care, politics, religion, construction, taxes—decisions, and more decisions. What an awesome responsibility for a young man, an inexperienced young man." Irish walked over to her chair and plopped down with her palms held up. "What to do...*what* is he to do?"

"Ask his father?" Mack said.

"Yes! You're right. But not his earthly father, his heavenly father. King David was on his deathbed when he appointed Solomon king, and he died shortly thereafter. So, Solomon was alone, without council, not knowing who to trust."

"But this is just a Bible story. No one knows if this really happened, right?"

"*WHAT!* Is this what you learned in catechism and Mass every morning of your life? Is this what I have being paying Father O'Brien all these years to teach you—*blasphemy*?" She stood up, towering over Mack, "Of course it happened, *stupid!*"

Blood rushed to her face, and her voice thundered inside Mack's head. He withered, expecting a blow, and looked up and saw a bulging vein, pulsating on the side of her head. He moved back quickly, almost tripping over his chair.

Irish sat down and dropped her head into her arms on the table, embarrassed that she lost her temper. She knew she would never reach him this way. She sensed him pulling away. She shook a cigarette out of the pack and stuck it in her mouth, lit it, and leaned back taking a deep draw.

She coughed, picked up her drink, and downed it in one swallow. "I'm sorry; it's in our blood—this Irish curse of passion and impatience—please forgive me.

"You are certainly not stupid, just young and..." she started coughing again, looked at her cigarette, and dropped it into her empty glass. "You will have to learn some tact, avoid saying the first thing that comes into your mind; God knows I've failed that subject."

Irish stood, picked up her Bible, placed her arm over Mack's shoulder, and led him back to the fireplace and his chair. She sat her Bible on the side table and stared at him as she sat in her chair. She waited till his eyes met hers.

"You still love me, don't you?" she asked, with a slight smile.

Mack, caught off guard by the question, had no answer, but the tension in the room diminished.

"Have you ever lost your temper like that?" A grin broke at the corner of Mack's mouth. "Can we continue?" Mack nodded.

"Let's see, where were we? Okay, in Solomon's day, there were no Bibles—there were some biblical manuscripts written on parchment and papyrus, but they were only available for scholars—so God spoke to his people in dreams, through angels, sometimes through signs, and sometimes through other people. I don't expect you to understand all this; it has taken me years, and I still don't have all the answers. But let me ask you something, okay?"

"Yeah. I mean, yes ma'am."

"What nationality was Solomon?" Mack shrugged his shoulders.

"Was he an Irishman? An Englishman? An Italian, like Pope Paul?" Irish asked smiling.

"I don't know."

"He was a Jew, the King of Israel. God promised the Jews, starting with Abraham, that they would all prosper as long as they obeyed his laws. It is all in this book right here." She patted the Bible, which was now in her lap, and then she leaned back in her chair with her arms crossed. "You've walked down Main Street in Memphis, haven't you? You've shopped in the department stores, looked in the windows, gone to the movies, right?"

"Yes ma'am."

"Have you ever noticed the names of the businesses on Main Street? Like Goldsmith's, Lowenstein's, Gerbers, Levy's, Julius Lewis, Shainberg's, Broadnax, Mednikow, Dreyfus, Perel and Lowenstein's, Fortas, Samuel's, on and on...and the movie houses: Lowes State, Lowes Palace, Warner Brothers, and the Malco, all owned by descendants of Abraham, in other words, Jews. What is the population of Memphis, a little over half a million? Well, guess how many Jews there are in Memphis? Barely one per cent, maybe six thousand Jews. With one percent of all the people in Memphis, guess who runs the city? A Jew. You question the Bible, that it's only a book of unsubstantiated stories? Listen to this." Irish opened her Bible to a marked page, "This is the angel of the Lord speaking for God to Abraham, *'That in blessing I will bless thee, and in multiplying I will multiply thy seed as the stars of the heaven, and as the sand which is upon the sea shore.'*

"The Lord is telling Abraham that his descendants, that means all Jews, now and in the future, will take possession of the cities, and all nations on earth will be blessed by Abraham's children, his offspring, all the way down the line. So, let's look at the mathematics here. For every one Jew in Memphis, there are twenty-five Irishmen. Now, is something wrong with that figure? Do you see any signs on Main Street with the names of Kelly, O'Brien, Fitzgerald or O'Sullivan?"

"Malloy?" Mack spoke up.

"*Damn right!* Now you're talking. And that's what we're here to talk about, the Malloys and the Shannons. We're not on Main Street, but we own a couple of warehouses on Front Street one block away, and if we plan correctly we can own whatever we want from Main Street down to the river. Come here, let me show you something." Irish walked over, pulled a sliding shelf out, and rifled through some large papers until she found what she was looking for. She lifted a handful of colored maps and placed them on the table and picked up a wooden ruler.

"This is a map of Shamrock and the surrounding properties. All that is colored green is my property."

"All that is yours?"

"This is *your* future. I've spent my life buying land, good investments, more than a hundred thousand acres. You see this blacktop road," Irish traced the road with her ruler across the map. "I own all the frontage on this side of that road. Now, you see the gravel road running off the blacktop, the one you came through the gate on? I own fourteen miles of all the land on both sides of that road, not mortgaged. I own it, and every acre pays for itself."

Irish changed the maps. "This is the Mississippi River, 2,500 miles long, running from St. Paul, Minnesota down past New Orleans into the Gulf of Mexico." Dragging her ruler from the top of the map to the bottom, "You see the red triangles along the river? Those are locations of businesses I own, Marine Service Centers, in major ports."

Irish walked back to the table and sat down. "I'm an old woman—Mickey's old too, but I'm older—I don't like it, but that's the way it is. Both of us could drop dead tomorrow. I know you have some questions about God and his holy words." She pointed to her Bible. "Just think of it as history—that's what it is—a true history of the world, and throughout your lifetime you'll find most of the answers to your questions inside."

God, I've got to have a cigarette. She got up and walked around looking for her cigarettes. She noticed Mack getting restless in his chair. "I know—I'm being long-winded." She hurried but couldn't find her cigarettes.

"Mickey and me..." she said, still looking for her cigarettes, "we never even finished high school, and so I'm plowing new ground here. Years ago I thought I would have a passel of kids. I promised myself that every generation, I would better our family's social station in life. Now I have no children, and you're my only hope. When you were just a wee one, God snatched you from that inferno—from the devil's hands—the only one that He saved. I knew then, and I know now, like Solomon, He has special plans for you."

Mack now understood why they had shipped him off down here. True, maybe ahead of schedule, but here regardless—*God's plan? I doubt it. Aunt Irish's plan? Damn straight.*

"So Mack, as King David told Solomon, 'You are young and inexperienced and have a great task before you.' The big question is...are *you* up to the task?" She saw her pack of cigarettes on the floor and picked it up; it was empty. She crushed the package, tossed it in the fireplace, and dropped into her chair.

Stop talking; let's see what he's got to say. Irish was determined not to break the silence. Her eyes were locked in on her future. *God, he's a handsome boy, just like his granddaddy—a heartbreaker.*

Mack's eyes darted back and forth on Irish, waiting. *She won't take her eyes off me.* He fought the soundlessness, the pressure. All he could hear was his own breathing. He looked at the door. "Do I have to give you an answer now?"

"Now," she said.

Fight or flight? That's always the question, "What if I say no? What happens?"

"Nothing. Mickey and I have wills, and there's a sizable amount set up in a trust for your education.

"And if I said yes?"

"We would change our wills to reflect the agreement you're to sign, and your task would start immediately."

"What task?"

"Your responsibilities that are listed in the agreement here." She picked up the lizard boot box and placed it on the table. "As we discussed, ten years for millions of dollars."

"You said something about preparing me. I thought I was headed for the Marines."

"You are. The Marine Corps is a plus, unexpected, but an important training opportunity for you. This problem you had in Memphis is over; forget about it. I shouldn't have brought it up. There's no record. After boot camp or even before, it depends when they call you, we could start your advanced studies and continue throughout your three years in the Marines Corps. Not only academic studies, but also private tutors and professional instructors to teach you many other things, things that make a man well rounded, a man of the world."

"What things?" Mack asked.

"Many things, not the least academic, but things like we talked about; flying an airplane, riding a horse, snow skiing, learning to tango—what's the name of the man in this latest movie? He's a secret agent. James Bond, that's it. Wouldn't you want to be like him, not a secret agent, but a man with his sophistication?"

Mack shrugged his shoulders. "What I don't understand, if you and Mickey have all this money and you have been planning my future, why have I lived in an orphanage all my life? Why, when my school friends went off to a summer camp or on vacations, was I working on a riverboat all my summers or on a construction site? And after school, why did I have to work loading boats on the river?" Mack asked these questions feeling somewhat betrayed.

"The simple answer is, I got sick. So weak I could no longer work the river businesses or even in the construction office. My doctors advised me to move down here to the farm. I tried to take you with me, to Shamrock—you were such a wee package—but Mickey would hear no argument on the subject. The doctors had told him I was to have no stress under any circumstances. So Mickey had to do it all, and he always said he would not turn this business over to some spoiled, snotty-nosed brat. He saw to it that you could operate and repair any construction equipment, pilot a towboat, hook up barges, and hold your own in a fight. Everything that he knew and more—worked you hard. He was determined to see that you were tempered to the task that lay ahead and now the time has come for you to make a choice. It's a big responsibility, probably the biggest decision in your life."

"Why college then?"

"Mickey did his part, as much as he knew. Now it's my time, my responsibility, to prepare you to take over this business."

She pushed the boot box across the table to Mack. "When I spoke with the Marine recruiter in Jackson, he told me after you've signed the paperwork, it could be anywhere from a month to six months before you get your orders to report to boot camp. Remember, before you decide, the contract is an agreement, your *word* that you will do what you say. This is your future, not Mickey's or mine; we're at the end. Your schedule, the contract, everything you need to know is in that box, year to year, for the next ten years. After that you're on your own with a net worth of around ten million dollars or more; that's my word. As someone once said, 'The teacher will appear when the student is ready.' The question is, are you ready?"

Mack stared at the faded name on the top of the box, "Heritage Boots—Austin, Texas," and looked down at her handmade lizard cowboy boots. *The best damn cowboy boots on the planet,* she had said. He thought of how long she had been planning this meeting and how important it must be to her. He also thought of how he had been living all those years at the orphanage, alone, no family. And when he was younger, the lonely nights, all those questions and no one there. Then, he thought about the ten million dollars, struggling with the concept.

Irish couldn't wait any longer. "So, do we call you King Solomon or what?" She held back from smiling. *I like the way he thinks, the way he asks questions and worked things down to its common denominator. He's very quick, analytical, calculating—qualities hard to teach. Mickey was right in keeping him in Memphis. Hard work never killed anyone. Plus, he's a good-looking kid with good physical genes and plenty of street smarts. Like a diamond in the rough—*

I just need to polish the edges.

Her instincts were going to prove her right. It was in his Irish blood; he would never avoid a challenge or a good fight.

Mack stood up, both hands in his pockets, shaking his head, "No, this is not for me."

Irish was waylaid; it couldn't have hurt any more if Ebony's Storm had kicked her in the stomach. As much as she tried, she couldn't hold her poker face. The pain was like a shattered mirror on her face. All this time...she could not believe her ears.

Mack leaned forward, both hands planted firmly on top of the table, staring, locked into her eyes, *vis-à-vis.*

"Oh. Sorry about that. I meant, '*No Ma'am.*' You cannot call me King Solomon...but *King Mack* will do nicely." He leaned over and kissed her on the cheek, picked up the boot box and sauntered out the door.

CHAPTER 8

MACK COULDN'T SLEEP; too much was going on in his head. Over and over he replayed his meeting with Irish—had he made the right decision? Ten years is a long time.

He sat up and leaned back against the headboard, the boot box that Irish gave him lay on the bed next to him, unopened. He watched as the breeze from the open window moved the curtains in and out, allowing a slash of moonlight to cross his bed. The open window brought back memories of his night with Ruby; no sleep that night. What a wild woman—no gentle instructions or teaching techniques, as he was led to believe. After the second time, she got out of the bed and closed the window. Mack had closed his eyes and kicked back, thinking it was all over. But it was not over; in her mind it hadn't even started.

Mack bolted upright from a deep sleep, grabbing each side of his mattress. He held on as his bed bounced up and down off the floor.

"Off your ass and on your feet. I'm Sergeant Major Buck Jones, United States Marine Corps. Your ass is mine for the next twelve weeks. Grab your jockstrap and tennis shoes and be out front in five minutes. You won't like it if I have to come back." Buck dropped the bed and stormed out of the room, slamming the door behind him.

The lights were on, and the bedsprings still shook. Mack's brain was not telling him if this was an earthquake or a nightmare. Before he knew it, his instinct had overpowered his senses, and he had hustled his butt out front and stood at attention before Sgt. Buck in tee shirt, shorts, and tennis shoes.

Buck stood in the shadow of the front porch light with his hands on his hips, legs apart, dressed in camouflage utilities. He was short and wide and wore a black patch over his left eye. His pistol belt held a M1911 Colt 45 auto pistol and a canteen.

In a flash, like the click of a camera lens, Mack *remembered* seeing this man with the black patch over his eye. It was when he first saw Irish riding up on her horse. He was the rider in the background who watched from the edge of the woods and then vanished.

"You may have noticed there is *no one* around at 0400. That's when Marines do their best work. I could kill you without a sound, bury you in the woods, and no one would ever know. Before I'm finished with you, *you* will be able to do the same. I have been hired to do a job, and *I will* do my job, and *you will* do your job. Your job is to graduate number one in your platoon from the Marine Corps basic training at Parris Island. In the past, you have been taught right and wrong, fair and unfair; forget that bullshit. You are training to be a warrior, not a lawyer. In this profession, if you hesitate a split second, you're dead. You operate on instinct and, to be the very best, you've got to prepare for the very worst. Follow me and don't stop unless I stop." Buck took off running with Mack right behind him.

That was how it all started, that and a haircut. Mack's hair was gone, like his old life, and his head shaved—the start of a new life. For the next three months, he trained on more than what was required at boot camp, much more. It wasn't long before Buck realized he had underestimated Mack's abilities; he found him to be tough and aggressive. Mack loved a challenge and took all that Buck could dish out.

Time flew by, and Buck was surprised when Mack had finished his training in half the time of the Marine Corps' basic training on Parris Island. Though his was an abbreviated schedule, Buck was at a loss to find something he had left out. Regardless, Buck kept pushing, moving past basic training into a combination of Infantry School with combat training. For another two weeks they raced up and down the river in a Zodiac combat raft, planting and disarming all kinds of booby traps and IEDs, and blowing up beaver dams with high explosives.

Mack was a natural when it came to flying. With Irish's insistence, Buck's instructions, and Mack's mechanical inclination, he was soon soloing all the planes at Shamrock. Still, there was no word on Mack reporting to boot camp.

Buck met with Irish the day she got back from Memphis. He gave her Mack's high school diploma and a bill from the Ole Miss grad student who had tutored him.

Irish didn't look good; she was pale, weak, and still had the hacking cough. She asked Buck how much longer he thought they had before Mack got his call to boot camp.

"Mack's good to go, ready for anything," Buck said. "But it's typical of the Corps to 'hurry up and wait.' It could be a week or another eight weeks."

Mack heard his name as he left his upstairs bedroom and halfway down he stopped, sat on one of the steps, and listened.

"Well, I hired a retired professor, a Dr. Kennedy, who lives in Natchez, to prep him for the ACT and the SAT. I need to know how smart he is." The only drawback is that Mack would have to go to her place. I offered her more money to come here, but she refused to drive out this far."

What? What is she doing? Mack thought. *I'm going into the Marine Corps.*

Buck poured coffee for both of them and sat down at the kitchen table. "Getting him there won't be a problem if you decide to go in that direction. Studying is not Mack's strong suit, but he's disciplined enough now to do what you tell him, and he has an excellent memory. But I'm more concerned about his physical condition, which is more important *now*. He's in peak condition, how do I keep him that way? Studying English and History at this point is not going to help him in the Corps. I could bribe two or three instructors from Force Recon and at least *start* some Special Ops training."

"Thank-you-Buck," Mack whispered to himself.

"I don't disagree...how about both? I'll pay for your recon men and Dr. Kennedy gets Mack on the weekends—Friday at noon till Monday morning. She's retired, may go for that; it won't hurt to ask. Do you think he's ready for Special Ops training?"

"Oh yeah. He's primed, and I want to keep him that way. This kid is a natural gunslinger, and they will train him to kill. It's a rare opportunity, one that could save his life and others, over and over again."

A gunslinger? Mack stood up on the steps.

"A gunslinger...not really what I had in mind." Irish said.

"That's right, *gunslinger!* What do you think I've been doing day and night for the last 12 weeks, training a ballerina? He's not going to dance, act, or sing; he's going to kill bad guys or get killed. That's a Marine's job. Gunslinger? Hell, yeah; first in last out. I want him to be the best *gunslinger* there is, so he doesn't *lose* that job."

"Okay, okay, don't get your skivvies wadded in a knot." For the first time Irish realized that Mack meant more to Buck than just someone he was training. "I agree. When you're right, you're right. I just hope we're not overloading the cart."

"Yeah, me too," Mack said, walking into the kitchen.

It was 0525 Monday. Buck and Mack were deep in the woods, squatting over a small fire, drinking coffee. It was still dark, and the ground was wet from the morning dew, but the sun was rising, and rays of light broke through under the tree limbs. It was very quiet, with only the popping sound of burning wood. They had been walking on a deer trail for over an hour before coming into this clearing where Buck stopped and started the fire. Mack knew better than to ask what was going on. It was always the same answer: *need-to-know basis.* What Buck did tell him, before he left for New Orleans, was to be prepared

Monday morning to start Special Ops training with some elite Marine instructors.

"Whatever you *think* you know about what is happening now, forget it," Buck said. "If Irish told you something about this training, forget that, too; she doesn't know. This is nothing like anything else you will ever experience, and only a select few have had the privilege. There is no doubt in my mind that you are ready; I trained you, so I know. You only have one disadvantage—you don't have other grunts training with you."

"Why would that be a disadvantage?"

"When you think you have no more gas, that you are totally spent, finished, then, at that very instance, the 'runt of grunts' runs by you, swims further than you, or keeps getting up after being knocked down more times than you. That's when you say to yourself, 'If that little shit can do it, I can too'…that's an advantage. But for the past 12 weeks you did great training by yourself, which has its advantages, too. You're a loner, like me. You don't talk much and you don't need people. Loners make the best warriors. What was it you told me you read in that book Father O'Brien gave you, 'Whatever the human mind can believe and conceive, he can achieve'? That's the mantra you want tattooed on one of your brain cells when you have no more in you to give; that will save your life.

"Will you still be training me?"

"No, I have to spend some time in Memphis, at the downtown airport, but I will be here some of the weekends. You won't be able to make contact with anyone during the week. These are 1st Force Recon instructors; it's all they do when not on a mission, and they have fasttracked this training just for you, 24/7, Monday through Friday. We don't know how much time you have, so they will cram as much in as fast as they can."

"What is Special Ops?"

"Basically, deep reconnaissance. For green operations: silence, stealth, surveillance and avoiding contact, and just the opposite is direct action for black operations: shock and awe. That's all you need to know. You don't want to spoil all your fun, do you? As I told you, it is an elite group of Marines, sometimes referred to as Silent Warriors. A lot will be advanced training of what you've had, but most will be the latest training in modern warfare worldwide, like Bomb Detection and Disposal, High-Altitude Low-Opening (HALO) parachuting at night, Survival Evasion Resistance Escape, Scout and Sniper training, and Amphibious Underwater Recon. You will fire thousands of rounds from every weapon from around the world and use all the latest electronic attachments of Night Vision, Infra-Red Target Pointer, and Long-Range Telescopes. You will practice Helicopter Insertion and Extraction, Rope Suspension, and hundreds of other things like Mapping, GPS and Radio Communications."

They heard a voice almost next to them, "Didn't I hear you say a minute ago '*You don't need to know?*'"

Mack jumped up, almost spilling his coffee, but Buck stayed squatted, poking at the fire. "It's about time, Shithead. I heard you monkeys coming through the jungle five minutes ago."

"Bull shit, we've been here waiting on your slow ass, right guys?" Three men stood just inside the tree line in full camouflage, including painted faces. They blended in so well that Mack could not see them unless they were talking.

The big one, Shooter, stepped out of the tree line, grabbed Mack's canteen cup from his hand, and downed his coffee, tossing the cup to the ground.

"Is this the fresh meat, Bucky?"

"He's all yours."

"Okay, Grunt, say *toodle-oo* to Daddy War-BUCKY...v*ámonos!*"

As quick as they came, they were gone. Buck shook his thumb, as if hitch-hiking, for Mack to "get going." Mack hurried through the trees right behind the men, but they were gone. He stood listening but could hear no sound and saw no movement. He felt a tap on his shoulder and a whisper, "First rule, stay close." Shooter shoved Mack, and they took off, double time, to catch the other two men.

Buck was proud of Mack and had never trained anyone that worked harder or with more desire. It was hard turning him over to someone else, but this was a once-in-a-lifetime opportunity. There was only *one way*, tried and proven, the Marine Corps way; the harder you trained, the better chance you had of surviving. There had been many complaints of brutality, but this advanced combat training separated the wheat from the chaff and had been successful in the Corps since 1775. Buck's answers to complaints were simple; the Marine Corps didn't draft men: they're all volunteers. If you don't like their philosophy, don't join. The Marine Corps poster said it succinctly, "A *Few* Good Men."

The extreme training and the intensity of having three instructors, compared to having just Buck one-on-one, had a tremendous effect on Mack. There was no shouting or criticism this time around. If he didn't understand or made a mistake, they stopped and went over it again, until he mastered the task.

Mack and Shooter, the Team Leader, had recently completed a forced march, tracking an enemy patrol (Shooter's other two instructors were the *enemy patrol*) for three days and three nights without sleep. They both carried a 60-pound pack with M16 rifles and Colt 45 pistols. Mack's body was rock hard, but the biggest change was in his mind. He kept "singing" the mantra "tattooed" in his head and was shocked by surpassing every personal goal he had set.

His attitude had changed, and the stories of Solomon helped him understand a lot about himself and more of what he wanted out of life. Every day he was more confident and secure and loved that feeling and the power it generated. He compared himself to others from his past and was proud that he couldn't think of one person who could do what he had done in all these weeks. There was nothing he couldn't do—he was a Marine and vowed that no one would ever take that feeling away from him.

Late at night, while looking at a sky full of stars, his body aching and too tired to sleep, the question of *why* he was doing all this would creep in. The money Irish promised was one reason, but the truth was he hadn't thought of the money in weeks. He believed it was fear—fear of how he would measure up, *mano-a-mano*. He knew he was good at what he was doing—damn good and getting better—and he loved the challenge of testing himself every day. One thing was for certain: Every day he felt less fearful and more courageous. If he didn't learn another thing, he learned that he always wanted to be around men like Buck and that crazy Shooter.

This was Mack's first weekend home. What he thought he would dislike the most, he found he liked best—his tutor, Dr. Loretta Leigh Kennedy. She was from England but had retired from teaching at the University of Mississippi. If he had to pick one word to describe her, it would be class. Everything about her was sophisticated—her mannerisms, the way she dressed, her well-coiffed white hair—and yet she was still friendly and unpretentious.

Their first meeting was Saturday morning at 9 a.m. Mack was running late, and parked Red's pickup on the brick driveway, and hurried down the path to the English-style cottage covered in wisteria and ivy. He rapped the doorknocker, and the door opened.

"Mr. Shannon, I presume?" Dr. Kennedy said. She was dressed up in a bright long-sleeved print dress and wore a matching amethyst necklace and earrings.

Mack, feeling somewhat underdressed in jeans, wondered if they were going out. Then, she hooked her arm through his and pulled him inside.

"Come, come, your tea is getting cold." A fat gray cat followed them into the kitchen. "Did you have any trouble finding me?"

Mack noticed an accent. "No, ma'am. I had to stop for gas." It was not a big house, but it was intimate, with everything neatly in its place. They sat at a round wooden table, and, while she poured tea from a knit-covered teapot, she insisted Mack call her by her middle name, Leigh. From her oven, she removed a pan of crumpets and insisted he try one with her freshly made fig preserves.

They talked for hours getting to know one another. Leigh listened and evaluated what Mack knew and didn't know, plotting her course of action. Mack, not usually comfortable around women, was relaxed and talkative for the first time as he scratched the big cat's neck, purring in his lap. And before he knew it, he had a second go around with the hot tea, cream and honey, and Leigh's crumpets and preserves.

Leigh explained that she would best serve him as an "informal mentor," rather than a tutor or a typical teacher. She would incorporate some basic techniques to help him develop, not just academically, but as a whole person. "According to your Aunt Irish, all this is time-sensitive, so it would have to be condensed and accelerated," Leigh added.

From then on, every weekend there was something new and exciting to learn. He now had a leather folder full of Irish's index cards. A whole new world had opened up to him, and he found himself excited about his future meetings with Leigh. For Mack, the weekends were a great respite after his grueling Monday through Friday schedule of Special Ops training.

Mack had no memory of his mother, and most of his experiences with women—like the nuns at the orphanage, his lay teachers, and even his Aunt Irish—were more businesslike. Leigh was warm and demonstrative. Now, when greeting Mack, she hugged him, and sometimes she kissed him on his cheeks.

On their last weekend together, Leigh and Mack walked along the river while Mack read to her his orders to report to Parris Island. Leigh's fat gray cat, his belly dragging the ground, tried to keep up with them.

The scuttlebutt in the Marine Corps has always been that a Marine sergeant major is equal to that of a general, especially when it comes to getting things done. Retired, after thirty years in the Marine Corps, Buck was not without his contacts and didn't hesitate when he picked up the phone and called his old CO, Colonel Jesse Butcher, Sr., Commanding Officer of 1st Force Recon, Camp Pendleton, California. While waiting to be connected, Buck perused Mack's orders again; he was to report to Parris Island in a week. Buck hadn't figured out what he was going to do with Mack, but he had no intentions of letting him report to Parris Island. That would be a waste of talent, time, and money.

He was somewhat glad when the Colonel's sergeant came on the phone and told him the Colonel was in a meeting and would return his call ASAP. He had forgotten one of his old CO's pet peeves; the Colonel hated it when one of his staff would bring him a problem without a recommended solution. He needed some time to think about all this.

The first problem would be the logistics. Natchez was east of the Mississippi River, meaning Mack would have to take his basic training at Parris Island. If Mack were on the west side of the Mississippi when he enlisted, he would take his basic training at Camp Pendleton, California. Buck realized that Mack was from Memphis not Natchez, but Memphis was east of the Mississippi as well; that still wouldn't work. Buck looked over the orders again and noticed they were not from the Jackson recruiter but from a Sgt. Earl Z. Washington, Jr. in West Memphis, Arkansas; was this some kind of screw-up? Buck served with an Earl Z. Washington in Viet Nam. They had to be related. West Memphis was *west* of the Mississippi...*aha, a crack in the dam*. Buck knew if he could get Mack's orders changed from Parris Island to Camp Pendleton it would be a lot less complicated for the Colonel to help Buck.

By the time Colonel Butcher returned Buck's phone call, Buck had already worked out a solution, and Mack's new orders would be faxed to Camp Pendleton tomorrow. He didn't want to say too much to the Colonel, just that he was flying out to Southern California and would like to see him while he was there. Later, he worked into the conversation that he was bringing with him an excellent recruit with orders to report to Camp Pendleton. The Colonel was curious and agreed to meet with Buck.

Buck told Mack they were leaving for Camp Pendleton the next day and wanted him to get Carmen to cut his hair high and tight before they left and that he would meet Mack at the airstrip, ready to leave, at 0630.

At 0600 the next morning, Mack stepped out on the front porch. It was unusually quiet. Irish was normally up at this time in the mornings, and she knew he was leaving. He stood on the front steps, the same duffel bag hanging from his shoulder just like when he first walked up the driveway months ago. It was cloudy and overcast, with a light rain falling. He had mixed emotions; so much had happened to him, and so fast, but now, another unknown adventure was about to start. He walked down the driveway to the gravel road and turned toward the barn. As he came around the curve at the barn, he saw something dark standing in the middle of the road; it was Bear.

"At least *you* came to say goodbye, huh, Pal?" They walked the rest of the way, about a mile to the airstrip, while Bear periodically bumped his leg with his body to let him know he was there. Mack often thought that there was something about Bear that was almost human; he was so intuitive.

"Hey," Buck hollered, "is that big *bear* going with us?"

Mack looked up and saw Buck on the wing of the black Aero Commander, filling the gas tanks. "I wish."

"I'm all loaded up and ready to go, just topping these off. Throw your gear in the back. Irish says it's too far for the 172 and wants you to fly the Commander." Buck looked up at the sky. "But there's a front moving in from the west. Maybe it will pass through in about an hour. Call flight service, check the weather, and re-file our flight plan while I finish up here. We'll ride back up to the house and eat some breakfast before we leave."

Mack loved flying the 500S Commander; it was big, bold, and beautiful. After flying the Cessna 172 and most of his time in the ag planes, flying the Commander was like driving Irish's big Caddie. He didn't have a multi-engine rating yet, but the truth was he didn't have *any* flying licenses. Irish's flying philosophy was simple, "No one ever pulled me over and asked to see my pilot license."

Mack was driving the pick-up back to the house. It was raining hard now, and he turned the wipers on full speed and looked over at Buck, "Where is everyone this morning? There were no lights on at the house or the barn."

"Beats me; there's not a lot to do on a rainy morning—probably all sleeping in."

Mack turned into the driveway.

"Park around back, and we'll go in the kitchen door," Buck said.

Bear leaped from the back of the truck before it stopped. Mack walked up the back steps and opened the kitchen door with Buck and Bear behind him. The lights flashed on and everyone shouted, "Surprise!"

Mack *was* surprised. Irish walked over and hugged him. "Did you think we would let you go without saying goodbye?" Red, his wife Carmen, their seven children, including Stormy, and Dr. Leigh Kennedy were all crammed into the kitchen. Stormy threw herself into Mack's arms.

"Okay, let's all move to the dining room; the food is on the table and getting cold," Irish said.

Mack was happy to see everyone together again but was disappointed not to see Kate. He was not going to ask Irish because he knew she didn't approve of their being together, and neither did Kate's family.

After breakfast, Irish thought it best for everyone to say their goodbyes at the house, but not Stormy. She threw her little fit, while they all watched from the front porch, as Bear chased the pickup back to the airstrip.

Mack had finished walking around the plane, doing his visual checklist, and climbed in the left seat, buckling his seatbelt. Buck, looking out the right side, gave a thumbs-up. Mack checked the left side and started the engines. He eased off the brakes and taxied over to the grass strip, checking the windsock one more time. As he turned left onto the strip, he noticed a movement at the edge of the woods and stopped the plane at the threshold. Shooter and his team took one step, all together, out of the woods and snapped to rigid attention, each holding a salute. Mack was surprised and a little overwhelmed. Buck had to remind him to return their salute. Mack turned in his seat as much as he could and snapped off the best salute he had.

In unison, they took one step back and disappeared into the woods.

Mack took a deep breath and mumbled, "Damn, I'll miss those guys."

"You okay?" Buck asked.

"Yeah. Let's go see some palm trees."

Buck called off the checklist while Mack completed his run-up, flaps up, mixture rich, and pushed both throttles all the way forward. As the plane lifted and climbed above the tree tops, Mack banked to the left, scanning the road, barn, and then the house one last time.

"She failed to show, huh?" Buck said.

Mack didn't want to talk about Kate; he just shook his head and busied himself at the controls. He raised the wheels, throttled back a little on both engines, set his mixture, and turned west, for sunny, southern California.

After reaching his cruising altitude, Mack set the S-Tec autopilot. "I figured to stay just north of Dallas, gas up in Roswell, then over to Phoenix and straight west to Oceanside?"

"Sounds good to me," Buck said, dropping his utility cap over his eyes and sliding down in his seat. "Wake me when you see Roswell."

Buck and Mack were waiting outside the office of Colonel Jesse Butcher, Sr., Commander of 1st Force Reconnaissance Company. They had landed at the small Oceanside Municipal Airport and as soon as Mack cut the engines, he saw the car coming across the tarmac that would take them over to Camp Pendleton.

Buck was dressed in neatly pressed, camouflage utilities, and Mack had on jeans, a tee shirt, and an old flight jacket Buck had given him. The door flew open, and the Colonel stood blocking the light from the doorway. He was built like a tight end, tall and wide at the shoulders.

"Buck, you salty old devil-dog, how the hell are you?"

Buck jumped up at attention, startling Mack to his feet. The Colonel threw his arm around Buck's shoulder and pulled him into his office. "Come on in here, I ought to be saluting you; you're the one who saved *my* ass."

Mack was left standing outside as the door closed, and then he heard the Colonel shout, "Get in here, son." Mack tried to remember what all Buck had told him when reporting for duty. He entered the office, shut the door, put his back to the door, and took two steps forward, starting with his left foot, "Sir..."

"Knock it off and grab a chair; you're not in the Corps yet..." he looked over at Buck, "Is he?"

"Well, technically no, but he's got orders."

The Colonel stared at Buck, "What's with the eye patch? I thought you got a glass eye."

"I did, it was one of those new, experimental, floating gyro tube they called it—they sewed it to the muscles in the eye socket, and it was supposed to follow wherever your good eye goes. The one I had kept moving on me. I'd be talking to someone, looking them straight in the eye with my good eye, and this gyro eye would start looking around the room."

The Colonel burst out laughing, "I can't believe you..."

"It scared the hell out of some folks."

"Buck, you haven't changed a bit. You still a drinking man?"

"Only if the first round is on me?"

"Well, let's get the hell out of here; it's happy hour over at the Slop-Chute."

Mack was sure he held the sole distinction of being the only recruit in the Marine Corps ever to drink with a full bird Colonel in the Officer's Club. He sat quietly at the table, sipping his beer, listening. The old adage, "Alcohol is a laxative for the mouth," is true. Mack learned more about Buck that one night of drinking than he did in all the time they had been together. One surprise was when the Colonel asked Buck about Irish, and Mack learned that Buck and Irish were lovers, or ex-lovers. He wasn't sure which. Mack figured that while he was sneaking out of the big house to meet Kate in the barn, Buck was sneaking into the big house to meet Irish—a whole lot of stealth going on.

The Colonel was an avid hunter, especially deer and birds, and had stayed at Buck's "Delta Hunting and Fishing Lodge" three or four times a year. Mack had seen the multi-level A-framed lodge many times but had never been close and had no idea that Buck owned the lodge. It was secluded high on a bluff overlooking the Mississippi River on one side and the Yazoo River on the other. But that night he learned that it was more than just a lodge; it was also a front for the Marines' 2nd Force Reconnaissance Company. The 1st Force Reconnaissance Company had moved half of their company from the west coast to establish an east coast operation. The government leased all of Buck's 500 plus acres, the lodge, sections of the 189,000 acres of Homochitto National Forest, and over 5,000 acres of Irish's land that bordered the National Forest.

It all started when Buck retired and had this dream of a cabin in the woods. He bought the property, built a small cabin, got bored, and started a hunting and fishing guide service. It wasn't long before he had more business than he could handle. Then one night, after a successful day of hunting, Buck and his friends and some invited guests—most were Marines or former Marines—were sitting outside around a fire, drinking and talking about the day's hunt. The most distinguished guest was Colonel Butcher's old college roommate and native Mississippian, the Under Secretary of the Navy, John Cross.

Buck was unaware that the Colonel and Secretary Cross had been hunting more than wild game; they had been scouting locations up and down the east coast for a clandestine training site for the newly formed 2nd Force Recon.

Within a short time an agreement was brokered between the Marine Corps, Buck, and Irish for the leasing and improvements of their land. Immediately, the government started the installation of an eight-foot chain link fence around the entire leased property. Next was to extend and pave the landing strip to 4,000 feet. Every year after the lodge was built, there seemed to be some form of construction going on continuously. Pretty much everything stayed the same; Buck ran the airfield and the hunting lodge as a business, by invitation only. Any problems Irish had, he handled those as well. The government paid all the expenses and had right of first refusal (ROFR) on almost everything. It was not a one-way contract; it was an agreement based on the principle of concept of rights, which amounted to the simplest version of the Golden Rule, "Do unto others as you would have them do unto you."

The last thing Mack remembered before he passed out at the Officer's Club was a table full of Marines toasting shots of Scotch, chasing it with beer, telling "war stories," and pulling off their clothes showing who had the most bullet or shrapnel wounds. He woke up in the middle of the night, ran to the head, vomited, took a leak, staggered back, and fell into his bed. Buck woke him up at 1130 with a cup of black coffee and, while sitting on the bottom bunk bed across from Mack, told him how, over breakfast this morning, he and the Colonel worked on the options open for Mack and for the Corps. The Colonel liked the way Mack looked and carried himself, except when he passed out at the table last night. He was impressed with all the training he had completed. No, he would not have to go through Basic Training or Infantry School, but he didn't qualify for 1st Force Recon; that required a five-year commitment, and Irish was emphatic about three and out. He handed Mack his temporary orders and told him that on Monday morning, 0700, he was to report to the Colonel's office to get sworn in and get his permanent orders. The first thing was to go wash his face and brush his teeth. He smelled like a drunk, and then they were going to the supply office to get his uniforms and meal tickets and have lunch in the mess hall.

Mack stood looking in the mirror, in deep thought, while brushing his teeth. At first, he was very gung ho about the Corps. Getting paid to shoot almost every weapon known to man and blowing up things was pretty adventurous. But now, after six months, he realized that he had given up his independence and freedom. He had always been on his own, making his own decisions, working out his own problems. Now, the Marines told him what time to get up, what time to eat, what to do from hour to hour, and what time to go to bed. He had nothing to say about that, no input. He rinsed his mouth, washed his face, and ran his wet hands over his buzz cut. What Irish had told him was true, "The Corps is not your career; it's a stopgap, that's all. Stay focused on your life's future and don't get caught up playing Marine."

All that *sounded* good, but the Corps always has its own plans. He was in the Marines now and needed to understand that they owned him for the next three years. Well, two and half now and would send him wherever and whenever they needed him.

Buck had worked the best deal he could for Mack, but it looked as if he were headed for Iraq. Irish would never forgive him if something happened to Mack. Regardless, what did people think—you could not be a gunslinger without a gunfight! Mack needed combat experience.

Buck wanted to send him right away, but the Colonel had other priorities—one being an order on his desk stamped urgent from his commanding general. Attached to the order was a copy of a letter from Secretary of Defense to assemble an accelerated Direct Action (Black Ops) advanced course, ASAP, for a team of Israeli Special Forces that would leave from California for Iraq. The Colonel's next group of Force Recon Marines would be graduating and shipping out in five weeks. His problem was logistics, especially timing, so that they could all be on one plane, leaving at the same time. Another piece of the puzzle was his own son, Captain Jesse Butcher, Jr., who had completely recovered from his wounds and was biting at the bit to get back to his command headed for Iraq.

The Colonel sought Buck's experience as a Special Ops instructor and his leadership in six tours of combat duty. After many cups of coffee, the Colonel agreed with Buck's solution to let each Force Recon instructor create his own specialized fast-tracked course. The Colonel would throw them all in together: Mack, Captain Jess, and the Israelis. That way, Captain Jess could get a refresher course and at the same time, monitor Mack's performance and report whether he was good to go. If so, and Buck had no doubts, Captain Jess would have the first shot at the most trained recruit in the Marine Corps for his company.

They both laughed at their Machiavellian strategy.

CHAPTER 9

I T WAS SNOWING hard, and visibility faded fast as Mack lifted his ski tips and scooted off the swaying chairlift at the Aspen Highlands. He skated around the lift-terminal and down to the edge of Loge Peak.

"Hey, Mack?"

Mack pushed his goggles up on his head and saw the lift operator waving at him.

"We're shutting down...big storm coming. Cloud Nine's still open," he shouted.

Mack waved, nodding his head, and pointed that he was headed downhill. Cloud Nine was the next chairlift, 1,000 feet below, but that wasn't his plan. He leaned forward, knees together, and turned his skis downhill, opposite the side of Cloud Nine. Picking up speed down the catwalk, he spotted the patch of aspen trees above him, the only ones up this high, and turned back uphill, slowing, zigzagging through the trees, and coasted to a stop at the foot of the hiking trail. He punched the release on his bindings with one of his ski poles, kicked out of his skis, pulled his goggles down, and started hiking the narrow ridge 700 feet up to Highland Peak, his skis over his shoulder. The wind had picked up, and the snow was deep, up to his calves, and getting deeper. *No one had hiked up here today.* If he could reach the top for his last run of the day there would be some deep powder inside the bowl.

But about half way up, around 12,000 feet, he stopped and removed his goggles; it was a total whiteout. The horizon was gone, and the descending clouds floated over the terrain dropping cotton-ball-sized snowflakes.

It was a mercurial moment. Mack stood entranced in the middle of it all, listening to the total silences of the falling snow while watching the landscape change before his eyes. Not another soul...completely alone, a microdot on a mountaintop. This was the majestic Rocky Mountain high you get hooked on—life-changing for thousands of people who come here each year.

He looked behind him, downhill, and saw no tracks; it was time to go. He unzipped the inside pocket of his ski jacket and checked to make sure his avalanche beacon was working, then placed the string holding his compass around his neck and unfolded his trail map. He sighted a line the best he could, from where he was standing, to where he thought the foot of the hiking trail should be, and started slowly back down the trail. The clouds had surrounded him, visibility was zero, and he couldn't see his ski boots, which were now knee deep in the snow. He couldn't tell if he was walking up or down, left or right— he stopped walking. Maybe he could wait it out, and the clouds would blow over. He brushed the snow off his head and ski jacket, but the temperature had dropped, and a layer of ice crystals and snow stuck to him. There were no trees up here to hide under, and, if he didn't move now, it wouldn't be long before he would be a *frozen* snowman.

He knew his skis were the same height as he was, so he planted one out in front of him at arm's length—the tip of the ski even with his shoulders. Walking slowly with a ski in each hand, he planted one ski out in front of the other, feeling his way downhill. With each step, he dropped a few inches below the cloud line, and his visibility increased as did his desire to hurry, but he realized that one misstep could be fatal.

He knew he was safe when he saw the bottom half of the patch of Aspen trees on the side of the mountain. A panoramic whiteout line, as if an artist swiped white paint across the sky, slowly drifted down from the mountaintop. Mack banged his skis together, cleared the snow and ice from his bindings, stepped into his skis, and turned downhill for St. Moritz.

He could feel the tension draining as he unwound, and like an escaped bird from his cage, he soared across the deep bowl—side to side—carving long curves through the fresh powder, a rooster tail trailing behind him while humming an old song from the movie "Alfie." The song asked the question stewing in Mack's mind for days: *What's it all about?*

He stopped on the ridge of The Wall, a double black diamond run, and the beginning of his last run of today. Looking straight down, he planned his descent, mapping each run in his head so that he could make it down to the base area, a three-and-a-half-mile run, non-stop. He pushed off the ridge; knees bent as he gained speed instantly, flying in and out of the moguls, legs pumping up and down like pistons. Closer to the bottom, his turns got longer as he checked his speed. The Wall was a short run, but his thighs were wasted as he stood up and shifted his weight from one leg to the other, resting while cruising down to the next run. Big snowflakes were still falling, but the visibility was clear as Mack attacked the long and steep run, Moment of Truth.

Halfway down the run, while skiing underneath a jutting rock formation, Mack sensed something flying off the top of a large pillow of snow above his head. He squatted, and made a wide parallel turn to avoid crashing. When he looked up, he saw the familiar white cross on the back of the skier's red jacket, identifying him as a ski patrolman. He landed in front of Mack and waved for him to follow. It was Doc Kris, the one who had taught him how to ski deep powder, his trademark chartreuse scarf trailing behind him. Mack turned down the fall line racing to catch up, then fell into Kris's deep tracks, and synchronized his turns with Kris', leaving a beautiful chain of powder 8s behind them.

They first met on a chairlift, and when Mack found out that Kris had been a Marine Corpsman, they became fast skiing and hunting buddies. Kris was a Nurse Practitioner in the emergency room at the Aspen Valley Hospital and an honorary ski patrolman who schooled the other patrolmen in emergencies, from heart attacks and broken bones to frostbite.

Mack watched Kris turn into the trees and knew he was taking a short cut to ski the Powder Bowl, the last run. Crossing under two lifts, Mack raced Kris down P-Chute Road and decided to take a short cut himself. He turned on Audacious and shot straight down the double black diamond run, flying out the bottom almost out of control. Racing across the ridge, he saw Kris uphill bearing down in fast pursuit. Mack flew off the ridge, catching big air, and landed into the waist deep Powder Bowl.

It was quiet inside the bowl, empty of people and all sounds; he couldn't even hear his own skis, or hear Kris directly behind him. This was the goods: floating up and down on untracked, billowing clouds of fresh powder—pure fluff, one face shot after the other. As the bowl narrowed into a chute and dumped them out onto a steep glade, Kris pulled up beside Mack and they skied—side by side—to the bottom, both covered head to toe in fresh powder.

The base was crowded as they checked their speed and cruised into the swarm of skiers coming downhill from all angles; some out of control, some just standing in the middle of the run chit-chatting—a dangerous game, like standing in the middle of an expressway.

Kris waved to Mack as he headed back up Exhibition chairlift to meet the other patrolmen for their last sweep of the day.

Mack skated the last few feet over behind a dumpster next to the Ritz where he had parked his old VW pickup truck. He kicked his skis loose from the bindings, unsnapped his shell ski pants, unbuckled his boots, removed his coat, and threw everything onto the passenger seat. He pulled on his cowboy boots and a down vest and looked at himself in the side mirror. Snow and icicles caked his beard and hair.

He removed his gloves, rubbed the ice from his beard, combed his wet fingers through his long hair, and headed to the bar inside the Willows.

Mack scanned the packed bar looking for Erica, a girl he had met earlier on the lift and agreed to meet for a drink when the lifts closed. He noticed the bartender, Amy, holding up a drink of hot buttered rum, his favorite after-ski drink. He waved back holding up two fingers and worked his way to the end of the bar. After getting his drinks, he moved over to the windows, but it was snowing so hard he couldn't see, so he went up the steps to the fireplace where he could watch for Erica when she came through the door. He sat on one of the cushions on the hearth and slipped off his boots to warm his feet.

This was Mack's second winter at the Highlands working as a snowcat operator. He first applied for a job on the Ski Patrol, however, because he refused to cut his hair or shave his beard, he wasn't hired. But, because of his experience operating heavy equipment for Shamrock Construction and being a Marine veteran, the maintenance manager, a former Marine, offered him a job operating a snowcat—compacting and grooming the ski runs and trails. That was fine with him because the job included a free lift ticket so he could ski days and groom the slopes at night. He leaned back against the stone fireplace, sipping his hot rum, and thought about the many changes his life had taken since his time in the Marine Corps. He had dark memories from the black-op missions his platoon had been on; the *shock* and *awe* had always been kill or be killed. *Sure, killing in self-defense made it easier, but what the hell were we doing thousands of miles away killing in another country?* These memories had changed his life and his way of thinking. One day he was gung-ho and now, in retrospect, he had many questions about carrying out orders to kill someone. Especially orders from some boot lieutenant who didn't know any more than he did *why* they were doing the killing. But when you see a whole squad of your Marines blown into small pieces from a roadside IED—you don't ask why you're killing, you just kill.

But now, high up in the mountains, sitting by a burning fireplace inside the Willows' bar, he just shook his head as if to erase the thoughts, and looked up to see Erica standing inside the doorway waving at him. She had her skis and poles with her and shrugged her shoulders in a question like, "What should I do with these?"

Mack pointed to a place away from the door where they could keep an eye on her skies and lifted up the two hot rum drinks.

Erica smiled and climbed around the people sitting on the steps to the fireplace and took off her coat and hat. Still smiling, she fluffed up her short hair with both hands.

"The snow is so beautiful; a lot of deep powder for skiing tomorrow."

She was prettier than Mack remembered—fair, with natural blond hair and an athletic body. "Here, warm your hands with this," he said, handing her the hot rum drink.

She sipped the drink, holding it with both hands. "Oh, did I need that. Thank you."

Mack took a cushion, and placed it behind her, and said, "Lean back, and I'll take your boots off, and you can warm your feet." He kneeled down and unzipped her ski pants at the ankles, unbuckled and removed her boots, and rubbed each foot.

"Now this is something I could get used to. Do all the women you meet get this kind of treatment?"

Mack stopped rubbing her feet and stood up. After a pause he said, "No, they don't. I was probably a little too eager to please."

"No, *no*, don't stop, *please*. I'm sorry. Why do I always open my mouth at the wrong time? See, I lost my foot massage. Let's start all over, Mack—it is Mack, right? I *love* you being 'eager to please.' I promise I won't say a word, just nice moans and groans. Instead of a hair shirt, how about we start over with me rubbing your feet?"

What the heck is a hair shirt? "That won't be necessary. How about starting over with another drink?"

She gave out a moan and moved her thumb and finger across her lips, imitating zipping her mouth shut, and nodded her head.

Mack moved through the crowd and was back in short order with two drinks. "I noticed you have a little bit of an accent. Are you Dutch?"

"Farther north—I was born in the States but raised in Sweden. I live in Massachusetts now." She took a sip of the hot rum. "Thank you, these could become addictive. How about you, is that a Southern accent I detect?"

"It shooow is," Mack exaggerated. "Memphis, born and raised."

"Is this the Southern hospitality they talk about?" She held up her feet and wiggled her toes.

"Well, Miss Scarlet, we do like to please our women folk."

"I must confess—I definitely misjudged you."

"Why's that?"

"When I first saw you skiing over to the lift, I thought, 'This is a burly mountain man:' the big down ski jacket, all that hair and beard, and with the sunglasses. I couldn't tell if..."

"And now?" Mack asked.

"Well, when the lift operator called out for a single, and you skied right up and got in the chair with me, it was a little intimidating. You didn't say anything for quite a while. Then I saw all those kiddies from the Snow Puppy Ski School winding down the hill and, when they skied under the lift, I heard them shouting and waving at you. That's when I saw that big smile of yours and knew you weren't the big bad wolf."

"Those puppies are a lot of my friends' kids. I try to ski with them at least once a day and, of course, lots of snowball fights."

"Oh, look!" Erica called out. As people were leaving, the door was caught open and a blast of snow blew through the bar. "I rode the bus here; I better get home while I can." Erica pulled on her ski boots.

"Come on, let's get your skis, and I'll take you home in my truck."

Mack took her arm, led her down the steps, and picked up her skis and poles.

"Last call, last call," the bartenders shouted. The manager was opening and shutting the door for everyone. "Big snow storm coming, Mack, you guys be careful."

Erica rushed through the door. "Look at the size of those snowflakes." Over a foot of snow had fallen since Mack had been inside. "Do you think your truck can make it up there?"

"Is a bluebird blue?"

"What does this bluebird mean?"

"Never mind, it means nothing. It's just a saying, 'Is-a-bluebird-blue'?" She had her head cocked and had a puzzled look on her face. "Okay, look, just answer me. Is a bluebird blue?"

"Yes, a bluebird is blue." Erica laughed.

"Okay, good—now, if a bluebird is blue, then my truck can make it up to your house, understand?" Mack laughed.

"No, I don't understand." Erica giggled. "When I asked you the question, 'Can your truck make it up the mountain?' you could say, 'No, I don't think so,' or 'Yes, it can," or 'I don't know.' What has a bluebird got to do with anything? Is it the name of your truck?"

"No. The name of my truck is *Hair Shirt*." He roared with laughter so hard he didn't see the snowball coming. It hit him right in the ear. Erica took off running behind the truck shouting, "I'm sorry, I'm sorry, I didn't mean to hit you in the head." She stopped running and looked back but couldn't see him. She eased from around the back of the truck and saw Mack on his knees holding his head, moaning. She ran through the heavy snow falling to her knees beside him, "Mack, Mack...did I hurt you?"

Mack roared like a grizzly, grabbed her and rolled in the snow. Straddling her, he wrapped his arms around a huge snowdrift next to him and dropped it on her head. She bucked him off, howling. He tried to get up but slipped and fell with her jumping on his back. She took a handful of snow and tried to stuff it down the collar of his vest. A loud horn blowing caused them to roll over and sit up. Staring into the high-beamed headlights of the Highlands' bus, they heard the bartender, Amy, and some of the waiters hollering at them and throwing snowballs as they ran to get on the bus. Mack and Erica jumped up and threw snowballs at the bus, chasing it down the road, as it edged past them. On the way back, Erica jumped on Mack's back, and he carried her up the road.

Mack cranked up the Volkswagen pickup and turned on the heater while Erica cleaned the snow off the windshield and windows. He put the pickup in four-wheel drive and shifted down into first gear. Erica jumped in as the truck rocked out of its frozen tracks. The wind had died a little, but the snow still came down hard as ever. The old truck crawled up the road in second gear without any strain, pushing the deep snow to the side and compacting what was left. A few snow-covered cars left in the parking lot looked like sand dunes.

Mack loved Aspen and had worked hard in the past couple of years to simplify his life, keeping things uncomplicated, basic, and debt free. He had very few possessions, and if he didn't absolutely love it, he didn't own it. He often thought if he ever were to get something as permanent as a tattoo, it would be *his* acronym for "KISS." Keep It Simple Sweetheart.

When Erica asked about his truck, he bragged about how pragmatic the Germans were in their engineering and design: his truck had never failed to start, no matter how cold it was, the heater and defroster were like a sauna in minutes, it was rugged, yet lightweight, no maintenance required, and it burned very little gas. Another unique thing Mack loved about the design was the drop-sides of the bed that folded down like the tailgate on all sides, making a flatbed truck for ease of loading and unloading.

"Stop," Erica shouted. "I think we just passed my driveway, but I didn't see the mailbox."

Mack stopped the truck and put it in reverse but couldn't see his truck's tracks to back up. Erica got out and walked back to see if it was her driveway.

The snow was up to Erica's knees as she trudged back to the truck. "That's my drive, but the mailbox is gone, covered with snow, I guess. Do you want to leave the truck here and walk up?"

"No, they will have the snow-plows out before long. Here, take this light and walk back between the tracks while I back up." Mack rolled down the window, wiped off the side-view mirror, and shifted into reverse, slowly backing down the hill 'til he was past where he thought the driveway was. Erica got in, and he turned up the mountain, staying in the middle by judging the equal distance between the trees on each side. At the top was a circle drive, and Mack drove around so that the front of the truck was headed back down the driveway. He parked and got out in front of a log house—an older house—but certainly not a cabin. It was a split-level A-frame, with part of the house built into the side of the mountain. The rest was cantilevered, in a fan-design, hanging off the side of the mountain.

Mack thought, *Location, location, location—a lot of money here.*

Mack followed Erica inside the house, carrying her skis and poles. There were no lights on inside, but outside there was indirect lighting high up in the trees and rays of light coming from the corners of the roof. Mack stood in the living room, looking at the large timbers at the top of the A-frame. A glass wall, from ceiling to the floor and wall to wall, gave you the impression that you were outside.

Erica was over at the fireplace and already had some small kindling burning. She stood on the raised hearth and placed a large log in the firebox behind the kindling.

"Why don't you pour us a cognac while I get out of these boots and ski clothes? I have Remy Martin Napoleon or Grand Marnier—you pick the drink."

The long, L-shaped bar separated the kitchen from the living room. Mack found two snifters and filled each about one-third full, one with Napoleon and the other with Grand Marnier. He walked over to the glass wall and watched the snow falling. With the help of the outside lights, his eyes followed a ski trail winding down from the top, through the woods, right across the sun deck, and out the other side down to a cleared ski run. *Wow, ski in and ski out: with that little feature you could add another hundred grand to the value.*

"Isn't that a beautiful view? Is it still snowing?" Erica asked. She walked toward Mack in a white terrycloth robe and had another one hanging over her arm with some towels. She placed the towels on the end of the couch and handed Mack the other robe. "I'll trade you for the drinks. The hot tub is out on the deck. You bring the towels." She turned to open the sliding doors.

"I don't have a bathing suit," Mack said.

Erica looked back smiling, "They're not allowed in the hot tub."

Mack removed his clothes, folded them neatly, and placed them on the couch. Throwing the robe on, he grabbed the towels and headed to the hot tub. Outside he saw Erica in black rubber boots shoveling a path to the hot tub. He hurried, took the snow shovel, finished clearing a path, then raked the snow off the top of the hot tub and removed the insulated cover. Steam rose from the whirling water as Mack finished shoveling the snow from around the tub. Erica placed the drinks on the edge of the hot tub, removed her robe, and stood with both hands on her hips, turning in a slow circle, posing in her black rubber boots. Mack removed his robe and eased into the hot water. Erica sat on her robe and stuck her boots out. Mack pulled each boot off. He took her hand as she stepped over the edge onto one of the seats and eased into the tub. She handed Mack his drink, and they toasted each other.

"I love these redwood hot tubs. You can stand up in them, and the water is up to your neck," Mack said.

"Does this feel great or what?" Erica said as she reached over to the pocket of her robe and removed a small, frosted glass bong and a lighter. She packed the glass with snow, and the bowl with a nice size bud of marijuana, and fired the lighter, working the flame across the bowl as she inhaled and handed it to Mack. She held the flame while he took a long hit.

"Hmmm, hmmm, *good*," Mack said, as he floated on his back, exhaling the smoke.

"Hydroponic. In a basement, right down the road."

"Potent." Mack took another hit. "Look, you can see some stars and part of the moon." The snow clouds were moving across the sky and breaking up. "A bluebird day for skiing tomorrow."

"There you go with that bluebird again."

"No, this is a different saying...never mind." They both laughed.

Erica took Mack's feet and started rubbing them. "Oh, they are still cold; you should have put some boots on."

"Feels great to me. This is something I could get used to. Do all the men you meet get this kind of treatment?"

"Ahhh, you're a cruel man, Mack Shannon." She splashed water in his face.

Mack grabbed a handful of snow and darted across the tub, trying to rub it on Erica's head. They struggled—ack and forth—breathing hard, then surrendered to an embrace. Mack slowly eased her down under the water as they kissed—her legs locked around his waist.

Not wanting to wake Erica, Mack slipped out of bed and down the hallway to the living room. It was almost daylight, and he knew the Highlands had been calling him to work all night. While putting on his clothes and looking out through the glass wall, he saw the lights of a snowcat moving up the mountain under the Exhibition chairlift. He did a quick triangulation of Erica's house in case he decided to ski in for his next visit. He stopped at a table next to the door and picked up an opened envelope to write a message. When he turned it over, he saw it was a Mountain Bell telephone bill with the name of Erica Vasa. Vasa, he thought, sounded more Spanish than Swedish; then he remembered a trail off Exhibition named Vasa Lane. He tore a piece of paper from the envelope, wrote her phone number on it, and then wrote on the back of the bill, "What a night it was, it really was...*a bluebird night!*"

Outside, as the sun was peeping over the mountain ridge without a cloud in the sky, the streetlights down in Highlands Village still burned.

CHAPTER 10

I T WAS EARLY morning, before the lifts were opened, and Mack steered the big snowcat straight up the mountain to Vasa Lane. He packed and groomed the left side first, then worked the cat over to the right, searching for the unmarked trail down to Erica's house. He parked at an opening in some trees, jumped down, and trudged through the deep snow until he saw the roof of Erica's house. He hustled back to the snowcat and drove along the edge of the tree line about thirty feet and stopped again. He took a red rag he used for checking fluids and tore it in half, climbed on top of the snowcat, and tied the rag around a limb high in a tree. Back in the snowcat he headed over to groom Exhibition and thought about last night and how he had failed to follow an old maxim he had committed to memory: *I have often regretted what I said but never my silence.*

They had stayed up most of the night talking, huddled on the couch in front of the fireplace. She had asked him where he had been before Aspen, and he told her a little about the Marine Corps and his time in college.

"Where did you go to college?" she asked.

"Up in Boston."

"In *Boston?* What school?"

"Why?"

"I went to school in Boston, well, in Cambridge, at Harvard. Did you go to Boston U?"

"No, I went to Harvard."

See...see that look. They all think, A Marine, at Harvard, and not even an officer, and driving a snowplow—how did he even get into Harvard?

She wanted to know why he quit school. He told her that after the

Marine Corps, he couldn't focus because there were too many things going on in his mind. He didn't want to be negative, but she insisted on knowing what he thought about Harvard. He squeezed his nose for his best New England accent, held up his snifter, and made a "toast" he had heard many times:

And this is good old Boston,
The home of the bean and the cod,
Where the Lowells talk only to the Cabots, And the Cabots talk only to God.
She laughed, "It couldn't have been that bad."

He was candid and told her it was the worst experience of his life. Being from the South, and never having been in the North, he felt like he was in a foreign country, a culture shock. Most students were immature spoiled brats who had this innate elitism—this preconceived entitlement as if they were members of some British royalty still in power. And a lot of the professors did, too. He had never experienced such prejudice toward the South and the Marines Corps. He was called a racist and a murderer to his face and, when he retaliated, it was *always* his fault.

He had promised his Aunt Irish, who paid for his tuition, and his tutor, Dr. Leigh Kennedy, who had pulled a lot of strings to get him accepted into Harvard, that he would stay a full year to give it a good chance. But when his uncle Mickey died of a heart attack and he went home for his funeral, he knew then that he was never going back. He'd be damned if he was going to waste another day sitting on his ass in a stuffy classroom listening to some dogmatic, atheist egghead. After the funeral, he traded his old car in for the pickup truck and headed west, telling no one.

Erica listened while Mack talked way too much. Toking on the pipe and sipping cognac is a combination guaranteed to provoke at least a couple of humiliating, foot-in-mouth faux pas. After he had finished dismembering the oldest university in the USA, with the largest endowment and the highest ranking in the world, he asked her about her house.

She told him a long history about Aspen skiing. How two Swedish silver miners, back in 1879, pulled people up the mountain on horses and taught them how to ski back down on wood planks. One of those Swedes was her gypsy great-grandfather, Gustav Vasa, who bought the mining rights and built a small shack where the house sits now.

When Gustav died, he left the shack and mining rights to his son in Sweden, Erica's grandfather, Karl Vasa, who had skied for Sweden in the 1936 Winter Olympic Games. While in Berlin, Karl, a teacher at Stockholm University, heard one of Adolph Hitler's many speeches on Germany acquiring new living space (Austria, Czechoslovakia, Poland, Hungry, etc.) for his Aryan master race. A few years later, when he learned that the Nazi Party had taken over and closed all the universities in Germany, he realized there was going to be a war and it was time to leave Europe. He contacted an Olympian friend of his in the United States, a professor at Harvard, who wrote him back that Harvard was seeking a more diverse and/or international faculty. He sent his application, and unlike many, his timing was exact.

Karl had been reading a lot about the opening of Aspen Mountain for skiing and, when it opened in the winter of 1946, he was there not only to ski but also to rebuild the little cabin built by his father, Gus. While skiing Aspen Mountain, he met Whip Jones, a Harvard graduate, and they became inseparable skiing buddies.

"Is this the original cabin of your great grandfather?" Mack asked.

"Oh no. Mr. Whipple owned the land at the base of this mountain and when he developed Aspen Highlands, in 1956, they tore down the original, and built this house."

"You mean *the* Whip Jones, the owner of the Highlands, is your father's best bud?"

"No, not my father, my grandfather. I have a lifetime lift pass."

"No you don't." Mack said.

Erica walked over and removed a laminated card from her backpack and handed it to Mack. "All the Vasa's have them. Guess what else Mr. Whipple did...he gave Aspen Highlands to Harvard."

"What?"

"The largest gift in the history of Harvard, 18.3 million."

Of course, when Mack ran his mouth off about Harvard, he had no way of knowing the Vasas were members of the "Kremlin on the Charles," a name he had heard describing Harvard, and that the Vasas had also donated a lot of money to Harvard. After hearing the history of Mr. Whipple Jones and the Vasa's Harvard connections, he thought seriously about swearing to a year of silence.

Mack parked the snowcat at the end of the catwalk and left the yellow lights flashing. *Erica should be up by now.* It was noontime and there was a long line at the Merry-go-Round restaurant. Every chair on Exhibition chairlift was full and dumping skiers out like a conveyer belt. It was a beautiful sunny day. Although it was 25 degrees, there was no wind, and many sat outside on the sun deck, some without shirts. Mack entered the restaurant from the back door of the kitchen, and one of the short order cooks shouted, "Mack, you want a burger?" Mack shook his head and pointed to the wall phone. He dialed Erica's number and was about to hang up when she answered in a muffled voice, "Hello."

"Good morning, Sleeping Beauty."

"Ohhh, Mack. Why did you leave?"

"Some of us have to work. Did I wake you?"

"No, no, I was just getting up."

"Liar, liar, pants on fire."

"Okay, you caught me. I slept like a baby; thank you. I had a *wonderful* time last night."

"You are a babe. Want to do it again tonight?"

"I'd love to."

"I've got to get back to work, but I'll pick you up at seven. Dress warm. We'll be outside, and Erica?"

"Yes?"

"Your pants *were* on fire last night."

If you wanted to live in Aspen during the ski season, the hardest thing was *not* finding a job but finding an affordable place to live. Mack was lucky; he found a job in less than a week, but it took a little over three weeks to find his apartment. According to his friends, that was in record time.

He had been reading the "Want Ads" and watching the bulletin boards without much success and decided he would try a different tactic. He had been staying in a small room downtown at the old Jerome Hotel for five bucks a night. The place was pretty rundown, but the J-bar was a local watering hole and information center. His plan was to use Napoleon Hill's philosophy of the three P's: Positive thinking, Perseverance, and Patience. He would knock on every door downtown and ask if they knew of a place for rent that was reasonable. This was his third day, and it was right after a two-day snowstorm with the snow plowed into knee walls against the curbs on Main Street. Mack pulled into a parking space in front of a building at the corner of Galena and Main. A wooden sign was hanging over the sidewalk above the door with the sandblasted name, "White River Forest Realty." Underneath the name, painted in small red, white, and blue were the words, "A Blue Chip Investment You Can Live In." At the bottom of the sign was the name "Bella Luca, Proprietor."

"Hey, Buffalo Bill, you can't park there unless you got business in here, and you don't look like you have business here."

Standing outside the door of the real estate company, smoking a cigarette, was a large, middle-aged redheaded woman, dressed in a full-length mink coat. She was taller than Mack and probably weighed more.

Mack was halfway out of his truck and stopped, reached back inside a grocery sack, and removed a large navel orange. He got out and walked over to the woman, tossing the orange and catching it with one hand.

"You can't judge a book by its cover."

"Oh, yes I can. I've done it many times, and I'm batting a thousand." She leaned against the door-jam with her legs crossed and tapped the long cigarette holder on the doorframe, knocking off the ashes.

"Are you the owner?"

"Who wants to know?"

"Mack Shannon. I work out at the Highlands."

"And so?"

Mack handed the lady the fat orange. "Good morning, Mrs. Luca, this is for you. I'm looking for a reasonable place to rent and thought..."

"You and about a thousand other people. What's this?" She turned the orange in her hand. Mack had written his name, the Highlands' phone number, and drew a "smiley face" on the orange with a black felt pen.

"Ingenious. Look, *Mack*, it's Ms. not Mrs., and I don't do rentals. I sell high-end real estate and—"

The office door opened, and Mack heard a lady say, "Bella, your conference call to New York. They are all on the line waiting." Bella took a long draw on her cigarette holder, removed the cigarette, and dropped it in the snow. She stared at Mack a few seconds, scoped his ink-black long hair and beard, then turned and walked into the office and shut the door.

Remember, no negative thinking. Mack walked back over to his truck, stuck some oranges in his backpack, and started to walk down the sidewalk, when a lady stuck her head out the office door, "Is your name Mack?"

She motioned for him to come inside and pointed for him to wait outside Ms. Luca's office at the end of the hall. Bella was waiting for him in the doorway with her hand covering the mouth of the phone.

"Can you do carpenter work?" she whispered.

Mack nodded his head and reached inside of his backpack, removed a handful of index cards he had printed and posted all over town, and gave her one.

"RENT-A-MAN"

*Snow Removal * Home Repairs * Mechanic*

*Chauffeur * Bodyguard * Escort*

Leave message: Mack Shannon 925.2555

Bella shook her head, smiling, and motioned for Mack to wait outside. She shut her door and said over the phone, "Ladies, I have just found the man for you. Don't worry about a thing."

Bella, dressed in jeans and cowboy boots, grabbed her fur coat and dashed out of her office door, "Come on Mack, I didn't finish my cigarette. You're one lucky son-of-a-bitch."

Mack knew it had nothing to do with luck. All his life, he had heard the saying, "luck-of- the-Irish," but he had learned in most cases it was just like Napoleon Hill said: *perseverance.*

Bella explained while driving up the winding road that four professional women from New York had formed a limited partnership and purchased an old eight-unit apartment building over a year ago. Bella had completely remodeled the building into four condominiums: two on the second floor and two at ground level with a full basement, partly below grade. The basement had not been remodeled and was used as a laundry room with a commercial washer and dryer and a mechanical room with a huge industrial boiler furnace. The rest of the basement was partitioned off into eight storage rooms stuffed with leftovers from the renovation: kitchen cabinets, stoves, refrigerators, claw foot bathtubs, toilets, sinks, doors and windows, furniture, and clothes—a little bit of everything—even an old snowmobile.

Driving back from looking at the condos, Bella told Mack the deal she had worked out for him. He was to clean out the basement, haul everything off to the dump, and turn the basement into an apartment. The owners would pay for all the materials and he would furnish the labor. In exchange for continued free rent of the basement, Mack was to make sure he took care of the security and maintenance of the building, and the basic needs of the four absentee owners when they came into town, she half-teasingly added.

"What exactly does basic needs cover?" Mack asked.

"You are naïve, aren't you? Just a puppy, a Tennessee hillbilly." Mack didn't say anything.

"Your card does say escort service and bodyguard, right?"

"Yes."

"A little false advertisement, huh?"

"There's nothing on that card that's not true."

"*Really?*" Bella reached over, turned the volume up on the radio, and started tapping her fingers on the steering wheel to some old song about *"tiptoeing through the tulips."*

Naïve? Yeah, just keep thinking that—let these judgmental know-it-alls spend a year tiptoeing through mines and booby traps. You can damn well bet they won't be shrilling about any tulips.

Bella cut the radio off. "Do you dance?"

"A little."

"You have to know how to dance if you're going to be an escort. What dances do you know?"

"The slow dances, the Cha Cha, Swing, a little of the Hustle."

"I love to tango, Argentine Tango. We have practice sessions at my house; I'll have to teach you. I told the girls you could dance, and they will want *you* to teach them."

"When I wrote escort on the card, I meant, like, if some lady needed a date."

"Let me ask you something. If a woman gave you a card that said Rent-A-Woman and Escort Service you would expect to get laid, right? I made the best deal for you I could; if you don't like it, don't take it."

He apologized, expressed his thankfulness for what she had done, and swore an allegiance to pay her back anytime she needed his help. He knew this was one sweet deal, and he had almost blown it. He would be grateful; whatever it took.

What Mack failed to realize was that Bella—first and foremost— was a businesswoman, and *never* did anything for nothing. His first clue should have been, after expressing his gratitude more than once, Bella said, "In Italy, my father had a saying, *Il mio giorno verrà qualche notte.*"

"What does that mean?"

"*My day will come one night.*"

It's not like he didn't hear what she said. He heard her loud and clear. He just didn't know what it meant and was afraid to ask.

It was happy hour at the J-Bar, and the Jerome Hotel was packed two rows deep, as Mack celebrated his good fortune of finding such a great place to live. He bought the first round of beers for a group from the Highlands and then ran up the steps, two at a time, to eat dinner with his neighbors in the room next to his.

Two days before, in the parking lot of the Jerome, a young, babyfaced hippie, tall and skinny, with straight white hair down to his waist, invited Mack to dinner.

"My wife and me noticed your Mississippi license plate and thought you might appreciate a good Southern meal. She's cooking fried chicken, mashed potatoes and gravy, homemade biscuits, and fried turnip greens. She's a good cook." He stuck out his hand, "I'm Cotton from Dallas, Texas."

Mack was surprised when Cotton's wife answered his knock on their door. They were complete opposites in looks; where he was very fair, she was dark brown, short, with long black hair—a total contrast. Cotton called her Tex. She was sixteen, and he was seventeen. Mack had never seen two happier lovebirds. Although, come to find out, Cotton's father, a wildcatter that hit it big in the oilfields of Texas, didn't agree. He had disowned Cotton for marrying a Mexican.

The supper was the best food he had eaten in years, and it was a mystery to Mack how this little girl prepared all this food on a two-burner stove, a cast iron Dutch oven, and an ice chest they kept out on the fire escape. Their room was the same size as Mack's, but Cotton had installed a piece of plywood onto the wall that, when raised, made a table, countertop, ironing board, whatever. Cotton and Mack sat on two worn cane-back chairs, and Tex sat in a lawn chair.

"What time is it, Tex?" Cotton said.

"4:20?"

Cotton nodded his head. Waited, staring at Mack. Mack didn't have a watch, but it was dark outside and he knew it was later than 4:20.

Cotton continued to stare at Mack, then asked, "You ever get high?"

"Sure."

Tex handed Cotton a cigar box. "You ever smoke any Thai sticks?" Cotton said.

"No, but I've heard a lot about them." Mack had heard that the THC level in Thai sticks was much higher than regular weed, very trippy. He had to be careful; he had a hypersensitivity to most drugs, legal or non-legal. *Go slow, Mack.*

Cotton opened a cigar box and, neatly stuffed, side-by-side, were over three dozen Thai sticks. He removed one from the box and unraveled some of the hemp thread that tied the marijuana to a sliver of bamboo, then pulled a couple of buds off the stick and handed it to Tex. She rolled a perfect joint the size of her little finger, and after firing it up, she passed it to Cotton.

Around the table it went and, on the second round, Mack took a bigger hit and held the smoke down in his lungs longer. Nothing happened. *All the hype I've heard about Thai sticks...and nothing.*

Mack no sooner had that thought when it felt like someone stuck his tailbone with a cattle prod. He shivered and fought to stay in a safe zone, shaking his head as if that might help, but it was too late; he was off and running. The insulation was off the wiring and the transformer, his brain, was firing arcs and sparks. Then it stopped, as quickly as it started. Cotton's face came back into focus, his eyeballs blood shot, his stare locked in on Mack. But the telltale sign was the diabolical grin on Cotton's face, and Mack knew then, that this trip was not over. In fact, it was just pulling out of the station.

The brain is a remarkable organ, with its billions of neurons encased in a shell of thick bones, so protective that even the bloodstream is isolated by a barrier. Yet two little puffs of smoke can take over this organ and send you to places unknown.

He wished he had someone to hold on to and talk him down; like an astronaut in space, he was terrified of being untethered,

"Remember your Creator before the silver cord is cut." *Wow!* What did that mean? He remembered they were Solomon's words.

It was instant, a loud gunshot like a starter pistol, a forewarning of another transition. He fell, whirling down a funnel of flashing colors and abstract images.

The unknown, that was the scary part; *where* was he going, and *how* was he getting there?

He saw Cotton and Tex staring at him as if his hair were on fire. His body shuddered as he watched a miniature mountain climber, slamming his ice axe into his T12 vertebra and jamming the toe points of his crampon in his lumbar. Up his back he climbed, all 24 vertebrae, from the lumbar to the cervical, until the ice axe dug into the delicate atlas, right below his skull, then all things ceased to exist.

Once upon a time, I, Chuang Chou, dreamt I was a butterfly, fluttering hither and thither, to all intents and purposes a butterfly. I was conscious only of my happiness as a butterfly, unaware that I was Chou. Soon I awaked, and there I was, veritably myself again. Now I do not know whether I was then a man dreaming I was a butterfly, or whether I am now a butterfly, dreaming I am a man.

Mack was flat on his back watching Tex jumping up and down, screaming, "Cotton! Cotton! DO something. He's bleeding!"

Cotton, laid-back in his chair, feeling no pain, jabbed Mack with the toe of his shoe,

"You cool, man?"

When Mack passed out and hit the floor, he bit his tongue, and that's where the blood was coming from. Other than that, he felt great. "Wow!" he said, with a dubious smile on his face.

The Roaring Fork River, if you want to call 15-feet-wide and two-feet-deep a river, snaked its way within ten feet of Mack's apartment door. This was a big plus to Mack, hearing the sound of flowing water and watching rare river otters chase the small rainbow trout along the rocky bottom.

Priority One for Mack was to make the basement livable so he could move out of the Jerome and stop paying rent. He first removed everything from the basement out into the yard, separating what to keep, what to sell or trade, and what to throw away. He tore out the storage room and gutted the building, leaving the large ceiling beams and columns exposed, and reused the lumber to build a long workbench and small storage bins for all the tools and equipment. He got the name of the mechanical contractor in Glenwood Springs off a metal tag riveted to the boiler furnace and negotiated a trade for a new heat pump for the parts from the old furnace. He traded six of the eight claw-foot bathtubs for two large glass windows. He installed the picture windows in the opening of the two overhead doors he removed. After cutting some trees, he had a beautiful view of the skiers coming down Ajax Mountain. In less than a month Mack moved into the basement with heat, a bathroom, a bedroom, and a kitchen. It was nowhere near finished, but during the summer he bartered and worked long hours building an intimate sanctuary, inside and out.

The four female owners praised Bella's management skills and thanked her over and over for Mack. He was a perfect gentleman, and there was nothing he couldn't do or fix. The owners were expected to contact Bella when there were maintenance problems, but now that Mack had a phone, they just called him direct, from New York or wherever, even to pick them up from the airport. They brought him gifts from around the world and always invited him to their house parties.

One night, when he was leaving the Highlands, his supervisor gave him a note that said Bella had an emergency and needed him at her home right away. He had never been to Bella's house but had heard about her estate on the mountaintop and how lavishly it was furnished. He tried to call her home and office, but no answer. He jumped into his truck and headed up to her house in Starwood. Driving up the unlit mountain road, Mack realized why it was named Starwood. At 8,400 feet high the stars were so close, you could almost reach out and touch them.

He drove through the opened double gates and up the winding drive lined with Aspen trees on both sides. He passed the barn and the outdoor riding arena and parked his truck around the back in front of the four-car garage. The stone house was huge and surrounded by a swimming pool, a tennis court, and a caretaker's house that was about 100-yards away with a sentinel view of the property. He walked around to the front door and rang the bell. After a few minutes, he tried again and waited, sticking his ear against the door to hear if someone was coming. He looked around the porch, then up at the hanging light and saw the small security camera lens and decided he had better leave. He walked back to his truck thinking what if something had happened; maybe she had fallen or was sick? He leaned back against the hood of his truck and zipped up his down vest tight around his neck and listened. A freezing wind blew down the snow-covered valley rustling the leaves. There were no lights on in the caretaker's house. He pulled the note from his pocket and read it again. Maybe she had to leave or was at the office when she called? Regardless, he was not going to leave until he walked around the perimeter of the house and, if the police came, he would show them the note. He started at the patio gate and, while crossing the patio, he thought he saw something move inside, behind the French doors. He moved closer and leaned against the glass door, both hands cupped around his eyes. An explosive sound against the glass door caused Mack to stumble backward and fall onto the snow-covered patio. He sat up and stared at the huge head of a black and white Great Dane who continued to bark. Mack stood up, embarrassed, and brushed the snow off the seat of his pants. Then he heard the voice of Bella over the door speaker, "Mack, is that you on the patio? Come in the front door; it's open. Duce won't bother you; he's locked in the den, just come straight back down the hall."

Mack opened the front door and stuck his head in, looking for the dog. He walked down the dark hallway to the end and stopped. To the right was a dining room with a long table lined with high-back chairs. He turned left and walked down another hallway to a door partially opened and emitting a red glowing light and a familiar smell, the sweet aroma of marijuana. He eased the door open with his foot and stepped inside a banquet-size bedroom.

Mack stood mummified in the dimly lit bedroom, looking up at Belle, all six feet of her, towering over him as she stood in the middle of a round, king-size waterbed, a joint burning in a cigarette holder in the corner of her mouth. She was dressed in a black, studded leather teddy with a riveted leather choker, armbands, and thigh high spider web stockings. The pink recessed lights highlighted her long bushy red hair, her wide shoulders, her massive breasts, and her long muscular legs. She stared down at Mack, her legs apart with the same flaming-red bush of hair bulging out the sides of her teddy. She had an ancient gold sword in one hand and a black riding crop in the other. Mack didn't know if she was an Amazon warrior or dominatrix sex-goddess, or whether to run, fight, or call for an emergency himself.

One thing for sure, he no longer wondered how he was going to express his gratitude for all the favors Bella had done for him. Like a light switch turned on in his memory bank, he *now* understood the words of Bella's father: *My day will come some night.*

CHAPTER 11

MACK BACKED OFF the throttle of his snowmobile and coasted downhill under the Exhibition chairlift. He didn't need his headlights; he had picked this specific night, the first night of the Super Moon, to take Erica across the mountaintops. He spotted Vasa Lane on the right, headed for the tree line, and stopped when he saw the red rag hanging from the tree limb. He continued to the opening and turned into the woods, cutting the engine and headlights, and coasted down the narrow run onto the roof's sundeck to surprise her. All he had told Erica was to "Dress warm. We'll be outside."

He sneaked through the deep snow and looked into the windows but didn't see her. He tried the door, but it was locked. So he put his hands up to the crack in the door and did his famous "wolf call" a couple times to scare her, but he got no response.

"Are you the Big Bad Wolf?"

Mack jerked around; surprised she had sneaked up on him. She had a red blanket wrapped around her, was wearing her rubber boots, and had a long-barreled shotgun pointed at him.

"Are you Little Red Riding Hood?" he asked.

"Have you come to eat me?"

"You betcha."

She placed the shotgun against the wall and dropped the red blanket onto the snow, offering her nude body. "Time's a-wasting, Mr. Wolf."

After an hour of traversing ridges and valleys on the snowmobile, Mack thought he had made a wrong turn at the last trailhead and was lost. It was isolated and hard to find, especially since he had never been up here at night, but that was part of the attraction. He had stopped on a ridge top of a long valley, climbed off his machine, and helped Erica off the backseat.

"Is this it?" she asked.

Mack removed a folded paper from his inside coat pocket. The Super Moon was so bright he could read his notes as if it were daylight, with its yellow and orange hues hanging over the entire mesa, so close and overpowering. Tonight it was closer to the earth than any other time of the year and blotted out the stars.

He took a reading with his compass and checked his notes again. He had been on top of the mesa once before in daylight but had never been to where he was taking Erica now. He scanned the mountain range while using his scarf to wipe the ice crystals from his goggles.

"Nope," he pointed west. "You see that dark patch of woods in the middle of that mesa over there? That's our destination: Tabletop."

"How come it's so flat?"

"Hello—because it's a *mesa?*"

She hit him on the arm with her fist. "I know that. I mean, how did it *get* flat?"

"Weathering. Thousands of years of erosion by water, wind, and ice, leaving nothing but bedrock, hence the name, Tabletop."

"Now that wasn't too hard, was it?"

"Saddle up cowgirl, let's ride." Mack was tempted to shortcut across some of the valleys and ridges, but he knew to stay on the trails he could see and recognize. Otherwise he would be flirting with triggering an avalanche with speeds too fast to outrun. Before he fitted his goggles, he studied the terrain and the angle of the slopes ahead.

He knew to traverse the concave, not the convex, and needed to stay away from sunny exposures since thawing and refreezing during the day and night was a hidden invitation for an avalanche. Staying on the windward side of the trees was always a good bet. Mack checked both their beacons to make sure they were turned to send, and they both had their avalanche cords. But what he reminded himself of was what was written in bold print in the Ski Patrol's shack:

"A slope that is flat enough to hold snow but steep enough to ski has the potential to generate an avalanche regardless of the angle."

This was not rocket science, but mostly common sense, a lot like avoiding hidden mines and booby traps while on recon patrol—both potentially deadly, but navigational.

A half-hour later Mack reached the top of the mesa, got his bearing, and headed for the thick forest at the end, weaving between knee-high rocks and snow mounds. He stopped the snowmobile just inside the tree line, under hanging limbs.

Erica had both arms wrapped around Mack, and her cold face was buried into the back of his down ski jacket.

"Okay, sleepyhead, we're here."

Erica dismounted and sunk into snow up to her knees. "That's not fair, you're wearing gaiters." She fell back onto the snow and looked at the stars and the Super Moon. It was so close now that its edges spread to each side of the mountain. "How beautiful is this? Look, there's a shooting star...right across the face of the moon."

"That's a good omen; we might need it going down that ledge." Mack removed his backpack from the cargo carrier mounted on the rear, then a long, coiled mountain-climbing rope and two pairs of aluminum snowshoes. He handed Erica a pair, "You know how to snap those on?"

She stood up with both gloved hands on her hips. "Mister *Shannon*, how much snow do you have in Memphis? *My* baby shoes were snow shoes."

"Okay, okay...Ms. Sweden; don't blow the hatch open on your long johns, just trying to help." He tossed her a pair of snow gaiters. "We have about a mile hike to the other side of those trees, then a steep trek down the side of the mountain on an elk trail, about 50 feet below the mesa."

"Where are you taking me?"

"If I told you, it wouldn't be a surprise." He stuck his arm through one of the straps, and swung the pack over his shoulder, and snap hooked the coiled rope onto his backpack. "Tally-ho."

Erica followed Mack along the perimeter of the thick stand of Colorado blue spruce and Douglas fir with their limbs extended and laden with fresh snow. She thought of Sweden and the times walking home from school with her classmates and started singing, "Winter Wonderland."

And it *was* a wonderland; the moon rays highlighted the long reddish-brown cones hanging like Christmas ornaments from each blue spruce. They walked in the stillness, absorbing the beauty, yet feeling like trespassers, afraid they would awaken God's ire for disturbing such splendor.

Mack stopped close to the edge of the mesa where an old elk trail meandered down the side of the mountain. He dropped his backpack, removed his climbing rope, and turned back into the woods, stopping at the first large tree. He tied one end around the tree, and added a safety knot. He backtracked, feeding out the rope with each step while Erica sat on his pack with a puzzled look on her face.

"A lot of snow has fallen, and there are some narrow spots on this trail; we need to be tied off just in case."

"In case of what?" she asked.

"Weathering or erosion," Mack smiled, "you know, seeing this is a mesa and all. A snowstorm could blow up or a cave-in; it's always nice to have a lifeline to get you out of trouble. Reach in my pack and give me those two red harnesses. We can get tied off and head down the trail."

Mack busied himself tying two butterfly knots to snap into the D-rings on the harnesses. She tossed the two webbed harnesses to Mack. "What all do you have in this pack? Hmm, something in here smells good."

"Stay out of there. That's for later."

Mack led the way down the trail, feeding the rope out with each step. The snow was fresh and clean, no animal tracks, tree limbs, or rocks had fallen. The short snowshoes were perfect for the deep snow.

"Step into my footsteps...unless I fall through, of course."

"You're so funny."

Mack stepped down and around the side of the mountain.

"Where's that smoke coming from?" Erica asked.

"What smoke? Oh, that. It must be from the lost tribe we're looking for."

"What lost tribe?"

"The tribe that invited us to dinner tonight. They're descendants of the Ice Age."

"The last Ice Age was two and a half million years ago."

"That's why they're called a lost tribe."

"You are so full of Irish malarkey."

Mack noticed the snow was melting off the trail and patches of ice were forming. He tightened the slack in the rope and stomped hard with each step, "Careful, watch your step; ice down here."

Mack came to the end of the trail where the side of the mountain broke into a staircase pattern of benches that led down to the mouth of a shallow cave. Above the opening was a large ledge, cantilevered out, with a row of giant icicles hanging, one over the other from the top. With each step down, Mack disappeared into the sea of fog.

"Mack! Where–are–you? I can't see you. You're scaring me."

Mack had passed through a layer of fog and stood on a cap rock shelf that extended out from the cave. He stepped inside the cave and found what he was looking for: a deep cratered pool of hot spring water with light, wispy vapors rising to the ceiling and escaping out the mouth of the cave.

"You're okay. Don't panic," Mack shouted up to Erica.

"I'm not panicking! I'm hanging off the side of a mountain, in the dark, freezing my ass off, and covered in smoke or whatever this is.

Where are you?"

"Just stay where you are, and I'll come get you. I'm taking off my snowshoes." Mack removed his backpack, snowshoes, and placed his flashlight on a ledge above the hot springs. He took the slack out of the rope until he was at the foot of the first step and started up.

"I'm just below you. It's clear down here, no *smoke*." Mack suppressed a chuckle. "There are some stairs, about four steps, and you will be on level ground." He felt her leg. "Here, take my hand." He guided her down to the floor of the shelf and removed the rope from her harness. "Sit on the step and I'll take your snowshoes off."

"This is beautiful. Look at those icicles! It's so warm. Is this a hot spring?"

Mack pointed to the pool of water in the cave.

She jumped up, kicking out of her harness, and walked into the cave, and bent over to feel the water with her hand. She stood up and took off her clothes. "Can we get in?"

"I've rented it for the night." Mack dug through his pack, finding the candles. After lighting them, he set them high up on a ledge above the pool. Erica sat on the side with her feet dangling in while Mack undressed.

"This is hot. Is it deep? I can't see the bottom."

"I don't know." Mack dug in his pack again.

"You've never been here before?"

Mack shook his head, "Nope, never. I've been on Tabletop before and used the hot pools above us, but this is my first time down here." He picked up the backpack, carried it over to the pool, and untied the two rolled Mylar space blankets from his pack. He spread out one of them and placed his and Erica's down coats and other clothes on top of the blanket, then spread the second blanket over the clothes. He removed his leather bota bag of wine, a small brick of Gorgonzola cheese wrapped in cheesecloth, and a round loaf of sweet rye bread with two ripe pears. He took his old Ka-Bar knife from his leg holster and placed it on top of the bread.

"The grandfather of one of the mechanics at the Highlands was a silver miner. He saw the cave across from a ridge top he was prospecting and drew a crude map of the location. I made a copy of the map and found Tabletop but couldn't find the trail to the cave. There was no trail on the map, but there had to be a trail down to the cave. I looked all day and started to leave when I thought about the old timer. If he saw the mouth of the cave from a ridge across from Tabletop, then the only ridge at that elevation would have to be on the top of Elk Mountain, and it was directly across from the southeast side of Tabletop."

"Is that when you found the trail?"

"Yeah, I found the trailhead, but it was getting dark, I was by myself and didn't have my climbing rope. That was six months ago, in the summer. I wouldn't have tried going down tonight if the moon hadn't been so bright."

"I'm glad you did." Erica stuck the cheese under her nose and removed the cheesecloth. "Hmmm, that's what I've been smelling. Look at the blue veins in that cheese. I'm so hungry I could eat the cheesecloth."

Mack handed Erica the knife and eased into the hot spring pool.

"Ohhh man, does this feel good."

"It's like a private suite in the Alps. I love it. Look at that view." Erica broke off a chunk of the bread and a piece of Gorgonzola and gave it to Mack. She sliced one of the pears in quarters. "Let's save the other pear for breakfast." She looked over at the blankets and smiled. She sliced the bread and cheese in half, and bundled it up with the pear, and stuffed it all in Mack's backpack. She pushed off the side of the pool onto Mack's back, forcing him under the water.

It was almost daylight when they finally fell asleep in each other's arms. Outside, hours later, the sun had taken its time climbing above the neighboring ridge top, and a golden shaft lit up the mouth of the cave. The snow and ice on Tabletop was melting, and a flow of water washed down the side and thawed out the icicles hanging over the front of the cave, creating a waterfall across the opening.

Erica, with her head on Mack's chest, opened her eyes to the rays of sunlight shining through the waterfall. It could be the beginning of time, like Adam and Eve, she thought. Waking up and being the only man and woman on earth, secluded in a beautiful wilderness. Certainly, this was the most inimitable date she had ever had. She closed her eyes, drifting, listening to the music of the waterfall...until she heard the scream and bolted upright.

"Mack! Mack, wake up, someone's screaming," Erica whispered intensely, shaking Mack. "Listen."

Mack rose up on his elbows, still a little groggy from the red wine, listening. "Bugling," he said and fell back with his eyes closed.

"What do you mean *bugling*?" Erica shook Mack again.

"Mating season...a bull elk is crying out, trying to get him some early morning loving."

"An elk? It sounds more like a woman being raped."

He rolled over on his back. "It's a high-pitched shriek, then at the end, listen...he grunts, four or five times."

"Come on, let's go watch," Erica said. She grabbed the blanket, pulled him by his hand, and led him to the opening of the cave. "The sun feels great, and most of the ice on the steps has melted." She guided him around the waterfall and up the rock stair steps. After they cleared the flow of the waterfall, they heard the bull elk bugle again, followed by four loud grunts.

"Look, over there," Mack pointed across to Elk Mountain. A small herd of elk above the tree line was foraging through the melting snow. One, an old granddaddy bull, with a rack of antlers like a treetop, followed a cow, pushing her with his nose and flicking his tongue, grunting, snorting, and humping.

Erica laid the blanket over the soft spongy moss that covered the ledge, eased herself down, her legs dangling over the side, and watched the cow lead the bull down a long alpine chute until they were out of sight.

"She wants a little privacy," Erica said.

Mack sat down next to her, sliding his arm around her shoulder and leaned over to kiss each erect nipple, "Thank you cold weather."

She snuggled into the crook of his shoulder. The sun, like a warm blanket, covered their naked bodies. Erica's fingers trailed the hair on Mack's chest: around his nipples, down the center of his abdomen, through his pubic hair...ending between his legs.

"Listen to that old bull; you think *we* have enough privacy? I've never done it hanging off the side of a mountain," She whispered.

They had drifted into a dream-like state, mesmerized by the panoramic view of the majestic Rocky Mountains; like Gothic cathedrals, their skeletal spires reaching for the heavens. Puffs of snow-white clouds lazily floated below them, as Mother Nature opened her doors and windows.

Hearing the booming "hoo, hoo" of a snowy owl, Mack opened his eyes to the bright sunlight. He didn't know how long he had been snoozing and looked down at Erica to make sure she was not sunburned. She was sleeping like a newborn in a crib, a nice golden glow on her face. He listened for the mating call of the owl again but only heard the sweet and clear sounds of the bluebirds and chickadees.

Mack turned, looked up into the rising sun when he heard a high-pitched shrill, and saw a huge black bird diving straight at him full force. He was defenseless and swung his body to cover Erica and shield his face. He waited, but nothing happened. Erica moved, "What's wrong?"

"Shhh, listen." There was nothing to hear, not one sound. The birds had stopped singing, and nothing moved. Then, right above them, Mack heard loud twittering and chirping, and a huge bald eagle jumped from the top of the mesa with his wings fully extended, blocking the sun. As he floated down in front of them searching for a thermal wave, his wingtip almost touched their legs. Mack stared in awe at the closeness of this magnificent bird with his dark-brown plumed body, snow-white head and tail, and fierce golden eyes, challenging anything that moved. Erica let out a small whimper when she saw the long snowshoe rabbit dangling from the eagle's talons. They watched as he caught a thermal wave and rode it up high, then turned and fell to a ledge jutting out, across from them on Elk Mountain. He flared his tail to check his speed and landed on the edge of a nest large enough for Mack and Erica to sleep in. Three baby eaglets fought to get to the rabbit first. The father handed the rabbit off to the mother and soared off, free to hunt again.

"Wow, that's what you call up close and personal. This is like watching a nature movie," Erica said.

Mack relaxed against the mountain, still holding Erica. Without warning, she pulled away, stood up with her legs apart, arms stretched wide, and shouted to the skies:

"He clasps the crag with crooked hands;

Close to the sun in lonely lands,

He watches from his mountain walls,

And like a thunderbolt he falls."

"Miss Julie Andrews!" Mack clapped his hands loudly. "That was great, Erica. Did you write that?"

"One of your Irishmen, Tennyson," and added with a sly smile, "another *Harvard* graduate."

Mack untied his climbing rope from the tree and took his time walking back to where Erica was bent over, cleaning the snow off the snowmobile. He watched her for a while and then grabbed her by the hips and started humping her from the rear, bugling and shrieking, mimicking the bull elk, then grunted four times as her legs gave way and she fell face-first into the snow with him on top of her. She bucked wildly, throwing him off, and sat upright, pissed, her face covered in snow.

Mack just stared at her, snorted a couple of times, and asked, "Did *you* get off?"

Erica roared laughing, falling back into the snow, swinging her arms and legs making a snow angel.

Mack loaded the snowmobile and they sat waiting for it to warm up. He was in no hurry to get back. Erica had her arms wrapped around Mack's waist and her head snug against his down jacket, humming a song. She was happy, and he was too. He had been looking for a woman who loved the outdoors as much as he did. There was something sensual about eating, sleeping, and making love al fresco.

He eased the clutch out and added gas as they started cruising across the mesa at a leisurely speed. Erica started singing the lyrics in Swedish to the song she had been humming, and Mack recognized some of the words: meadow, snowman, and something about a preacher. *What were the lyrics about?* He started humming the tune, and then the words came to him, "Marriage! Parson Brown!" *NO! No way!*

Erica squeezed him and started singing louder, "Are you married? We'll say, No man. But Parson Brown can do the job when you're in town!"

Mack instinctively increased the throttle until they were racing at full speed across the mesa. He hardly heard Erica when she rose up, both hands on his shoulder and shouted in his ear,

"Are we in a rush?"

CHAPTER 12

MACK NOTICED THAT most of the furniture in Bella's living room had been moved to other parts of the house or pushed back against the walls to create a long rectangular dance floor. This was her first *milonga* (meeting place to dance the tango) without her tango partner.

Mack *nosed* the crystal snifter of single malt Scotch. He smiled when he remembered how he used to judge people as pretentious, showing off, when he saw someone do this very thing. But Bella had taught him why: "The nose is a far more acute organ than the tongue. There are 32 primary smells and only four primary tastes," she preached.

He surveyed the dance floor. The room was packed with people, mostly with tango aficionados from Aspen and the neighboring towns like Leadville, Glenwood Springs, Grand Junction, even as far as Denver.

Prior to the first set of music, Bella and her old dancing partner typically put on an exhibition, not a lesson, but a performance of the latest steps, turns, and *adronos* (embellishments). At the bottom of the invitation was a special offer; each guest could bring a newcomer for his or her first romantic encounter with the tango. This, for Bella, was the reason for the exhibition, to show the beginner the beauty, passion, and different styles of the dance.

Mack had committed to be Bella's new tango partner; what choice did he have? But he knew nothing about an exhibition. When they first started, he thought, *Ballroom dancing, a lot of choreography, with fancy and exaggerated moves;* he hated that. Bella assured him they would dance *Argentine* Tango, and that he would grow to love the elegance of the close embrace and the passionate *salon* style tango that they danced in the crowded halls, clubs, and bars of Buenos Aires.

She insisted that they practice three times a week and gave Mack a cassette tape of the music, *La Cumparsita*, to practice by himself. He listened to the tape over and over inside his snowcat and later, after Bella gave him a portable cassette recorder with earphones, he found himself skiing to the music, long swirling turns and short quick steps.

Mack had to admit, Bella was right. He came to love the tango and the music too, which could not be one without the other. It was a lot like the Memphis blues, soulful and earthy, and yet the tango had a touch of sophistication with a dash of mystique.

Mack savored the Scotch whiskey, rolling it over his tongue until it was coated.

Everyone was dressed to the hilt: coat and tie for the men and long and short dresses with deep slits up the sides and spiked heels for the women.

He took a slow deep breath through his mouth; the pungent, peaty, aged Scotch flooded his taste receptors, leaving a lingering, smoky flavor.

Mack was dressed in a dead man's suit. It was a beautiful, navy blue pinstripe Brioni, that he found when Bella took him to her Starwood neighbor's estate sale, whose husband had recently died. Mack thought a hundred dollars was too much for a used suit even if it did fit perfectly. Of course, he didn't know Brioni from baloney. But after Bella told him what the original had cost, he agreed to Bella's bartering for the suit, a sport coat, and a couple of Zega dress shirts just for keeping her neighbor's driveway clear of snow the rest of the season. No big deal for Mack, since he snow plowed Bella's driveway once a week anyway.

The finishing taste was almost too smooth, losing some of its earthy Islay character, but holding a great balance.

Mack had learned a few Spanish words, like *codigos*, meaning codes or rules of Tango. Another word he particularly liked was *cabeceo*. That's when a man invites a woman to dance—he waits to make eye contact from a distance, tilts or nods his head toward the dance floor, and she answers by a slight nod or rejects the offer by looking away. You never walk over and ask a woman to dance; that could be very embarrassing.

The lights flickered on and off and dimmed down to darkness.

"Okay, Valentino, you ready to show these yokels how it's done?" Bella whispered, slipping up behind Mack.

"You talking to me, Señora?"

"Who did you think I was talking to, you *burro*!"

"You cannot *ask* me to dance! You must wait for me to *cabeceo* you first."

Bella reached under Mack's coattail and grabbed the crotch of his pants, lifting him slightly, and walked him out onto the dance floor, "I'll make you think *cabeceo*."

"Sí, Sí, Señora Bella!" Mack said in a faked high-pitched voice. He downed his drink and placed the snifter on a side table against the wall.

They both stood erect but relaxed, facing each other in the middle of the dance floor. In a high whisper Bella said, "I don't know how you stand to drink that stuff. It smells medicinal."

"You were the one who taught me how to appreciate the full measure of that *stuff*.

"I know, but I was mainly talking about wines."

"Too late, I'm addicted and it's your fault; you serve the very best single malt."

"I *am* the very best."

La Cumparsita started to play. The lights came up to a pink glow. She stared into his eyes.

The tango is a dance of seduction, and, as the Scotch warmed through his bloodstream, it erased all inhibitions of "performing" before an audience. This was like waiting in the ring before his championship fight. There were just the two of them. He wrapped his arm around her torso and moved her in close, chest to chest. He felt her heart beat against his and felt her quiver. She placed her right hand in his and draped her left arm around his shoulders, the two bodies now becoming one.

Mack heard the noise first, a loud crash followed by a constant car horn blowing as if it was stuck. He hurried down the hall and out the front door with Bella following. He saw a red sports car convertible smashed into a tree. It had skidded off the drive, over the snow bank, and across the yard. *Stupid ass must have been flying.* The top was down, and the driver was leaning forward pressing on the horn. Mack jerked the door open.

"You hurt, man?"

"What's it to *you*, asshole?" the driver shouted and then tipped backward against the seat, releasing the horn and laughing. Blood trickled down his forehead, and the smell of alcohol was overpowering. "Don't just stand there looking stupid, help me out of this tin can." Bella came up from behind Mack when she heard the loud laugh. She stood looking down into the car with both hands on her hips,

"Angus McGregor, what are you doing here?"

"Tango!" he shouted, laughing, "Tango, Big Momma, me and you."

"I mean, what are you doing in Aspen?"

"Am I in Aspen?"

"Come on, Mack, help me with this beached beluga. This is my old tango partner. Angus, you better not get blood on my new dress."

"Who's bleeding? Did this hippie hit me when I wasn't looking?"

Mack helped, unwillingly, with Bella's urging. Angus was huge, at least 250 pounds and a head taller than Mack. *How did someone this big get into this car, which wasn't a foot off the ground?* As soon as they got him on his feet, he wobbled and fell to his knees. *Concussion,* Mack thought.

Angus laughed, grabbed two hands of snow, and roughly washed the blood from his face. He stood up, staggered a little, and Mack reached out to keep him from falling.

Angus shouted, "Who are *you?*" and shoved Mack so hard he fell backward, stumbling over the snow bank.

"Let's tango, Big Momma," he said, seizing Bella by the arm.

Mack stood up, brushing the snow off his *new* Brioni, and watched as they strolled up the driveway, Bella leading him. A lot of the guests stood outside and, when they saw it was Angus, they ran shouting, all gathering around him. Obviously, he was well known and the life of many past parties. Like a school of herring, they moved back inside.

Bella never looked back at Mack.

What the hell? No, thank you, kiss my ass...nothing?

He looked at the smashed nose on this classic car with a hood that seemed to stretch forever, even when crumpled in the middle. The crash was only a minor distraction from the streamlined beauty years ahead of its time. He knew his cars; this old classic, with its powerful V-12 engine, came off the showroom floor ready for the racetrack.

He eased himself into the driver's seat of the vintage Jag, the smell of leather still strong as he ran his hands around the polished wooden steering wheel. Leaning forward, he flipped a toggle switch, and turned the key in the ignition—nothing happened. He wanted to listen to that distinctive sound of a 12-cylinder engine that generated enough horsepower that rocketed this—*what did they call it back in its day?* A racecar in a mini skirt, top end speed, 160 mph. Instead, he got steam pouring out underneath the hood.

Men and their cars. Yeah, I'm one of them too...freedom and power.

He crawled out of the car, walked around the back, and saw the name on the trunk: JAGUAR – E TYPE – V12. Well, if nothing else, Angus had excellent taste in cars.

He looked over at his old pickup, parked in the trees, just off the driveway. *What am I doing here? This is not my type of people.*

He smelled trouble, fight or flight...stay or go? *The hell with it, I'm having one more drink before I go.*

Mack sipped his Scotch and watched as Bella and Angus glided over the dance floor. He couldn't believe Angus, a stumbling drunk earlier, now a big cat moving across the floor in perfect balance. His posture and embrace were picture perfect. Mack had made a serious misjudgment. He had underestimated Angus, and he knew better.

The first round of songs ended, and he watched Bella work her way through the crowd over to him. "Shall we finish our dance?"

"Ooh no, follow him? You've got to be joking."

"He's good, isn't he? He studied in Buenos Aires for a year."

"I've never seen a man that big move like that."

"He tells everyone the tango is the reason he was voted All-Pro middle linebacker."

"He plays for the NFL?"

"The Denver Broncos."

"You would need to have a large set of gonads to follow his dancing."

"You have them."

"Yeah? Well, they just shriveled up. I'm staying my distance from that guy."

The second round of songs, *Tanda,* began, and Bella backed out onto the dance floor, wiggling her fingers for Mack to follow. Two lines of dancers were circling the dance floor. Mack hesitated and then walked through the first line into the inner-circle where the beginners danced and waited for Bella, motioning with his fingers. She stood in the outer circle, her hands on her hips, demanding, and holding up the line of dance. He hurried over to her and pulled her into a close embrace. The dancers behind them danced in place, waiting for the line of dance to continue. Mack walked to the rhythm of the music. He was going to keep it simple and focus on his posture, the embrace, the cadence, and his walk. "A good dancer you recognize by the way he walks. The beginning and the end of the tango is the walk." How many times had he heard Bella say those words?

Okay, no fancy moves, none of the embellishments he had practiced. It was way too crowded, just Caminada, a continuous walk.

After *walking* once around the dance floor Mack felt pretty good. Bella and he were in sync with the music. The separation between dancing couples had increased, and Mack thought he would do the first part of a *paso basico*. He stopped, did a side step with his left foot, crossed his right foot to the outside of Bella's, then walked on the outside a few steps before crossing back into the line of dance.

"Nice move, twinkle toes." Bella kissed him in the ear and whispered, "Angus is one of the best *technical* Milonguero, who knows all the tango moves, but you, my little Tanguero, you are the pure one, the one who dances the tango with *passion*."

Mack was caught up in the music now, and in a sensual communion with Bella, dancing without thought or effort, the feeling of one body, four legs. He decided to add a little turn, a simple *medio giro a la derecha*, a half turn to the right. He shortened his steps and waited for the couple in front to move forward. In the middle of his turn, he felt a bump to his back shoulder and turned to apologize. The woman that bumped him was spinning, her partner rotating her with increasing speed, a whirling blur. He saw the man's forearm, but it was too late. The next thing Mack remembered was being on the floor with the warm taste of blood in his mouth. Choking, he felt someone turn him on his side, and he threw up. Blood and Scotch is not a good cocktail. He heard Bella scream, "You son-of-a-bitch! You did that on purpose."

He heard Angus say, "The asshole should have been in the inner circle with all the other beginners."

"He will kill you for this!"

"Naaaw, I don't think so."

"Can you sit up?" Bella asked, lifting Mack to a seated position. She wiped his face with a wet bar towel.

Mack couldn't talk; the pain was unbearable until he felt his head disconnected from his body and saw it rolling across the dance floor. The last thing he remembered was counting his wobbly front teeth with his tongue.

When Mack's skiing buddy, "Doc" Kris, who worked in the emergency room, came in late the next morning, Mack was sitting up in the hospital bed.

"Damn, what did he hit you with, a baseball bat?" He walked over and stuck an X-ray in a wall-hung reader. "I borrowed these from radiology."

Both of Mack's eyes were black, his nose and lips were swollen, and tape crisscrossed the bridge of his nose and under his chin. Ice packs were held in place on each side of his face with an Ace bandage.

"You got any pain?" Kris was small, and wore a perpetual smile and Marshwood-style glasses like John Denver's.

Mack shook his head.

"Good news, no concussion. You can take a pretty good punch, Buddy."

Mack mumbled something.

"I talked with the doctor who saw you last night, and the radiologist and I examined your x-rays. We both agree that your jaws and teeth will tighten up on their own; just no steaks for a while. You want to look at the x-rays?"

"Took you long enough to get here; I'm ready to go home." Mack wasn't sure what a nurse practitioner was or how much authority he had, but he knew that Kris had a lot of dedicated patients in Aspen. More importantly, Kris was a Marine corpsman; that alone was good enough for him.

Kris moved over to the bed, removed the pillows from behind Mack, and eased him down on the bed. After taking off the Ace bandages and the ice packs, he rubbed his hands together and placed them over Mack's face.

Mack felt the energy and warmth penetrate the pores of his skin, like an injection of Niacin, draining the tension from his face.

"Close your eyes and picture this," Kris said in a low singsong voice. "It's early morning. You can't see it yet, but the fingers of the sun are climbing over the mountaintops. You take a deep breath, inhaling the fresh, clean, cold air. You are the first on the chair lift as you rise to the top of the mountain." *Good, most of his swelling is subsiding. The icepacks are doing their job.*

"You ease off the chair lift. You're alone, the sun is full and radiant, and everything is in slow motion as you stand on top of the mountain, awestruck by one of God's wonders of the world—the majestic Rocky Mountains. You take a deep breath and taste the snow crystals riding on the sunrays." *His nose and mandibular feel okay.*

"You push off with your poles, skating down to Steeplechase, picking up speed, turn left and point your tips down the fall line at St. Moritz. The powder is deep; you stay over your skis, not too far back, as you carve through a field of faceted ice crystals, snowflakes engulfing you, while you vanish in and out of the pristine powder in perfect rhythm. Undefiled by lust and emotional impurities, unclouded by any dualistic perceptions, this ethereal space is luminous consciousness."

"What the *hell* have you been smoking?" Mack squeaked out between his taped jaws.

"Then I asked myself, what would my friend Mack do, the one who loves deep powder as much as I do? Would he take one more run through Nirvana? Or would he rush to the hospital to attend to his injured friend?" *Salt water will take care of his loose teeth.*

"Nay, not my friend, he'd understand. My Karma is in balance, without guilt."

"Okay, Siddhartha, you're forgiven. Help me up, I gotta pee." Mack said.

When Mack came out of the bathroom, Kris said, "Here, sit in the chair while I take the tape off. You'll have to eat through a straw for a couple of days, a lot of smoothies. The black eyes, nose, teeth, and jaws...everything, about a week, and you'll be like new. Other than that, you're good to go. Rinse with warm salt water four times a day, and your teeth will tighten up before you know it. No work for a couple days, stay home, and I'll come by and see you tomorrow. *No* skiing. Now, let me re-tape your nose."

There was a knock on the door, and Bella walked in.

"You come to get this, guy?" Kris said. "He can go back to work in two days, but no more tango unless he wears a catcher's mask, okay?"

Bella didn't find that funny. She stood at the end of the bed with a sad look on her face.

They both stood looking at her. "What?" Mack asked.

"I've got some bad news," Bella said.

Mack waited.

"I got a long distance call in the real estate office this morning from a Li Fang in Natchez, Mississippi. They had my number down as your landlord. There's been a death in your family. I'm sorry, Mack, it seems when it rains, it pours."

CHAPTER 13

I T WAS VERY cold, bone-chilling, and the dark gray skies that loomed over the horizon mirrored Mack's feelings as he turned off Highway 82 at Glenwood Springs, Colorado, onto I-70 east, headed for Natchez, Mississippi, and a warmer climate. He normally would have taken Highway 82 South, but Independence Pass was snowed in and no one would be able to get through until spring.

In his long distance call with Li, Mack learned that Irish had died in her sleep. Carmen, Red's wife, had found her when she brought her coffee that morning.

"According to the doctor, she died from a ruptured pulmonary artery, caused by lung cancer," Li said. "When they removed her body, they found a burned-out cigarette fused between her charred fingers."

"God...didn't anyone know she had cancer?" Mack asked.

"Buck and Carmen were the only two, and they were sworn to secrecy, the only way they could get her to go to the doctor. She had cancer years ago. They thought they had got it all, but this time they found a tumor the size of a lemon and it had metastasized. She refused all treatment and told Buck to take her home and keep his mouth shut," Li said.

"Where is she now?" Mack said.

"At the funeral home in Natchez, I told them tentatively to set her burial for Sunday, but that could change after I talk to you. Irish's attorney in Memphis said he would drive down and go over her will with you Monday, if those days are good for you."

Mack asked Li to move the burial to Monday, and said he would meet with the attorney afterward. Bella had already cleaned the blood from his suit, and it was hanging in one of her garment bags. She told him that she had dropped Angus off at the airport, and he had caught a red-eye flight back to Denver. He had apologized for his drunken behavior and wanted her to tell him to send him a bill for any cost he incurred.

The headlights on Mack's old pickup highlighted a highway sign that read, "Vail 10 miles." He had a problem and needed to make a decision, now. He also needed a cup of coffee. He saw the off ramp up ahead where Highway 24 intersects I-70, and there was a country store. If he was going to take the southern route, he would have to turn here and follow the Arkansas River southeast on 24. But if he was going through Denver, he should keep on driving. Mack had a bill he needed to collect, and it was for a lot more than "the cost he incurred." It wasn't good business to let things slide: Payback had a tendency to eat away at Mack until the books were balanced. His problem was he didn't have much time, and he didn't know where Angus lived in Denver. Bella wouldn't give him Angus' address. She suggested he give her the bills, and she would collect from Angus.

Mack slowed down and veered right, up the off-ramp. He would have a cup of coffee and make his decision.

Standing outside, sipping his large cup of coffee and trying to reach a decision, he noticed a pickup truck with a car hauler pulling into the parking lot. Mack couldn't believe his eyes. He pulled the tape from his nose, crumpled it up and threw it in a trashcan, and started walking around back following the truck to the diesel pumps. He ambled over, sipping his coffee.

"Beautiful car. Is that yours?" Mack said to the young man pumping gas into the truck.

"I wish. I could have all the women in Aspen with this baby."

"I know what you mean. I drive an old pickup, and it's hard to get any girls with that. This baby must belong to someone important."

"I heard it was a big football player. He was drunk and ran into a tree. I got his name on the delivery ticket. Maybe you know him?" He opened the truck door and pulled out a clipboard. "Boy, you sure got a couple of shiners! What happened, car wreck?"

"No, a skiing accident. Did you recognize the name?"

"Naw, his name is McGregor," he handed the clipboard to Mack as he put the gas pump back in its cradle.

Mack read the name, "Angus McGregor. Yeah, I've heard of him, believe he plays for the Denver Broncos, a middle linebacker," Mack said.

"Really?"

"Is this address where you're delivering the car?"

"Yeah, sometimes I drop them off at a body shop but this is where he lives. They told me to roll it off in his driveway if no one was there."

"Man, that wind is cold." Mack zipped up his vest and started walking off. "Well, I got to get back on the road."

"You live in Aspen?"

"Yeah."

"Maybe we could get together and chase some chicks?"

"Sure thing. Aspen Towing, right?" Mack said, looking at the side of the truck.

"They call me Tee, man. Just ask for Tee."

"Okay Tee...I have to run."

He backed up his truck and re-parked where he could watch for Tee's truck. He turned the heater up, removed two Darvocet from a bottle "Doc" Kris had given him, and downed them with his coffee; his face was hurting. He leaned back and stared out his windshield, watching the twilight above the horizon trying to break through the gray clouds of the eastern sky.

There was no decision for Mack to make now. *What did they call that, "serendipity?" Or was it, "the luck of the Irish?"*

Mack patiently followed Tee through all the construction on I-70 into Denver, staying two or three cars back. Tee turned onto I-25, and Mack followed for a couple of miles, then saw Tee take the off-ramp onto Colorado Boulevard. A drizzling rain had started. Mack turned on the wipers and saw the right turn signal on Tee's truck blinking. Tee turned on Dartmouth, the name of the street printed on the delivery ticket, and stopped two streets down at the corner of Garfield. The house faced a golf course, but the driveway was off Garfield. He drove by the house and saw an old Honda parked in the driveway and smoke coming from the chimney; somebody was home. He stopped under a tree on the side of the golf course across from the front of the house and cut the engine. It was an expensive house, custom built in a posh neighborhood amid mature trees and shrubs with manicured hedgerows for privacy. He noticed an older Hispanic lady with an umbrella walking a Chihuahua on a leash. The Chihuahua wore a red, fleece-lined dog coat. Mack put on his sunglasses as she passed the front of his truck, crossed the street, and walked up the steps of the corner house. She never looked toward Mack or even his truck but focused on Tee standing on the front porch holding his clipboard. Mack watched as Tee pointed to the Jaguar on his tilt trailer and handed her the clipboard and a pen, the Chihuahua yapping the whole time.

Mack watched as the overhead garage door opened, and Tee backed in the trailer, rolled off the Jaguar, and drove off as the overhead door closed. He started his truck and turned on the defroster. The windows were fogging up inside, and the rain was turning to a mixture of sleet and snow; he would wait and watch for a while. He turned on his wipers to clear his view and saw the Hispanic lady backing out the front door, her umbrella under her arm. She must be his housekeeper. He turned off his wipers and cracked his window, watching as she locked the door, opened the top of the mailbox, and dropped in the key. She opened the umbrella, walked to her Honda still parked in the driveway, and drove off.

He couldn't believe his eyes. *This* was going to be a piece of cake, but where was Angus? He removed the oak ax handle from the gun rack behind him; did Angus have a second car, rent a car from the airport, or take a cab?

Mack eased the gearshift into first and drove down Dartmouth, turned back up Colorado Boulevard, and stopped at a grocery market he had spotted coming in. He bought a large cup of coffee, an egg and cheese sandwich, a cinnamon roll, and a bag of beef tips. Outside he saw a pay phone and looked up McGregor on Dartmouth and called the number—no one answered. Next to the pay phone was a Denver Post paper rack, and Mack bought a copy when he saw "BRONCOS" printed across the front page. He drove back to the house, turned into the driveway of the golf course, and parked in the empty parking lot. The golf course, its rolling hills covered in heavy snow, and the tall Christmas tree-like blue spruce would have made a great image for a Christmas card.

He watched the front of the house and down the side street as he removed his sandwich, dipped it in his coffee, and chewed carefully. He removed the sports page from the newspaper and stared at bold, colorful letters across the top of the page, "BRONCOS v STEELERS." Turning the page, he read where Denver was playing the Steelers at Three Rivers Stadium in Pittsburgh tomorrow, and they had left early this morning to avoid a snowstorm headed for Denver. He looked out the windshield at the huge snowflakes falling. No Angus, huh? Watching the smoke coming out of the chimney, he realized he'd just missed him. How lucky for the Scotsman.

Mack's jaws hurt from eating the sandwich, but the sweet taste of revenge dominated his thoughts. He was still hungry and looked at the cinnamon roll...*why not?* He leaned back, staring out the window as he dipped the roll in his coffee and took small bites.

He pulled his ski hat low over his head, put on his sunglasses, grabbed the bag of beef tips and the ax handle, and headed for the house. Walking around the perimeter of the house, he checked under the cornice and gables for an alarm horn or surveillance cameras; there were none. On the front steps he looked up and down the street and over the golf course but saw no one. It was snowing so hard he could hardly see his truck. He hurried to the front porch, stomped the snow from his boots, removed the key from the mailbox, and unlocked the door. He stood in a hallway with his back against the door and removed his sunglasses. His heart raced as his eyes adjusted to the darkness; he felt like a burglar. It was warm. You could smell the wood left burning in the fireplace and melting snow from his hat ran down the back of his neck...*where was that Chihuahua?*

He took a couple of steps down the hallway and stopped. On the wall was a framed photo of the front page of *The Denver Post* showing Angus McGregor in a Denver Broncos uniform, a menacing look on his face. Both arms were stretched out. In one hand was a football and in the palm of his other hand was a two-pound, black and tan Chihuahua puppy, named "Bronco."

Mack heard a low growl. When he looked down, he saw what resembled a rat staring up at him, lips curled back, teeth bared. The two canines looked like snake fangs. *Hello Bronco, Angus' little baby.* He thought of the scene from the movie, *The Godfather*, where this guy wakes up with the severed head of his beloved horse in bed with him; something like that would get Angus' attention. He looked back at the photo on the wall, paying no attention to Bronco, and flipped one of the beef tips down the hall. He watched as Bronco fought between his natural instincts, watch dog or olfactory? His sense of smell won out, and he tipped across the hardwood floor to the meat, woofing it down in one bite. *Angus must be a vegetarian.* Mack threw another beef tip at Bronco and walked into the living room....*so much for being known as a one-person watchdog.*

Across the room, a high-backed couch faced the fireplace with a leather wingback chair at each end. A fire screen covered the fireplace where a couple of small logs still burned in a bed of dying embers. Mack saw a gold football mounted upright on a pedestal and walked over to read the award, "Defense Player of the Year." Bronco barked for more meat.

"Don't push your luck, rat dog; I may mount your head on top of this football." Bronco barked again and edged toward Mack. Mack leaned the ax handle against the pedestal, and reached into his pocket for the bag of beef tips, and stopped in mid-motion. His internal alarm was going off, firing on all cylinders: *Danger! Beware!* Threat was a close relative of Mack; he knew it well and had experienced it many times, beginning as a child with the loss of his whole family. His reaction was immediate and innate. He stopped breathing, stood still, listening. His heart rate doubled. Someone else was in the house.

A deep, guttural sound broke the silence.

Mack twitched as a chill ran up his back. He turned and watched: rising from the cushions of the couch was a Rottweiler, his black face not twelve feet from Mack. His bloodshot eyes locked in on Mack like a laser, half his body hanging over the back of the couch, enraged and ready to pounce.

Mack could hear Buck shouting inside his head "Don't PANIC! You're dead if you panic. Improvise. Adapt. Overcome."

Mack submitted to the Rottweiler's stare, lowering his head, half looking at the floor. Taking a deep breath and exhaling, he removed his down vest and wrapped it around his left forearm.

Without any warning, the Rottweiler exploded from the back of the couch like a rabid panther, saliva dripping from its jagged teeth.

Mack threw his left arm up to protect his face and with his right hand grabbed the gold football, pedestal and all, slamming it in front of the dog, deflecting his attack. The dog landed on his back on the hardwood floor with a thud; but he bounced back up like a basketball, in full attack mode. Mack darted around the edge of the couch, knocking over the wingback chair behind him to slow the onslaught, but the Rottweiler must have been a trained guard dog, because he was not to be denied his instinctual responsibilities—seek and destroy. He leaped over the chair and lunged, his powerful jaws wide open, and baring deadly teeth ready to rip meat from bone.

Mack shoved his wrapped forearm into the dog's mouth, but the momentum of a hundred pounds of muscle and bone knocked him back, and he tripped over the hearth, crashing through the fire screen into the firebox. Mack's arm felt as if it was in a steel vise as he grabbed the massive neck with his right hand to push the dog away from his face. He smelled the foul breath and stared at the mucus running from his flared nostrils. He felt something tugging at his pants leg and then a sharp bite into his leg—*Damn, a two-point attack. Bronco had joined the assault.*

Mack was on his back, halfway into the firebox with the dog on his chest, when he smelled his hat burning. He rolled to his right side, and with his hip, shoulder, and all his power, he threw the heel of his right hand against the head of the dog, knocking him off his chest. He reached back with his right hand to push himself out of the firebox, and his hand landed on a burning log that had rolled out onto the hearth. He grabbed the log, and, at the same time, the dog released Mack's arm and lunged for his throat. Mack swung the log as hard as he could, catching the dog in the face. Burning embers flew everywhere, and the log disintegrated in his hand. The dog dropped to the floor howling, shaking his head, and pawing at his nose frantically. Bronco stopped his attack, stunned, watching the Rottweiler roll on the floor in agony. Mack smelled burned flesh, looked at his hand, and felt the pain. The first layer of skin was peeled back in a couple of places, and white patches of blisters were forming. He removed the tattered vest from his arm while walking to the kitchen, but the Rottweiler was rolling on the floor, blocking the kitchen doorway. Mack kicked him in his side.

"Shut up that howling. I didn't hit you that hard; you tried to kill me." Mack stepped over him and opened a kitchen cabinet, removed a bowl, filled it with ice and water, and submerged his hand. He checked his left forearm—just bruised bite marks, no broken skin. He pulled up his pants leg, checked where Bronco had been gnawing, and found blood trickling out of two small punctures.

Mack found a drawer in the bathroom full of first aid remedies. He opened a bottle of peroxide, poured it over his leg, and watched as white foam bubbled out of the two holes. *That little shit better not have rabies.* He looked at his hand; it was throbbing, the pain intense.

Digging around in the drawer, he found a spray bottle of antiseptic with Lidocaine and a pair of scissors. He cut a face towel in strips, sprayed his hand, then wrapped it and stuck the bottle in his pocket. The Lidocaine eased the pain almost immediately.

Loud moans continued from the Rottweiler as Mack walked back into the living room. The dog was spread out on the floor, pawing his nose with his front feet and shaking his head back and forth. Mack pushed him with his foot; there was no fight left in him. He kneeled down, grabbed his snout with both hands, locking his jaw, and looked down his nose. Inside one of his nostrils, lodged deep, was a glowing ember. Mack walked over and removed an ice cube from the bowl in the sink. He sat on the floor holding the dog's head in his lap with his legs wrapped around the dog's body and forced the ice cube down his nostril. The dog struggled, wiggling his head trying to get up, but Mack held him tight, releasing his jaws so he could breathe out his mouth. The dog stopped resisting and relaxed in Mack's grip, the ice doing its job.

Mack remembered seeing a toolbox in the kitchen pantry. He went to the pantry, opened the toolbox, and found a pair of long needle-nose pliers. Holding the dog in his lap again, he carefully inserted the pliers and removed a two-inch long piece of smoldering charcoal. The dog jumped up, shook his head, snorted a couple of times, and locked his bloodshot eyes on Mack again. The hair on the back of Mack's neck bristled as he studied the dog. *Not another attack?* But the dog relaxed, lowered his head, and with a low whine came to Mack, dropping his huge head in his lap. Mack removed the bottle of antiseptic from his pocket, turned the dog's head sideways, and sprayed the inside of his burned nose. The dog didn't resist; he lay perfectly still, while Bronco ran around them jumping up and down, yipping.

Later, Mack sat on the couch and sipped on a cold beer after downing four Darvocet. As in combat, the adrenaline made him forget about his injuries, but now his whole body was in pain.

He had hand-fed both of the dogs the remaining beef tips. Now the Rottweiler was stretched out with his head resting in Mack's lap, and Bronco was cuddled up between the Rottweiler's front legs. He was trying to figure out what to do next. He saw a copy of *GQ* magazine with the new Mercedes Benz sedan on the front cover, tore out the two-page centerfold, and stuffed it into his pocket.

He looked around the house, surveying the damages and comparing them to his injuries, and concluded it was not enough payback. *Maybe if I burned the house down? No, that's a little overkill. I need to get out of here.*

He stood up, "Sorry, boys, it's time for me to go." He toasted the half-finished beer towards the two dogs, "Good fight though," and poured the remaining beer over some embers on the wood floor. He hated light beer. He picked up his torn vest and headed for the door, the dogs on his heels.

"No. Stay. You can't go with me."

The dogs barked as if they were talking back and jumping on Mack's leg. Mack looked at the framed photo of Angus in *The Denver Post* again and noticed an article at the bottom. While reading the article, he stopped and reread a statement made by Angus, "No, I'm not married and I don't have any kids. I guess my kids are my two dogs, Rebel and Bronco." *His two kids, huh?* Mack continued to read and learned that Rebel was a gift to Angus from his parents when he graduated from the University of Mississippi.

Mack opened the door, "Okay, boys, consider yourselves kidnapped." Rebel darted out the door with Bronco biting at his heels.

Mack slammed the door. *Vengeance—sweet vengeance.*

CHAPTER 14

MACK THOUGHT OF the last time he was in this bed, years ago, staring at this same Legacy Boot box beside him now.

He had been young and confused, wondering if he had made the right decision when he accepted Irish's agreement—*her* plans for *his* future.

It didn't take long for Sgt. Buck Jones to "un-confuse" him. He stared at the boot box, plus the two file storage boxes that Li had marked "Immediate Attention." In one storage box, according to Li, were legal folders containing threatening letters, notices, lawsuits, subpoenas, foreclosures, etc. The other box contained financials prepared by Li and a couple of tax men: balance sheets, profit and loss statements, statements of retained earnings, cash flow on all the businesses—corporate and personal—including lists of investments, equipment, and real estate.

Rebel snored, his chin across Mack's leg, while Bronco slept between Rebel's legs. The dogs felt good close to him. On his drive to Shamrock, he thought there might be some trouble between the alpha dogs, especially Bear and Rebel, but he soon learned that Bear had died the day after Irish died. Carmen said nothing was wrong with him, "You know how he loved to jump and play. He just stopped eating and would not leave her bedroom. He died of a broken heart, and part of my heart died too."

Mack drove straight through to Natchez. He was tired and looking to grab a couple of hours sack time. He had figured two, three days at the most, and he would be headed back to Aspen. But when Li met him at the door and spent hours at the kitchen table bringing him up to date on all the financial problems of Irish's estate, he knew this was not going to be a quick turnaround trip.

After the funeral, he met with the estate lawyer, and they went over Irish's will; most of her estate had been left to him. It wasn't just that they were broke; they were drowning in debt and lawsuits by everyone who had enough money to hire a lawyer. According to Li, the liabilities far outweighed the value of the assets. Mack's immediate thought was, *How do I get out of this quagmire and back to my simple, carefree lifestyle in Aspen?*

He lifted the boot box and placed it in his lap. It was bound in duct tape with "MACK SHANNON ONLY" printed across the top. He opened the box and dumped the contents on the bed: a white envelope with his name printed on the front, a clear plastic bag with a key inside, a copy of her will and the old contract between Irish and him.

He leaned back against the headboard, opened the envelope, and read the shaky, handwritten letter:

Dear Mack, I was diagnosed with lung cancer years ago and, after chemo and radiation, the new tests were NED (no evidence of disease). Now, it's back in full force. My doctors in Memphis have diagnosed stage-4 lung cancer, and those cancer cells have now spread throughout my body. I left the hospital because I want to die here at Shamrock, my home. I'm confined to my bed with a hose running up my nose to breathe for me, an IV that feeds me, and 30 mg of mind-altering morphine every four hours. The most dehumanizing aspect of all this is having to wear diapers at my age. I have stopped taking the morphine so I can write this letter; although between the hallucinations, the constant pain and my rambling, I might write just about anything. I have to stop a lot, so be patient. You are all that's left of this family, and these are my last words. You have always had an inquiring mind, asking questions about religion—especially Catholicism—heaven or hell, a merciful God or a God of eternal damnation. I have prayed a hundred prayers begging God to take me, but He has not heard my prayers. He gave all of us the freedom of choice, and I'm taking mine while I'm able.

I wanted you to understand that after Mickey died and the economy crashed, I was too sick to take care of the businesses. When the banks failed and the prime rate skyrocketed, it was all too much. Li tried, he worked hard, but he's not a leader. I feel I let you down and didn't live up to our agreement. I'm sorry I forced you to go to Harvard. That was my dream, not yours. Regardless, it's over now, and it is what it is. What I want to say is how much I love you and wish I had told you that a 1,000 times. But no, I went along with Mickey and the old Irish traditions of developing an "alpha male." No spoiled sissy or girly girl in this Irish family, no sir. A couple of hugs and kisses now and then wouldn't have robbed any of your virility—God knows you have more than enough of that. But in the end, I do see the wisdom of those traditions. Look at the financial mess I have left you with. Only a powerful, tenacious alpha male, with a lot of fight, could pull this debacle out of the fire. This is an opportunity, Mack, not a disaster. You are trained for the fight. You're young and tough, love competition, and you're starting with nothing. So you have nothing to lose and everything to gain. Remember what we talked about, "Money is power; the more money, the more power, and you shouldn't go through life without that experience."

The safe deposit box key is from American Security Vault Company in Memphis. It is not a bank. See Mary Singer, the manager, and show her the papers in the bag with the key. Since I own the box (it's not rented) Mary will transfer it into your name; what's in it is yours. Li and my sweet man Buck are taken care of; enclosed you will find the titles to the properties now in their names. NEVER, never trust a banker. Those lying vultures circled outside my hospital door waiting to pick my bones...I'll never forgive those bastards. Have I forgotten anything? Oh, sweet Jesus, Mary mother of God—Carmen! I almost forgot. Mack, please, please take care of her as long as you can. What a saint; she bathed my soiled body like an infant, such gentle hands. I could not have endured the pain without her loving care—such a Godly women. Please pray for my absolution.

Mack removed the pillows from the headboard, turned off the table light, and scooted down in the bed, pulling the covers over him—he was beat. *Man, what a letter. I shouldn't have read it before going to bed. This was not a good time to make important decisions.*

Rebel lifted his head, waited until Mack settled in, and dropped his head back onto Mack's leg. Mack dozed off to the rhythm of the Rottweiler's heartbeat against his leg, but then started turning from one side to the other. After repositioning his pillow numerous times, his brain won out over his sleep-starved body and he sat up. He had this image in his mind of vultures circling Irish's body. He threw back the covers, grabbed his shaving kit, and headed for the bathroom, both dogs at his heels. If he was going to "kill some buzzards," he needed an outline for his battle strategy, and no better way to kick it off than with a hot shower, a shave, and a haircut.

Downstairs, he sat the boxes on the kitchen table and put on a pot of coffee.

"Can I help?" Li asked, standing in the door opening. "I couldn't sleep and heard you come down the steps."

"I've decided to stay...for a while. I'm not going to let them take everything Irish and Mickey worked for their whole lives."

"You sure? You're taking on a heavy load," Li said, removing two cups from the cabinet. "Cream and sugar?"

"Just sugar." Mack smiled at Li dressed in red flannel pajamas. He was bald now with a thin Fu Manchu mustache and thick, rimless glasses that replaced the old, black horn-rimmed ones.

"All cleaned up for the battle, huh?"

"I feel like I cut off ten pounds."

Li brought the two cups of steaming coffee over to the table. "It was a nice funeral. I've never seen so many flowers."

"Yeah, I'm glad it was a closed casket; she didn't look anything like herself."

"Cancer has a way of doing that."

"Buck seemed to handle it okay, don't you think?"

"He's been watching her die a little each day. Like you; I guess death is no stranger to Marines."

"It doesn't make it easier."

Li looked back at the door and in a low whisper said, "You know the day she died, Buck and Bear were the only ones in her room for the last 24 hours."

"What...you think he...assisted in her death?"

"He was devoted to her, would have done anything she wanted."

"Why would God let someone suffer all those years and then send her to hell for taking her own life? I don't believe that shit...dead's dead."

"Who's to judge? It would have been a blessing," Li said.

"Easier said than done. I can understand killing in the heat of passion, like war or self-defense, but a cold, calculating execution of someone you love—that's hardcore."

Li filled their coffee cups again and looked down at the blank legal pad in front of Mack. "So, what's your plan?"

"Why, you want in?"

"In for a penny, in for a pound, right?"

"Great, I need you. First thing is to stop the bleeding. For me, I got to keep it simple, so let's start with a master sheet, one for each box. I'll take the legal documents, and you take the financials; that'll help me a lot. Basically, I need the name, rank, and serial number on everything we own. We need a copy of every title to see if there's a brick on it and, if no liens, can we sell it? And whose name the title is in: Mickey's, Irish's, a third party, corporation, or a company. Is there any money in those bank accounts...information like that? Everything is on the selling block. We need operating capital."

"Everything?"

"Everything," Mack said, "airplanes, horses, boats, barges, equipment, property...anything and everything." He noticed a concerned look on Li's face and remembered Irish had quitclaimed the old Magnolia Farm to Li. Irish held the mortgage on the 100-acre property, along the river, 40 miles north of Memphis. Li had been paying a monthly note to Irish for years and remodeling the farmhouse for his and his wife's retirement. He decided to hold off telling him Irish had torn up their mortgage agreement and titled the property in his name.

Mack removed the legal folders from the box. "One thing for sure, we're going to need some lawyers immediately. Do we have any?"

"None that we don't owe money to. There's a folder in that box, marked *Attorneys,* of the ones who are suing us."

"That figures. Well, at least we'll know who not to call."

Mack enjoyed working with Li. He was not a big talker, and before long morning light was coming through the kitchen windows. They had worked all night on the two master sheets. Mack had gone through every folder in the box and listed each lawsuit that had been filed, the name of the lawyer or law firm, the date it was filed, the status, and the amount. Li was still working on his box when Carmen stuck her head through the kitchen door.

"Mr. Mack, am I disturbing you? I saw the lights on. I bet you all have been up all night working and would like a big breakfast?"

Mack got up and hugged her, "That would be nice, and could you finish trimming my hair in the back?" Carmen cut everyone's hair at Shamrock.

"Let me turn the oven on, and you sit over here. It will only take me five minutes to shape it up."

She smiled as he handed her the scissors, and she slipped a towel around Mack's shoulders and started cutting.

After she finished, Mack looked over at Li, "I'm going to run upstairs and get packed while Carmen's cooking. I need to get to Memphis. Are you driving back today?"

"I can. You want a ride?"

"No, but I would like for us to get together in Memphis so we can go over these master sheets and talk about strategy. Is there a place for me down on the barge we could lock those files up? Maybe Mickey's old office?"

"No problem. I'll get dressed, finish this box by the time you're packed, and have the car loaded." Li didn't want to tell Mack that *he* had moved into Mickey's office. It was a little over a six-hour drive back to Memphis. He would call and have the guys move his stuff back to his old office.

Mack came down the steps with his suit bag and his old Marine duffel bag and sat them by the door with Li's files and boxes.

The smell of the hot biscuits made his stomach growl. Buck stood at the stove pouring a cup of coffee. Rebel and Bronco were on their haunches waiting for another handout from Carmen.

"Well, well, you look like a *real* Marine now," Buck said, inspecting Mack's haircut and clean shave. He moved to the table with the coffee pot and filled Mack's cup. "Still black with sugar?"

"Thanks." Mack sat at the table and Carmen put a plate in front of him with eggs, bacon, grits, and biscuits.

"Mr. Mack, I need to run and check on the kids, and I'll be right back. Do you need anything before I go?"

"No, you go right ahead; take your time."

Buck sat at the table with his plate, "We have that new aerial map of Shamrock that the surveyors marked up, and I thought you might want to fly over and eyeball everything you now own. Afterwards we could check the service centers on the way back to Memphis and..."

"You mean everything that owns *me*; I've seen very little in those boxes that *I* own."

"She didn't mean to leave it that way, Mack."

"She sure fooled me."

Li walked in and stood at the door, listening.

Mack looked at both of them. "I'm not saying she did. I just can't get my head around how she lost *everything*."

Li and Buck looked at each other until Li started shaking his head toward Mack, "Irish didn't just have that name 'cause she was from Ireland. She was known up and down the river for her Irish tales. She'd get real excited telling stories and had a tendency to embellish each one, especially after a couple of drinks. There never was 100,000 acres here, more like half of that. Every time she told the story of how she bought Shamrock—each section at a time—it grew 3,000 to 5,000 acres. I guess she stopped at a 100,000 because it was a good round number for her to remember. I've heard it so many times I believed it myself.

"Shamrock has always had a mortgage; everything has. She was a great lady, give you the shirt off her back, but when it came to money, she was like a rich kid in a candy store. If she wanted something, for herself or anyone else, she bought it, no matter the cost. It never seemed to bother her that she was always chin deep in debt, standing on her toes to keep from drowning. And when this past recession hit, it was like the 'great flood.' Prime rate went to 21%, inflation 15%, and the price of gas tripled. We all drowned."

"Not yet, we haven't." Mack nodded toward the files and boxes by the door. "According to those legal documents, nothing has changed ownership yet. We've lost a couple of battles but not the war. They have a head start, but now it's our time to kick ass."

As they were leaving, Carmen came up to Mack and asked if she could talk to him alone. Mack told Li and Buck he would catch up with them.

"Did I forget something?" Mack asked.

"Oh no, it's not that. It's just...well...Red and I, we know things are in trouble around here and...well, we was wondering, do we still have a job? Are we going to have to move?"

Mack put his arm around Carmen, her face showing the strain and fear of not knowing if she was going to have a place to sleep or enough to feed her family. "I will take care of you, all of you. I promise you that. We all will have to cut back, and we might have to move from here, but it won't be anytime soon. Right now, I need time to figure out what's what, okay?" Mack kissed her on the cheek. "I need you to do me a favor."

"Anything. You know that."

"I need you to take care of Rebel and Bronco?"

"Oh, thank you Mr. Mack. I miss Bear so much and those two give me great company. That little Bronco has no idea he's smaller than Rebel; they're a mess. Don't worry, I will treat them just like they're mine."

Mack was in the copilot's seat looking at a marked-up aerial map of the Shamrock property. His first instinct was to sell it all, but after careful calculations, he figured if he cut out about 80 acres and got an easement from the main road, he could keep the house, the barn, the hangars, and the airstrip. But on second thought he knew he didn't have a chance fighting for Shamrock. There were too many lawyers and courts involved from Nashville to Natchez and in Federal court for the acres Irish had leased to the government. It would take years to untangle the paper chase caused by this legal storm.

Mack showed the map to Buck, "I don't want to spend a lot of time on Shamrock. I'm going to let the lawyers fight it out; it'll take years. We'll watch from the sidelines, save our resources, and focus on our construction business and our service centers."

"Do you want to head on down to the service center in New Orleans?"

"Yeah, this place is locked up tight for years. We'll keep running everything the way we've always done, except we pay *no* bills; we're just caretakers now."

"Whatever you say. Buckle up," Buck shouted over the noise of the prop and the river banging against the aluminum floats as the Cessna 150G, an amphibious plane, pulled away from the dock. Buck explained how and why he traded their Cessna 172 Skyhawk for the much cheaper 150. With the many trips back and forth to Memphis for Irish's treatments, it was convenient to land and tie down at the Memphis Service Center. Plus, Buck was paid $5,000 cash to boot, which was the amount they owed to pay off the loan on the Skyhawk. "It's light, about 1,500 loaded, climbs fast, and with the extra 50 horsepower, 25 to 30 knots faster. Having wheels and floats we can land it just about anywhere, water or land, day or night."

One question still bothered Mack; did Buck have anything to do with Irish's death?

Buck taxied out into the middle of the river, cut the power to idle, pulled up the water rudders, and let the plane weather vane into the wind. Holding the stick all the way back, he shoved the throttle to full power. The plane lifted off the water, cleared the treetops, and turned back south toward the house and barn.

Buck leaned over and traced his finger down the map along the Yazoo River, the natural boundary between Shamrock and the Willingham's property. Mack looked out his side of the window at the Willingham's house. He thought Kate Willingham would have attended Irish's funeral, but she hadn't. She had written him a couple of intimate letters while he was in the Marines, but he wasn't much of a letter writer, and it wasn't as if he carried stamps and envelopes around with him at that time.

"What about you and Kate Willingham? I didn't see her at the funeral. Have you talked to her?"

Mack looked over at Buck. *Is he reading my mind?* "No, I thought I would see her at the funeral, but I didn't see any Willinghams."

"Irish didn't care for them. They are English, and she didn't trust them. Always trying to steal her land, she'd say, just like they did with the six counties of Northern Ireland."

"Yeah, she could never let that go."

"You think the Willinghams will jump at the chance to buy Shamrock now?" Buck asked.

"Maybe, but if they did, Irish would have every spirit, fairy, and leprechaun over from Ireland casting spells 24/7. Buck, I got to get something off my chest; it's been bugging me since Irish's funeral. The only way I know is to ask straight out."

"Fire away. We've never held back with each other."

"Did Carmen really find Irish already dead that morning...or was she helped in any way with her death?"

Mack waited, thinking Buck wasn't going to answer.

"The first part of your question is yes. That's the legal answer, 'died in her sleep' and that's on her death certificate, signed by her doctor. An autopsy wasn't required because she was terminally ill. Now, that *should* answer the second part of your question, as well."

"Buck, are you holding back?"

"Yes."

"Why?"

"Because others may be involved."

"Who?"

"I can tell you're not going to let this go. You have to swear that you will never breathe a word of what I tell you."

"I swear!"

"Technically, she killed herself. Planned it all for weeks. Called Carmen and me in the day before and told us she needed our help in case she passed out or was too weak to finish."

"What did you say?"

"At first I was against it, but the three of us stayed up all night talking about everything you could imagine. She was in great spirits, at peace with her decision and with God."

"How did she...?"

"Late the next morning after Carmen had bathed Irish, Carmen came and got me, and we sat on each side of Irish's bed. We all had one of her favorite drinks, the green fairy, except she had four La Fée Verte to our one, plus ten Valium."

"What?"

"Yeah, she took 10 Valium at one time. 10 milligrams, and I left."

"Why?"

"Well, on her bedside table was a box of 12 suppositories of 30 milligrams of morphine, and she didn't want me in the bedroom while they were all being inserted."

CHAPTER 15

"MEMPHIS TOWER, THIS is Cessna November 368 niner Sierra."

"Go ahead, Cessna niner Sierra, Memphis tower."

"Just letting you know I'm VFR in a Cessna 150 floatplane, ten miles south of you over the Mississippi River at 1,000 feet, landing at Memphis Harbor."

"You're on your own, niner Sierra. Wind out of the SW at six knots. Don't run over any of those big yachts down there."

"Thanks Memphis, Cessna 368 niner."

Buck looked over to Mack and said, "Yeah, and we don't want any of this Memphis air traffic running over *us*, either."

"Let's circle over King's Island and look around before we land." Mack said, while looking at an aerial map. "You know where it is, don't you?"

"No. Is it this side of the new bridge?"

Mack pointed straight ahead. "That's President Island up ahead, the big one, with the channels and buildings on it. The smaller one on the right is Treasure Island. King's Island is right in the middle of the river just north of the new bridge—about the same size as President Island. You can't miss it."

"Did Irish own it?" Buck asked.

Mack rummaged through the folder. "I couldn't find the title.

The original should be in the register's office, but according to these documents Mickey owned it and had been paying the taxes, but here's a notice where a tax lien was filed. Everything of Mickey's was left to Irish, but I don't know what it's worth. It's all vacant land.

"Here's a large newspaper article from the *Commercial Appeal* about the history of the island. I've hunted on it with Mickey and his friends. The duck hunting's great—right in the middle of the Mississippi Flyway. I remember standing in a duck blind calling ducks while watching deer swim across the river from that island," Mack said as he removed the newspaper clipping from the folder.

"It says here, 'the soil on the island is among the most fertile in the Memphis area thanks to long years of flooding.' I remember walking through acres of old soybean fields to get to the duck blinds.

We kicked up a lot of quail too."

"That must be it up ahead. What are those large mounds?"

"I don't know. Maybe burial grounds? You want to buzz those two guys working on the bridge?"

"Over it or under?"

"Under."

"Oh sure, we're probably the only floatplane in a hundred miles, and I just told Memphis where we are. The FAA would lock both of us up and keep the plane...tempting though."

"Chicken," Mack said.

"You pay the fine?"

"With what? I'm flat broke."

Buck flew the plane a couple hundred feet above the new bridge and nosedived down the other side, gliding over King's Island at treetop level.

"How big is this island?" Buck asked.

"The article says about 10,000 acres. Listen to this,

Memphis had run out of riverfront property for companies that wanted to take advantage of barge transportation. The city wanted to buy the island with the stipulation that the government builds a road over to the island. A Senator from Memphis, who was chairman of the Appropriations Committee, got the project funded for the construction of a bridge over to the island, but when it reached the island, it was left unfinished with a twenty-foot drop-off. For years Memphians called it BTN, the "bridge to nowhere," and it has been barricaded ever since. This birthed the first big environmental revolt that drew national attention. The leader was the powerful editor of the Memphis Press-Scimitar—an evening daily newspaper—and a staunch environmentalist, who vowed to dedicate a front-page article every day to stop the development of King's Island—a Chickasaw Indian burial site.

Mack continued to read and ad-lib, "Here's the kicker. This gets pretty interesting. The bridge is funded, right? So they go ahead with the construction. A lawsuit is filed by the National Association of American Indians, and here comes the government with all its power and pre-sells some of the land before the ruling of the court. The Corps of Engineers leased a dredge called the *Terra Firma* to dredge the river around the island so the towboats and barges can dock to load and unload their goods. This *Terra Firma* cuts and sucks up the floor of the Mississippi to widen the river and, at the same time, pumps the mud, sand, and whatever through floating pipes, and stockpiles it on the island. Then bulldozers level it out, raising the elevation above the 100-year flood plain. They also cut and dredge a canal into the center of the island. Somebody was preparing to make a killing. Guess what the *Terra Firma* cost the Corps of Engineers, fully manned, per day?"

"How long ago was that? 30 years...say about, $500?" Buck said.

"How about $5,000 a day, a lot of money back then. Hell, it's a lot of money now. That same land that had been valued at $20 an acre is now being sold for $6,000 an acre."

"So what happened?" Buck said.

"Well, it says here the courts ruled against the City and the Federal government. This same Tennessee Senator, through some Flood Control Act, saved all their butts and got funded an additional twenty million dollars to develop President Island, the big one we just flew over. Then the Wilson family, owners of a worldwide timber and lumber company, and long-time owners of King's Island, sued everybody involved—the City, County, State, and Federal governments. Finally, they settled the case with the Wilsons owning the BTN with all the improvements, and the City having to maintain the bridge for life."

Buck banked the plane and circled back over the island, low and slow. "Uh-oh, we've got company." He pointed below as they passed over a group of people working in a cleared field.

"What are they doing?" Mack said, looking down.

"Beats me. Let's take a closer look." Buck circled back, flew over the treetops at the edge of the cleared field, and, like a crop duster, dropped down to about twenty feet above the freshly plowed rows of black soil, but no people. "What the hell...?"

"Where'd they go?"

"You want to make another pass?"

"Yeah, fly around the perimeter. There has to be a boat somewhere."

Buck pulled back on the stick, gained a little altitude, and circled the riverbanks of the island.

"Look, there are two other cleared fields, but no boats. You want to put her down and check it out?"

"You bet. How about that boat landing there on the east side?"

"Looks good to me." Buck flew south over the treetops to the end of the island, turned left, and on final approach cut back his throttle while adding 10 degrees to the flaps. Then he cut the throttle and held back on the yoke, letting the plane settle onto the water. He lowered his water rudders, taxied up to the boat landing, and parked the plane.

"You strapped?" Mack asked as the prop stopped turning.

Buck patted his right hip, covered by his tiger-striped combat fatigues. "You?"

Mack reached behind Buck's seat, lifted his duffel bag up front, and removed his 1911 Colt 45. He racked a shell into the chamber, flipped the safety on, and pushed the pistol down in his waistband. "Let's check it out."

They stepped down out of the plane onto the concrete landing. Mack walked over to the edge of the woods where a weathered 4' x

4' plywood sign was nailed onto two trees. He read the faded red letters:

NO TRESPASSING
VIOLATORS AGGRESSIVELY PROSECUTED

Buck stayed back, observing, scanning the treetops down to the ground and the thick underbrush, looking for any signs of an entrance to a trail.

Mack stood listening, heard no sounds, not even a bird, saw no tracks, but could feel eyes watching him. A light rain began to fall. He noticed the buds on the limbs of bushes—*the start of spring.* He looked back at Buck, watched him remove his hat and scratch his bald head, sending him a signal—*be careful, I've got an itch.*

Mack nodded, turned, and took the point, a position he had taken many times on patrols. He walked along the edge of the woods, noticing the posted *No Trespassing* signs nailed to trees. He looked behind him to see what kind of tracks he was leaving and watched Buck walking along the edge of the riverbank, stopping and looking back. He waited, caught Buck's eyes, but made no signals, and started walking again.

They had gone about a mile like this when Mack stopped, raising his left hand balled into a fist. He waited, took a deep breath through his nose, and grimaced at the odor hanging in the air. He looked back at Buck, who was like a statue, waiting for a signal. The woods here had grown out closer to the water's edge, the riverbank almost gone now. Buck walked the bank, easing up beside Mack, took a couple of sniffs, and shrugged his shoulders.

They walked a few more yards until there was no more riverbank. Mack pushed underbrush and limbs aside as they turned into the woods. Buck walked behind him until they stopped at a wide chute, turned, and followed the chute as it cut back deeper into the island. The chute was covered with overhanging limbs and kudzu vines. As they worked their way inland the chute widened into a deep-water canal. They followed what looked to be a deer trail, the stink growing stronger. Mack felt his muscles tighten. It was way too quiet for a place known for so much wild game. He saw a large bushy fir tree lying across the trail in front of him and thought what a perfect place for an ambush; the leaves were still green, not brown. He turned to see if Buck had the same feeling when a loud explosion erupted. They both dropped to the ground, their heads down. A chill went through Mack when he looked up, saw the expression on Buck's face, and jerked his head back to see, but it was too late. With the explosion still ringing in their ears, out of nowhere emerged a large dark man, at least six-feet-six-inches tall, cloaked perfectly in jungle fatigues.

Mack eased his right hand up to his waistband.

The dark man shook his head as he racked another shell in the chamber of the pump shotgun to replace the one he had just fired. "Are you two so stupid you can't read, or do you just like to live dangerously?" he asked with a slight Hispanic accent.

Mack lowered his hand back down to his side and said,

"Listen..."

Buck jumped in, cutting Mack off, "We were just scouting out a place to hunt," moving up beside Mack. "We have permission from the owner to hunt on this island."

"You don't look much like hunters to me."

No one said anything. They all just stood staring at each other, at an impasse. Finally, the large man said to Buck, "Where'd you get the Marine tiger stripes?" The emblem of the eagle, globe, and anchor was on Buck's cap.

"Nam," Buck said.

"What company?"

"Special Ops, 1st Force Recon."

"Semper Fi, brother," the man said, hanging the shotgun over his shoulder, six extra shells attached to the sling. "Miguel Estrada, 2nd Battalion, 3rd Marine Division, Bravo Company." He stuck out his right hand. "You Recon guys saved my ass, up north outside of Dong Ha; my platoon was shot all to hell. Listen, you want to hunt...you two can hunt anytime you want, in or out of season, it don't matter."

"We may not want to; what the hell is that smell?" Buck said.

"Zoo shit: elephants, hippos, big cats, everything from the zoo we pick up to make compost. It's free, a great fertilizer for our truck farming business."

"We saw a lot of men out in the field when we flew over." Buck said.

A man stepped out from the edge of the woods, a long machete in his hand. In a low voice he said something to Miguel in Spanish and merged back into the woods.

"He's one of my laborers you saw in the fields. It's planting season, and they're spreading fertilizer. That's what brings out the aroma, that and the rain."

"They sure disappeared quickly when we flew over." Mack said.

"Well, you know," Miguel said smiling, "some of them may not have their green cards with them." Putting his arm around Mack's shoulders, he turned him toward the river. "You're too young for Nam; were you in the corps?"

Buck spoke up quickly, "Yeah, he was Black Ops in Panama and Desert Storm."

"Ooh-rah! Listen, mis amigos, there's a little problem with some equipment back at one of the fields that I need to take care of, so let me show you a shortcut back to your plane." Not waiting for an answer Estrada moved out onto a path leading them through the woods, still talking. "I owe you guys big time for saving my ass. Let me plan an all-day hunt for us: lunch, drinks, everything. Deer, quail, rabbit, whatever you want to hunt. How's that sound?"

A roar of thunder exploded overhead, followed by a streak of lightning across the sky, and the bottom fell out with pouring rain. Miguel hesitated, then turned and started walking back in the other direction. "I got a lean-to about a half a klick this way; let's get out of the rain."

Mack noticed Estrada's limp as they followed him alongside the river chute until they came to a long barge and a pontoon boat camouflaged with overhanging trees anchored at the end of the chute. They rushed across a gangplank and hurried under a huge tent-like tarpaulin stretched over a rope and tied off between two trees. A coffee pot sat on the cook-top wood-burning stove in the middle of the sheltered area surrounded by men. To the side of the stove was a brick fire pit with chunks of meat, large jalapeño peppers, onions, and tortillas cooking on a flat sheet of metal. Some of the men were squatting and moved to the wood benches, eating their tacos.

"Sit, my friends, and have some deer meat and coffee. We can't go anywhere in this storm. Buck, tell me about your tours in Nam."

Mack was hungry, but the overpowering smell of manure was so strong, he was afraid he would barf if he ate anything. He was doing well to sip black coffee from an old bean can. He watched Buck, smiling at him, as he chowed down on a taco. The heat from the stove felt good as the rain continued to come down in force. He listened half-heartedly to their Vietnam war stories, his eyes growing heavy. He still hadn't recovered from the 22-hour drive straight through from Aspen.

"I'll never forget that day..." Mack heard Miguel say and watched him take a machete and spread a pile of ashes over the floor of the barge, drawing out a map. He used pieces of wood and rocks to mark specific locations. "We'd been out patrolling along the DMZ, humping it all day, when we got orders to check out this *deserted* hamlet, one hill over from our designated LZ Pickup. The men were tired, hot, and ready to go back to camp. I overheard the Captain's voice over the radio talking to our Lieutenant—"*I don't like these orders, but they came down from Battalion. Just be careful. I wouldn't be surprised if Charlie or the NVA had crossed over the river and set up shop there...*"

Mack felt a tap on his shoulder, and heard a whisper, "Senor, mas café?" Mack had no idea how long he had been catnapping. He saw his spilled coffee can on the ground between his legs and picked it up.

"Gracias," Mack said, sticking out his can.

"Muy caliente, Senor," the man said as he poured.

Mack noticed that Buck and Miguel were drinking shots of tequila with their coffee. Miguel was still talking.

"Man, it was like the sound track in that Apocalypse movie when those helicopters attacked the beach hamlets. The Hueys hovered above, steadily sweeping the hedgerows on each side of the field with their four M-60 machine guns. Right behind the Hueys, Zeus Leader in his huge CH-53 descended like a house coming down on us, both door gunners firing their machine guns on full automatic.

"There was no hesitation, no fear. The 53 landed directly into the middle of the battlefield and before the rear ramp hit the ground, a pack of Devil Dog Marines raced each other to the fight. It was a death squad of combat-loaded Recon Marines trained for precision bloodletting. Half of them set up a line of fire on each side of the chopper, and the others loaded the dead and wounded.

"In the middle of all the noise and the heavy rotor wash, we heard the sonic boom of two Marine F-4 Phantom jets break the sound barrier. Following the air traffic directions of Spooky, they dropped out of the blackish sky like a fireball meteor and leveled off at 200 feet, releasing their napalm bombs that exploded over the hedgerows like molten lava. Man, this was all split second timing, a perfectly executed operation. Your Recon guys carried our wounded and dead while bullets tore through both sides of the chopper. LT, DD, and I leaned on each other as we hobbled up the back ramp. We all sat on the deck trance-like, bloodied and bandaged, next to the stacked litters of bodies hanging from the bulkhead.

"As the chopper lifted off into the dark, I counted what was left of our platoon: eight Wounded-In-Action (WIA), all sedated from shots of morphine.

"I watched the rear-loading ramp close as we headed for the NSA hospital in Da Nang, then I removed a morphine syrette that DD had given me and popped it in my thigh. As my eyes adjusted to the dim lighting inside, I removed my helmet and stretched out on the aluminum deck, when a sudden downdraft jerked the chopper a quarter turn to the left, rolling me against the port bulkhead. I tried to move back but kept slipping, and realized I was lying in a large pool of blood that had dripped from the bodies of my men hanging above. The morphine kicked in, and I closed my eyes and started counting the 21 names KIA to the beat of the rotor blades: whomp, whomp, whomp, whomp...."

CHAPTER 16

BUCK WAS FLYING copilot so he could check Mack out in the 150G floatplane. Mack taxied the Cessna from King's Island over to the Memphis Service Center.

"What about Miguel Estrada's war story, the farther from the battle, the thicker the flak?" Mack asked.

"He's a bullshitter alright, exaggerated his part a little, tequila will do that sometimes, but it happened. There's an official record of the twenty-one Marines, KIA. They interviewed every one of the survivors, and even teach this screw-up—of what not to do—at Quantico, in Officer Candidates School. They tried to keep it quiet, but there was a war correspondent there when the Super Bird landed at the hospital. Shortly after that, a photo of the bodies being unloaded was all over the front page of *Time* magazine with a story of the whole fiasco. The staff officer who gave the stupid order retired a month after the story broke.

"You got the water rudders down?"

Mack flipped the rudder switch, and the pedals tightened up.

"Hold out your hand." Buck dropped a handful of seeds into Mack's palm.

"What's this?"

"Weed seeds."

"Marijuana?"

Buck nodded his head.

"Are you planning on growing your own?" Mack asked as he taxied down river at idle speed, touching the rudder pedals now and then to keep the plane straight.

"Nope. You know where I got these seeds?"

"No idea."

"From one of those five-gallon paint buckets on Sergeant Estrada's barge."

"No shit? They're not planting corn?"

"Oh yeah, they're planting corn, but next to every other stalk of corn, there's going to be a stalk of *Mary Jane*. Remember that article from the newspaper you read to me about King's Island—'The soil on the island is among the most fertile in the Memphis area thanks to long years of flooding.'"

"How many buckets were there?" Mack asked.

"Five that I saw."

"25 gallons...that's a lot of weed."

"That's a lot of money."

Mack reached the foot of Beale Street, and made a wide U-turn, and taxied up the Wolf River Lagoon. He saw a deckhand waving from one of the barges with the sign, *MALLOY MARINE SERVICE* above the marina, but he taxied past the barge, throttled back to idle, and let the current push him over to the end of the barge. "Nice move," Buck said.

The deckhand grabbed the wing of the plane as one of the floats banged against the rubber tires hanging over the side of the barge.

Buck tied the plane off while the deckhand held the wing. Li met them halfway across the barge, "How'd it go?"

"Interesting. Very top heavy," Mack said as they walked toward the offices. "Too much overhead, too many employees, too much payroll. As Irish used to say, 'If it ain't paying for itself, get rid of it.' I need you to get me the P and L statements on all the service centers; we'll start with this one."

"I've got your office all set up, and ah...there's some big, ragged-looking guy, waiting for you. He wouldn't tell me his name or what he wanted, just said you knew him."

Mack stopped walking and stared at both of them, shaking his head, "Listen up, I don't care if it's the Pope, I don't want no one, ever, in my office without me being there. I can't be bothered with putting out grass fires while the whole damn city is burning down around me. You're going to have to take some initiative, understand?"

Mack stormed off without waiting for an answer. Buck hurried behind him, catching the door before it shut, and followed him down the hallway. Mack jerked the door open to his office and stared at the *last* person he expected to see...Angus McGregor, wrinkled clothes and unshaven.

Mack still had his Colt 45 stuck in his front waistband, and when Buck saw the heated look on Mack's face he stepped out in front.

"What do you want?" Buck asked.

"Easy, guys," Angus said, looking at Mack's gun. "I'm not looking for trouble. The Oriental fellow said I could wait here for Mack Shannon."

Mack realized Angus didn't recognize him without his beard and long hair. He walked behind his desk, removed the pistol from his waistband, and placed it on his desktop, the barrel pointed toward Angus. "I'm Mack Shannon. What do you want?" He said, still standing.

"Sorry Buddy, you're not Mack Shannon," Angus said, starting to get up from the chair.

"Stay seated, *Buddy!*" Buck ordered, pulling the corner of his utility jacket up and resting his hand on his pistol.

Angus dropped back down in the chair, "What's with all the guns?"

Mack stared at Angus, remembering the night Angus blindsided him.

"He will kill you for this!" Bella said.

"Naw, I don't think so," Angus said.

I will kill him for this, Mack swore.

Mack, still staring at Angus, picked up the 45 automatic, ejected the clip, inserted it back into the butt of the handle, and banged it with the heel of his hand. *I've got to pay him back for that. Don't kill him; maybe blow his kneecap off.*

"Do you realize how close I came to killing you and your two dogs and burning your house down? Be thankful you were not home. You might want to think about that before you break the next guy's face with a sucker punch. Vengeance is much more powerful than a forearm."

Dr. Kris Nanda had explained to Mack. "Let me show you something. See this line. That's your bottom jaw and, last night, with all the swelling, it was over here. This latest film shows it here, right where it belongs. I'm going to take the tape off, but you'll have to eat through a straw for a couple of days, lots of smoothies. The black eyes, nose, teeth, jaws...." Angus now realized it *was* Mack Shannon behind the desk.

Mack continued, "Crime *does* pay, Angus. Only about 13% are caught...and most of those are dumbasses. Take a methodical person, like Buck here, trained with first-hand experience. He could slit your throat in a second, but that would be very messy, or he could just shoot you. But guess what his specialty is? Strangulation—swift...silent...deadly—and within a few steps you'd be rolling down the river, weighed down with a log chain wrapped around you." Mack waited, staring at Angus. "What's wrong? You're not so brave now...the odds a little different, huh?"

"You're right...do what you want. I don't give a damn," Angus said, standing up. "I have no excuses. I was drunk, stupid. Go ahead, beat the hell out of me, I don't care. But I'm not going to stand still while you do it. We'll tear this office up, and I will get some licks in, but you can't beat me down any more than I am now. I've lost my job, my house, car, wife, and my dogs; so just go ahead and shoot my ass, I don't care."

"I thought you played football for Denver?" Mack asked.

"I did...they fired me." Angus dropped back down into the chair. "I was drunk at practice, the second time. I laid up drunk for two weeks after that, then my wife left me, closed my bank accounts, and took all the furniture, even the light bulbs and the toilet paper from the holders. I was drunk when served with the divorce papers and fell down the front steps chasing the process server. The bank foreclosed on my house, and I'm down to less than twenty bucks to my name."

"What do you want from me?" Mack asked.

"Don't get me wrong. I'm not trying to have a pity party here. It's my fault. I have a big- time drinking problem, and I brought it on myself. The team doctor said it best, 'You're a drunk and will stay a drunk until *you* decide to do something about it.' I'm trying to do something about it now, and I thought if I had my dogs...well, I came here to apologize and beg, if necessary, for my dogs."

Mack sat down behind his desk and put his pistol in one of the drawers.

"I don't know. I just woke up on a park bench one morning with an empty bottle of vodka and throwing up blood. Everything I had was gone. I started hitchhiking back to Oxford to see my mom and dad and figured I'd start there. When the trucker dropped me off on Riverside out there, I remembered Bella telling me someone in your family died and left you a business on Riverside, towboats and barges, she said."

Mack picked up the phone on his desk and pushed one of the buttons. "Ask Li to come to my office, please."

Buck backed off and took a seat on the other side of the room as Li entered the office.

"Li, this is Angus McGregor. Show him to the kitchen and make sure he's taken care of. We'll talk some more after you've finished eating."

"What are you now, Mother Teresa?" Buck said after Li and Angus had left the office. "He puts you in the hospital, and you *console* him?"

"He's down and out. What? You want me to do a toe dance on his head?"

"Don't lose that warrior instinct."

"Buck, we've all had too much to drink at one time or another and made stupid mistakes."

"Not the same. He's a drunk, an alcoholic, and *you* can't help him."

"I like him. He's got guts. I respect that, and he needs help."

Buck shrugged his shoulders, "Remember, no good deed goes unpunished."

Mack stood up and checked his pockets, "You got any money on you?"

Buck reached into his pockets and shook his head, "Couple of bucks, maybe."

"Have Li get someone to run up on Beale to Lansky's Brothers and buy Angus a double extra-large sweat suit. After he's through eating get him showered and his clothes cleaned. He smells like a goat. Then I want to see him. And Buck, tell Li to put you on the payroll and get us some pocket money. I'm broke."

Mack sat behind his desk, looking at more file boxes stacked on the floor. He opened one of the folders on his desk and removed the master sheets Li and he had been working on. *I hate doing this. Okay, okay, just take small bites at a time.*

There was a knock on the door, and Li walked in. "Angus is in the shower. I got him some coveralls to wear while his clothes are in the washer. He's a nice fellow."

"Did you talk to Buck?"

"Mack, there is *no* money, not even for a sweat suit or pocket money. The banks have closed most of our accounts, and the few we have open, I'm afraid if I put in any money someone would put a lien on the account. We've got a lot of judgments against us already, and the attorney fees and interest on what we owe are mounting up every day. I've been operating on a cash basis, giving everyone a 5% discount that pays us in cash, and I've let half our workers go; we're barely breaking even. I haven't had a paycheck in the last two months."

"Damn!" Mack said under his breath. "What have I gotten myself into?" He felt a migraine building. *What was Irish's favorite saying? "Throw up a bullet prayer, like King Solomon did, ask your father, your heavenly Father." Why not, I got nothing to lose. Oh Lord, if you can help me I'd appreciate it.*

"You okay?" Li asked.

"Yeah, a little headache, that's all." *What was the name of that vault company in Irish's letter?* He started looking through one of the folders on his desk. "Do we have Mickey's car?"

"It's up in the warehouse, a little dusty but a great car."

"Have Angus clean it up and come get me when he's finished. I'm going to be gone for a couple of hours. Oh, and have someone put a lock on my door with four keys, one for you and Buck and two for me, thanks."

Mack searched his desk drawers until he found the phone book. Looking under American Security Vault Company, he wrote the address down and called the number, asking for Mary Singer. He was told she wasn't in.

Later, he had a long talk with Angus, and at the end, he offered him a job. But Mack told him the company was broke but could give him room and board and a little pocket change, and later it may lead into something more *if* he stopped drinking. Angus jumped at the offer. He told Mack he would do anything to keep busy and swore he was going to join AA.

Angus was cleaning out file cabinets while Mack labeled folders he wanted filed. There was a knock on the door, and Buck came in.

"Guess who's outside wanting to see you?"

"I'll bite, Michael Anthony?"

"Who's Michael Anthony?"

"*The Millionaire.* The name of an old TV show...where Michael Anthony gave away a million dollars to a total stranger...never mind."

"Well, you got the first name right, but I don't think he's bringing you a million dollars. It's Miguel Estrada."

"The Sergeant?"

"One and only."

"Well, Semper Fi, show the brother in."

The Mexican walked in smiling, carrying a brown paper sack wrapped with tape under his arm.

"Mis amigos. When are we all going hunting?" Miguel placed the sack on the corner of Mack's desk, and they shook hands. Buck introduced Angus to Miguel and after some small talk, Miguel asked Mack if he could talk to him alone, no offense to Buck and Angus, just business.

With a slight nod from Mack, Buck and Angus left the room. Miguel told Mack of the business arrangement his boss had with Mack's Uncle Mickey on renting King's Island. And now that Mickey had passed away, Miguel's boss was wondering who to pay the past couple of years' rent to and if Mack would continue to honor the same deal. Miguel stood up and placed a sealed letter from his boss on top of the package and said it was all in the letter.

"I wrote my phone number on the back of the envelope in case you wanted to talk to me, privately you know, in case you have any questions or whatever. I have no idea what's in the letter or the package; today I'm just the deliveryman." Miguel reached across the desk and shook Mack's hand and walked out the door.

Mack opened and read the letter:

Hey Mack, it's been a long time. You still have that wicked left hook? I realize the last time we had any dealings with each other, it turned out badly. But the past is the past, and we all have scars from the past, right? I hope there are no hard feelings. None on my part, that's for sure. Your Uncle Mickey rented me King's Island, but when he died I didn't know who to send the rent money to or if they sold the island or what. My lawyer tells me you inherited the island and that the estate is in financial trouble. I would like to talk to you about buying the island. I'll help you and you help me. Meanwhile, I have sent you a token of my sincerity to show you I mean business. Let the big Mex know when you want to meet.
— Ray Flynn

"Ray Flynn...*Crazy Ray Flynn?*" Mack looked up as if asking the question to someone in the room. He stared at the paper bag, lifted it, and set it down, then removed the tape and opened it cautiously. He jerked his chair back and jumped up, as if a coiled rattlesnake was hissing at him. He lifted the sack and turned it upside down on the desk. He couldn't believe his eyes as they focused on the pile of hundred dollar bills spilled out over his desk. He walked across the room and locked his door, then stood in front of his desk looking at the money. *How much is there?* he wondered. He started counting.

Twenty-five stacks of one hundred dollar bills, each stack wrapped with $1,000 printed on the paper wrapper—$25,000! *Wait till Buck and Angus see this.* He headed for the door, then stopped—*wait a minute, not so fast—THINK!* He went back to his desk, cleaned out one of the bottom drawers, and scooped the money inside.

He leaned back in his chair...why is Crazy Ray giving me $25,000? I know he's a crook. Is it back rent for leasing the island? Maybe his lawyer told him to make the payments current. Or it's hush money because he knows now that we know about him growing marijuana on the island. If he's paying me 25 grand, what kind of money is he making? Or did one bullet prayer cause all this? I don't think so, but what if? Mack looked up at the ceiling, put his hands together as he had done when he was a child at Mass every morning, and prayed, *Thank you Lord.* He made the sign of the cross and added—*just make sure the money is real.*

He unlocked the door and walked to the kitchen, found Angus, and told him to get Buck and meet him back in his office.

Buck and Angus sat in front of Mack's desk. "You know I don't believe in voodoo or any other mystical powers. But I've been reading this book that Father O'Brien gave me years ago, *Think and Grow Rich.*

It preaches this philosophy: *Whatever the human mind can conceive and believe it can achieve.* Also, there's this chapter called, 'The Master Mind Group.' Napoleon Hill, the author, talks about if you get two or more people together who think the same and focus on the same concept—long enough and hard enough—it will happen. I know it sounds strange, but I tried it by myself last week, and it happened."

"What happened?" Angus asked.

"Hold your horses. I want to try it with us three and see what happens, okay?"

Buck and Angus looked at each other, shrugged their shoulders, and nodded their heads.

"Now don't interrupt me, just do what I say. What do we need more than anything right now, *money*, lots of it, right? So, let's focus on money. Remember, 'whatever the human mind can conceive and believe it can achieve.' *Mooooney!*"

Angus looked over at Buck, smiling.

"I'm serious. Close your eyes, and don't open them till I tell you. I want you to *think...focus* on nothing but money. Picture it in your mind, lots of it. Green...hundred dollar bills." Mack opened the bottom drawer of his desk and grabbed four stacks and removed the paper wrappers. "Keep your eyes closed, now think, think money! Let me hear you say MONEY!" All three shouted MOOOONEY at the same time, and Mack threw the hundred dollar bills high in the air and grabbed another handful, and threw that. Hundred dollar bills were floating all over the room, falling on Buck and Angus as they opened their eyes.

"Manna from heaven," Mack shouted, his feet propped up on his desk, taking a couple of stacks and throwing them directly at Buck and Angus.

"What in the world? What did you do, rob a bank?" Buck asked.

"My God, Mack, how much money is this? How much?" Angus asked, picking the money up with both hands.

Mack told them about his past history with Crazy Ray and his meeting today with Miguel, as they all picked up the money and stacked it on Mack's desk. Buck told Angus about the marijuana farm and how Miguel was planting corn and marijuana together on King's Island.

"Okay," Mack said, "let's think about this. We're drowning, and one of the biggest crooks in Memphis just threw us a life raft, but crooks like Crazy Ray don't give away twenty- five grand for nothing. Obviously, he wanted to get my attention, but why? We all know there's a rope attached to that raft."

"How many acres did you say is on this island?" Angus asked.

"10,000."

"At a dollar an acre, which is dirt cheap, is $10,000 a year."

"Yeah, and that's all that's on the island, just dirt," Mack said.

"Not now," Buck said.

"How much of that is planted?" Angus asked.

"We saw at least three cleared fields and each were about two-to three-acre patches," Buck said.

Angus picked up a pen and piece of paper from Mack's desk. "Let's figure everything on the low end and say the growing fields are two-acre patches. If you planted 1,000 plants, mixed in with corn, say every four feet—that will give you a bushy, high yield plant—which should produce a little over 1,000 pounds per patch. You multiply that by the three cleared fields gives you 3,000 pounds. Multiply that by a farm gate price, wholesale, of good stuff, say $800 to $1,000...."

"Three *million* a year!" Mack said.

"That's conservatively speaking. If he has his own distributors, retailing instead of selling it wholesale, he could double that. Your friend Crazy Ray is not so crazy."

"How do you know all this?" Buck asked.

"I worked on a pot farm when I was in college."

"Where?"

"Ole Miss. They have the only legal—paid for by the US Government—seven-acre marijuana research farm in the country."

"In Oxford, Mississippi? Unbelievable," Mack said.

"You can believe it," Angus said, "and primo weed."

Mack was excited; he felt something developing from the chapter he had read about the power of a mastermind group. "I want to try something. I want us to focus on nothing but what to do with this money...and with Crazy Ray. Let's meet tomorrow and see who comes up with the best idea."

"What about Li?" Buck asked.

"Not just now. We'll talk about that tomorrow. Later on we can include anyone we agree on. But they must have a positive attitude and the same goals as all of us," Mack said.

"And what goal is that?" Angus asked.

"M & M Baby—*making money*," Mack said, throwing a handful of hundred dollar bills at them as they were leaving. "Hold on a minute." Mack picked up the bills from the floor and handed them to Buck. "Split this, pocket money, no reason for us to be completely broke. Hey, don't forget, loose-lips-sink-ships. Say nothing to no one; for now it's only the three of us."

The black Fleetwood Cadillac stopped at the front door of the American Security Vault Company. Mack got out of the car and watched as Angus drove off to wait in the parking lot. He had called and made an appointment with Mary Singer and was dressed in his only suit, the navy Brioni; he felt empowered when wearing it, especially when the pockets were stuffed with hundred dollar bills. The building was three stories tall and to Mack, unassuming, except for the disguised security cameras surrounding the building. Inside it was just the opposite: all plush, lots of polished brass, floors covered in marble and thick carpet, and what appeared to be bullet-proof glass. A guard met Mack as he stepped inside and asked him to wait while he called for Mary Singer. After talking on the phone, the guard motioned for him to walk through a thick glass vestibule. Another guard watched on a monitor as Mack stood inside the enclosed glassed area until a buzzer went off. A door on the other side opened, and the guard motioned for him to pass on through. Mary Singer introduced herself, and Mack followed her into her office. Once all the paperwork was finished and Mack had signed a signature card, he followed Singer into a huge steel vault filled with automatic sliding walls on rollers. She walked down about twenty feet, hit a button, and the walls parted. Mack followed her between the two walls, stopped about halfway down, and faced a wall of safe deposit boxes of all sizes. She asked Mack for his key, opened the locks with his and her key, and gave him back his key. Mack removed the metal box, and followed her to a private room.

He closed and locked the door, looked around and above his head, suspicious of a hidden camera, then lifted the top of the box. He removed a handful of envelopes, made a quick inspection, and found real estate titles and some deeds of trust. On the bottom of the box he found a velvet jewelry bag with a diamond ring, a diamond bracelet, and a diamond necklace. He dumped the box over, and a red paisley bandana tumbled out. He untied the handkerchief and found gold; twenty Krugerrands and fifteen $20 dollar U.S. gold coins. He looked in the desk drawer and found a stack of canvas bags with drawstrings. Printed across the front was American Security Vault Company. He grabbed a bag and stuffed everything inside, removed the money from his pockets, and stacked it inside the safe deposit box and took it back to the vault. No one was there, so he slid the box back in its hole and locked the door. The glass doors were locked when Mack tried to leave. He stood waiting, the guard staring at him. The buzzer went off, the door opened, and Mack walked in. When the door shut behind him, the front glass door opened, and he walked out of the vault area saying, "good-day" to the guard at the door as he left the building.

Back in the car, Mack removed a card from an envelope he had taken from the safe deposit box. "Let's head for a jewelry store downtown, a Julius Goodman and Sons on Madison."

"I know that store. My family always shopped there when they came to Memphis. They bought my watch there," Angus said. Mack looked at Angus's wrist, "Where is it now?"

"I pawned it for a case of vodka."

"You know if they buy jewelry?"

"Don't they all? Honest Abe, that's how my parents referred to him."

"I thought it was *Julius* Goodman?" Mack was looking at the card.

"It is, you know, but Honest Abe, they just called him that 'cause he's honest. A lot of Jews are named Abraham."

"I thought Honest Abe referred to Abraham Lincoln?"

"Yes, but..." Angus shrugged his shoulders. *Damn...and he went to Harvard?*

Angus parked in front of Julius Goodman & Son on Madison, and Mack went inside. The sign read "Memphis Jewelers Since 1862." A bunch of old guys worked in the store, and when Mack asked for Mr. Julius Goodman, they walked him to a small room in the back. Mr. Goodman was as old as the others but got up from his desk and shook Mack's hand, saying he was *Joseph* Goodman. After looking at the jewelry, he told Mack that his father, Julius, had made the diamond ring for a lady in Mississippi over fifty years ago and that I should not sell it. He said that the diamond was a flawless five-carat, one of a kind, and that he should save it for when he got married. Mr. Goodman didn't allow how he knew Mack wasn't married. He said the bracelet was worth about $1,800 and the necklace was very pretty costume jewelry. He told Mack that gold was bidding for $358.32 an ounce and offered Mack $7,100.00 for the 20 gold Krugerrands, which included his $60.00 fee between bid and ask. He added that he should keep the $20 dollar gold pieces for his kids, as they were excellent coins. Honest Abe, or as Mack found out, Honest Joe, was like his father, Julius, and their last name, *Good*-man. Mack stuck the ring and the $20 dollar gold coins in his pocket and walked out with $8,900.00, in cash. At the door, Mack asked Mr. Goodman why he had charged him $60.00 for *buying* the Krugerrands. Joseph whispered, "Never stop a man from making a little profit off you," and held up his thumb and index finger, almost touching, "jus' a little, it makes for good business."

By the time Mack and Angus got back to the office, Buck and Li were waiting for their first "Master Mind Group" meeting.

When Buck and Angus left Mack's office the other day, Mack had walked down to Li's office and asked if he wanted to walk-and-talk, a term he used a lot. While walking out on the barges, Mack told Li most of everything about the money, Crazy Ray, Miguel, and he touched a little on how fast and profitable the *farming* business could be.

Li, not a big talker unless it was about his family history, had told Mack before about his grandfather's boat business along the South China coast. He said that his grandfather had many subcontractors, individual boat owners that operated all along the coast, in and out of small ports, docks, inlets, and coves. They bought, sold, and traded a variety of merchandise, but the more profitable were the black market goods, like alcohol and tobacco. In many countries, especially in the Muslim world, alcohol was forbidden, but the big profit was in opium, which was legal in China at the time, and that's where his grandfather made a fortune. But around 1917 the Emperor's ten-year plan of outlawing opium had worked. After years of steady demoralization, with half the population addicted to opium and making enormous profits out of the trade, all opium fields were destroyed and all import of opium was banned from China. That same year Li's grandfather retired and moved his family to America. Walking back to the office from the barge that day, Mack invited Li to join the "Master Mind Group."

Mack stood behind his desk and reached inside a paper bag. "I bought five of these paperbacks, *Think and Grow Rich*, and I want each of you to have a copy. There are 15 chapters and we are starting off on Chapter 10, 'Power Of The Master Mind.' Read that first so we all can be on the same page. I could talk for hours about Napoleon Hill, his 20 years of research, and his personal interviews with the richest men in the world, but I want you to read and experience the simplicity of his principals of making money.

"Immediately, the questions we need to answer today, or at least discuss: What to do with the $25,000, what to do with Crazy Ray, and what about the *farming* business over on King's Island? Li, tell us what you think."

"I'm going to throw this out to all of you—it's just for discussion and my opinion only. If you want to make money and make it fast, you've got to go into business for yourself, not work for someone else. Let's don't beat around the bush here. We all know what that the big question is, do we want to go into the *farming* business?"

There was immediate talking among the four of them.

"Let me add one more thing," Li said. "Angus knows more about this type of farming than any of us, but I think it comes down to this: For all four of us and for *this* time and place, this would be the fastest way to make the most money with the least liability—again, just my opinion. The problem with the liability is it's illegal, but not the same thing as robbing a bank."

Mack said, "Let's hear what Angus has to say."

"God knows I've thought about it, especially after looking at fields of it every day being grown legally. Everybody that toked a doobie or blazed a blunt has thought about it, and I know plenty who have made a lot of money growing it. It paid for their four years of college, and a lot of professors at school bought their product. The reason most legitimate people, I mean people who are not pot heads or criminals, *don't* go into the business is because of the risk. If caught, there is the stigma of having a record as a drug dealer. The truth is alcohol kills over 100,000 people a year and, as far as I know, no one has ever died from smoking weed. The main factor to consider is the odds on the risk, and they're pretty low. Some other factors would be: Do you want to grow it or transport it? Do you want to wholesale or retail? And how long do you want to operate the business? The longer you're in, the higher the chances of someone finding out. What do you think, Buck?"

"Those are good questions. All of you know I've spent most of my life in the Marine Corps, in and out of combat, and I don't have a penny to show for it. True, I didn't save much, but then again I never thought I would live this long. I don't need a lot of money to live, but I'll *never* let them foreclose on my hunting club and the little bit that I do own. The risks don't bother me a damn."

Mack told the group he had put most of the $25,000 in a safe deposit box for the time being, and they spent another hour discussing what to do about Crazy Ray. Li wanted to think about it some more; Buck's suggestion was for him to have an accident. Angus reminded everyone that *Mack* now owned the island, that they should just take possession, right after planting season of course, and hire Miguel to run the business. What could Crazy Ray do? Go to the police?

"Why do anything?" Mack asked.

"What do you mean?" Buck said.

"Just don't respond, as if I never got the money. As Angus said, 'What's he going to do, go to the police?'"

CHAPTER 17

MIGUEL ESTRADA PLACED his umbrella in the corner of Mack's office before sitting down. Outside a strong wind and hard rain caused the barge to bob up and down.

"Not good planting weather huh, Miguel?"

"No, Mr. Shannon, not good at all."

"Is this a business call or pleasure?"

"It is always a pleasure to see you, my friend, but my boss sent me. He was wondering when you would like to meet with him?"

"About what?"

"Maybe the package he sent you?"

"What package?"

Miguel's peaceful eyes became alert; the pupils contracted to black dots, like two bullets boring in on Mack.

Mack continued to stare at Miguel.

A smile grew on Miguel's face, showing a row of white teeth against his dark complexion. "I understand...this is a joke, right? You two are old friends."

"Friends? No we have never been friends."

The smile disappeared and, after a long pause, Miguel said, "This could cause me a lot of trouble."

"You're in a dangerous business. How long have you worked for Crazy Ray?"

"He doesn't like to be called that."

"I'll bet he doesn't. What do you call him?"

"Mr. Flynn."

"What all do you do for *Mr.* Flynn?"

"Mr. Shannon, I'm walking on thin ice here. Ray Flynn is not someone to toy with. He's a very rich man with a short fuse...let me just say, I'm paid well."

"Good for you, Miguel. What else can I do for you today?"

"I didn't mean to piss you off."

"No, I have a lot of work to finish up here."

"What do you want me to tell Mr. Flynn?"

"Tell Crazy Ray whatever you want." Mack stood up, "Nice seeing you again Miguel, adios."

Miguel stood up with a puzzled look on his face. He shrugged his shoulders and left Mack's office.

The next day Mack opened the blinds in his office and saw a new S600 Mercedes park at an angle, taking up two parking spaces. This was the car he coveted. He'd even torn out the centerfold ad from Angus' *GQ* magazine. But like a beautiful virgin you've dreamed of, only later to find is no more than a whore, Crazy Ray stepped from the Mercedes and spoiled Mack's desire of ever owning this model.

Crazy Ray looked like a survivor from one of Auschwitz's concentration camps. His suit hung from a bony body; he couldn't have weighed more than a hundred pounds. Mack only recognized him because Dago was helping him from the car.

There was a knock on the door, and Angus stuck his head in, smiling, "There's a Ray Flynn here to see you."

"Show them in," Mack said, then motioned for Angus to stay, "Keep your eye on the big guy."

Crazy Ray and Dago entered Mack's office and stood looking around, then walked over to shake Mack's hand. Mack did not get up from his chair nor offer his hand.

"Oookay," Crazy Ray said, easing himself into a chair across the desk from Mack. Dago continued to stand. "You look great, Mack."

"I can't say the same for you." Mack assumed he was bald. He couldn't see any sideburns or hair in the back below his baseball cap. He was emaciated, even with the cover of pancake makeup he had on.

"Stomach cancer, but they caught it, cut it all out, and I've had my last chemo treatment." He removed the cap and rubbed his head. "Little fuzz back already."

They both waited for the other to say something. Finally Crazy Ray spoke up. "I thought it would be better if we talked face to face."

"About what?"

"About the package and letter I sent you."

"I don't know what you're talking about."

"The hell you don't!" Crazy Ray exploded.

Mack knew that Crazy Ray and Dago were always armed. He opened his desk drawer and placed his Colt 45 automatic on the top of his desk. "Are you calling me a liar? If you are, you'd better leave now and take your girlfriend with you."

Dago went to move, and Angus stepped between him and Mack. Crazy Ray reached up and grabbed Dago's arm. "Wait! Wait a minute...I spoke too quickly. Let's start all over. It's my medicine, makes me nervous, jumpy. Forget the letter. It was a bad idea anyway. I should have come here myself. Let's just focus on business."

"I don't have any business with you and, if I did, it wouldn't be in front of Bozo, here."

"Dago's okay. He knows my business."

"No, it's not okay. He doesn't know my business, and he's not going to. If you want to talk to me, he waits outside."

Crazy Ray looked up at Dago and nodded his head toward the door. Dago puffed up and snarled like a trained dog on a leash but left the room with Angus close behind.

"This is exactly what I didn't want to happen...us getting off on the wrong foot. It's not good business." After a coughing spell, he removed a bottle of red liquid from his coat pocket, and sprayed inside his throat. "I can't get rid of this cough or sore throat; it keeps hanging on.

"Mack, I've always liked you. You're smarter than the rest and tougher too. I should have brought the twenty-five grand to you personally. We can make a lot of money together."

"Yeah, like the American Snuff Company, huh?"

"That was Dago; the cops beat the hell out of him, made him talk."

"I'm not interested in going into business with anyone."

"I'm into a lot of things now, own different businesses, legit businesses. I could help you get started in your own business."

"Why?"

"I help you. You help me."

"Help you what?"

"You need money. That's why I sent you the twenty-five thousand deposit for the island, to show you my good faith. The taxes are overdue on the island, and it's just sitting there. I'll pay you a fair price, in cash."

"How much?"

"You tell me. I'm easy."

"You're the one who wants the island. What's your *fair* price?"

"I'll tell you what I'll do...you keep the twenty-five grand and I'll add another, say two hundred and twenty five thousand. That's more than fair, two hundred and fifty thousand total."

"Twenty-five bucks an acre? You're joking, right?"

"See, that's what I'm talking about, Mack. You're quick. You have Harvard book smarts, but more important, you have street smarts. You're also smart enough to know no one wants to buy that land; it's been vacant for years, and a lot of it's in the flood plain.

"Okay, no more bullshit...I should know better than to try to fool you. My last offer, but don't give me an answer today. Think about it and then call me. Five hundred thousand dollars! Half a million, Mack; you'd be set for life." With a little trouble he pushed himself up out of the chair and walked to the door. "Check on it; it's a good offer."

"Is that cash and the twenty-five grand included?"

"Yeah, all in hundred dollar bills," Crazy Ray said as he left Mack's office.

Later, Mack met with Li, Buck, and Angus to talk about the offer of a half a million dollars. At first, Mack agreed with the others to take the money, "a bird in the hand is worth two in the bush," they were all singing. Mack thought about it for a long time. He could put out a lot of fires with half a million—pay everyone off and have plenty of money left to rejuvenate the Marine Service Centers, Shamrock Farms, and what he was personally interested in, expanding the commercial and industrial side of the construction business. If Angus' numbers were right, and Crazy Ray wasn't just "dangling the carrot before a starving rabbit...."

But he had this nagging suspicion he could be walking across a minefield. He leaned back in his chair, closed his eyes, and took a deep breath...*what to do, what to do?* When he opened his eyes, he noticed Napoleon Hill's book on his desk and picked it up. Fanning the pages he stopped on the chapter about the three P's—positive thinking, patience, and persistence. That's what he needed, *patience*; he was always quick to make a decision, maybe too quick in this case...*why the rush?*

Napoleon was right. Two day later, Crazy Ray called and offered Mack one million dollars for King's Island. He said his real estate attorney had drawn up a contract with a purchase price of five hundred thousand dollars and, at closing, Crazy Ray would hand Mack another package with half a million dollars in undisclosed cash. There was only one stipulation; he had to have an answer in twenty-four hours.

All day Mack argued with himself about that damn axiom "a bird in the hand" but continued to focus on *patience* again. Look what just happened; the offer doubled. No telling what another twenty-four hours would bring!

That evening as Mack and Angus walked to the car, a black Chevy Suburban with dark windows pulled up beside them. Mack waited as the driver's window was lowered.

"Hola, Señor Shannon."

"Hola, Miguel. What happened to your face?" Miguel had a white bandage over his left eye, and his bottom lip was swollen with stitches almost down to his chin.

"Can we talk?" Miguel asked.

Mack invited Miguel to follow them to Finnegan's Wake, a pub at the foot of Beale Street overlooking the river. Once inside, they ordered drinks and Miguel told them how Crazy Ray had blamed him for the mix up with the money. The twenty-five thousand was not for back rent, but a deposit if Mack agreed to sell the island. Miguel argued he knew nothing about what was in the letter or the package and did exactly what he was told to do—he had delivered it. Crazy Ray had gone berserk and had ordered him out of his office, screaming he was fired. Miguel demanded the money he was owed, and Dago hit him in the back of the head knocking him down, and they dragged him outside. Dago and another goon, pistol-whipped him, and almost kicked his eye out.

After another round of drinks, Miguel told them he knew everything about Crazy Ray's businesses and why he wanted to buy King's Island. But he would not give up any detailed information without being assured that he would be included in any businesses he brought to the table. Mack agreed in principle but needed to know what businesses he had in mind.

Miguel stated he was aware that Mack knew they were growing marijuana on the island. One of his men saw Buck take a handful of seeds from one of their buckets and hide it in his pocket. Miguel wanted to continue running that business for Mack, that is, *if* he had any interest in going in that direction. Planting season was on top of them, and he had a lot of orders to fill. They could work out the details later.

Mack told Miguel to get with Angus on the details, and that his immediate concern was the million dollars offered by Crazy Ray.

Miguel answered, "You'll make twice that much in one season."

"What about Crazy Ray if you take over his business?" Mack said.

"That will be *your* business, and Crazy Ray will be *your* problem.

I've got the men to keep him off the island, but I don't want to be looking over my shoulder for his crazy ass the whole time I'm working."

"Why would Crazy Ray pay a million dollars for 10,000 acres and only use less than ten acres planting?" Angus asked.

"He doesn't want to buy the island to grow marijuana," Miguel said.

"What? Why then?"

"He wants to build a casino on it."

"A *casino*?" Mack and Angus said at the same time.

"It's a long story, but...my older brother, Marcus, lives in Mexico and works for the Diaz Brothers. Have you heard of them?" Both shook their heads.

"They are one of the largest producers of marijuana in the world, very powerful. It is a family affair with five brothers: Cesar, the oldest, is the Boss, nice guy, you would like him. He paid for Marcus' college, and his Master's degree in finance. They used to be in the wine business and owned hundreds of hectares of vineyards, including a whole township. Everyone in the town, over 3,000 people, worked for the Diaz Brothers."

A waitress sat another round of drinks on the table. Miguel picked up his drink, took a long swallow, and continued.

"A few years back, the Supreme Court ruled against the State of Florida in favor of the Seminole Indians. It basically confirmed their rights to operate a gaming hall because they were considered a sovereign entity by the United States. As a result, the operation of a casino could not be prohibited by the state. Some way or another, Ray—Crazy Ray—found out about this decision, probably from his lawyer. He had been buying small shipments of marijuana from the Diaz Brothers and even had been to their farms in Mexico. He asked me if I knew any big money people that might want to go into the casino business with him. I was certainly interested and saw a great opportunity for myself; so I talked to my brother, and he talked to

Cesar; yes, they were interested. They were always looking to buy what they called Laundromats, a business to launder money, and casinos were the biggest "washing machines" you could buy.

"I set up the meeting in Dallas. Crazy Ray and I drove down, and Little Tony, the youngest brother, and Marcus flew in from Mexico. The meeting was a disaster. Crazy Ray played the big shot, insisting on paying for everything, was loud, self-promoting, and ate like a field hand at the dinner table. He was totally unprepared: no site plans, building plans, or any financial figures. Later, in our room, I tried to salvage the deal and said something about putting together a pro forma to send Cesar. His response was, 'What the hell do a bunch of wetback drug dealers need with all that paperwork?' I was embarrassed. It made me look like a fool in front of my brother and Tony Diaz."

Miguel continued, "I worked for Señor Carlos, the father, in their vineyards for over five years. In Mexico, as well as other countries, the Diaz family is highly respected. The family property was at one time all vineyards, and the five brothers worked in the fields before school and after. Cesar was the first to go to college at the University of California Davis, and graduated with a degree in viticulture and enology—wine growing and wine making. He worked his summers and weekends at the Gallo Wineries, the largest family-owned winery in the world and where the Diazes sold their grapes. Cesar's dream was to have his own family-owned winery and be the first major producer of Mexican wine. Unfortunately, one summer a double tragedy hit. Just before harvest, Señor Carlos was visiting Cesar at the Gallo's winery and received an emergency phone call. A lightning storm had struck, and the whole side of a mountain range, adjacent to the Diaz vineyards, was ablaze and being fueled by a 45 mile per hour wind. Señor Carlos and Cesar flew home, but it was too late. Driving through their vineyards, it looked like a war zone. The fire was gone, there was no wind, ashes covered everything, and only black twisted vines cloaked in white smoke stood like headstones on the hillside. One day a flowering and vibrant green valley, the next day a graveyard. Then the second tragedy hit; the next morning they found Señor Carlos dead in his chair in front of his picture-window, overlooking the destruction of his life's work."

"Where does all this leave Crazy Ray?" Mack asked.

"Dead! Like Senor Carlos as far as the Diaz Brothers are concerned. On the drive back from Dallas, Crazy Ray said to me, 'I think the meeting went really good, don't you?'

"But to answer your question, the latest rumor is that Mississippi has voted in favor of riverboat gambling, down at a place called Tunica Cut-off, about 30 miles south of here. Memphis city leaders are worried they will lose their millions of tourist dollars, their conventions, and money from their own residents, and they're primed for a solution. I think Crazy Ray is now wining and dining the Governor of Tennessee trying to beat Mississippi to the punch."

"He looked awful sick to me, like the cancer was killing him." Mack said.

"Cancer? He doesn't have cancer."

"He told me he did! He's lost all his hair and..."

"What's wrong with him then?" Angus asked.

"Nobody knows for sure, even Dago. He shaved his head to make everyone think he has cancer."

"Why would he want people to think he has cancer?" Mack asked.

"He was seeing a cancer doctor, and that doctor sent him to a specialist out in California. The nurse who took his blood here refused to go back in the same room, and rumors spread like the clap in a whorehouse. Did you see that old newsreel on TV the other night about Rock Hudson, the actor? His agent and the press were saying at the time that *he* had liver cancer, but the Hollywood gossip was he has this deadly virus, the same as Crazy Ray. It's highly contagious between members of the 4-H Club."

"What the hell is the 4-H Club?" Mack asked.

"Homosexuals, Hookers, Heroin addicts, and Haitians. They think that's the way the virus spreads. You knew Crazy Ray was acey-deucey, likes it both ways?"

"I knew he was weird. He always wore makeup; they didn't call him Crazy Ray for nothing. *Man,* he was coughing all over my office," Mack said.

"And I sat in the same chair right after he left," Angus said.

"Relax," Miguel said. "It's only contagious through blood shared from one of the Four-H's—I checked."

Mack wiped his hands on his pants leg. "You never know who's got what...people sneeze in their hands, then you shake hands with them, then unaware, you rub your eyes, pick your nose or wipe your mouth. You can't blame that guy, what's his name? He locked himself up in a hermetically sealed, germ-free hotel room in Hollywood. He wouldn't touch anything without a Kleenex in his hand."

"How did the Diaz Brothers go from the wine business to..." Angus stopped and looked around the pub to see if anyone was listening, "the farming business?"

"It was a likely progression," Miguel said. "They had the land, equipment, labor, irrigation, and transportation. It was a trade-off, a plant for drinking to one for smoking."

"Are you the one who got them started?" Mack asked.

"Oh no, it was their little brother, Tony. He started smoking weed in high school, liked it but had trouble buying it, so he planted a couple of seeds in a milk carton and, *Voila!*

"That's how it all started, from a milk carton?" Mack said.

"Well, once they became seedlings, he transplanted them to a hilltop adjacent to their farm. Like I said earlier, it's a long story..."

"You can't stop there," Angus said. "Waitress," Angus held up three fingers for another round.

"Okay, here's the short version of what Cesar told me," Miguel paused, looked at Mack, who nodded his head to continue. "After the father's funeral, the three middle boys went back to college, leaving Cesar and Tony at the farm. Cesar was at a loss for what to do with thousands of hectares in ashes. It was never a profitable business; it paid the bills, but was more a family addiction, a love affair with the vine and the wine. And now it was all gone, plus the soil was overworked and worn-out like his father's heart, and Cesar had no intention of following in his footsteps.

Tony had his own plans but wasn't sure if he should include his brothers in something so esoteric. He knew Cesar was hurting, weighed down with the family's future, but he wanted to help. So one morning, he persuaded Cesar to go trail riding with him through the Islas del Cielo National Forest that adjoined the backside of their property, unscathed by the recent fire storm. Tony led the way, each on their Honda three-wheelers, climbing the hillside of the vineyard, racing to see who would eat the trail dust while ashes roiled up behind them.

Tony had decided it would be easier to show Cesar than try to tell him. As they entered the national forest, the trail narrowed and the underbrush grew thick, closing in around them. The tall pines and oak trees blocked out the sun as they crossed a small stream that zigzagged down from above. They parked their ATVs, and Tony motioned for Cesar to follow him as he hiked up a deer trail that ended on the rim of a large, bowl-shaped depression. Cesar walked over and stood at the edge, looking down in amazement. It was like a gigantic bouquet of flowers; as if God had reached down from heaven and scooped a handful of earth from the forest—and created a flower garden in a meteorite crater. They both sat on the rim of the crater watching a squadron of squawking, Red-head Amazon parrots, flying in formation then diving into the crater to feed off the fruit trees. The sun was bright, directly overhead, highlighting the multi colors in the bottom of the bowl. Cesar noticed a large clump of red flowering trees across the crater and asked Tony if they were mangos blooming? Tony had remained reluctant, actually scared, to tell his big brother what he had been doing for the past couple of years, but he had come this far and now it was time to show him. They walked down into the crater and around to the other side, stopping one tier above the blooming plants.

Large red buds, the size of a pine cone, frosted all over with a glittery crimson and gold dust, sagged with heavily laden trichomes, gleaming in the sunlight. Cesar reached over and pinched one of the colas. He rubbed his thumb and fingers together, feeling the sticky resin all over his hand. He looked over at Tony, "Is this what I think it is?"

"What it *is,* my big brother is thirty of the finest sensi plants available. Red Lady is what I named her, Dama de Rojo. It took me three years to develop this strain. These thirty ladies will bring me a net profit of one hundred thousand this seas..."

Tony never finished his sentence. The next thing he knew, he was on his back in the dirt, choking on the blood gushing out of his mouth, and splattered over the front of his shirt. He sat up, shook his head, spit, and checked his mouth with his finger to make sure none of his braces were broken.

"I ought to kill you!" Cesar shouted, standing over him. "I've got a brother that is a *drug dealer!"*

Tony stood up and removed his shirt, holding it to his mouth. "These braces cost me a thousand dollars," he mumbled. Then he walked over to a piece of black plastic irrigation pipe, running down from above, and turned on a small spigot. The water trickled out from a gravity flow as he cupped his hands and washed his mouth, then his shirt. He climbed up one tier and sat next to a large boulder, his small teenage body not fully developed yet, wrung out his shirt, and spread it over the hot boulder. He ran his tongue across the inside of his lip and felt the cuts, spat again, and saw that the bleeding had almost stopped. "I'll pay for your braces if any are broken. You okay?" Tony didn't answer.

Cesar climbed up and sat next to Tony, putting his arm around him. "I'm sorry; I shouldn't have hit you. I've got a lot on my mind and the thought of you going to jail...I just snapped."

Tony laid back and closed his eyes. Cesar removed his shirt, spread it out, and leaned back against the dirt bank. "The sun feels good."

After a short time in the sun, Tony walked over to one of the plants and pinched a thumb-size red bud from one of the plants. He removed some Zig-Zag rolling paper from his pocket, moved back over on the rock next to Cesar, and rolled a joint. "I know you didn't go through those years of college in California without smoking a bud, but I bet you've never smoked anything like this." Tony lit the joint, held his breath, and handed it to Cesar. "There's no harsh taste; it's smooth with a THC level way up there, rocking, around fifteen percent."

They passed it back and forth to each other, leaned back against the dirt bank, and watched the hummingbirds fight each other over the wild Mexican Firebush that covered the hillside. Thousands of Monarch butterflies covered the crater, flying in and out of the bushes and trees, alighting on their hands, head, and legs.

"This is a hidden paradise. I never thought I would be smoking a joint with my baby brother and enjoying it so much."

Tony leaned up on his elbow, facing Cesar, "Do you remember the year Papa planted the Chardonnay vines that Senor Gallo gave him? They were planted up on that shaded hill behind the house? The grapes turned out to be the best ever grown and Gallo used them for a special Champagne—Cuvee Speciale Reserve he called it? Well, brother, that's what you're smoking, Lady en Rojo, a Cuvee Speciale Reserve."

"You won't get any argument from me," Cesar said, falling back, following a low moving cloud pushed by a warm tropical breeze. "You *really* made over a hundred thousand in one year off these thirty plants...Un-Be-Leeeve-Able."

Cesar, looking at the sky, slowly exhaled and watched the small smoke-rings break up as the light breeze carried them upward from the crater, the *Sweet Smell of Success.*

Back at the house, Tony didn't answer any of Cesar's questions about his Lady Rojo. As he said, it was his private reserve—his *experiential* garden. He did propose a partnership with his brothers and volunteered a one hundred thousand dollar loan, interest free, as seed money, no pun intended. He explained that the family farm was a perfect location in a perfect climate. Tucked away in a valley, hidden from the main road, the irrigation was already in place, and they had all the equipment they needed. After ripping out the vines, disking in the right fertilizer, planting the right seeds, they could have a profitable crop in less than a year. Not Lady Rojo—she required special-attention—but something less demanding, although certainly desirable and marketable on both sides of the border. Tony estimated if they planted only one-quarter of the farm the first year and planted the grapevines they could salvage on every other row, they should easily gross around ten million dollars.

"*Ten million dollars?*" Angus said, a little too loud.

"Shhh," Mack put a finger to his lips, looked around the bar and leaned forward, "So, are you suggesting I partner up with the Diaz Brothers and go into the casino business?"

"Why not?" Miguel asked. "Stall Crazy Ray on selling and let me get a crop in. We can make a lot of money while waiting. He won't bother us if he thinks he still has a chance of buying your island. I assure you he's in no rush to spend a million dollars until he has a deal with zoning. Time is on our side; a lot of things can change between now and then. Let him do all the schmoozing up in Nashville, and if he gets a casino bill passed, you can jump on it."

"What about Crazy Ray's twenty-five thousand?" Angus said.

"*Angus!* You disappoint me," Mack said. "Surely you're not talking about *our* twenty-five thousand of *seed money* for our new *farming* partnership on King's Island?"

CHAPTER 18

MACK AND MIGUEL walked along the Mississippi River bluff in Tom Lee Park. Robotic rush hour traffic raced north and south on Riverside Drive, unaware of the magnificent blood orange sunset suspended over the western shoreline on the Arkansas side.

"You are a good man, Miguel, and a damn good friend. I'll hate to see you go." Mack said.

Miguel had called and asked Mack if he could meet him at the river park. They stopped and sat on a park bench that jutted out over the river.

"You know that I feel the same way. We had a great run, and I never thought I would say this, but I'm worn out. It's time for me to get out of this business, and you need to get out too. I built that big ass ranch in Mexico, and I've never spent more than two weeks there at one time."

"You're going to get bored down there all by yourself, just fishing and hunting."

"Who said I was going to be by myself?"

"Ahh, you have a little señorita stashed away, huh?"

"I've got a long list of beauties that are waiting for me to pay their bills. They can smell the US dollar as far away as Mexico City." They both laughed. "I just hope I've put away enough."

"Have you?"

"Has any of us...what's enough?"

They leaned back on the bench, and Mack unzipped his jacket, thinking about the question. *How much was enough? Good question.* He stared into the setting sun, falling fast now, the rays glazing over the milk-chocolate color of the swift flowing Mississippi River.

"You said something about your brother, Marcus?"

"He and Cesar want to meet with you. You know Cesar. He's paranoid about talking business over the phone."

"Is it about the casino? Is he flying up here?"

"I don't know what it's about, but I know he's not leaving Mexico. He thinks the DEA is watching him and trusts no one but the few of us."

Mack had visited Cesar many times in the past couple of years, and they had become fast friends. They hunted and fished together, rode three-wheelers, and talked long hours into the night about their favorite subjects—money, wine, and women.

Mack relaxed while his mind drifted, his eyes closed, legs extended, and his hands behind his head. There was something tranquil about the beginning of spring: the mixture of cool air and warm sun, the moving water, the purple buds blooming on the redbud trees, and the multiple songs of the mockingbird.

The soft beep of his phone brought him back to reality. "That's Buck," he said, standing up and reading the message. "Come on, let's go see my new plane. He's bringing it in at the downtown airport."

Memphis's downtown airport had no tower and only one runway, 17/35, which ran 3,800 feet along the banks of the Mississippi River. Buck had been the Fixed Base Operator for over twenty years. He was hardly ever there but had a great crew that managed the operations better than he could. He had signed a five-year lease with the Memphis Airport Authority for one dollar a year rental that had an automatic renewal clause as long as both parties agreed. It wasn't a very profitable business, but it offered him the convenience of flying in and out with no parking fees and free gas and maintenance on his Ag-planes. For Buck it was like owning your own private airport, and with the sale of Avgas, hangar leasing, flight school, pilot training, aircraft rentals, and repairs, it at least paid for itself.

Buck was in the co-pilot's seat in Mack's new Super King Air-200 as it lifted off the downtown airport runway with a whole lot of power but very little noise. At six years old, it was not a new plane, but it was *new* to Mack and, at a cost of two million dollars, the most expensive toy he had ever owned. With its turbojet props, the King Air was the top of the line; the next step up would be a jet—possibly.

Buck had already checked Mack out on the plane and had no problem with him in the pilot seat. Mack had practiced a couple of touch and go's at the downtown airport the day they got the plane. They flew over to Memphis International, longer runways and more congested, and did a couple of touch and go's there, but this King Air had the latest avionics with more instruments and controls than Mack had ever seen.

"Boy, what a sweet ride! It practically flies itself. It's a lot different than flying the Commander," Mack said.

Buck adjusted the knob on the Stormscope, "The weather looks good all the way to the border. Just keep the heading stabilization on auto, and it will continue to adjust itself." Buck looked to the rear of the plane and saw Miguel and Angus playing cards and drinking beer. "If you've got everything under control up here, I'm going to try to get some shuteye in one of those reclining Corinthian leather seats. You need anything?" Buck asked.

"Yeah, see if Miguel wants to sit up front and bring me one of those cold brewskis, I'm dry as a bone." He checked his instruments: air speed was 305 knots, altitude 26,000, RPM 1,800, and heading indicator was 195. He would change that heading in a few minutes and start a slow descent. He wanted to level off at about a 1,000 feet when he started over the gulf. Flying on autopilot was like driving with cruise control and soon, he knew he would be bored.

"You lonely up here by yourself?" Miguel handed Mack a beer and a package of peanuts. "I figured you were like me and hadn't had time to eat anything. Mack, this is a beauty. You did good: all this leather, plush carpet, and the most important thing, a pisser. That's number one on the list for an enlarged prostate."

"What's that?"

"You'll know soon enough."

Mack held up his beer and nodded toward the co-pilot's seat. "You want to ride up front for a while; we're getting close to the Gulf. I may need your Spanish when we cross into Mexico's air space."

Miguel eased into the seat. "Your Spanish is good enough; you just need to talk more. I thought all those tower guys had to speak English anyway?"

"Sure, but sometimes they speak too fast."

Miguel leaned forward searching all the instruments. "How fast are we flying?"

Mack pointed to the airspeed indicator, "We've had a good tail wind, so about 300 miles an hour. We've been on a slow descent; I want to get down pretty low over the Gulf.

"Are you going to land this baby at Cesar's place?"

"Yep, his airstrip is long enough, and they keep it well maintained. We'll do a fly-over first and make sure everything is okay; no tractors or wandering livestock."

"Cesar still didn't tell you what he wanted?" Miguel asked.

"No idea. He just said, 'not on the phone.' Have you heard anything?"

"I asked Marcus, but he said he didn't even know we were flying down."

"There's the Gulf up ahead." Mack called Houston Center and canceled his IFR flight plan. He descended to 500 feet above the water, turned right, and followed the coastline, staying about thirty miles out and under the radar. He wasn't smuggling anything, but it amused him to see if he could fly without being detected.

He was over the oil and gas fields now with derricks of all sizes, shapes, and colors. Oil tankers from many parts of the world maneuvered for entrance into Galveston Bay to unload their crude oil.

The super tankers, too large for the bay, anchored in the gulf and offloaded into smaller tankers.

"That long strip out your window is Padre Island. Flying this low we'll need to keep a lookout for air traffic coming out of Brownsville and Matamoros Airports. As soon as we hit the Rio Grande, we'll head inland." Mack started a right turn, southwest, a heading of 236. The Diaz's place was located in the valley of the Pilon River, surrounded by the Madre Oriental and Los Nogales mountain ranges. It wasn't long before Mack spotted the river and followed it until he saw the grass landing strip and the Hacienda Diaz. He flew over the house and down the length of the airstrip. Seeing that the windsock was lifeless, he turned for his final approach. There was plenty of runway, and the King Air floated down to a soft landing on the grass strip. Mack taxied to the end, turned into the parking area, and shut down both engines. As he exited the plane, he saw half a dozen vaqueros on horses racing a pickup truck down to the plane. It appeared all the Diaz brothers were here, standing on the veranda, waving.

The servants hurried to beat the dying sun as they lit lanterns hanging from trees and the overhead trellis of the pergola that was covered with blooming wisteria. A long rectangular table was set with colorful dishware, and two men busied themselves swabbing a dark sauce over a large pig on a turning spit.

The truck stopped, and Mack leaped from the back, the sweet smell of the sizzling sauce of brown sugar and molasses triggered his hunger. Angus and Miguel each carried two cases of Coors beer onto the porch.

"Hey, lookie-here, lookie-here...Pure-Rocky-Mountain-Spring-Water." Tony helped Angus with one of the cases of Coors.

"Let me see your ID, Baby Face," Angus teased Tony.

"Fat Man, you want me to punch you in that beer belly?"

Angus, a foot taller and two feet wider, but lightning quick, grabbed Tony in a bear hug, lifting him off the ground and swinging him around and around. "I'll make you think, Fat Man."

When Tony first found out Angus studied at the University of Mississippi's Marijuana Research Farm, he couldn't wait to introduce Angus to some of the "new and unique" breeding strains he had developed. From that day forward, they were practically inseparable. At the same time Mack and Cesar's friendship developed. Both alpha males, they shared their love of exploring new and unique-tasting wines, fine art, and beautiful women from around the world.

"Okay, *boys,* knock off the horseplay. Time to eat," Cesar said.

After supper, Mack and Cesar lounged under a gazebo down on the river with oak logs burning in a fire pit. Dark shadows of gnarled bougainvillea vines encircled each column with flame-colored flowers, while a slight breeze carried the perfume of night-blooming jasmine.

"Thank you, my friend, for the excellent wine." Cesar set his glass down and picked up the bottle. "Chateaux Haut Brion."

"I know you don't drink a lot of Bordeaux, but I thought you would like this. A friend of mine brought back some vintage bottles for me while on a wine tasting tour of Châteaux in France. This one placed first in the World Wine Competition. I've never had it before, but I agree, it is...outstanding."

Cesar held his glass under his nose and inhaled. "Ahhh, the nectar of the gods. I'm a simple man, Mack. All I ever wanted out of life was to make a bottle of wine like this."

They clicked their wine glasses. Mack said, "Life is short...you're here today and gone tomorrow."

"You're so right about that—my friend, Jose Castro died less than two years ago in his fifties—a year after he had retired. He was a professor at UC Davis and wrote *the* book on Viticulture and Enology. I spent many weekends at his family's vineyard studying his experiments in wine growing. About six months after his funeral, his wife called and asked if I knew anyone who might be interested in buying the vineyard. She wanted to keep a low profile that she was moving—no signs or realtors. I told her I would ask around discreetly.

"Jose had inherited a section of land, approximately 100 acres up in Napa Valley. It had been in his family since the mid-1800s and had been patented under Mexican land grants. It never occurred to me that my life's desire was staring me in the face. Two weeks ago I bought Jose's 200-year-old Spanish-style house, the vineyard, and his new state-of-the-art winery."

"That's great." Mack emptied the Chateaux Haut-Brion into their glasses and made a toast to his new venture. "Congratulations!"

"Gracias, Amigo. This brings us to why I asked you to fly down. You know, I never considered what we do as criminal. I compared it to Prohibition, a Sumptuary Law that was repealed. I believed and still believe, like Prohibition, the laws against marijuana will eventually be repealed. But now a lot of criminals—Colombians, Guatemalans, Salvadorians, all bad guys, low-life peons, guns for hire, they're being pushed into Mexico. The DEA and even the US Military AWAC are involved with their eye-in-the-sky surveillance system. They're all over the coast of Florida, and it won't be long before they'll be down here. The business has changed. It's no longer just marijuana. Now they're dealing in cocaine, heroin, kidnapping, and even murder. It's all moving this way and I want no part of it."

"We all knew this day would come."

"True, but you're never fully prepared for it. We all made a lot of money, but where did it go?"

"It just goes. Expenses: employees, transportation, inducements, houses, cars..." Mack nodded towards the airstrip, "Airplanes, it all adds up. Do you need money?"

"Are you offering?"

"I am. Tell me how much you need."

"Maybe none; it all depends. I figure we have about a year, maybe two, before the DEA has spies all over this farm. I'm not worried about any of the family turning; it'll be one of the distributors they squeeze—some of those would sell their mothers to stay out of La Mesa prison. Fortunately, I still have powerful friends in the Federal Security Directorate, including the Director, who just received a FedEx package with the keys to a bright red Mercedes convertible for his daughter's graduation. So, it is not that we are without protection or a warning system, but we need to be proactive in planning our immediate future."

"Do you have a plan?"

"Sí, Señor, albeit tentative...Operación code word: *CODA*—the end of a piece of music."

Mack looked puzzled. "You lost me there, pal."

"How many stories have we heard about people in this business staying too long and not knowing when to walk away? Do we know of anyone that was in this business that is not in jail or has been at one time or another? I'm convinced, Mack, that it's time for us to get out. But before we go, I would like to have a grand—how do they say it in the States—'Last Hurrah,' a going-out-of-business sale, and I'll need your help."

Mack banked the King Air into a left turn as the landing gear retracted and the plane started its climb. He had a lot on his mind and flying was not one of them as he turned on the autopilot master switch. He set a heading of 090, then the climb rate and the altitude.

Cesar was right. Mack had made some good money since he had taken over the distribution of Diaz's shipments to the United States but nothing like the money Cesar had made. Of course, Mack didn't have the same overhead and only distributed wholesale, which brought in less money, but the risk was also smaller. The Diaz's Brothers now owned over 100,000 hectares of timberland and vineyard—from the state of Tamaulipas to the state of Chihuahua—but most important were the rich valleys, now planted with the daughters and granddaughters of Lady Rojo, an inventory that would change all of their financial futures. He needed to clear his mind and tie up any loose ends so he could focus on Cesar's Operación: *CODA*. First thing would be to close down King's Island. Although extremely profitable, it was an unnecessary risk—too close to home. The only other outstanding problem was this unsettled business with Crazy Ray—a volatile situation that could blow up anytime and send them all to jail. Crazy Ray was not going to take a loss of $25,000 without some form of retaliation. The last he heard, Crazy Ray had died in some AIDS Hospice in San Francisco. But if he was still alive, he knew that Mack had stolen his King's Island business and the business with the Diaz Brothers.

Why not send Miguel—no, send Angus—with $25,000 to give back to Crazy Ray? No, that wouldn't work. Crazy Ray is not a dummy; he would just take it and still retaliate. First thing was to find out if he was still alive and, if so, where he was.

The wheels inside his head kept turning, as in a precision watch, ticking away. So much had happened in his short life. He was lucky; he could be serving a jail sentence after pulling such a stupid stunt as agreeing to drive a car in an armed burglary. *Such juvenile judgment!* And for what...a meager hundred dollars, silver dollars at that...*how stupid was that?* Crazy Ray Flynn had always been trouble, as long as Mack had known him.

He needed a woman; or did he? Sometimes he was lonely for a female companionship, not just as a bed buddy, but someone he could share his intimate thoughts with. Yeah, Ruby was intimate, between the legs for sure, but not between the ears.

He might have been in love with Kate Willingham, but he didn't return her letters while he was away and she never returned his calls when he came back from Aspen. The last he heard she had graduated from veterinarian school at Mississippi State and was practicing in Memphis. He checked information and looked in the yellow pages but found nothing. He would look a little harder when he got back home.

But overall, his best times were with Erica. She was funny, smart, pretty, sexy and a lot of fun to be with. But she wanted to get married and all her family was in Boston and that's where she wanted to live.

He had talked to her a couple of times and they were going to meet, but it never happened.

The last thing he needed now was any distraction. The only woman he should be focusing on was named *CODA*. It would be a huge gamble, a life-changing decision, a dangerous decision. He looked over at Buck in the co-pilot's seat. After their long night of drinking, he was fast asleep. It was time for another Master Mind Group meeting.

"We all have a vote," Mack said, "in or out, without anyone judging your decision. But regardless of your vote, Cesar is shutting the doors. He's out of the business for good, and he's offering us a once-in-a-lifetime opportunity. We can't stay afloat much longer without his product and capital. What we've made has been invested, and the way I see it, either we get out now and sell our investments or we stay for this last hurrah." Mack had been explaining Cesar's plan, Operación: *CODA*. Well, not quite a plan yet; that would be up to Mack to formulate. "What we need now is a vote, yes or no, in or out?"

Buck leaned against the door. "It's between you and Angus, Mack. You're the young bucks. Me, Miguel and Li are old farts, ready to hang it up. But speaking for myself, I don't have that much saved up and could use one more big paycheck. So, Semper Fi little brother—if you're in, I'm in."

"How big of a paycheck are you talking about?" Angus asked.

"One hundred million dollars. If the five of us are in, we walk away with ten million each. The Diaz brothers have agreed to a split of fifty-fifty of the profit. That's the payout Cesar and I came up with, fifty million for each side of the Rio."

"*Ten million* dollars...each! Who do we have to kill, the President of Mexico?" Miguel asked.

"If we plan and execute it right, no one should get hurt," Mack said.

"What exactly are we planning to do?" Angus asked.

"We're going to sell all of Cesar's current and future inventory and our own; we're getting out of the farming business. I have some ideas, but I've told you all of what I know now. The rest will be up to you. As soon as I find out who's in and who's not, we can have a Master Mind Group meeting to lay out a concrete plan."

Mack looked over at Li sitting on the couch, closest to the door, writing in a notebook. He continued, "I need to let Cesar know soon, 'cause as they say, time is of the essence. Li, we haven't heard a word from you. Don't feel pressured to be a part of this. If you want to walk away now, no problem, no judging."

Li looked up from his notebook. "You've always calculated your gambles, success versus failure. How did you rate this one?"

Mack did not hesitate, "80%."

"And the chance of going to jail?"

"To jail, less than 10% if we move fast. We all have been contributing to the contingency fund set up for legal fees and expenses in case one or all of us got in trouble; it's grown substantially. I doubt if any of us would ever see the inside of a jail."

"I'm in," Angus said.

Mack looked at Miguel who was nodding his head, "Count me in."

"Okay, everybody's in?" Mack asked.

"Everybody's in," Li said and scribbled in his notebook.

"One more thing; we will have to use all our savings to capitalize the operation. The Diaz Brothers are furnishing the entire product and all the expenses on their side of the Rio Grande."

"Does that include the contingency fund setup for our protection if this all blows up?" Angus asked.

"No, that's a cash fund set up years ago when we first started growing on King's Island and is for one thing and one thing only. It's our 'stay-out-of-jail' card. Is everybody still in?" All four nodded their heads.

"Good. First thing, let's get King's Island cleaned up. Sell what we've got; discount it if you have to. We'll use that money to start the operation. Disk up every field, grade it, and compact the field closest to the Wolf River. I'll need a large pad there, approximately the size of a football field. I don't want any residue of our past on that island. We may need to use the island in our operation, and I don't want to take any chances. We may want to plant some corn; how long before standing stalks?" Everyone looked at Miguel.

"Some as early as 60 days."

"Cut the size of the pad in half and let's go ahead and plant the corn; we may need that for cover."

It was early morning, and commuters from Mississippi and across the bridges in Arkansas had already started their race into Memphis. The sky was clear, and a southwest wind picked up the moisture from the river and carried it across the barge. Five chairs were placed around an overturned cable reel in the middle of one of the barges. Long towropes, fore and aft, stretched tight from the barge to wrap around embedded bollard buttons, which looked like huge mushrooms pushed up from the cobblestones. Mack and Buck, early risers, marched side by side across the barge. Li, Angus, and Miguel followed close behind. A boat steward followed the group with a tray of coffee that he sat on top of the cable reel.

"Gooood morning, *sun!*" Mack, in a playful mood, shouted with both hands in the air and bowed to the sun rising between the office buildings that towered over the bluff. He had just finished a five-mile run, shaved and showered, and came straight out to the barge. The steward poured steaming coffee into each mug and returned to the galley. Mack stretched, popping his neck and spine, picked up his mug, and took a long slurp.

"Ahhh, there's something primitive about being on the river in the early morning." He smiled at Li, knowing how he appreciated early mornings out on the barge. Mack waited 'til everyone fixed his coffee.

"Okay, D-day is almost here, so let's get started. Buck, in our last meeting we left off with you and security. Oh yeah, same as before, everyone try to hold your questions till the end."

Buck set his mug down. "First thing, no discussions or even a hint of this operation over the office or home phones. Keep change with you at all times to use the pay phones, and limit what you say over the cell phones. Also, put nothing in writing unless absolutely necessary, then memorize it and burn it. The five of us and some of the men from Mexico will be armed. Everyone else will be searched, and, if a weapon is found, you confiscate it. The last thing I want is a misfire or a shootout. We have off-duty policemen—some being paid a year's salary for one night of work—to protect our operating perimeter that will be completely locked down. The perimeter will encompass the Wolf River, King's Island, and all of the area around the downtown airport. Mack will tell you more about our perimeter later. No one is to enter or leave this perimeter during the operation without orders from one of us." Buck stood up, reached in his pocket, removed a handful of jewelry-like pins, each one embossed with a green enamel shamrock, and handed one to each of the group.

"Like the Secret Service, these are lapel pins for us to pass through security. We'll wear them on our shirt collars. 'Shamrock' will be the password for backup; security is going to be tight." Buck sat back down in his chair. "I'll have more information as we go along."

Mack nodded his head to Miguel who had agreed to handle the transportation and logistics.

"How do you transport 365,000 pounds of weed undetected? That's over 182 tons in one load." Miguel looked at each face to see if there were any answers. He then stood up and looked down at the barge and stomped his foot hard three times. The men stared at him as if he were a child having a tantrum.

"A barge!" he shouted, smiling. "Ain't that great? A Hopper Barge is 195-feet long, 35 feet wide, and 12 feet deep. It will hold 1,500 tons or three million pounds; over 8 times what we're hauling. Our product will be packed in Garden Mulch bags and sealed—each weighing 50 pounds. Each wooden pallet will hold 50 bags, six feet high, and wrapped in plastic. A crane will lower each pallet into the bottom of the hoppers with a large tent-like canvas spread over the bags. The barge will then be moved to the docks at Puerto Lucero, just south of Matamoros, at the Cemento Hermoso Company, and each hopper will be topped off with dry cement—six feet of weed under three feet of dry cement. At the same time, our own *Irish Mist II* will be pushing 14 empty hopper barges along the Gulf Coast and will rendezvous with the cement-loaded barges in the middle of the night at an old deserted oil rig somewhere offshore of the Padre Islands. Our crew will lash together the loaded barge in the middle of the empty barges, five long and three wide, and then head for the Mississippi River. We are allowing five days, once on the Mississippi, to get to Memphis. That's about it for right now. Oh, not to be outdone by the Sergeant Major here, you know how competitive we Marines are…" Miguel opened a brown bag that was on the table and removed a handful of watches and passed them out among the group. Strapping one on his wrist, he said, "This is the new Timex Ironman Triathlon Digital watch. It's water resistant to over 300 feet but try not to fall in the river to test it. It's also a stopwatch, has a timer, and 3 alarms. An added feature is the backlight. It's bright enough so you can read a newspaper. Wear the watch and get familiar with it; you'll need it. Timing will be critical in this operation." Miguel filled his mug and sat down.

"Who's next?" Mack said.

Angus stood up, looking at Li to see if he wanted to go next. Li nodded for him to go ahead.

"First, credit where credit is due; without Tony Diaz's incredible development of Lady Rojo none of what I'm going to tell you could ever have happened.

"Tony and I have traveled a lot: Colombia, Jamaica, Panama, Hawaii, India, and Amsterdam. We visited secret pot farms up and down the coast of California, the lab at the University of Mississippi, and most farms in Mexico. From these places we've gathered soil samples, calculated the hours of sun, the levels of rain, irrigation, and the mixtures of fertilizers, and most important, we collected seeds from all over the world to experiment with—from germination of sprouts to a 20-foot plant. In the last three years we've transplanted, cloned, pruned, and manipulated gene frequencies, cross-bred, topped, and trimmed, until we perfected the growth of this female into the world's most potent and prolific plant—THC levels over 20% that produce *two* full crops a year—and in all her naked splendor, the most beautiful specimen ever." Angus lifted a grocery sack from under the table, sat it on top, and removed a bundle wrapped with butcher paper.

"Since we're all having 'Show 'n Tell.' I brought one of the granddaughters of Lady Rojo. Talk is cheap...but seeing *is* believing." He unrolled the ball of paper, and the smell was overpowering, not unpleasant, but heady, sweet, and seductive. He lifted the super bud, the size of a wine bottle, like a new baby; one hand held the bottom of the stem, the other cradled against the waxed side of the paper, keeping the syrupy resin from sticking to his hand.

"Gentlemen, let me introduce you to this lovely newborn, Amazon Lady!"

Miguel jumped up, spilling his coffee. "Santa Madre, *cola de zorra.* What a *foxtail!* I've never seen one like that even in High Times." He walked closer. The plant was dusted with honey-colored resin that glistened in the sunlight and fused together in bright red cones.

Angus placed the foxtail on the table and removed some plastic baggies from his pocket. He pulled some of the red buds from the plant, dropped them in the baggies, and handed them out. "This is the highest quality weed ever, Sinsemilla, without seeds, all protected virgins. We had around-the-clock vigilantes on all five farms, ripping up the first sight of a male plant. Enjoy gentlemen; this is like a rare wine that comes around once in a lifetime. I shipped a sample by FedEx, a small hermetically sealed nickel bag, about 0.5 grams, to every one of our distributors. A primo product the streets have never experienced. Like Cleopatra, with her sexual conquests, Amazon Lady will sell herself. Angus rolled the plant back up, and placed it in his grocery bag, and sat down.

Li closed his notebook. "Good job, Angus. Unlike the rest of you, I must take notes, but rest easy, everything is in Chinese." Li smiled and continued, "Miguel asked the question, 'How do you transport 365,000 pounds of weed in one load, undetected?' Well, I ask you the same question; how do you distribute $109,500,000.00 undetected? The short answer is, slowly and carefully. Normally, I would play these cards close to my chest and keep this information undisclosed. Mack and I have talked extensively about this, and he concluded we are the Master Mind Group, equally in risk and reward, so he wants everything disclosed and on the table in case something should happen. I will add the old axiom that Mack stated earlier, 'Loose lips sink ships' and, *remember*, we are *all* on the same ship.

"The FBI, CIA, DEA, and the IRS all have the same saying when investigating a crime, 'follow the money.' I've studied the way these agencies track the money, and I've designed a plan without any tracks. For me, this is my last chance at ever having a good life for my family, and I intend to protect every penny we bring in. The best way to do that is to spread it out and keep it moving. When Mack lived in Aspen, he made a friend while skiing; she was from Switzerland. From that relationship we opened an account for our *farming* business on King's Island with Clearwater, a Swiss private banking group based in Vaduz, Liechtenstein..."

Only a couple of people knew that Mack's friend was Madeline Neuhaus, whose father was Ludwig Neuhaus, the founder of UBS in Switzerland. Mack met Maddie while skiing in Aspen. One day he had just skied down to the base restaurant to eat lunch, punched the release on his bindings, and when he looked up he saw this young girl, maybe 17 or 18 years old, sitting on the steps crying. He eased up and sat down beside her, unbuckled his ski boots, and whispered, 'I'm the official Host on this mountain and crying is absolutely verboten while in Winter Wonderland.' She forced a smile, wiped her tears, and told him someone in the restaurant had stolen her backpack with her passport, driver's license, credit card, money, plane ticket, everything. Mack told her he was sorry but not to worry, he would help. As they walked to the Customer Service Center, Maddie told him she *was from Switzerland and was in graduate school studying International Finance and Banking at Stanford. She was on Christmas vacation and had to catch a plane to Zurich leaving Denver at 8:30 that night. Mack helped her return her rental skis, checked her out of her hotel, took her to the Aspen Airport, and waited with her until they called her connecting flight to Denver. At the gate he gave her $67.00 in cash, all that he had on him. Then, surprisingly, she threw her arms around his neck and kissed him on the lips, a kiss that extended beyond appreciation. Mack was a kisser; he liked to kiss and realized that he had underestimated her age. Her lips were on fire, and he could feel her rapid heartbeat under her breast pressed hard against his chest. She hurried to the gate, stopped, and turned back looking at Mack. He read her lips as she mouthed the words, 'I'm glad someone stole my backpack.'*

"Clearwater International Exchange is more than a bank," Li said. "They offer ironclad financial privacy, asset protection, confidential international investments, real estate, undisclosed gold, diamonds, and currency exchange, and especially one service that we've taken advantage of, unregistered business transactions. We've had too much cash on hand with the money we brought in from King's Island and needed a depository. Through them we started buying, with down payments, small businesses in other countries, $100,000 here and there. In Zurich we bought, *Diamanté Brut*, a small, unassuming jewelry store that was established in 1861. In Panama, we bought an active commercial construction company where the owner had died of a heart attack with six million dollars under contract. By the time we finish with this operation we will own two more businesses, one in the Cayman Islands and one in Luxembourg. We will comingle our cash into these businesses and, after a short period of time, two years or more, we'll close the doors and write the investments off as failures.

"I'll turn this over to Mack. We've covered a lot of information this morning, and I know you have questions."

Mack stood up, his hands on his hips, "So far so good. Everything is running on schedule and without any problems. Look how far we've come in such a short time. We all contributed to Buck's plan of security, Miguel's plan of transportation, Tony's and Angus' research and development, and Li's money management. From the beginning, we laid this operation out as if we were on a Marine recon mission. There are two types of reconnaissance: Black Ops, which is direct action, and Green Ops, which is deep reconnaissance and surveillance: There will be *no* Black Ops on this mission. Avoid all contact with anyone not a member of this operation—do not confront. Run, hide, whatever you have to do to avoid being seen or having any communication. Buck and I will do all of the recon, way out in front of the operation. I'll get more into our recon as we get closer.

"Let me warn you though, *beware,* there *is* an enemy out there. You don't deal in a hundred million dollars' worth of drugs without attracting attention from all types of criminals waiting to rip you off. The word will be on the streets soon—there's no way to stop it—and there are too many bodies involved in this operation already. The key to success will be *speed* and *mobility.* Our lives and future are at stake here, so let's continue to stay focused from start to finish.

"Miguel, will you go over the transporting after it arrives here at Memphis?"

"The plan is to use six tractor-trailer trucks, four loaded with 26 pallets of *mulch* each, about 65,000 pounds. So, 104 pallets will leave Memphis for warehouses in Atlanta, Little Rock, St. Louis, and Knoxville. Those are the major distribution points for our distributors. The balance of 42 pallets, 21 in each truck, will be transported to warehouses here in Memphis and will be distributed locally into east Arkansas, north Mississippi, west Tennessee, and the Missouri Bootheel. If any of those sites are compromised, we have backup sites for the other warehouses. As you can see, one of my primary concerns will be managing the logistics. Remember, no one but us knows how much we are transporting. It could be one pallet or 146 pallets, so if there's a problem, don't panic. Call Mack; he's the firefighter, the one to put out any fires."

There was a recent change of plans from Cesar. He increased

Mack's operating budget to nine and a half million dollars to cover the cost of *CODA* and to insure a higher percentage of a successful outcome. He didn't want Mack to have to skimp or leave any bases uncovered. Mack offered Clearwater as collateral, but Cesar refused, "I'll take it out of the profits at the end."

Mack stood up, "Payment from our distributors are simple: POD, *paid on delivery*, in one-hundred-dollar bills, *only*. The timing, distance, and schedules were laid out so Buck in one chopper and I in the other will be at every delivery to collect from the buyers. As Miguel said, if there's a fire, call me."

The ship's bell rang, and Mack clapped his hands. "I know you have questions, but breakfast is ready, and I can smell those biscuits from here; let's eat."

CHAPTER 19

THE TREETOPS HAD grown over the narrow gravel road and blocked out the sky; it was like driving through a tunnel. The headlights bounced all over the place, making it hard to dodge the potholes and keep the truck in the middle of the road. Miguel lifted his foot off the gas pedal and slowed to a crawl; he was lost. There hadn't been a crossroad for the last hour, and he was low on petrol. He should have filled up before crossing the border and cursed himself for not stopping. He had to take a leak. He stopped his truck, shut the lights off, and waited for his eyes to adjust to the darkness. On second thought, he turned the lights back on, stepped outside the truck, and walked to the side of the road. He unzipped his pants and relieved himself, "Ohhh, man," he said out loud, stretching and closing his eyes, "does that feel good." When he opened his eyes he saw white lights flashing through the treetops and his first thought was falling stars until he heard the roar of a powerful engine. Two spotlights covered him, and he heard men shouting in Spanish, "Hands in the air! Hands in the air!"

Miguel could not stop the flow of relieving himself, but when he heard the rapid fire of automatic weapons, his hands went up, and his urethral sphincter sealed shut, cutting the flow as if a spigot was wrenched closed. The four-wheel drive monster truck towered over him, the tires stopped at chest level, while a man ran to him and jabbed him in the chest with an AK-47 rifle. The second man exited the truck, carrying the same Russian-made rifle and swaggered over to Miguel. They both wore camouflage fatigues; the second one wore a cap with a gold oak leaf pinned on the front. Two other men, without guns or camouflage clothing, searched his truck, opened his suitcase, and scattered everything over the road. *Some kind of militia or highway bandits,* he thought.

"Look, the turtle's head has gone back in its shell," The first man said, laughing and pointing his rifle at Miguel's penis. Miguel was a head taller than both of them and wanted to bang their heads together, but when he tried to zip his pants they both shouted at him, pointing their rifles to keep his hands above his head.

"I am *Major* Juan Carlos Jimenez," he said, looking up to Miguel, tapping the barrel of the rifle against his leg. He had a small birdlike head that kept twitching left and right. "Who are *you?* What are you doing on this road?"

"*Major* huh, no shit," Miguel shouted, "Well, I am Pancho Villa, Supreme Leader of the Division del Norte, and I'm on this road to rob and kill...and rape your wife and daughters."

Major Juan, stepped back with a look of fear on his face, "You gringo?" he asked, raising his AK-47. "Search him."

The other man leaned his rifle against the bumper of Miguel's truck and started searching him. The Major, with his rifle tapping Miguel's chest, peppered him with questions.

"Aha!" The other man shouted. He had Miguel's wallet and found two thousand dollars in hundred dollar bills. Miguel knew they would kill him now and dump his body in the woods for the dogs to eat.

Juan stepped forward to pick up some of the money that had fallen from the wallet and, in that split second, with both hands still in the air, using one swift motion, Miguel half turned and delivered a full swinging kick to the Major's knee. His knee buckled and he flew backward to the ground, both hands still clutching the rifle. Miguel was on him, snatching the rifle by the hand guard, but Juan was holding on with a death grip and fired off a couple of rounds. Miguel took the heel of his hand and slammed the bottom of the AK-47's magazine as hard as he could, forcing the carrying handle on top to smash Juan's nose, opening a cut from his forehead down to his chin. He turned around, the rifle in his hand now, flipping the selector switch forward with his thumb to full automatic. The other man reached for his rifle, and Miguel screamed a loud cry and fired off a blast of ten rounds that tore up the gravel road in front of both trucks. The man dropped his rifle as if it were on fire and threw both hands in the air. The two unarmed men that were searching Miguel's truck now ran full speed down the gravel road, disappearing into the dark. Miguel, with one hand on the AK-47, let loose a six-round blast of fire over their heads. He then stepped over to the front of his bumper, picked up the other rifle, and said to the man in Spanish, "Get him up," pointing to Juan.

Juan was standing now, his cap knocked from his head and long black hair covering most of his face. He used both hands to wipe the blood from his eyes. His lips were busted, his nose broken and smashed to the left side of his face.

"Where does this road go? How far is it to the next petrol station?" Miguel shouted.

Juan threw his head back, his long hair uncovering his face, and stared at Miguel with bloodshot eyes and raging anger. He spit a stream of blood on the ground in front of him and hissed, "You will pay for this, Gringo."

Miguel's first instinct was to shoot him, but he grabbed his long hair and drove his knee up hard between his legs. Juan bounced off the truck and fell forward to his knees, both hands between his legs, groaning and gasping for air. Miguel kicked him, and he rolled over, face down. "Stand up," Miguel said.

The best he could do was roll over, the back of his head on the ground with his knees drawn up and both hands still between his legs.

"Listen up, shithead," Miguel planted his boot on Juan's throat and rested the end of the barrel of the AK-47 into the large gash opened in his forehead. "I ask you a question, you answer my question. Now, where does this road go?"

He couldn't speak. Miguel's boot was pressed too hard against his Adam's apple, shutting off his larynx. Miguel lifted his boot, and Juan took a deep breath. In a low measured voice he told him the road ended about ten kilometers at the Gulf of Mexico. And yes the Diaz Brother's warehouse was there too.

Miguel told them both to take off their boots and remove the laces. He tied Juan's hands behind his back and put him in his truck. He pointed down the gravel road to the other man, in the direction the other two had escaped, lifted his rifle, and told him to run. He then walked over to the monster truck and removed a red Jerry can full of gas strapped to the side, placed it in the back of his truck, and drove off with the *Major* beside him.

Miguel could see the lights on the eaves of the metal warehouse and at the entrance gate. Two guards were posted on each side of the closed gate.

"Are those your men at the gate?" Miguel asked.

He was slow to nod his head.

Miguel stuck the end of the AK-47 into Juan's belly, "If you're lying, you're dead. Tell them to open the gate."

When the guards saw Juan's face, they drew their pistols, but Juan ordered the gates opened, and they drove through. Miguel drove around the back of the warehouse and down to the end of the dock, passing posted guards along the way. He saw forklifts coming and going through the tall plastic strip doors of the refrigerated warehouse, each carrying pallets and stacking them on the dock next to a Hopper barge. A large crane lifted and lowered each pallet into the belly of the barge; the warehouse buzzed with activity. Miguel estimated a quick count of 20 men hustling about, not counting the guards. He saw Cesar standing on the barge talking into a handheld radio, directing the crane and forklift traffic. He turned and saw two guards running toward his truck and stepped out of the truck, waving. Cesar shouted, and the two guards stopped as Cesar walked up to Miguel.

"Running a little late, aren't you, Big Man—didn't get lost, did you?" Cesar laughed as he embraced Miguel. "What do we have here?"

he asked, looking at Juan, still tied and sitting in the front seat. "Someone have an accident?"

Miguel walked around to the passenger side, opened the door, and pulled Juan out. He untied his hands from behind his back and shoved him forward toward the barge. The other guards started laughing and pointing at him as he hobbled off bootless while two other guards ran to help him. Miguel and Cesar walked to the warehouse as Miguel explained his run-in with the Major's road patrol.

"That guy's a loose cannon. He was an indentured laborer my father got from the prison, and when his time was up, he wouldn't leave. My father liked him because he spoke English, so we kept him. I don't know where he got the gold leaf insignia. He went from Captain to Major. I think your old boss, Ray Flynn, promoted him," Cesar laughed. "Flynn convinced us that we needed a security patrol, and we all kind of went along with it. When he left, he put Juan in charge."

Miguel followed Cesar as he pushed through the strip doors of the warehouse. "This feels good," Miguel said. "I didn't know you had cold storage."

"We converted it. The first crop is stored here while we harvest the second crop. As with a good grape, heat and moisture are critical factors. Without refrigeration, the potency would drop about 5% per month for six months, then down to 2%, according to Tony."

"He should know; I never could grow anything close to his Lady Rojo."

"Yeah, he should have been a botanist," Cesar said.

"He is. This Amazon Lady, this super strain, he created from Lady Rojo will be historical, a world-wide success."

"I wouldn't doubt it; it's mighty potent."

"Is Marcus here?"

"He's in the back, with Francisco. You know how your brother is, counting every bag while they're being loaded; he's hands-on, that boy. Lazaro is in the hole of the barge, supervising the tying down of the pallets, and will ride back with us."

"Is Marcus still driving my truck back?"

"As soon as we leave here he's headed to our distributors in Houston and Dallas. Then he'll wait for us in Memphis. Benito is staying to plow the fields under and handle the cleanup. All the guards we're using in Memphis are crossing the border at Matamoros, meeting Francisco in Houston, and will report to Buck in Memphis."

"Good, so everything is still on schedule?"

"Time wise, yes, but there's one small change. We decided to add two more barges, just another precaution. They're loaded and waiting at the cement plant. It's better to have three barges moving up river at the same water level. I've sent word to Mack, and they'll have 12 empty barges when they push out of Galveston Bay. That will give us 15 total—3 wide and 5 long—when they start up the Mississippi."

Cesar and Miguel had been going over the maps and charts in the warehouse office when the phone rang. Cesar picked it up, said a couple of words in Spanish, and turned to Miguel, "We're loaded. You ready?"

The *CODA* barge, as Cesar's brother Lazaro had called it, was loaded, and a towboat pushed it down the inland canal to the cement plant where the other two loaded barges waited. The fiberglass lids were pushed open and a flexible hose hanging from a tall storage silo swiveled from one hopper to the next, covering the bags of *mulch* with dry cement. A white cloud of dust boiled up from inside the hoppers, leaving a thin coat of powder over the barges.

"Are we riding on the towboat?" Miguel asked.

"Oh no, we are going to run interference." Miguel followed Cesar to the end of the warehouse and entered a passage door, then down some stairs to a boathouse. A lift was lowering a boat into the water while two men on top were removing the cover from the 38-foot long, Cigarette Top Gun, custom-built boat. From front to back, the painted design was of a great white shark, with its torpedo-shaped body and long pointed nose. The color was a dark, flat gunmetal gray mixed with poly-graphite to deflect radar and blend in with the dark water. The bottom hull, below the water line, was white and, when powered up, it leapt out of the water like the Great White when attacking.

"The eye on that shark looks as if it's staring at me; it looks real," Miguel said.

"Menacing, huh?"

"Where did you get this?"

"Some airbrush specialist in Texas City called the Wizard builds these high performance boats and custom paints them. It was Mack's idea, the gunmetal gray; he didn't want anything that would show up, like the bright colors they are normally painted. This gray blends perfectly at dusk, night, and dawn; he got one for each of us, to ride shotgun on the barges. Wait till you see his; it's like something out of a Jules Verne novel. One thing for sure, if something happens along the way, we can intercede or run. Nothing is going to catch us."

Miguel sat in the bucket seat across from Cesar as the overhead door started rolling up. Cesar eased the throttle forward, the Twin Mercury engines, 1,400 total horse power, purred at idle speed as the boat exited from the warehouse, silently cutting through the dark water underneath the wooden docks.

Lazaro waited out on the end of a barge anchored to the dock as Cesar stopped against the rubber tire bumpers on the side. Lazaro handed Miguel his duffel bag and moved down into the boat. Chico, a tall, broad-shouldered man with his head shaved, handed Miguel a golf club travel bag and then a duffel bag. Miguel had met him once before but was never sure what he did for the Diaz family. Chico stepped onto the front of the boat and pushed the boat away from the barge. They both were dressed in dark windbreakers, jeans, and black deck shoes.

Cesar flipped the red and green running lights on, leaving the stern light off, pulled away from the barge, and idled down the canal to open water. The crescent moon allowed only a small sliver of light, but the stars were bright and lent plenty of light.

Cesar, under the map light, double checked his navigation chart and set his GPS for Point Penascal, off the middle of Padre Island,

Texas. "What we're going to do is run interference for the barges following the east side of the island, staying about ten miles out, scouting port and starboard. We'll stay out in the Gulf until we hook up with Mack at the oil rig. We are looking for bad guys: pirates, DEA, Coast Guard, anybody who attempts to get close to those barges." Cesar and Miguel were in the two bucket seats up front, and Lazaro and Chico were on the bench seat in the back. Miguel looked back when he heard a familiar metallic click and watched Chico shove a magazine into an M-16 automatic rifle and hand it to Lazaro. Chico then removed the second M-16 from the golf club travel bag and inserted a magazine. Miguel looked over at Cesar who shrugged his shoulders, "Mack's idea. You Marines are all alike. What's that saying of yours?"

"Semper Fi." Miguel said.

"No, the other one, 'Don't be caught with your pants down.'"

"Is that what we're looking for?" Miguel asked, pointing to a white light on the horizon as he pulled back on the throttles; the powerful 5-ton boat came to a stop almost immediately. As her bow eased back into the water, Cesar stuck his head out from inside the small cabin,

"Is there a problem?"

"Miguel spotted a marker," Lazaro said.

Cesar flipped on the cabin light, wiped the sleep from his eyes and unfolded a navigation chart, and checked the time. He stepped out of the cabin, looked at the compass heading, and checked his charts again.

"Is that the oil rig?" Miguel said.

"Could be," Cesar was looking through the binoculars, "Good eyes, Miguel. You heard from the *CODA* barge towboat?"

"About 20 minutes ago. They're close behind. I've been slowly circling them, letting them catch up," Miguel said.

"Take a heading of 047. If that white light is on top of the derrick, we're close, maybe ten miles out. When you see red lights, start slowing her down. I'm going to get a cup of coffee and then I'll give you a break."

"Recon-Two to Recon-One," Cesar recognized Mack's voice and picked up the hand-held radio. Miguel gave Cesar the helm seat,

"Recon-One."

"I've landed. What's your ETA?"

"15 minutes." They had agreed to keep all radio talk to a minimum.

"Caution. Light fog. Recon-Two, over."

"Roger. Recon-One, out."

Cesar radioed the towboat their location and ETA. "Everybody hold on." He shoved both throttles all the way forward, and the boat reacted instantly, leaping out of the calm water and racing across the top as if flying.

Mack loved high performance anything: boats, cars, planes, and of course, women. But, owning them was something different. He would sell both boats as soon as this operation was completed. Ever since his return from the Marines—for some reason or another—he guarded his privacy more and more and avoided any part of the public limelight. On the other hand, he enjoyed the attention when people appreciated the artistry of his boat and the craftsmanship of the King Air, his Birona suit; it was just one of his dichotomies.

The fog was breaking up, rising from the water as the boat bobbled on the slow moving waves. Like a giant stingray spread out on top of the water, the boat lifted and fell, in and out of the fog. Angus had tied one line off on a buoy with a blinking red light, about 30 feet north of the oil rig. White lights were all around the platform of the deserted oil rig, which was mostly under water, except for what was left of the hurricane-twisted derrick, 70 feet high with a white light on top, shining through the vanishing fog.

Mack heard the fog bell from the *Irish Mist*, clanging in the distance, north of him. He responded with a hand held foghorn and radioed the towboat, "Slow and easy." *The last thing we need now is a four-way pileup.*

Cesar's boat moved through the water just above idle speed. He heard Mack's foghorn on the starboard side and gave out two short blasts in response. He turned the wheel a couple degrees to the right and pulled back the throttle to idle speed as he broke in and out of the lifting fog.

Mack heard Cesar's foghorn and focused on the direction of the sound until he saw the green side of their navigation lights. "Recon-One straight ahead, slow and easy. I'm tied to the red blinking buoy."

"Recon-Two, I see your lights. I'm coming in on your starboard." Cesar eased forward while Miguel edged out on the bow of the boat to throw an anchor line when Mack's boat broke out of the fog. Miguel stepped back. Looming above him was a dark gray *ghost,* riding a wake with huge bat-like wings. His foot slipped on the wet deck, and he landed in a sitting position. He threw his arm up to protect his face and rolled across the deck holding on to the anchor line. A large wave splashed over the bow of the boat as it settled low in the trough. Cesar was right. It could be something from a Jules Verne novel, but Miguel had seen one before, in an Air Force Base in New Mexico. The Wizard had done a masterful paint job on Mack's boat. It was an identical replica of the F-117 Nighthawk Stealth Fighter jet: with a raised fiberglass pyramid-shaped cockpit, a long rectangular air intake scoop painted down each side of the boat, and Delta swept wings.

"Miguel, throw me the line," Angus shouted as the boats washed alongside each other.

Miguel, hanging onto a deck cleat and trying not to slide off into the water, tossed the coiled line in a long overhead hook shot. Angus grabbed the line and tied the two boats off, side by side.

Miguel stood up, wiping his eyes and studied the 38-foot long boat; it was a work of art. He remembered the F-117 was only for nighttime missions, hence the name, *Nighthawk.* The Wizard was not only creative but also a marketer—drug dealers would love this boat. It was almost undetectable at night and at 80 miles an hour could outrun 'most anything.

A fog bell from the *Irish Mist* started its steady ring, "ding-ding, ding-ding." The fog had lifted about six feet above the water now and Mack saw the lights on the lead barge approaching the far side of the oil rig. He got on the radio to Captain Nick, pilot of the *Irish Mist*, and talked him through the fog and alongside the oil rig. After tying off the 12 empty barges, the *Irish Mist* uncoupled and faced off. The Mexican towboat came around and faced up the three loaded barges to the stern of the empties, unfaced from the tow, and stood by. The *Irish Mist*, 200 feet long and 54 feet wide, moved into place, faced up to the 15-barge tow, finished the rigging, and turned the 1,000foot tow toward the rising sun. She did this with ease—with her Triple Screw, 9,000 plus horsepower engine, she could push four times this many barges. She was a workhorse, Long Hauler, operating around the clock, 24 hours a day every day of the year.

Mack set his compass for Aransas Pass, just north of Corpus Christi. This is where Recon-One, Recon-Two, and the *Irish Mist* with her tow would enter the Intracoastal Waterway. They would stay on the Intracoastal to Morgan City, turning north up the Atchafalaya River for a hundred miles, and then start the long run up the Mississippi River.

Buck hovered the Vietnam-era Huey helicopter above the Baton Rouge Marina parking lot that was stuck out over the water; he looked around but didn't see anyone. It was early Sunday morning, and this is where Mack said to pick him up. There were no cars in the parking lot, and Buck checked to make sure there were no wires or overhead obstructions and pushed the collective stick down until the chopper settled onto the parking lot. The rotor blades continued to turn, and he saw Mack walk out of the marina with a white paper sack and his duffel bag. He ducked under the blades, threw his duffel bag in the back seat, and climbed aboard in the front. Buck waited till Mack buckled up and put his headset on before lifting off. He hovered at about 20 feet, rotated 360 degrees, and looked over at Mack, who gave him a thumbs-up. He rotated the nose north, added full throttle, and in a slow climb headed for Memphis.

"Where did you get this antique?" Mack said into the microphone of his headset.

"Hey, no bitching, the price was right."

"How much?"

"Five thousand a day and no questions asked—just a heavy security deposit."

"Was the camouflage extra?" Mack asked, smiling as he handed Buck a Styrofoam cup of coffee from the sack.

"I like it. It brings back old memories, and I thought it would be a good cover for this operation."

Mack agreed. It certainly looked military, and that could be an asset.

"Everything go alright, hooking up the barges?" Buck asked.

"Yeah, we lost a little time 'cause of the fog, but the water was calm and the hand-off of the *CODA* barge was pretty routine."

"Is that what they're calling it, *CODA* barge?"

"Yeah, the barges are all alike so they mark *CODA* on the top in chalk so we can follow the goose-with-the-golden-eggs."

"Who's doing the recon in the speed boats?"

"Miguel was in Recon-One and took my place in Recon-Two with Angus. Cesar, Lazaro, and a bodyguard named Chico are all in Recon-One."

"*Cesar's* coming to the States? I thought he never left Mexico."

"I think he changed his mind at the last minute. While we were talking at the oil rig, he asked if I minded him tagging along. I said, 'Hell no, glad to have you.' I didn't blame him. I certainly couldn't sit on the sidelines a thousand miles away with a hundred million dollar deal going down."

"Why the bodyguard?" Buck asked.

"I found out he's an old friend of the family, lives on the ranch, and a longtime protector. The other brothers never let Cesar leave the hacienda without Chico.

"We're north enough now. Let's head over to the river and do a little scouting for our convoy."

"You want to drive?"

"Naw, you go ahead."

"I rented two of these, one for you and one for me. It was two for the price of one. I figured if something went wrong, we would need a backup."

"Good thinking," Mack nodded his head.

"Actually, I made the deal for $30,000 a week for both of them, and five grand a day if we need them more than a week."

"That's a hell of a deal."

"They've just had their annual inspections. I took both of them up, and they checked out clean, no problems."

"In that case you had better check me out, Captain. It's been a while."

"Just like riding a bicycle," Buck said.

Mack had flown helicopters before but never a Huey. He put his hands and feet on the controls, "I got it."

"It's all yours."

It took a few minutes of erratic flight before Mack coordinated the controls, lifted the collective, and pulled back on the cyclic climbing for some altitude. As he leveled off, he hovered, did a full 360 with the tail section stationary, rotated back with the axis of rotation in the center of the helicopter, then held the front stationary and rotated the body 360. Satisfied, he banked the chopper and headed over the river.

"How does she feel?" Buck asked.

"Powerful."

"You ok?"

"Like riding a bicycle," Mack smiled.

Buck reached down between them and flipped the engine switch off. The chopper dropped out of the sky.

Mack, without hesitation, shoved the collective stick downward, changing the pitch of the rotor blades, pressed hard on the right pedal, and eased the cyclic stick forward. He then checked his rotor RPM and the air speed and pulled up on the collective, holding the air speed to 70 knots. He set his glide angle and his rate of descent at 18 degrees and looked for a place to set the bird down.

Buck offered no assistance.

Mack spotted the levee on the far side of the river and turned on a final approach downwind. He looked for any wires or other obstacles and checked his instruments once more; his air speed was 65 knots as the Huey continued to fall. At fifty feet above the levee, Mack pulled back on the cyclic stick and up on the collective, flaring out to a hover with the nose up and floated the skids down on the grassy surface, a perfect autorotation. He looked over at Buck, "Thanks a lot."

"That's my boy."

"You could have waited a little longer, a little more altitude—you don't believe in foreplay at all, do you?"

"Why? You did great. Let's go check on the barges."

Mack lifted off and climbed to 500 feet over the river, looked around, but didn't see Angus and Miguel in Recon-Two. He figured he would catch them on his way back to Memphis. He turned downriver and, in a short time, he saw the barges and the *Irish Mist* about two miles out. He stayed at 500 feet and continued on downriver until he saw Cesar in Recon-One. He passed them and, after a mile, turned back upriver, moved slowly up behind them undetected, and descended to about ten feet above the water. Chico looked asleep stretched out across the bench seat in the back while Cesar was riding up front with Lazaro. They couldn't hear the chopper because of the two high-performance engines in the rear of the boat and the chopper was downwind. Mack inched forward until the Huey was over the twin engines. Chico raised his hand to block the sun from his eyes, then jumped to his feet and must have shouted to the others because they all stood staring up at the bird, somewhat in shock. Mack waggled his finger and shook his head, chastising them. When Lazaro pulled back on both throttles, and the boat came to a stop, Mack hovered over them, letting the Huey settle down until Buck was eye-level with them. When they saw it was Mack and Buck, they all "reached for the sky" laughing, as if to surrender.

Buck pointed his finger with his thumb up, simulating a pistol, and fired off three shots. With each shot he jerked his hand up like Clint Eastwood firing his 44-Magnum. Buck held up three fingers and pulled them across his throat.

"Three dead men," Mack said. "That's how easy it would be." He lifted off and headed upriver to the *Irish Mist.*

CHAPTER 20

THE HARDEST THING for Mack to do was to give up control—to delegate authority. All his life—over and over— he had heard and lived by the old axiom, "If you want it done right, do it yourself." Mainly, his was due to the fact that he was a multitasker and had never been in a supervisory position. But he *was* introspective, and the long boat ride across the Gulf allowed him plenty of time to analyze what he was doing and where he was headed. He quickly realized he would have to trust others with some of the responsibility; there was no way he could do it all. Leaving over a hundred million dollars in the hands of *others* would be a major challenge. They had another four days on the river, and Mack, after breaking it all down, concluded that he needed to be in Memphis and make sure everything was ready when they got there. Timing and speed were everything, and being organized was the engine that would ensure their success. His Force Recon training taught him that much, plus Cesar, who had much more business experience, was now riding a close shotgun on their product, and had everything shipshape before Mack left.

The first thing Mack wanted to check on was the dock they were constructing so the barge could anchor alongside. Directly across from King's Island was the confluence of the Wolf River and the Mississippi River. About 1,500 feet up the Wolf was a natural canal running north onto the downtown airport property; this is where they planned to unload the barge. Mack had left specific instructions not to cut the tops of the overhanging trees. Buck had posted guards around the clock, barricading the area and posting "Under Construction" signs.

Mack leveled the helicopter at 1,000 feet and followed the

Mississippi River into Memphis and over the massive span of treetops which covered the city as far as one could see. He saw the Wolf River on his right and lowered the chopper as he turned east toward the confluence and then north up the wooded canal. Most of the tree limbs had been cut back to the trunk, ten feet from ground level, while leaving an umbrella effect for any spying eyes in the sky. A large track-hoe was digging out the side of the canal, a motor grader was following a bulldozer smoothing the surface of a dirt road, and a front-end loader was filling dump trucks.

"Busy little bees," Buck said.

"Let's get down and have a look."

Mack circled back to the airport and hovered over a large H painted white on the ramp at the south end of the airport. He set the Huey down on the H, switched off the ignition and looked over at Buck.

"Like I said, 'Just like riding a bicycle.'" A tow tractor raced across the tarmac to meet them as Buck unbuckled his safety harness and handed Mack some keys, "Can you get the truck while I unload and help secure the rotor blades?"

There was no security inside. The guards were on the perimeter and only a four-foot chain link fence across the front separated the parking lot from the airfield. Other than aviation people, very few were aware the airport even existed. This would all change in a couple of days.

Mack drove out on the ramp, threw the bags in the back of the truck, and walked over to look at a small Citation parked up close to the operation building. He had never seen a jet at this airport, and it looked somewhat suspicious—not good timing for something to be *unusual.* He looked through all the windows but didn't see anything that would require a second look. He had been looking at a used Lear before he bought the King Air, but it was way too noisy and required a longer runway. Buck came out of the operation building and walked over to Mack.

"Everything okay?" Mack said.

"Same ole,' same ole,' employee problems."

"Who's Citation?"

"Don't worry, I've already checked it out. Some big-shot lawyer flew in for a one-day deposition. Let's go see our construction site."

When Mack first started planning *CODA*, he ran across an original construction document in Mickey's office titled, "Construction Schedule," which was basically a bar chart with a timeline. It was an oversized sheet of paper that listed the type of construction, start and finish dates, and slots for each day of the month, using legends and charts to show the progress of construction. On the left side of the page under Description was a title of work, i.e., from Site Work and Foundations to Structural Steel and all the way to the bottom to Close Out with the start and finish date for each one. Mack got the idea to adapt this form to *CODA* operation. Albeit, this was contrary to his orders of, "nothing in writing," he justified it by needing a timeline to follow each phase of the operation; plus, he would have the only copy.

When finished, he was not pleased with his work. He needed something more visual but couldn't think of anything, so he gave up and went for a run. When he came back, he sat with his feet propped up on his desk, relaxing so his right brain would come up with something. A long conference table was against the wall, a catchall for everything that didn't have a home: boxes, old typewriters, telephone books....He stared at the table for a long time then got up and cleared everything off, crawled underneath it, and was on his back studying the table when Buck walked in. "You playing hide-and-seek?"

Mack jumped up, found the measuring tape, gave one end to Buck and stretched the tape out, measuring the table.

"You want to tell me what you're doing?"

"I need a battle plan, something visual, maybe a physical model showing the area of the operation, the two rivers, King's Island...I could use a sheet of plywood, some 2 x 4s and sand." He picked up a yellow extension cord and pulled it across the table, "This is the Mississippi River." He took a stapler and a small box of paper clips, "This is the *Irish Mist* with her barges coming up the river." He grabbed a dictionary and two other books and a couple of scale rulers. "The dictionary is our headquarters, right here." He sat the book in the middle of the table, "and this coffee cup is the downtown airport, the ruler is the runway, and..."

"Wait a minute, wait a minute."

"No, wait...listen. This is the beauty of the plan. I remove the top from the base of the conference table, we set the 4' x 8' sheet of plywood..."

"Great idea...but the *Irish Mist* will be here in two days, and it would take you that long to build the model. Marcus will be in tonight, and Francisco and his men came in early this morning. We're going to need every minute of your time pulling all these men and their work together. How about I run over to Campbell Blueprinting? They can print us off any size map we want. I can pick up some color pens and map legends and we can mark it up in a couple of hours."

"You're right. What was I thinking? That was *stupid*. I got plenty to focus on." Mack made a couple of notes. "I'll work on a quick preliminary timeline, beginning when the *Irish Mist* starts its push up the Mississippi. I'll have it finished by the time you're back. It won't take me long, and we can put it all together for tomorrow's meeting."

"Did you talk to Angus and Miguel about the meeting?"

"Yeah, Angus called from the fishing camp at Tunica Cutoff. He said they were upriver about six miles in front of the *Irish Mist*. No problems, nothing suspicious, everything's been...routine. They're coming on in tonight for the meeting in the morning."

"What about Cesar?"

"He said he was close behind the *Irish Mist*, near West Helena, and as soon as Angus and Miguel head to Memphis, he's going to scout front and back of the *Irish Mist* all the way in. Everything's on schedule;

so far so good."

Buck left for Campbell Blueprint.

Mack thought about his phone conversation with Cesar; normally, somewhat stoic, he had been cheerful and talkative, especially about finally completing his life's ambition—growing grapes and making wine. He couldn't wait to move to his new home and vineyard in California and wanted Mack to move out there and go in the wine business with him. Mack was considering it. He and Cesar were so like-minded and could talk for hours, but Mack was a Southerner, born and raised. "Territorial instinct," some called it: every time he came back across the Mississippi he wanted to kiss the pavement of the bridge. But he had told Cesar he would give it some serious thought. Mack had planned a large celebration and a going-away party for Cesar at Justine's Restaurant, al fresco in their Rose Garden. He had ordered some rare bottles of wine and had a surprise, a very special gift for Cesar. Down at Shamrock, their world champion stallion, Ebony Storm, had fathered a new colt about six months ago. According to Red Bordeaux, the foal looked identical to Ebony Storm when he was born, hence the name, Carbon Copy. He was to be rolled out to the Rose Garden on a wheeled platform and uncovered.

The *Irish Mist* pushed her tow upstream through the midnight hour using her radar and swing indicator. The river was serpentine in this part of the Mississippi Delta, and from time to time the captain used spotlights to make some of the bends that were extremely tight.

Captain Nicholas Socrates Alissandratos sat in the wheelhouse of the *Irish Mist* perusing his nautical charts of the Mississippi River and making notes. He was a short man, and his legs used to dangle from the raised Captain's chair until the machinist's mate welded a second step to rest his feet. Printed on his Master Marnier Ticket was five feet, five inches tall, but he was much shorter. When asked, he always replied he had shrunk since taking the test years ago.

A Master's license allowed him to captain any vessel, any size, anywhere in the world, and he had: oil freighters, cargo vessels, and merchant ships. He had sailed from the Port of Singapore, where the largest tonnage in the world is shipped, to the Port of South Louisiana, the largest port in the world for bulk cargo.

Captain Nick picked up his binoculars and scanned his tow of 1,000 feet of barges in front of him. It was inky black with booming thunder and strikes of lightning flashing across the barges. He looked down at his radar and saw Horseshoe Bend, a long wide curve in the river. Looking through his binoculars again, he watched the lights on the lead barge disappear from view around the horseshoe curve. In his peripheral vision, he caught a flicker of a spot light crossing the water on his port side. He opened his side window, four stories above the water, and waved at Cesar in Recon-One as they passed the *Irish Mist*. They would run interference for the next hour to make sure there were no problems waiting for them around the bend. Captain Nick watched the white stern light of Recon-One as it turned into the beginning of the horseshoe curve and dissolved into the blackness.

Captain Nick could now see the lights on his lead barge as the *Irish Mist* came out of Horseshoe Bend. He looked down at the radar and saw that the next ten miles of the river ran straight, right alongside old Highway 61. He looked through his binoculars, and checked the face wire and bitts that tied the *Irish Mist* to the barges, then checked each barge from the push knees of the towboat to the lead barge, and found everything running straight and shipshape. He saw a white light about a mile in front of his lead barge and adjusted the focus on the binoculars; it was Cesar in Recon-One. He was anchored, probably waiting for him to catch up. He slowly steered the wheel to the right, hugging the east shore due to a buildup of sandbars on the west side, then checked the location of Recon-One again.

The *Irish Mist* had about an hour to go without any bends or curves in the river. Captain Nick leaned back in his chair drinking his umpteenth cup of coffee. He could relax now; there was no other traffic on his radar except Recon-One. He thought about Cesar, an interesting fellow that he had as a guest on the *Irish Mist* a number of times for coffee and dinner over the past five days. He was very cultured, soft spoken, down to earth. Certainly not what you would expect when you heard—"Mexican drug dealer." Truth be known, he had probably hauled more drugs back and forth across the continent than all of them put together. He was thinking of the movie, *The French Connection* with Gene Hackman, and the car with a load of heroin hidden in the rocker panels. There was no way anyone could know what was in all those shipping containers he had hauled.

Just like the cargo he was hauling now, inspected and certified by Cesar's customs broker, and furnished with the proper documentation. Comparably, his tow represented a pebble of sand in the Mississippi River. Over 630 million tons of cargo valued at over $73 billion dollars moved up and down the Mississippi each *year*. It was the largest inland transportation system in the world, transporting tremendous amounts of commodities, like agriculture, coal, petroleum, metals, aggregates for construction, and construction materials. The bill of lading, clamped to a clipboard inside the wheelhouse of the *Irish Mist*, stated that the cargo was dry cement and as far as Captain Nick was concerned, that's what the *Irish Mist* was pushing upriver...dry cement.

When Captain Nick lifted his binoculars to check on Cesar's location, the first thing he saw was a streak of light from the east bank of the river, and he thought, maybe a shooting star. But when he saw the second flash streaking across the sky, he lowered his binoculars for a larger picture. He followed the trail with his naked eye until he heard what he first thought was a sonic boom and then saw the explosion. Was it a plane crash? He grabbed his binoculars again..."Ohhh, my God." He watched the mushrooming inferno.

"Captain Nick, Captain Nick..." a deckhand came crashing up the steps into the wheelhouse.

"What the hell was *that?*" Captain Nick said.

"A LAW!"

"What?"

"A rocket—Light Anti-tank Weapon."

"Where did it come from? Did it hit...? Captain Nick continued to scan the river with his binoculars.

"Yeah, Recon-One is gone; blown to smithereens."

"Are you sure?"

"I'm sure, Captain. I was in Vietnam, I know a LAW when I see one. It came from the bank while I was out on the lead barge; I felt the explosion."

"Get the men and line the barges on each side with lights, maybe..."

"Yes sir," he hurried from the wheelhouse but paused at the door, "but...but Captain, everything was incinerated."

It was almost daylight when Mack climbed from the copilot's seat to the back of the Huey helicopter and opened the side door. Buck had made a couple of low passes over the *Irish Mist*, saw Captain Nick wave, and then hovered above the back of the boat. He maneuvered the helicopter in a 360 degree rotation, scanning the surroundings, but still didn't see anything unusual or out of place.

Earlier, a phone call from the night manager at the marine service center, had awakened Mack. They had received an SOS signal from the *Irish Mist* three times. While getting dressed, he had pulled his phone from the charger and flipped it on. Immediately it had vibrated. There were three messages, all from the *Irish Mist*: "911." Mack called Buck and told him there was trouble on the *Irish Mist*, to get the Huey ready, and he would be at the downtown airport in fifteen minutes. He then called Angus and told him to get Miguel and to head downriver in Recon-Two to the *Irish Mist*, full speed and dress for trouble.

"I don't see nothing," Buck shouted over the noise of the engine and the rotor blades. Mack pointed down to the deck of the *Irish Mist* and leaned out the door, giving hand signals as Buck lowered the helicopter closer to the boat. Mack stopped him about three feet from the upper deck and, while it hovered, he jumped. He was dressed in his old Battle Dress Uniform Marine Tiger Stripe, with his M-16 and Colt 45 automatic strapped in a chest holster.

Captain Nick hurried down the steps from the pilothouse to meet Mack, who was on one knee, scoping the area for the 911 emergency. Captain Nick assured Mack that he thought the attack was over and guided him down the steps to the galley. He told Mack he saw the rocket when fired and, one of the deckhands, a thousand feet out on the lead barge saw the rocket when it hit Cesar's boat. He explained how they had searched for them. Mack didn't believe him; there had to be some kind of a mistake. Cesar couldn't be dead. He was just talking to him. He demanded to talk to the deckhand. Yet the more he refused to believe, the sicker he got. He remembered something he said the last time he was at the hacienda while the two of them were out under the gazebo drinking a vintage wine. Cesar had said, "Mack, all I ever wanted out of life was to make a bottle of wine like this."

And his stupid response had been, "Life is short...you're here today and gone tomorrow." He felt as if a wild bull had gored him in the gut, and he swallowed hard to keep from throwing up.

The door opened, and the deckhand that Captain Nick ordered to the galley for Mack to question came in. "Later," Captain Nick said, waving him back out the door and then got a dishtowel, soaked it with cold water, and handed it to Mack.

Mack covered his face in the towel and took a couple of deep breaths. *Cesar dead...just like that. His new home, the vineyard, the winery— poof—extinct!* He hated that he could not control his emotions when it came to people he was close to. He had tried all sorts of digressions, and was a lot better than he used to be, but when it was personal, he was too sensitive. Sadness overwhelmed his thoughts, he choked, the hurt crushing the breath from him. But he had faced pain before, learned that emotions were a buildup of energy, and energy was power. There was *one* power that overpowered all emotions, though—the power of revenge.

CHAPTER 21

MACK WAS STILL in the galley drinking coffee and trying to get his focus back on the $100 million cargo he was pushing upriver. Two of his partners were dead, and someone was trying to sabotage or steal their shipment...or were they? The *Irish Mist* was unscathed and still on schedule. Was it a warning? They don't want the product. What are they going to do with 183 tons of marijuana? It took us almost a year to set up this operation—they're after the *money*. But why the attack? Why show your hand? He was writing in his notebook when the door banged open and Miguel barged in.

"They're really dead?"

Mack nodded his head.

"All of them?"

"Yeah."

"I should be too. If you hadn't called us in for the meeting, I'd be toast. Damn, why didn't Cesar stay in Mexico? He told me he was only going as far as the handoff at the oil rig? Whoever did this, Mack, we got to make 'em pay, big-time."

"I was thinking, maybe it was *me* they wanted to kill? No one knew I was getting off Recon-Two in Baton Rouge. I changed my mind at the last minute; there was no reason for Cesar and me both to ride shotgun on the barge.

"But now, we have a bigger problem. We've got a mole, a *rat* somewhere inside. It has to be. No one outside our group would know our schedule, know we would be passing Mhoon Landing at that exact time. The question is...is the mole from our camp or Cesar's?"

"None of our five, I'd bet on that. What would be the motive?

Same for Cesar; they're all brothers, and we're all paid the same. It wouldn't make sense."

"I can't get sidetracked on this; we have to stay on schedule. Can you find someone we can trust to handle this? Captain Nick has the coordinates pinned down exactly where the rocket was fired. He said it could only be Mhoon Landing unless they were in a boat, and he didn't see any boats. Before you leave, I want you and Angus to run by there, look it over, and see if you can find anything."

"We'll do that now, and I know just the person to handle this. Not cheap, a hundred an hour plus expenses, but mean as a pit bull and never gives up." Miguel stood up to leave.

"Good, but I need him to jump on it immediately. What's his name?"

"Zira."

"Zira? A woman?"

"One of the best."

"Well...why not? If you say so."

"Are you staying here?" Miguel asked.

"Buck is picking me up. I'm trying to figure out a way to tell Tony. Man, it's going to kill him."

"You want me to do it?"

"Thanks, I'd better handle it...but it wouldn't hurt to have Angus there. They've become best buds. While you're checking out Mhoon Landing, make sure there's...you know, nothing floating around, maybe washed up on the bank...for the funeral services. You guys be careful."

"You too, Boss."

Over the noise of the helicopter, Mack brought Buck up to date on everything that had happened. Some things he had already deciphered from all of the radio transmissions. Buck had seen a lot of hard deaths in the Marines, and like the armored vest, you learn to build a barrier of protection around the mind as well as the body.

"That's tough. I know you and Cesar..."

"He's gone. Nothing we can do about that except payback, and we'll damn well get that, tenfold."

"What now?"

"I'm not changing a thing; we stay on schedule just as we planned. At least until I find out why they showed their hand with this one attack."

"They were sending us a message."

"What message? They didn't touch the *Irish Mist* or the barge. They're not after the cargo. They're after the money."

"What then, another attack?"

"Yeah, I'm sure, but when and where?"

"After we collect the money? It's got to be."

"I agree, but only a few people know about the warehouse, and we're shipping the money out as fast as we get it. We need more security. I want you to get Shooter and his troops, at least a squad or more and two snipers. No one but you and I will know about this. I want to catch this snake and skin him alive. Make it enticing for Shooter so he can't say no. Say $20,000 cash for Shooter and $10,000 for each Marine he can hustle up. We'll need them maybe four days at the most, plus pay their expenses and a bonus if everything goes well.

But they have to be in Memphis before dark, sooner if possible."

"I'll fly down to the lodge as soon as I drop you off."

"I don't want anyone to know about Cesar or the attack. The last thing we need now is the Coast Guard or the police snooping around our barge. As far as we're concerned, Cesar, his bodyguard, and Lazarus all turned back to Mexico at the oil rig. I'll tell Tony, and he can tell his brothers *after,* when we give them their money. Same with Captain Nick and the deckhands, make sure they saw nothing. When this is over and all goes well, they'll get a bonus too."

Mack stood over the conference table moving pins and symbols on a blown-up map of the city. Coming into Memphis, he and Buck flew low over the exact route the *Irish Mist* would push the *CODA* barge up the Wolf River tonight. It was less than a mile up the Wolf River before they would turn back north for a short run up the canal where the new dock was located. They had cleared an area about the size of a football field for the parking and loading of five tractor-trailer trucks, two cranes, and two large forklifts. Mack had color-coded pins designating the locations and equipment on the map.

The phone on his desk buzzed, and he pressed the speaker button, "Mr. Shannon, a gentleman is calling you on the other line. Said he's an old friend."

Mack hesitated, thinking maybe it might be Shooter. He sat down behind his desk, "I'll take it." He paused a second time, then pressed the button, "This is Mack."

There was no answer. Mack could hear the line was still open.

"Who is this?"

"Like I told the woman...an old friend."

It wasn't Shooter, but the voice was somewhat familiar. "Well, *old* friend, I don't have time for games. If you don't tell me who you are, this conversation is over."

"I hear you're looking for some new partners?"

Mack felt like he had stepped on a high-voltage wire; he couldn't speak. *Looking for some new partners?* Is *that* what he said?

"Mack, get me off that damn speaker phone."

Mack jumped from his chair, snatching up the handset, as rage flooded his body. "You lowlife, scum sucking, son-of-a-bitch!" His lips were all over the mouthpiece, spraying it with spittle. "Mack, settle down, I..."

"I should've choked the life out of your useless ass years ago and thrown you in the river for fish bait!"

"Mack!" Crazy Ray shouted, "I didn't kill Miguel. He was a friend of mine too. Why do you think I'm calling you? Mack, are you still there? I know who killed them and I want to make you a deal."

"I don't make deals with *shit* like you."

"Calm down, Mack. I'm the one who should be mad. You *owe* me. I was dying of cancer, and you stole my $25,000. You robbed me of my men and cheated me out of King's Island. You think I would let you get away with that? Am *I* shouting and calling *you* names? We go way back to grammar school, man, just listen to what I got to say. I swear to God, I had nothing to do with killing those men.

"Let me tell you..." Mack started.

"*Hold it.* Let *me* finish. If I get what I want, I'll give you the person who killed Miguel."

He thinks Miguel was killed in the boat explosion?

"Remember this, Mack; I have the names of everyone involved in your deal with the Diaz brothers, in Mexico and in Memphis. I know all about this barge shipment coming upriver. I've had a man inside your operation since day one. I know everything. My deal is simple.

You owe me, and I want a percentage of the profits." A long pause followed.

"I know what you're thinking, Mack. Your brain's racing to figure how to get out of this shakedown, right? Well, it ain't gonna happen. I'll drop a dime on your ass so quick the DEA and the Feds will have you rotting in a federal prison for life."

Be cool, Mack, this is exactly what you didn't want to happen. You've got to hold this operation together. Damn, who's his snitch?

"What do you want?" Mack said.

"Listen close; I want ten million dollars, cash. Now don't be stupid. This way you and your partners still keep your take without any losses. Like I said, I know every move you make. I will call back in two hours.

Have an answer." Crazy Ray hung up the phone.

Mack slammed the handset down so hard all the push buttons started blinking. *What the hell else is going to happen?*

THINK! He took a deep breath. Okay. What was it Napoleon Hill said? *With every adversity there's an equal or greater benefit.* He repeated it out loud and then looked at his watch—*where is everybody?*

He remembered that Li was flying into Memphis International from Liechtenstein at noon, and Angus was picking him up.

Mack pressed the intercom to the receptionist, and, changing his mind, said, "Never mind," and flipped the intercom off. *The phones may be tapped.* He looked out the window and saw Miguel getting out of his car: *is Miguel the mole? At one time he and Crazy Ray were close. He's been down in Mexico and knew the schedule there and in Memphis. No, they think he's dead. No one knew that I was leaving Recon-One or that Miguel would ride in my place…or that Cesar changed his mind at the last minute? Is there really a mole? Is Crazy Ray bluffing?*

He met Miguel in the kitchen, and they walked outside on the barge to talk. "I found out who's after our money."

"*Who?*"

"Your old boss…Crazy Ray."

"You're kidding, right? I thought he was dead. How'd you find out?"

"He called me for a shakedown."

"He didn't kill Cesar…"

"Oh yeah, he's involved. He said he wasn't, but he knows who did and will tell us. He thinks *you* were on the boat and were killed."

"It will be my pleasure to prove him wrong when I slit his throat."

"He's crazy, but he's no fool. He told me if something happens to him, his attorney has two sealed envelopes addressed to the DEA and the FBI. We'll have to think of something special for him."

Miguel sat down across from Mack. "They used an M72, a LAW rocket. Angus found the sling wrapped around a tree limb underwater; he didn't know what it was. We got out and walked around after that and found where the blowback from the rocket had burned the grass black behind the pier. Zira is backtracking from there now. You want her to stay down there since we already know it was Crazy Ray?"

"Yes. Can she check for phone taps and bugs?"

"Sure, and plant them too. You thinking what I'm thinking, track down Crazy Ray?"

"If she can find him; but it's got to be quick."

"Like I said, she's the best."

"I'll believe you if she can find him. Tell her I'll pay her double if she does, but I need it yesterday. I want to know his every move, 24-hour surveillance, without detection for the next five days. Have her sweep our offices and, if she finds any bugs, leave them until she talks to me. And have her check out here too, around the barge."

"Zira's thorough; she'll make a clean sweep of everything," Miguel said, and hurried across the barge to call her.

Mack walked out to the end of the barge and stared at the fastmoving current. He tried to organize in his mind all the things he had to do in such a short period of time. He removed his pocket notebook and checked his list when a feeling of *fight-or-flight* came over him. A chill nipped the back of his neck, and he shrugged his shoulders, as if to erase the crosshairs of a sniper locked in on him. Turning back toward the riverbank, he adjusted his sunglasses so he could barely look over the top to scan the area. He searched along the river's edge, north and south up to Riverside Drive, and then checked each building on the other side of the railroad tracks. His eyes walked up the bluff of Union Avenue to Front Street as he continued to search every window of the buildings on the bluff overlooking the river. He stopped when he saw two shiny dots coming from a window on the top floor of a building on the southeast corner of Front and Union. He counted over from the corner—left to right—without raising his head. It was the third window. That had to be the old Memphis Cotton Exchange building that faced the river. He looked again, and the two silver dots were gone. *Damn, did I spook him?* He turned his back, facing the river, and removed his phone, acting as if he were dialing a number. After a few minutes, he turned, and there it was again, the sun reflecting off the binoculars, and he knew that someone was spying on him. He stopped walking when he saw the black Cadillac bump down the riverbank and park. Angus and Li got out, and Mack waved for them to come out on the barge.

Meeting them halfway, he put his arms around them as they walked toward the table. "Don't look back. Just act normal. Someone is watching us with binoculars from a building on top of the bluff."

They all sat around the table, Mack with his back to the riverbank. He explained his call from Crazy Ray, then stopped, bent over, and tied his shoe, casually looking under the spool table for a bug. "Okay, just be casual. Let's all walk over and check the mooring lines around the bitts while I'm thinking."

Li and Angus followed Mack out to the end of the barge. Mack stood with one foot on a bollard with a large rope tied securely around the double-bitt.

"Do you know who's watching us?" Li asked.

"No, the best I can tell they're on the top floor of the old Cotton Exchange building, but I'm pretty sure they work for Crazy Ray."

"Do you want me to check it out?" Angus said.

"No, I've got a PI coming, and she's looking for Crazy Ray."

"*She?*" Angus said.

Mack shrugged his shoulders, "Miguel has used her before and swears by her. It's an all-girl agency with a couple of men on call when they need muscle.

"Li, you don't look too good. You okay? Bad flight?" Mack had moved his foot from the bollard, and Li was resting on one of the bitts with his hand on the other.

Angus jumped in, "I told him about Cesar while driving back, the whole thing; he got sick, and we had to stop."

"You feel like telling me about your trip and your meeting with Maddie?" Mack said.

"I can't stop thinking about Cesar. What a waste of life and just for money. This is what I was afraid would happen."

Mack put his arm around Li's shoulder, "I know...I feel the same way, but there's nothing we can do now."

Li stood and took a few steps to the edge of the barge. There was a warm southeast breeze coming off the river. He removed his glasses and wiped his eyes with his handkerchief, turned back to Mack and Angus, and told them about his trip.

Maddie was a delight. To Li she was beautiful: fair skin, blonde hair, typical for that part of the country, and blue eyes that you got lost in and forgot what you were trying to say. But what impressed Li the most was her knowledge of international finance.

Li explained that when he landed at Zurich Airport, Maddie met him as he came off the plane. A tall, middle aged, official-looking man was with her and was introduced only as Hans. Li had no luggage except a folded garment bag and his briefcase. They followed Hans to a private lounge off the main corridor, and Maddie asked for his passport and gave it to Hans. A few minutes later Hans led them to an elevator, and they rode to the main floor and followed him out on the tarmac to a waiting limousine. He opened the door for Li, handed him his passport, and in perfect English said, "Welcome to Switzerland."

Maddie winked at Li as she slid in beside him and whispered, "You just went through customs."

The limo driver eased across the tarmac for about a mile and stopped in front of a helicopter, its rotor blades slowly turning. It was a Corporate VIP model, made in Italy and painted in high gloss green. Large gold letters flowed through a stream down the sides, spelling the name *CLEARWATER*. Li wondered if the colors were a subliminal icon for cash and gold. In less than thirty minutes, they were descending down the Rhine Valley to Vaduz, Liechtenstein. The rugged snowcapped Alps bordered one side of the city and the baby Rhine River flowed glacier-blue down the other side. A prominent landmark, perched atop a steep hill in the middle of the city, was Vaduz Castle, the home of the reigning prince of Liechtenstein.

They hovered over the roof of a four-story, green granite building and slowly lowered the helicopter onto a painted red H in the middle of the roof. When the door opened, Li inhaled the clean mountain air and listened to the hundreds of small wind chimes hanging from the necks of the grazing cows down in the valley.

Maddie explained to Li as they toured the building that there was no airport or even a train station in Vaduz, a tiny capital city of less than 5,000. Yet the whole country of Liechtenstein, with less than 30,000 people, managed over 100 billion dollars. Although this was Clearwater's headquarters, and she had an office and a small penthouse apartment on the top floor, she lived in Zurich, which was about equidistant between Basel and Vaduz. She explained to Li that FedEx flew direct from Memphis to the EuroAirport Basel-MulhouseFreiburg, the closest airport to Liechtenstein, because it was the international custom hub for freight and passengers into Switzerland, France, and Germany.

This was news to Li; he had assumed the money would be flown directly to Clearwater in Vaduz. This was his first time in Europe and, from all the signs and languages, he didn't know if he was in France, Germany, Switzerland, or Liechtenstein. Li learned that Hans was in charge of Swiss customs even though the airport was on French soil, but once the freight arrived at EuroAirport, Hans would personally walk the money from the FedEx hub to Clearwater's waiting freight helicopter. Maddie added that she and her security man would be close behind Hans the whole time. This was another reason Li was impressed with Maddie; her attention to details was amazing. She showed Li the vault in the basement that was dug out of the side of a mountain. It was about 100 feet long, 50 feet wide, and 10 feet high; everything inside, including the three-foot thick vault door, was polished brass. But the most interesting and revealing part of his whole tour was the third floor, the maximum-security area, called the *Kontengruppe*, the Account Group. Everyone inside wore a one-piece jumpsuit that was removed and checked, and then everyone was scanned before leaving the room. Cameras were everywhere—in the ceiling, floors, and under the clear Lexicon tables that lined the walls. In their "count room" there were currency machines of every size and type for sorting, counting, counterfeit detection, discriminating denominations, bill stacking, and strapping. These machines were duplicated in almost every foreign currency from the Dollar, the Franc, the Mark, the Pound, the Yen, and many others: a world of money.

Maddie gave Li clear instructions and asked him to repeat back to her how she wanted the money packaged. She had already FedExed two counting machines and two strapping machines, stamped *inspected*, to Mack. They wouldn't need a sorting machine since it was all hundred-dollar bills, but she was adamant about the packaging: 500 bills, two and half inches thick, double strapped. These packets of $50,000 each would be packed in double-lined plastic boxes, 12" x 12" x 20". Each box would hold $2,400,000. This first shipment would be 16-boxes, $38,400,000. Eight boxes fit squarely on a wood pallet, stacked two high, and would weigh approximately 836 pounds, not counting the boxes, but less than the maximum of 1,000 pounds per pallet. The balance of their $50-million would take less than a week to collect and ship. There was a 25% penalty for any late payments from their distributors. The product would be held in a different location for one day.

Li choked up when he talked about Cesar's money. Cesar had planned to pick up their money in Memphis and fly it to Mexico. Now, Li would need to count, strap, and box Cesar's money and deliver it to Tony unless he heard differently.

Mack reached in his pocket, removed his vibrating phone, and read, "911-Your office." He turned and ran across the barge, made a quick check of the windows in the Cotton Exchange Building, and saw no glare from binoculars. "Someone has broken into my office," he shouted back.

Buck was returning from his meeting with Shooter and drove across Riverside Drive onto the riverbank. As he coasted down the cobblestones, he saw Mack, Angus, and Li standing out on the barge; *another meeting,* he thought. At the same time, in his peripheral vision, he caught a movement in the window of Mack's office. *Who the hell was*

that? No one was supposed to be in Mack's office when he wasn't there. He noticed a dark green Chevrolet Suburban parked down at the end of the barge next to the water. It had no chrome, all the windows were tinted black, and the rear was facing the barge. *Something wasn't quite kosher here.* He texted Mack.

Hurrying over to the truck, he rubbed his hand over the hood—and the engine was still warm. He walked around, looking in the windows, and then noticed the tags were from Crittenden County, across the river in Arkansas. He crossed the gangplank, threw his leg over the handrail, and sneaked down the side of the barge to Mack's office window. The blinds were half- opened, and he saw the back of someone bent over Mack's desk, rummaging through the desk's drawers. Buck squatted and duck-walked under Mack's window, lost his balance and banged against the metal siding, then righted himself. He baby-stepped down to the end of the barge, entered through the back door to the hallway, and stopped at Mack's office. With his ear against the door, he turned the doorknob and pushed the door open. He stopped at the doorway when he saw a woman looking up from behind Mack's desk. She was dressed in a tight pair of black jeans, a white t-shirt, and a black jean vest.

"What are you doing in here?" Buck said, straddle-legged, both hands on his hips. "Who the hell are you?"

"None of your damn business," she said. "Who the hell are you?" She flipped her black hair out of her face and stood with her legs apart, both hands on her hips, mocking him.

"Listen, young lady, we can do this the hard wa...."

"Hard? You bald-headed, one-eyed old fart you haven't seen hard in 20 years and, when you did, you didn't know what to do with it."

Buck moved toward her. "Okay, you smart mouthed bitch, if that's the way you want it—I'm going to drag your ass out of here."

"You and who else, fatso," she scurried to the opposite corner of the desk.

Buck lunged across the desk, anticipating her move, and grabbed her by the wrist. She screamed, her other hand darted inside her vest, and jerked out nunchucks. Buck saw the pair of sticks as she swung wide with her hip and arm, and he threw up his hand, blocking the full force of the hardwood. But the blunt end of the stick bounced off his hand to his temple with enough force to stun him. He lay motionless, stretched out across the desk. She was on him immediately, spraying him in the face with pepper spray. Buck rolled off the desk to the floor, got up on his knees, coughing and holding both hands over his face.

Mack and Angus came rushing into the office, Li lingering behind. Everything on Mack's desk was strewn all over the floor, a chair was knocked over, and Buck was on his knees moaning. Mack stared at the girl in black, one hand holding the nunchucks and the other holding a can of Mace. "What are you doing in my office?"

"Are you Mack Shannon?"

"Answer me, woman."

"I'm Zira LeBlanc," she said, reaching in her vest pocket and tossing a handful of small, button-sized microphones on his desk.

"You have more bugs in this place than a flea circus."

"My door was locked. How did you get in here?"

"You call that a lock? It took me 10 seconds to get in. Miguel said you wanted the sweep done *immediately*. You pay me double, you get— *immediately*." She lifted herself up on his desk and dangled her feet back and forth.

"I told Miguel I didn't want the bugs removed."

"You want to tell *me* how to run *my* business?" Zira said.

Mack had about enough of her mouth, and Zira knew to back off.

"I left a couple bugs with off and on switches; they're off now."

Mack started coughing. "Angus, open that window and air this place out." He put his arm around Buck, "You okay, Bud?"

"Yeah, next time I'll shoot the little bitch for trespassing."

Zira jumped from Mack's desk, "You won't be shooting anyone, you one-eyed..."

Mack shouted, "ZIRA!" Then looked over to Li, "Take Buck down to the kitchen and get his eye washed out while I talk to this…"

"He started this, said he was going to *drag* my ass…"

"Quiet—*please!* I don't have the time." Mack stared at her with his hands on his hips and his legs apart.

"*Okay!*" she said, sitting back on Mack's desk. "What *is it* around here anyway? Something in the water, all of you guys challenging everyone with your John Wayne stance? It just pisses people off."

Angus was picking up papers from the floor and almost cracked up…*ballsy little maverick.*

Mack walked around the corner of his desk and righted his chair. "Get your butt off my desk," he said, as he sat down and put the receiver back on his phone. He watched her walk across the room while Angus held a chair for her.

"Damn, what happened to Buck?" Miguel said as he hurried into Mack's office. "One of the men in the kitchen is taking him to the eye doctor."

Zira jumped up, "Miguel. I saw him sneaking around outside and thought he was the one planting the bugs and…"

Mack jumped up and slammed his hand on top of his desk. "*Enough!* Don't you listen to people? I don't have time for this *shit.* We need a meeting, now. Everybody find a chair. Miguel, get Li in here."

Mack introduced Zira to everyone so there would be no more mistakes and showed them the bugs she had discovered. He looked over his notes and explained to Miguel and Zira about the binoculars on the top floor of the Cotton Exchange Building, and that it was probably Crazy Ray or his people who had been spying on them.

Zira made a note of the floor and window location, and then her phone vibrated. Mack nodded to his desk phone, but she shook her head.

She told the group she had never pulled off of a hot trail and had continued following their lead on the Mhoon Landing shooting. Not many places were open at the time of the shooting, and two of her girls had been checking places along the highway offering money for information. They got a hit at the Blue and White Restaurant. One of the kitchen help saw a Hispanic man, dressed in camouflage, outside in the parking lot and saw a black guy named Rocky pick him up in his truck. She thought that was odd that late at night and with hunting season closed, but didn't say anything to anyone. Another twenty dollars got them the location of Rocky Robinson's shack a mile down the road. They're sitting on his house now waiting for him.

CHAPTER 22

ZIRA HAD ONE of Mack's most admired traits, aggressiveness; she took care of business. He liked Zira, you didn't have to kick her in the butt to get her started.

Zira was animated while talking about her work; her dark eyes lit up with passion. Angus was practically drooling.

Mack told Zira he needed to find Crazy Ray ASAP and to start at the Cotton Exchange Building first.

"I'll have his location before the day is over," Zira said as she got up from her chair. Angus stood close behind her, and she turned and looked straight into his eyes, and whispered, "None of this is for you, big boy, you're way too hungry for me." She headed for the door, stopped and looked back at Mack, "A freebie—I'll install an electronic lock on your door that will take a cutting torch to open. You're still paying double, right?"

Buck walked in the door, and Zira stepped back to let him pass. They stared at each other, and Zira said, "*Biiiig* man," and hurried down the hallway.

Buck shook his head, "Tough little broad."

"I thought you went to the eye doctor." Mack said.

"It didn't hit my eye, just burned my face. One of the cops got a towel, soaked it with milk, and I held it on my face. Most of the burning has gone." Looking out the door he added, "I'd like to throw her across my knee and wear her ass out."

"Yeah, me too," Angus said.

Mack wanted to say to Buck, *I thought you tried that,* but bit his tongue instead. He looked at his watch, "I've got about ten minutes before Crazy Ray calls, so let's talk. Li, is everything on schedule at the warehouse?"

"Yes, the counting and strapping machines are ready; the packers, the boxes, the truck, and FedEx are all ready. I've checked and double-checked."

Mack stood up, "Buck and I will be flying the two Huey helicopters, and we'll collect the money at each distribution exchange and fly it back to the warehouse for Li to count, pack, and ship. There will only be one shipment for now, $24 million stacked on a wooden pallet with sixteen boxes bound in stretch wrap. It'll go out by FedEx tomorrow. Day after tomorrow, sixteen more boxes will go to Tony and his brothers. We offered our connections with Clearwater, but Tony and Marcus think that with over 20 million people in Mexico City alone, they would have no trouble making another couple of million exchanging dollars for the pesos. Cesar and Lazaro's money will be divided between the Diaz brothers with an uncertain amount going to Chico's family. Tony agreed to give Marcus five million for his part. I offered to chip in, but Tony said it wasn't necessary, that Cesar would have wanted it that way. For our part in this, my thinking is to remove us as far away and as fast as we can from the money and *don't get greedy*. Stay with our plan. With Maddie directing, we can all live on the interest alone—one million a year—for each of us. The last thing we want is any part of this money to be traced back to us."

"How will we get paid? Once a year or by the month?" Angus asked.

"Our objective is to collect the balance of the money as fast and as safely as possible, but it may take as long as a week. As the money comes in, Li will pay all of our expenses through the companies. After that each of us will get one million dollars in cash—I hope you will be cautious in your spending. Every year, on the first of February, a deposit of one million dollars will be paid into your account, or wherever you direct. I allowed some shortages from our distributors who don't pay, not much, but some. Remember, no rough stuff, if they can't pay or they're short, let *me* know. If it's small we may let it ride.

Regardless, the balance will be split equally with Tony, and then our share will be shipped by FedEx to Clearwater."

"What kind of insurance do we have on our 50 million, or do we?" Miguel asked.

"Well, there's no FDIC, but Li negotiated a good deal for us with Eurobonds. I'll let him tell you."

"Oh great, my *friend*. Thanks a lot," Li said. "*You* were doing just fine." Li gathered his thoughts. "As Mack said, there is no FDIC. Even if there were, they only insure for a hundred grand per account. A lot of money managers will offer you ten percent but without any real guarantee on the principal. Clearwater backs our full 50 million with Eurobonds that are traded worldwide, most through London, one of the largest centers of the Eurobond market. These bonds are held and traded within one of the clearing systems, like Euroclear and Clearwater, and are named after the currency they are denominated in, like Euroyen for the Japanese yen and the Eurodollar for the American dollar. These bonds are bearer bonds. No registered owner's name is printed on the face. Interest and principal will be paid without question to anyone tendering them. They are also tax free, and there are no official records. *You* hold the bonds. They're like cash. If you lose them, they're gone."

The telephone on Mack's desk buzzed; he knew it was Crazy Ray. He jabbed the blinking button and put it on speaker.

"Yeah?"

"Well, well, it's the *man* himself. Are you answering the phones now?"

"What do you want?" Mack put a finger to his lips for those in the room.

"You know what I want. Do we have a deal?"

"Not for ten million."

"Are you that dumb to risk the rest of your life in prison?"

"If you know all about my business, then you must know that's not going to happen."

"Why not?"

"I've taken certain precautions."

"Maaack, that's what I love about you: smart, with natural instincts. We could have a great partnership, call it B&B Unlimited, Brains and Brawn. What do you say?

"Yeah, sure."

"Then tell me, what's your ace in the hole? You don't want to do something stupid here."

"It would be you doing something stupid."

"So, what do we have here, a Mexican standoff?"

"No, what we have is a barge wired with 200 sticks of Hercules C dynamite and ten 50 gallon drums of napalm B."

"You wouldn't blow up...."

"Wait a minute, someone just came in." He put his hand over the mouthpiece. Angus cracked the door and pointed to the blinking button on Mack's desk phone and whispered, "It's Zira, says it's an emergency."

"I got a small crisis here," Mack said to Crazy Ray. "I'm going to put you on hold for a minute." Mack pushed the blinking button.

"Zira, this had better be good!"

"Guess where I'm at?"

"*Zira.* I don't have time for guessing games; I'm on the other line."

"Damn, you're a stick in the mud."

"*Zira.*"

"Ooookay. I'm looking at Crazy Ray as we speak. How about that?"

"What?"

"See there, I told you I would find him—*today.*" She told Mack she had followed Crazy Ray Flynn to the Leahy Trailer Park on Summer Avenue, and he was sitting at a table outside a doublewide trailer talking on a phone. Zira was in the trailer park's office and couldn't say too much, but when she inquired about renting a double-wide trailer, the manager told her that Miss Hazel Flynn, an award winning rose grower, was the only doublewide they had, and she owned it personally. It was a Christmas present from her son, Ray. "This whole trailer park is covered with blooming roses."

"How did you find him?"

She said she had just left the police station with his rap sheet, driver's license photo, and his car registration, a red Cadillac convertible. "I stop at this red light, and I see this red Cadillac convertible go by with this big yellow-headed goon driving. Guess who was next to him? None other than your perp, led me right to his mom's trailer park."

"Okay, stay with them and don't lose Crazy Ray; he's pretty sneaky." Mack thought he heard the line disconnect, "Hello? Hello?

Zira? You still there?"

After a long moment of silence, "*What?*"

"I thought you hung up. Is something wrong?" Mack asked.

"Yeah, there is. Who am I?"

"What?"

"Who the hell am I? You tell me. *Don't lose him.* If Crazy Ray is so damn *crafty* how did I find him so quickly? What's your problem? You don't appreciate my skills because I'm a woman?"

Oh shit. "I'm sorry, Zira. I've got a lot on my plate; work with me here, girl. *Okay*—I have no doubt that you could be the great, great, granddaughter of Sherlock Holmes."

"Please, none of that Irish bullshit."

"I'm sending Miguel to meet you now."

"If Crazy Ray leaves before then, do you want me to stay with him?"

"Absolutely, and keep me informed."

Mack started to hang up and Zira shouted, "Hang on. You can add this to my *Sherlock Holmes* skills. The lawyer that Crazy Ray gave those sealed envelopes to...I know him, and he owes me big time."

"Who is he?...Never mind, we'll talk later. That's great, Zira, smart girl." Mack hung up the phone and turned to Miguel.

"Got him! Zira is sitting on Crazy Ray and Dago at the Leahy Trailer Park on Summer Avenue; he's at his mother's. You were so right about that girl; she *is* good, real good. Take one of the men from Mexico and meet Zira now. Call me when you get there."

Miguel left, and Mack saw that the blinking light on the hold line was no longer blinking. The desk phone started ringing again while Mack was looking at it; he pushed the button.

"You think I'm going to just sit here on hold?" Crazy Ray said.

"I couldn't *talk* with people in my office. What do you want?"

"I'll tell you what I want. I want my cut or else. There's nothing to keep me from calling the Feds *after* you collect the money."

Mack wanted to keep him on the phone as long as he could. "That's true, but then you get nothing. I was thinking it might be worth a million dollars just to have you out of the way!"

"I bet you were. You take me for a fool, a drop from ten million to one million?"

"You were shooting for the moon with the ten million, and *you* know it. Be smart for a change; you have no exposure and could walk away clean with a cool million for doing *nothing*."

"Five million, and you've got a deal."

"I could easily have you removed permanently for a lot less than that."

"Are you threatening to kill me? You're not a murderer, Mack. You're such a Catholic you could never live with a mortal sin."

"In your case, I believe God Almighty would rocket down to Father O'Brien's confession booth to thank me."

"Very funny. Okay, this is my last offer, four million, or I send the letters."

"Now that is funny. Here's *my* last offer, take it or leave it: one million in cash and one million in product."

"When would I get the cash?"

"Same time all of us get paid, about a week from today."

"And the product, how much and when?"

"2,000 pounds and whenever you tell me the delivery location."

"We've got a deal, I'll be in touch." Crazy Ray hung up his mother's phone.

Mack checked his notes. He started to scratch through Crazy Ray's name and stopped. He wasn't quite through with him yet. The next item on the list was Shooter and his team. Now that he had resolved the threat of Crazy Ray, he may not need Shooter, but then decided to use him with their chopper as a backup in case there was an emergency.

The phone rang. It was Miguel. He told Mack he was outside the Leahy Trailer Park, and Zira was nowhere to be found. He was looking at the only doublewide in the park, where a lady was outside watering her roses, but no red Cadillac.

Mack told Miguel to make sure the old lady was Hazel Flynn. "Then show her your police badge and tell her Ray Flynn crashed his red Cadillac and the fire department is transporting him to the hospital downtown. Take her to our warehouse and I'll have Li meet you there."

"You want me to *kidnap* her?" Miguel asked.

"Exactly."

Why not have another backup for Crazy Ray, Mack thought. Listening to Zira about Hazel Ray's rose-growing talents made him think of Carmen and all the roses at Shamrock.

He sent Li to the warehouse to meet Miguel and Crazy Ray's mother. Li was to tell Hazel Ray they had made an unfortunate mistake and would compensate her with $10,000 in cash. All she had to do was spend a week at their farm, about a day's drive from Memphis, and help Carmen in Shamrock's prized rose garden. The contract she would have to sign had a couple of stipulations: no communication with anyone outside the farm, no questions to anyone about what they were doing or why, and lastly, she could never tell anyone about the contract. They would deliver a note, written by her to the trailer park manager, saying she was off to receive an award from the American Rose Society in Atlanta and would be back in one week. If she violated any of the terms of the contract she would receive no money, and they would deny ever knowing her.

Hazel Ray was euphoric and couldn't believe what was happening. It was like winning the lottery. Mack hoped the contract would protect them if kidnapping charges happened to be filed later.

He saw his unlisted phone line ringing and looked up at Buck, shooing him out the door, "Find Shooter, now," he said. He pushed the blinking button, thinking it was Li or Miguel, but it was Zira calling back. "Where are you? You're supposed to be at the trailer park. Miguel is looking for you. How did you get this private number?"

"Are we going there *again*? You Irishmen never learn. Shush! Listen, listen—two ears, one mouth." She continued talking without waiting for Mack's response. "I followed Crazy Ray and Dago from the trailer park to the Cottage Restaurant on Summer Avenue, just down from the trailer park, and I'm watching them from the parking lot."

Mack told her to sit tight, he had help on the way, and then told her Miguel had grabbed Hazel Flynn, and they needed one of her girls to sit with her down in Natchez. Her response was the same as Miguel's.

"You *kidnapped* his mother?"

Buck walked into the office as Mack hung up the phone. "Shooter was in the kitchen, and he's on his way here. The others are over at the downtown airport."

"Hold on a minute. I've got to call down to the farm." Buck listened as Mack told Carmen she would be having two guests for about a week. One was a famous rose grower to help her with her roses. He wanted someone watching Hazel full time and Zira had agreed to loan him one of her girls—an older lady named Norma— who Zira thought would be more compatible with Hazel. Mack agreed to a flat rate fee of $2,000 for the week.

Mack and Buck met Shooter in the hallway and they all headed outside and stopped on the riverbank. Mack had bought two black Chevrolet Suburbans for Miguel to handle transportation and asked Buck to get the keys for one of them. Mack told Shooter about Zira on stakeout at the small Mom and Pop restaurant, The Cottage, on Summer Avenue while they walked along the cobblestone. Mack removed a piece of paper showing the layout of the parking lot, the restaurant, and the front and back door—he had eaten there 3 or 4 times. After a quick rundown on Crazy Ray and Dago, Mack explained how he thought it should go down. Shooter and his men were not dressed in military camouflage but more like a SWAT team—all black assault and combat gear. They had left their equipment on the Huey, but each man had a Glock 30, subcompact, strapped to their thigh with two extra 13-round magazines.

Buck pulled up in one of the Suburbans and, while Shooter and three of his squad scrambled inside, Mack briefed Buck on what he had gone over with Shooter.

Zira waited in her green SUV in the parking lot on the Holmes Street side, watching Crazy Ray and Dago through her tinted windows. They were sitting in front of a large picture window just inside the main entrance of the restaurant in full view of their red Cadillac. Zira was parked where she could see the front and back doors of the restaurant and had no idea what Mack meant when he said "help is on the way." She unzipped the bottom of the inside leg of her black jeans and removed her .38 S&W Chiefs Special. Sliding the thumb-piece forward, she swung the cylinder out and pressed the extractor rod, ejecting five hollow point cartridges. She never took her eyes off the picture window as she rolled each bullet around in her hand, feeling the cool metal. She pushed each shell into a separate chamber, and once the gun was reloaded and the cylinder closed, she placed the gun on top of the center console.

Zira started her SUV while watching a black Suburban with dark tinted glass turn into the parking lot from Summer Avenue. It pulled up beside her, driver to driver. Without taking her eyes off the window, she eased the Chiefs Special from the top of the console and laid the two-inch barrel on the window ledge. They both lowered their windows halfway at the same time.

"Me and you are back-up only," Buck said. "Just sit and watch unless something goes wrong. You got a weapon?"

Zira lowered her window all the way, and Buck stared at the end of Zira's gun barrel, pointed at him. He frowned, shook his head, and raised his window. He drove around the back, let one of the men out, and then drove around to the front corner of the parking lot and shifted into park, leaving the engine running. He had a clear view of the front and back entrances and of Zira. He looked at his watch and pressed the stopwatch as three men, dressed in assault gear and vest with body armor, jumped from the truck. Two of the men headed to the front door.

The third man pulled the pin of a flash-bang grenade and, as he passed the red convertible, he released the lever and dropped the grenade in the rear floorboard while continuing to walk to the back entrance.

Inside, Crazy Ray walked to the back of the restaurant and entered the men's room. Dago had just taken the first bite of his burger when the grenade exploded. He threw his hands up to protect his face, but the window didn't break, just rattled. When he looked out the window, he saw fire and smoke pouring out of the Cadillac and rushed out the front door. He saw the two men with black ski masks and the black "nightstick" coming at his chest, as he reached for his pistol, but it was too late. His last thought before his legs crumbled was the nightstick penetrating his chest. With over three million volts in his body from the Equalizer stun baton, he lay moaning on his back, eyes opened, arms and legs rigid, his whole body in a seizure. The two men acted quickly and in unison: one removed Dago's pistol from his shoulder holster while the other took a gas-operated nail gun from his belt and fired off three quick shots, nailing the front door to the frame. They both rolled him facedown; one bound his hands behind his back with a zip tie while the other pulled a pillow case over his head and tied it around his neck with duct tape. He tossed the role of tape to his partner, who wrapped both feet together with the tape. Buck eased the Suburban up to the front door, jumped out, and opened both rear doors to load Dago.

Inside, Crazy Ray heard the explosions and hurried out of the men's room. He saw everybody bunched up, trying to get out the front door, but he didn't see Dago. He looked behind him and saw the exit sign and headed for the back door.

Zira, her mouth open, watched with amazement as the masked man stuck Crazy Ray in the chest with the stun baton, pinning him against the door. A bright electric current pulsated across the top of the baton, and you could hear the electrical sound popping like a broken overhead high-powered voltage line. Crazy Ray stood frozen from the shock. He didn't fall. His arms stiffened as if they were glued to his side. His whole body shook with convulsions. *Damn, that's gotta hurt,* she thought. Buck had pulled to the back of the restaurant and waited. He watched while they wrapped Crazy Ray up like Dago and tossed him in the back of the truck *God, they're good.*

Buck heard the sirens as he pulled out of the parking lot and turned south on Holmes. At the Broad Street stop sign, he looked left and saw the fire truck bearing down on him. He looked down at his stopwatch, 3 minutes and 36 seconds. He smiled, nodded his head, and turned west on Broad Street toward the river. In his side view mirror, he saw Zira close behind him. *Good, she's covering my rear; just in case.*

Mack took out his notebook and scratched through Crazy Ray's name. That threat was gone, and next on his list was the Mexican who killed Cesar. Zira had her girls tracking this guy Rocky now, and Miguel was awaiting her call. Mack told them both that he wanted to play a major part in that meeting. Meanwhile Zira went to meet Crazy Ray's lawyer for drinks after work to see if he really had two letters from Crazy Ray. Zira would call him after their meeting.

Crazy Ray and Dago were locked up and guarded at the Delta Hunting and Fishing Lodge. He would deal with them after all their transactions were completed. It was getting dark outside, and Cesar's "Last Hurrah," the finalization of *CODA*, was getting close—time for another meeting.

CHAPTER 23

LIKE THE OPENING curtain of a Broadway musical, the morning sun spread over the gabled skylight roof of the dark warehouse. Mack's head rested on his arms, folded over an old wooden desk. Startled, he jerked upright, confused as to where he was, his fingers tightening around his Colt 45, his eyes heavy and out of focus. He had been working for three days and three nights without sleep. A look at his watch, and he realized he had dozed off for less than an hour. The last thing he remembered was locking the warehouse doors after everyone had left. He rubbed his bloodshot eyes; his mouth was dry and bitter tasting. He looked around for something to drink and walked over to a galvanized washtub half-full of melting ice. He dug around the bottom and found a bottle of Budweiser, popped the cap, reached into his pocket, found his last amphetamine pill, and washed it down. Mack had twelve hours to go before Buck and Angus would be back to relieve him. He bent over the washtub, cupped both hands, and splashed his face with the icy water. He stood up, a little dizzy, and looked down the lines of cotton classing tables. Twenty-five tables, all about eight feet long, were lined up and down the warehouse floor. The tables had a six-inch lip turned up on all sides to keep the cotton samples from falling to the floor while grading.

Li had made his office in an enclosed area in the rear of the warehouse with windows on one wall to see out onto the warehouse floor. A single light bulb hanging from the ceiling still burned. Mack followed a ray of sunlight across the floor to Li's office and saw through the windows that he was still there, his head resting on stacks of paper, asleep. Rolls of adding machine tape spilled from his desktop and across the floor. Mack turned and walked up front, sliding his hand over the worn, turned-up edges of the tables. He had always had the "luck of the Irish" in making money buying and selling real estate, but in this case it was a blessing that he couldn't sell this warehouse when he needed the money. Sure, it was in a bad location, a rundown industrial site, but it *was* on the bluff overlooking the river and built like a fortress, with huge rafters, joists and columns of rough-sawn cypress. Despite its isolation, overgrown weeds, and broken glass windows, it was perfect for this part of the operation.

For the past 72 hours they had counted, wrapped, and shipped out over $89 million. At one time all 25 tables in the warehouse had overflowed with hundred-dollar bills. In the past, inside the walls of this warehouse, cotton was the King of the South, but for the last three days Benjamin Franklin had taken King Cotton's place.

Mack looked at his watch. The last shipments had gone out, everyone had been paid, and he was calculating how long Buck had been gone. Buck had helped Tony and his men load the King Air with their share of the money and flew them back to Mexico; figuring a quick turnaround with no problems, he should be close to Memphis by now.

It was all over, and the operation was a complete success—so far. They had underestimated the payments from the distributors, but that was before Angus came up with the brilliant idea to FedEx one bud of Amazona Rojo to each distributor so they could see, smell, and smoke a sample. Angus and Tony had convinced everyone it would sell itself, and it did, big time. The second phase of the operation: the offloading of the barge, the loading of the tractor-trailer trucks, the exchange of money for the product, and the shipment of the money to Clearwater all went off as planned and without a hitch. There was little doubt that teamwork and the discipline of their Marine Corps training were major factors in their execution. The one debacle of losing Cesar was a bitter pill Mack continued to choke on and could not swallow. He eagerly awaited his meeting with the Mexican who had killed them.

Mack walked along the width of the warehouse in the back, high on the bluff, overlooking the river. He was a very wealthy man now with unlimited possibilities, but he was reluctant to celebrate without Cesar.

Most of the windows on the back of the warehouse were in good shape, only a few with broken glass, but the overgrown weeds and budding saplings blocked the view of the river. Mack pushed open one of the windows, stuck his head out, and saw a guard at each of the corners. He turned and walked back across the warehouse and opened the front door; he saw no one guarding the front. He looked down the gravel road to the gate and saw two guards talking, but a banging noise caused him to whirl and draw his 45 automatic. A guard had kicked the door open on a Port-a-Potty about 20-feet away and was standing outside buckling his gun belt. He looked up and saw Mack's pistol pointed at him.

"Whoa!" The guard shouted, raising his hands and dropping his gun belt.

Mack pointed his pistol toward the two guards down by the gates. "Next time have one of your buddies on this door when you have to leave."

"Yes sir...sorry about that."

These were off-duty policemen, not in uniform, but armed. Mack had hired guards around the clock to patrol outside the fenced area as well, including along the river. If there was going to be any trouble, it would be while money was being exchanged. There might be a little overkill on the security, but with Mack seeing Benjamin Franklin's face on the bills covering the cotton classing tables, it reminded him of one of Ben's famous axioms: *An ounce of prevention is worth a pound of cure.*

He decided he would keep the guards for another week or until *all* the money was collected.

Mack heard the muffled ring of his telephone and jogged across the warehouse to answer his phone.

"Were you asleep?" Zira asked.

"No, I was outside."

"Can we meet? I've got some information and I need some directions."

"I'm pretty tied up. Can you tell me over the phone?"

"Sure, it's *your* information, but I don't think you want me telling you over the phone."

"Okay, hold on a sec." Mack checked his watch. Li had scheduled each distributor who still owed money to call every day at noon for a time and place to meet. The *Irish Mist* was docked at the foot of Beale Street, and that's where Li and Mack agreed to accept payments. It was out in the open, had a gangway, was easy to defend, and could break away instantly if needed. "I can meet you at Tom Lee Park in 15 minutes."

"I'll be there."

Mack's plan had always been to maintain a low profile. The fewer people who knew he was involved, the better. However, he wanted to be at these money exchanges in case something went wrong. This experience had answered his uncertainty about his future, and Cesar's death had sent a strong message—providence. He cared less about man-made law, but divine law was front and center, and that would be his guiding light for all future endeavors.

The pill had kicked in, and he was anxious and hungry. It was not that far to the park, and he needed a run. He opened a white paper sack on his desk, removed a half-eaten donut, and washed it down with the rest of the beer. He woke Li, told him what he was doing, and left for his meeting.

Mack jogged along the bluff of the river. The sun felt good on his face, and he started sweating. Wild daffodils lined the dirt path through Ashburn Park, and squirrels chased each other around and around the base of the trees. He slowed his pace as he headed downhill and saw Zira crossing Tom Lee Park. With each long stride he could see the fine shape of her body moving inside her translucent, sleeveless dress.

She stopped at a park bench that sat on a neck of land jutting out over the Mississippi and stood looking for Mack. She saw him jogging across the park between blooming redbuds.

Her smile was radiant when she waved, and it warmed him to see her so cheerful. He slowed to a walk, breathing heavily, as she moved to greet him. He extended his hand, but she moved inside, wrapped her arms around him, and kissed him on the cheek. He felt the softness of her breasts and her thighs pressing his, and whispered, "To what do I owe this pleasure?"

"I needed a hug."

Mack eased his arms around her.

She jerked back from him, "God, you *stink*."

Mack's first instinct was a denial, but instead he grabbed her and pulled her in tighter. He searched quickly to remember a memorable line from a movie he had seen. Finally, in a deep, dramatic voice said, "Breathe deep baby, I may never smell this good again."

Zira shrieked, laughed, and pounded on his chest. "You stole that line from *The Carpetbaggers*. I'll never forget that movie—I *loved* it."

Mack had a big grin on his face. "Yeah, and *he* hadn't washed in 91 hours."

"Ohhh, what was that other line?" She pounded on his chest again. "I read the book three times; it was the biggest scandal of the year, and they banned the book from all the libraries."

Mack pulled her close again, "Breathe deep..."

"*Yuck!* You're gross. Jump in the river." She pushed him toward the edge of the bluff.

"Okay, okay," he said, throwing up his hands. "I'll stay back, over here downwind, while you tell me your information—how's this?"

Zira stood in front of Mack while he sat on the bench. "First thing, my girls found the Mexican who did the killing, a man named Juan..." Zira saw Mack roll his eyes.

"I know—there's a million Mexicans named Juan. Do you want to hear what happened or not?" Mack nodded his head.

"You remember, the girls had this guy Rocky's shack staked out, well they caught Juan sneaking out in the middle of the night, and drove off in a raggedy-ass pickup. Come to find out, he stole Rocky's truck. One of the girls, Dot, has been following him ever since. She called from just this side of Houston, and thinks Juan is headed for the border."

"I don't want him crossing that border..."

"No worry. I talked to Miguel, and, luckily, they were just leaving the hacienda. He said they would land at Corpus Christi and rent a car. Dot called late yesterday and said she had met Miguel and Buck, and they followed Juan to this all-night truck stop in the middle of nowhere on Highway 77. Buck said to tell you they were all going shark fishing tonight, and they had plenty of fresh bait."

Zira noticed Mack had this disgusted look on his face again. "I tried to call *you* first. You didn't answer your phone, so I called Miguel." Mack didn't say anything.

"Do you want to hear what my other girl, Joyce, got out of Rocky...how Cesar and the others were killed? It's not pretty."

"How did she....Okay, tell me."

"Joyce is a big woman and fierce; not afraid to fight a bear." Mack waved his hand, motioning for her to hurry up.

"Damn, you're impatient. Okay, the short version. Rocky's door was not locked, Joyce found him across the bed drunk, passed out. She hit him with a stun gun anyway, stripped him naked and duct taped him in a chair. When he came around he saw his testicles were gift-wrapped with two small copper wires that were connected to the two prongs protruding from the stun gun. He gave up Juan without hesitation, saying he got a call that there was an envelope waiting for him at the Blue and White. There was $300 in the envelope and instructions to pick up a Mexican and take him wherever he wanted to go.

"Joyce told him she wanted details on who did the killing; how, when, and why, and who paid the money. Rocky said he would be dead within 24 hours if he gave up the name. Joyce told him that in *24 seconds* a million volts would hit his balls, and he would wish he were dead. He sputtered out the name—Ray Flynn had paid him the money, and he drove Juan to Mhoon Landing where the Mexican walked out to the end of the dilapidated pier, half underwater, with a duffel bag over his shoulder and a flashlight.

"Are you sure you want to hear this part?"

"Yeah, keep going."

"Well, Rocky said he got tired of waiting in the truck and sneaked down through weeds to the pier and stopped when he heard Juan talking. Juan was on one knee with a green pipe-like rifle on his shoulder. He moved down closer to the water's edge to hear what Juan was saying. It was quiet with a cool breeze coming off the river. Rocky heard the snap of the trigger pull and one word, uno."

Juan, his cap turned backward, rested the M72 Light Anti-tank Weapon (LAW) on his right shoulder. With his ear pressed against the side, his right eye almost touching the rear peep sight, he sighted down the barrel until Recon-One was lined up and then pressed down on the trigger, just like shooting a rifle, except there was a slight hesitation. He waited, listening until he heard the firing pin striking the primer and started counting in a low whisper:

"Uno"—the primer set fire to a small amount of black powder that flashed down the tube to the rear of the rocket.

"Dos"—the flash ignited the propellant in the rocket motor.

"Tres"—the rocket motor burned complete, producing gases around 1,400 degrees.

"Cuatro"—the rocket exploded out the front of the launcher carrying the warhead at a speed of 500 feet per second and a blowback of fire 45 feet long out the rear end of the tube.

"CINCO"—he shouted loudly. The explosion and the illumination of the blast were so instant and powerful, he froze, part shock and part awe. When the TEA, a pyrophoric substance in the warhead, fused with the gasoline, it blasted a blanket of fire over 200 feet wide across the surface of the river. The power of the gaseous vapors formed a fiery mushroom as it climbed, lighting up the sky like a night game at a football stadium. Then it was dark again, the black boiling smoke being pushed downriver by the wind and the current.

"That son-of-a-bitch!" Mack said.

"I'm sorry, Mack. Oh, one other thing. One of my guards down at the *Irish Mist* called this morning and said someone stopped by with a sealed envelope from your office with your name on it." She handed the note to Mack. "I stopped by the boat and picked it up on my way."

Mack opened the envelope and jumped up from the bench. "When was this?"

"About an hour ago."

"I've got to go." Mack hurried off, jogging across the park.

"You need to slow down; you can't do it all. *I'm sorry*," she shouted, "about calling you stinky." But Mack was too far away to hear her.

Mack was pissed. He had promised that the Mexican would pay a long slow death for killing Cesar...but reminded himself: *you've got to let go—delegate.*

Jogging faster now, he charged the hill at the foot of Ashburn Park. On top of the park he bent over, his hands resting on his knees, gasping for air. He was sweating profusely and looked down at his chest to see his heart pounding through his wet t-shirt. Alarmed, he jerked up his shirt, and put his hand over his heart, and watched his hand move in and out rapidly. *Am I having a heart attack? No, there's no pain.* He walked over to a park bench, took a couple of deep breaths and sat down. He looked at his digital watch, waited for the minute dial to roll over, and checked his pulse: 240 beats per minute. *Damn.*

Then he remembered the amphetamine. That's what was causing his runaway heartbeat, and no sleep, and running on empty. He hated speed; it did the job of keeping him awake, but every time he took it, his body reacted erratically. He leaned back on the bench and relaxed. Just knowing the cause of the rapid heartbeat made him feel better. He felt his heart again and could tell it was not beating as fast. He opened the crumbled note in his hand: *"Emergency at Buck's lodge."* He started a slow jog back to the warehouse.

Inside the warehouse he kneeled next to the #2 washtub and stuck his head in the icy water, then removed his t-shirt and washed his upper body. After drying off with his shirt, he felt a lot better and called down to Buck's lodge.

One of the guards told him Crazy Ray had had some kind of seizure and didn't think he would make it. The other guard had followed them to the emergency room at the University of Mississippi Medical Center in Jackson where he fell into a coma. An EMS helicopter transported him to the Baptist Hospital in Memphis where it was reported Crazy Ray had stopped breathing.

Please God, let the scum die and burn in hell.

As soon as Mack hung up the phone, it rang again. It was Li, and he was meeting with four distributors, one every hour, starting at 11:30, again at the *Irish Mist*. This should be the last of the distributors, and Li had figured after today they would have less than $3 million total unpaid. Miguel and Angus had set up a team the day before to hit the road to collect the balance owed from some of the smaller dealers.

Mack told Li he would meet him there at 11 o'clock. Li said he had just talked to Buck and Miguel and they had landed at the downtown airport. They had been trying to call, but kept getting a busy signal.

Mack walked back down the hill to Tom Lee Park and across the cobblestones on the riverbank to his office. If Crazy Ray died, it would save everyone a lot of trouble; they said he wasn't breathing on his own. That's a good sign. He would get Miguel to check the Baptist Hospital and see if Crazy Ray was dead or not...or maybe make sure he was dead? *Naw, with everything going so well, I don't need to go there, let him die on his own.*

Mack needed a hot shower and something to eat before meeting Li. Two of Zira's guards stood at the end of the walkway leading to the *Irish Mist*. Mack told the two guards there would be some visitors arriving for the next three hours to see Li. He also reminded them, that he, Mack Shannon, was *not* on the boat, and to ask each visitor if they were carrying a weapon, then discreetly search each one to make sure.

Mack sat inside the wheelhouse sipping a hot cup of coffee behind tinted windows. He was in familiar surroundings. Like Irish and Mickey before him, they had all piloted the *Irish Mist* up and down the Mississippi. He placed his holstered 45-automatic on the chart table in front of him while he scanned all sides of the *Irish Mist*. With clean clothes and food in his stomach, he felt 100 percent better. Li was downstairs with his last distributor, and all had gone well. Tony had left a couple of his men with Li, and they were in an adjacent cabin with one of the money counters and a wrapping machine.

His phone rang; it was Miguel. He told Mack that when the guards down in Mississippi went to check on Crazy Ray, he was balled up on the floor, delirious with a high fever, and coughing up blood. He stopped breathing, recovered, but then went into a coma while being transported. He was now hooked up to a ventilator and being treated for something the doctors called *pulmonary aspergillosis* a highly invasive fungal infection that attacks patients with immune system deficiencies. The doctors ordered injections of prednisone for inflammation of his lungs, and he was in an oxygen tent that was feeding blood to his brain. They can't treat the coma until they find out what caused it. Miguel said the doctor told him it would take a miracle for him to recover. When Miguel asked what were his odds, the doctor said, "90% he won't make it till morning."

Mack could feel the warm river breeze coming through the open windows, and occasionally a gust of wind would rock the boat. It was quiet and secluded, and he thought back to when he was a boy and would sneak off to this same wheelhouse and daydream about being a captain on this pirate ship, counting the gold in his treasure chest. He stared out the window, watching the fast current of the river and re-examined the past week. It was hard to believe. Last week he couldn't pay his bills; this week he was a very wealthy man. His eyelids grew heavy, and soon his head eased down onto the chart table. There was no more gas in his tank, and soon he was in a deep sleep.

When Li had finished and everything was secure, he shouted

upstairs to see if Mack was coming down. Not getting an answer, he climbed up to the wheelhouse and found Mack spread out over the chart table, snoring. Li removed the 45 automatic from Mack's hand and half lifted and guided him into the Captain's quarters behind the wheelhouse. Li removed Mack's shoes, socks, and pants, threw a sheet over him, and placed the 45 on the table. It was time for him to get some sleep too, before *he* passed out on his feet. He closed the window shutters and left.

Later the next day, Zira drove along Riverside Drive and, at the foot of Beale Street, turned onto the riverbank, bouncing down the cobblestones to the *Irish Mist*. She stopped in front of one of the guards standing by the gangway and rolled down her window.

"Good evening, Ms. LeBlanc. How are you?"

"Hello, Jerry. Where is, ah...your new man, what's his name?"

"Bobby. Bobby Frick," Jerry said, looking behind him at the *Irish Mist*. "Here he comes now. I sent him to check around the outside of the boat."

Zira watched Frick walk over to them. He was a big black man, a body builder, purposely wearing a shirt too small so as to accentuate his bulging muscles.

"Is anyone inside the boat?" Zira said.

Frick spoke up, "Naw, they all gone."

Jerry gave Frick a dirty look and said to Zira, "Yes ma'am, there's one person inside. Mr. Shannon came aboard yesterday and told us not to tell anyone he was here. And late yesterday, everyone left *but* Mr. Shannon, and the Oriental fellow told us not to go onto the boat or let anyone on the boat without Mr. Shannon's approval."

"Why was Frick on the boat then?"

"Oh, no ma'am, we've always been checking the outside of the boat every hour, but never go inside."

Zira nodded her head. "When was the last time you saw Mr. Shannon?"

"I saw him late yesterday in the glass house up there on top," Frick interrupted, pointing to the wheelhouse.

Jerry added, "When we relieved the other two guards this morning, they told us no one had been on or had left the boat on their shift."

"No one has seen or heard from Mr. Shannon since...what time did he come aboard yesterday?"

"Around 11 a.m."

"And no one has seen him since?"

"No ma'am."

Zira parked her SUV in front of the gangway and jumped from her truck. She was dressed in tight black jeans and a white cotton blouse. She propped her foot on the running board of the truck, removed the S&W Airweight Chiefs Special from her ankle holster, and headed for the gangway.

"You want us to come with you?" Jerry asked.

"No, I don't think anything is wrong, just being careful." As she passed Frick, she felt his eyes on her, turned quickly, and caught him holding his crotch. She walked back to him and stared up into his face, tapping the gun to his crotch, "You'd better hold them with both hands if you want to keep them, 'cause if I catch you *leering* again, at any woman, you're going to lose them and your job."

Zira turned and walked to the side of the boat, stepped up on the gunwale and jumped down onto the main deck. As she walked to the stern, she looked into each window and door as she passed, then climbed the stairs to the upper deck. She stood on the landing, listening and looking, before climbing up to the wheelhouse. She opened the door slowly with her gun in her hand, but no one was inside. Jerry watched her from down below, and she nodded her head in acknowledgement. She could see the orange ball of the sun setting on the shore across the river through the windows; it was a picture perfect setting. She stepped inside, saw a door opened to a narrow hallway, and in a low voice she called out Mack's name but got no response. On the right side of the hallway, she saw a bathroom and a galley. When she stuck her head in the room on the left side, she saw Mack tangled in a sheet, his face buried in a pillow. She stood looking at him, holding her breath until she heard his soft snoring. Relieved, she walked back from the hallway into the wheelhouse, opened the exterior door, and waved at Jerry, nodding her head that everything was okay. So this is the Captain's quarters, she asked herself; not much more than a walk-in closet. She opened the shutters, and a reddish, golden yellow hue from the setting sun seeped through each slat, lighting the walls in stripes like a tiger. Mack groaned something incoherent and lifted his head from the pillow, rolled out of the tangled sheet, leaving one leg and arm halfway off the bed, then fell back on his pillow with a soft snore.

Zira watched the sunrays drop down over Mack and across his face; *God he's handsome. He needs a haircut.* She combed her fingers through his hair, smoothing it back. His pants were thrown on the floor, and she picked them up and laid them across the foot of the bed. She stared at his leg, and without hesitation lifted the corner of the sheet to see if he was sleeping in the nude. He was wearing white boxer shorts, and dark hair covered his muscular body. The hair started on top of his foot, and she traced the tips with the back of her hand over his calf, his thigh, and up his chest. She bent over and touched her nose to his chest and breathed in his scent, hesitated, then placed her lips over one of his nipples. Trembling, she stood over him, her breathing shortened almost to a pant.

Mack opened his eyes.

She jerked up, "Just checking on you, making sure you're alive."

Mack sat up, noticed the tight-fitting slacks she had on, and the gun in her hand. "Were you going to shoot me or seduce me?"

Her thigh leaned against the side of the mattress, next to his hand. He cupped his fingers around the back of her thigh, close to her bottom, and nudged her forward. "Cat got your tongue?"

She didn't move, just stood there, as if balancing on a tightrope...staring at his naked chest.

"Seduce you first, and then maybe shoot you." She backed up, kicked off her shoes, unzipped and removed her pants, her blouse, and camisole, and crawled on top of Mack, kissing him wildly. Mack rolled her over and straddled her, holding each arm down while he kissed her lips, her neck, and brushed each breast with his tongue. She yelled out, like a cowboy riding a bronco, and bucked him off and jumped on top, pinning both his arms back while teasing his body with her flickering tongue. Her legs were tangled in the sheets, and she rose up, ripping the top sheet loose, threw it across the room, and then grabbed at Mack's boxer shorts, tearing at them with both hands. He twisted and turned, kicking with both legs in wild fury trying to help, while at the same time struggling not to lose his grip on the side of her panties.

Zira stopped, fell forward covering Mack, panting, with sweat dripping from her neck, then rolled over on her back laughing so hard she was shaking the bed.

Mack, with one leg out of his shorts and breathing hard, rose up on his elbow, "What?"

"I can't do this," she said.

"You got to be...." He watched her wrap the sheet around her. "What did I do?" Mack said.

"It's not you. We need to talk. Pull up your shorts and sit down." Zira sat in the chair by the table while Mack sat on the side of the bed.

"I have genital herpes; it's not active, and I haven't had any signs in over a year. But *some* medical experts say it is still contagious. My no-good husband gave it to me and never told me he had it before we married. His excuse was he thought he was cured; there is no cure. I have had sex, not that often, but always with a condom. It's not easy for me to tell you all this, but...it's your choice if you still want to. I have a condom."

"I ahh...Damn, Zira, I need to think about this."

Zira started putting on her clothes with her back to Mack. "I understand. I've learned to live with it and so have millions of others, but please don't mention this to anyone. I confided in you because I trust you, and we are friends, personal and business, and I would like to keep it that way."

"Of course. I feel the same way. I won't say a word...to anyone. And, ahh...well, thank you for telling me, it took a lot of guts to do that."

"Relax," Zira said as she stuffed the 38 special in her ankle holster, "It's not the end of the world having to do without a little sex." She reached out and brushed his hair from his forehead, opened the door and left.

Mack sat on the side of the bed, staring at the blank wall until he heard the wheelhouse door close. He stood up and looked outside at the darkness. *Did I just dodge a bullet or what?*

You have just read the first book of a trilogy.

In the sequel, *A Man's Hungry Heart*, Mack Shannon continues his search for the meaning of life.

The first book of his trilogy, *A Chasing After The Wind*, and the sequel, *A Man's Hungry Heart* are available in hardcover, paperback and e-book at Amazon.com or his website: www.jamesacarson.com. The third book of his trilogy, *The Right Choice*, is under construction and will be available for purchase in the spring of 2016.

From the Author: *"Out of millions of writers, only 2% make enough money to live on, so reviews are important and good ones fuel our egos. If you like my books, I would appreciate you telling your friends and if you write me a review on Amazon.com, I will send you a free e-book. Please email me at my website:* www.jamesacarson.com.*"*

ABOUT THE AUTHOR

JIM CARSON, a former Marine, studied Theatre Arts at various California universities where he won numerous awards in acting, directing, and speech. His pursuit of a vocation that would satisfy his dreams led him to many occupations: firefighter, soybean farmer, director of Underwater Rescue, night school teacher, and the job that always paid the bills, a commercial construction contractor.

Ask him to tell you about the time he was flying to his house in Key West and walked away after totaling his V-tail Bonanza on takeoff from the Destin Airport or the time when he was hired as a sparring partner, unaware it was Davy Moore, the Featherweight Champion of the World—he was paid $10 a round.

Jim was born and raised in Memphis, Tennessee. He has two adult children, one in Nashville, Tennessee and the other in Richmond, Virginia. He lives on 3 acres in a 1920 Italian Renaissance house with a small leak in the tile roof that nobody can find.

A sequel to *A CHASING AFTER THE WIND*
JIM
CARSON
A MAN'S
HUNGRY
HEART